ALL HAT

ALL HAT

A NOVEL

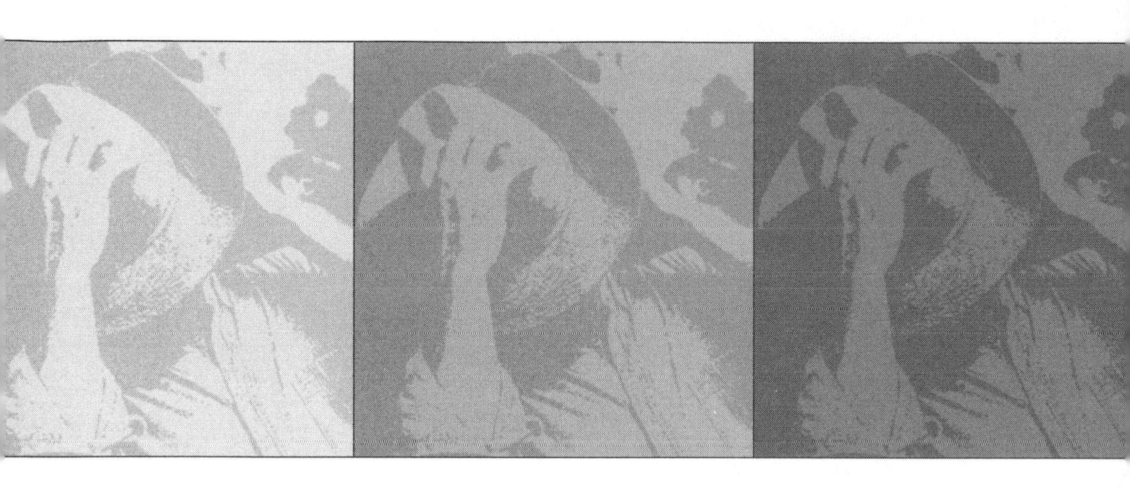

BRAD SMITH

HENRY HOLT AND COMPANY   NEW YORK

Henry Holt and Company, LLC
Publishers since 1866
115 West 18th Street
New York, New York 10011

Library of Congress Cataloging-in-Publication Data
Smith, B. J. (Brad J.)
All hat : a novel / Brad Smith.—1st ed.
p. cm.
ISBN: 0-8050-7217-9
1. Swindlers and swindling—Fiction. 2. Male friendship—Fiction. 3. Women jockeys—Fiction. 4. Horse racing—Fiction. 5. Ex-convicts—Fiction. 6. Canada—Fiction. I. Title.
PR9199.3.S55148 A45 2003
813'.54—dc21 2002027307

Henry Holt books are available for special promotions and premiums.
For details contact: Director, Special Markets.

First Edition 2003

Designed by Fritz Metsch

Printed in the United States of America
1 3 5 7 9 10 8 6 4 2

For Gibby and Hawk

ALL HAT

1

It was fall when they let him out. The first frost was a week gone, and the air was at once sharp and clean with the passing of summer and cool and gray with the promise of the season to come. The soybeans in Holden County were mostly harvested, a poor crop due to the long, wet spring and the short, dry summer, and the farmers were trying to get the corn off before the November rains. It was either that or wait until freeze-up, run the combines in the ice and the snow.

Ray Dokes shed his orange prison overalls like a copper head sheds its skin, walked out of the detention center in Niagara into sunlight, the day cold and clear, the sky bluer outside the fence than within, the air cleaner, somehow worthier even of breath. He stood on the steps outside, the sun on his face and this new morning before him.

He lit a cigarette and found the blue Ford pickup across the lot.

Pete Culpepper was behind the wheel of the truck, smoking a Marlboro nonfilter and listening to the country music station out of Toronto. Or at least what was passed off as country these days—pop singers looking more like lap dancers and fashion models than real country. If old Hank hadn't died in the back of that limo, he'd have shot himself after a hard look and a short listen to this bunch.

Pete pushed back his Stetson with his thumb and nodded at Ray—who tossed his bag in the back and climbed in—as if maybe Ray had been gone a couple days instead of a couple years; then Pete popped the truck into low gear and started off. Ray reached over and turned the radio off and rolled down the window, hung his right arm out over the door of the truck, flicked the ash from his smoke.

"How are you, Pete?"

"I'm all right. What about you?"

"Never better."

They took Route 20 west, through familiar ground, farm country interrupted by small towns and hamlets, the odd strip mall marring the landscape, speaking to what some would refer to as progress. There were new houses, gas stations, co-ops. Seems there'd been some prosperity after all, although you'd never know it reading the papers inside.

They entered Holden County outside of Middleburg. Ray glanced over to see the old Texan watching him instead of the road.

"You feel like the prodigal?"

"Not one bit," Ray said.

"Good thing," Pete said. "I wasn't fixin' to kill no calf anyhow."

They drove through the hamlet of Cook's Station. Ray watched as Pete double-clutched and punched the truck into second gear, checking his West Coast mirrors as he did. Pete liked to drive the pickup as if it was an eighteen-wheeler.

"You got some gray in your hair," Pete said.

"So have you."

"I'm supposed to. I'm old. What're you—forty?"

"Not yet, Pete. But I'm getting there."

They took the turnoff at the town line, headed north on the paved road. Ray turned and had a good look as they passed Homer Parr's place. There was a blue sedan in the driveway, and the grass needed cutting. The flag was up on the mailbox.

"She's still there," Pete said as they passed.

Ray nodded at the information. He wasn't going to ask about her, but he was glad to have heard just the same.

They topped the crest of the road a mile short of their destination. From that height Ray could see a series of subdivisions, like a nasty urban rash, scattered across the landscape to the west.

"What the hell is that?" he asked.

"That's Guelph," Pete told him.

"Goddamn."

"Yup. Civilization crowdin' me."

Ray looked at the rows of houses in the distance, their roof lines identical right down to the color of the shingles, stretched across the horizon like dominoes.

"What else have I missed?"

Pete reached over and turned the radio back on, punched a button, and got Lightfoot lamenting on some early morning precipitation. A lucky break—another of those pretty boys, and Ray might have pressed him for an answer.

It was noon when they reached Pete's farm. The field in front of the barn was cut, the hay lying in thin windrows, as sparse as a spinster's prospects.

"You baling hay this time of year?" Ray asked.

"Third cut," Pete said. "First two were so bad I had no choice."

"This one don't look like a world beater."

The house sat back a good two hundred yards from the road. Left and to the rear was a machinery shed of steel siding fading red to gray under a ribbed galvanized roof. The main barn was across the yard to the right; the building was large and hip-roofed, in decent repair although its walls and roof aspired to no color at all save that of pine planking and cedar shingles weathered by decades of just plain being there. There was a split-rail corral off the east end of the barn. The corral was empty, although Ray, when he got out of the truck, knew there were horses on the premises. He couldn't hear them, but he could smell them and somehow he could feel them.

The smokehouse was still standing, although the door was gone completely and it had been a lot of years since anyone had cured a ham inside. The building was constructed of red brick, and when Ray looked closely he could still make out the faint outline on the wall—a roughly painted figure of a right-handed batter with a rectangle alongside that represented the strike zone. Pete Culpepper had painted the wall when Ray was fourteen, after Ray had broken most of the boards out of the end of the barn. Now Ray looked at the faded batter and thought about the countless balls he'd fired at the wall. Fastballs inside and breaking stuff away, the balls growing soft as pulp from the constant pounding on the brick.

The old pump was still there too, atop the drilled well. The pump was coincidentally located sixty feet from the smokehouse. Ray had built a pitching mound alongside, and it was mostly gone now, worn away by the years. The pump had a broken hockey stick for a handle, and the water, when pumped, fell into an ancient clawfoot bathtub.

The house itself was a fieldstone story and a half built in the late 1800s and in need of some cosmetic attention. The wooden sashes of the windows were cracked, the paint flaking away to nothing, and the porch roof had a dip in it that resembled a swayback horse. There were a couple of ladderback chairs on the porch and a red refrigerator, which Ray had last seen in the kitchen. Pete's Walker hound was stretched out between the fridge and the chairs, and he raised his head and blinked sleepily as they approached.

They went into the house, the old hound at their heels. In the kitchen Ray leaned down to rub the dog's ears, the animal groaning with pleasure at the attention; then he headed to the rear staircase—there were two in the house—and carried his bag upstairs to his room.

The bed was made, and the room had been cleaned—at least as much as a crusty old man with little interest in house-cleaning could manage. Ray tossed his bag on the bed and looked out the window. There was a bush lot at the back of the farm, and between the house and the bush the fields were planted with corn. The hardwoods in the bush were just beginning to turn color, a flash of red or yellow dispersed indiscriminately among the green.

Ray's ball glove and Detroit Tigers' cap were on a shelf where he'd left them. He set the cap on his head and went back downstairs.

"You wanna beer?" Pete asked when Ray walked into the kitchen. He'd already opened two bottles of Old Vienna. "All I got is this Canadian stuff."

"Imagine that, us being in Canada and all."

Pete sat across the table, flopped his hat in the chair beside, and took a long drink of beer. Ray sipped at his and adjusted the ball cap on his head. Cold beer was one of the things he'd dreamed about these past two years, that and firm breasts, smooth buttocks, thick steaks, clam chowder, Scotch on the rocks. The beer in his hand was all right, but just all right. Like everything else as you got older, the getting never seemed to measure up to the anticipating.

"So how was it?" Pete asked, like Ray knew he would.

"Jail?" Ray asked, and he considered the question. "Well, it was like jail. It was exactly like jail."

"Anybody give you a hard time in there?"

"Not like they gave me out here."

Pete drank his beer, half gone already, looked at the younger man across the table, the table they'd sat at a thousand times before. A thousand beers like these, a thousand silences like this, a million words in between.

"Where'd you get the scar?" he asked.

"Defending my honor," Ray told him, and he looked out the window and saw the years settle on the farm like darkness settles on a long and honest day.

2

Etta stopped on her way out of town and bought the largest take-out coffee that Tim Horton's would sell her without a prescription. Even with the caffeine kick, her eyes were heavy as she drove. It had been a slow night at the hospital, and she found that the shifts when she sat around doing nothing were more wearying than the hectic nights when there were babies to birth, drunks to stitch, crazies to inject.

She drank the coffee and concentrated on the meandering center line. It wasn't as if she could go home and flop into bed like a normal person. But then, Etta had long ago abandoned any hope of living a normal life. In truth, it wasn't something she aspired to or desired.

It was a cold fall morning—she'd seen her breath in the air as she walked across the hospital parking lot—and she drove with the odd combination of the heater on to keep her warm, and the window down to keep her awake. It was cold enough that the chimneys of the farmhouses on her road trailed wood smoke in the early morning air. Cold enough that the sheep on the McKellar place were bunched together in the lee of the pine grove of the pasture field.

And too cold for her father to be sitting on the side porch in his underwear. But that's where she found him.

He didn't seem to notice the chattering of his own teeth as she led him into the kitchen and sat him down. He was cranky and looking for a fight, glaring across the room as Etta took her coat off and hung it on the hook inside the door.

"Where the hell you been all night?"

Etta looked down at her scrubs. "Ballroom dancing," she told him. "Want some breakfast?"

She went up to his room and brought down pants and a shirt and socks and forced him into them, and then she made coffee and gave him a cup while she scrambled eggs and fried some leftover ham from the night before.

"Did Jim do the milking?" he asked while she cooked.

She glanced over; he was sipping the coffee with an unsteady hand, watching out the window toward the barn. Jim had been their hired hand when Etta was growing up. He'd been dead now maybe ten years.

"Yeah, Jim did the milking," she told him, setting his breakfast in front of him.

She showered and changed while he ate. Then she went into his room and jotted down the names of the various prescriptions there. He was seeing a new doctor later that morning and she wanted to be sure of everything he'd been taking.

She was hoping for some answers today. Or rather, she was hoping for some different answers today. She still wasn't convinced of his specific ailment. She was confused by the fact that he had good days and bad. On the bad days he was a virtual child; on the good he appeared to be as healthy mentally as he'd ever been, although she reminded herself that that was a qualified statement if ever there was one. She clung to the hope that he—with his short-term memory loss and frequent returns to normal behavior—was suffering from some form of dementia other than Alzheimer's. His chronic alcohol abuse could also point to this, she'd discovered, and as such might mean that his condition was treatable.

Now she sat on his bed and looked out the dormer window to the outbuildings and the fields beyond. The farm had fallen into great disrepair in recent years. There were leaky roofs and sunken foundations, fallen fences and rusted equipment. Homer had never been any great shakes as a farmer in his salad days, and now that his mind was beginning to slide into oblivion it only seemed natural that the farm was following suit.

Etta had moved home three years earlier, and she'd been pretending to be a farmer ever since. Without the proper equipment, though, she'd been forced to hire most work out, and the numbers weren't really supporting the effort. She'd recently taken a job as a nurse's aide at the hospital, three shifts a week, twelve hours each, and the unusual hours had required some adjustment to her inner clock.

What she hadn't anticipated, moving back, was the strange and strong attachment she'd developed for the farm itself. Growing up, she'd rarely considered the land as anything but acreage. In spite of the fact that her family had been here for more than a hundred years, it had never occurred to her that that might account for anything. Hell, everybody had to be somewhere. She had, in fits and starts, begun the long and painstaking task of bringing the place back from the brink. So far, her efforts had manifested themselves in small ways, painting and caulking, cutting grass and raking leaves. Her meager funds and her schedule, at work and with her father, left her with few resources, fiscal and physical, to accomplish much more at this time. Still, the deterioration of the place weighed heavily on her mind.

She suspected that she was equating the farm's state with her father's. If she could restore the place to its—if not magnificent then competent—past, then perhaps the same could be available for her father. It was an absurd notion, she knew, but still she couldn't shake it.

His doctor's appointment was at nine—just enough time to get him showered and dressed, if he was cooperative. When she went downstairs he was sitting stock-still in his chair, and—except for the rivulet of egg yolk on his whiskered chin—his breakfast was gone. She washed the dishes quickly and left them in the drainer to dry.

"Time to get you in the shower, Dad."

"I just had a bath."

"That was yesterday."

"Liar."

"I'm not a liar," she told him. "You have an appointment with Doctor Nichols. You have to shower and shave," she added, throwing the shave in as a bargaining point.

"No."

"You have to shower and shave."

"I'll shower, but I'm not gonna shave."

"Okay," she said quickly. She turned and started to lead the way to the bathroom, hoping to get him moving while the thought was still fresh in his brain.

"But first I want my breakfast."

It was a long morning at the medical center. First they had to fill out forms, and then they had to wait, and then there were the standard tests for Homer to undergo—tests that he'd been through before but that the new doctor wanted to administer firsthand. So Homer did the thirty questions again, and he did the memory tests, and he had his heart, lungs, kidneys, liver, ears, eyes, and throat prodded and poked and listened to and studied. Etta was in the examining room for some of it and exiled to the waiting room for the rest. Of course, when all was said and done, more was said than done, and they were sent home with the assurance that they'd hear back from the doctor in a few days.

Homer was tired from all this examining, and when they got back to the farm he lay down on the couch and was asleep in a heartbeat. Etta thought briefly of napping herself, but she found that she wasn't in the least tired. She changed her clothes and retrieved a Swede saw from the shed and then walked down to the orchard.

She'd mounted a campaign the past couple of years to bring the apple trees back from the brink and she had, this fall, experienced at least enough success to convince herself to carry on. There were branches that were weak sisters, though, and now she went to work culling them, using a Swede saw, which she'd bought at Lee's Hardware a year ago, and her grandfather's ancient hatchet, quite possibly purchased at the same store a few decades earlier.

The work quickly warmed her in spite of the cold autumn breeze. She made a pile of the limbs in the corner of the orchard along the fencerow. A friend of Homer's would pick them up later—he used apple chips in his smoker, and one day soon Etta would be repaid with a cured salmon or two.

She lost herself in the menial labor, humming tunelessly as she trimmed and toted and stacked. It was midafternoon when she finished up. Kneeling to place the last of the dead wood on the pile she realized that she was tired at last—it seemed that fatigue had crept up on her.

When she straightened and turned toward the house, Sonny Stanton was standing there, directly in her path.

"Jesus!" she exclaimed.

Sonny smiled at her but he didn't speak. He had his long hair tied back and was wearing jeans and a leather coat. He had on ugly aviator sunglasses, and she couldn't see his eyes. His cane was in his hand.

Etta's heart was pounding. "What the fuck do you think you're doing?"

"I was just out walking my property," Sonny said, and he nodded toward the fence to the east.

"Well, *this* is my property," Etta said.

He stepped closer to her and she instinctively moved back. He was wearing cologne, and the smell enveloped him. Something he would deem suitable, she guessed, for traipsing around the countryside. She glanced toward the gate to the orchard, where she'd left her tools.

"Actually, it's your old man's property," he reminded her.

"The point is, it's not yours," she said, and she stepped sideways as she spoke, moving tentatively toward the entrance.

He gestured at the farm again. "I was just looking over my crop."

"Yeah?" Etta said, judging the distance to the gate. "What exactly have you got planted there, Sonny?"

He shrugged. "Why—don't you know?"

"I do. What I don't know is what you're trying to pull," she said and she moved again. "You're no farmer. And even if you were—you're not getting this place."

"That'll be up to Homer," Sonny said. He was walking with her now. "And he's my good buddy. I was just gonna stop at the house and say hello."

"No, you're not. He's sleeping."

Sonny took the sunglasses off then. "Etta, why can't we try and get along?"

"I'd settle for half of that," Etta said, and she pointed her chin toward the fence line. "I'd be happy if you got along."

He looked where she indicated, and when he did she moved quickly to the gate. When he turned back she had the hatchet in her hand.

He smiled. "Come on, Etta. There's no need for that."

"Just picking up my tools."

He shook his head. "You don't know me, Etta."

"And I'd like to keep it that way. Now, why don't you limp back to wherever you came from?"

He flinched when she made the reference to his leg. "Shouldn't believe everything you hear. You're a smart girl, I thought you'd know that."

"It's not what I heard. It's what I've seen."

"And what would that be?" Sonny asked. "A mentally unstable woman talking a lot of unsubstantiated shit."

"Really? And what was Elizabeth's motive, Sonny? Why would she lie?"

"Christ, I don't know," he said. "She's fucking crazy."

He was whining now and his whining made her less afraid. She picked up the saw and walked through the gate. "Funny—all this time I've been thinking that was your excuse."

She left him standing in the orchard and headed for the house.

3

Ray stood in the mow window and watched the last half dozen of the bales come up the elevator. Pete Culpepper, on the wagon below, removed his hat and wiped the sweatband with his handkerchief, waited until the last bale disappeared into the barn, then climbed stiff-legged to the ground and unplugged the elevator.

Ray stacked the bales near the ladder drop. The hay was good, especially for a fall cutting; it hadn't been rained on, and it was pretty clean, and it smelled the way hay should smell—sweetly green and pungent—an odor that always reminded Ray of the summers he'd spent as a kid on this very farm. The first hay bale he'd ever lifted had belonged to Pete Culpepper. Thinking back, Ray doubted if he'd managed to get the bale six inches off the ground at the time, but he'd carried it the length of the barn while his father and Pete had watched, the muscles in his thin arms screaming at him to drop the load, his pride overruling the notion.

When Ray climbed down, Pete was standing in the front stall with the gelding Fast Market, the gelding's right front hoof between his knees. The bay mare in the next stall had her head over the top rail, watching the proceedings. There was a second broodmare, a roan, in the back stall.

The gelding was a beautiful horse, a shade off chestnut with darker brown in the mane and lower legs. He had a good head, with cheeks like a stud, and he had sharp, intelligent eyes. He wasn't a tall horse, but he was deep in the chest and nicely muscled across the shoulders and haunches. He stood as quiet as could be while Pete examined the hoof.

"When you running him?" Ray asked.

"Claimer in a couple of weeks."

"What's he done?"

"Well, he won in July. Next time out, he came up with this crack in the hoof. Had to shut him down. I epoxied it a couple times, but it wouldn't hold. I couldn't work him, so I just let him be 'til about ten days ago. I been working him over to Granger's since. It looks all right now, but we'll see."

Ray walked along the stalls, reaching in to rub the mare's forehead as he passed. The second mare was standing hip-shot in the back corner, sleeping on her feet, her breathing slightly labored. Ray looked her over, then said, "You got a foal coming."

"I guess I do," Pete said tersely. He climbed out of the gelding's stall and walked over.

"You're not exactly doing cartwheels about it."

"Why would I do cartwheels when my thoroughbred mare gets impregnated by a quarter-horse stud?"

"You're kidding."

"You know Tom Stackwood, down the side road?" Pete said. "Well, he's got this quarter-horse stallion. Black as coal—calls him Smoky."

"Got one eye," Ray said, remembering.

"That's the horse. Well, I had these two in that front field last winter. This one came in season, and I don't know—I reckon the wind was just right or something, but that stud ran through a plank fence at the home farm and a wire fence here and jumped my mare, and now I'm gonna end up with a foal whose two halves ain't gonna add up to nothin'."

Their voices had awakened the mare. She stood blinking at them.

"You could've aborted it," Ray said.

"No sir, I don't believe I could've."

Ray walked outside into the midday sun. The hound was sprawled on its stomach on the side porch, its jowls splayed across its front paws. The dog's eyes opened a moment, flicked on Ray, then closed slowly, like a curtain going down.

Ray walked to the paddock, leaned his elbows there, smoking. The barn was failing fast, and the house wasn't far behind. Three horses in the barn, a couple of mares whose running days were past and a nine-year-old gelding with a cracked hoof.

The sport of kings.

Pete came out of the barn, carrying a hackamore with a broken strap.

"How the hell you making a living off this?" Ray asked.

"Who said I was making a living?"

"Then how are you managing?"

"Well," Pete said, and he pulled the buckle from the halter. "I got my corn to come off, and could be I'll get a couple wins out of that gelding yet this year."

"Could be he'll break down next time out, too. That's not exactly a young horse you got in there."

"You're a pessimistic sonofabitch for somebody who just got out of jail." Pete showed Ray his crooked smile. "I'll have you know I'm fixin' to make a comeback."

"Yeah?"

"Martin Augustine is selling out. You know the place—next concession over. There's an auction next week—the farm, brood stock, everything."

"Yeah?"

Pete dropped his voice to a whisper, as if someone might be listening. "He's got a two-year-old colt, out of Canfield Dancer, and the word's out that the colt's damaged goods. Bowed tendon. But I know different. Jack Wilson's been training him in that swimming pool down at Fort Erie, and he says it wasn't never a tendon. He's had him out on the track a couple times, and he says the animal's as sound as a double eagle. Jack's my old pal—Augustine owes him money he's got no intention of paying, so Jack's keeping this to himself."

"He's still not gonna go cheap, with that blood."

"Damaged goods, Ray. You know how people are. I figure I can buy him for ten grand, maybe eight or nine if I get lucky."

"You're telling me you got ten grand?"

"If I did, it'd go for taxes. But I found a realtor who'll put up the ten against that little piece of land down front there." He pointed toward the northeast corner of the farm. "See where the creek angles across there. Well, that's considered a natural severance. There's about an acre there."

"An acre building lot is worth a hell of a lot more than ten grand," Ray said.

"True, but it takes about three months to get it severed. The sale is next week. I'll take the bird in the hand. Just think, Ray, I could be running a real nice three-year-old come spring. I could run him against the big boys."

Ray smiled. "You're still a dreamer, Pete."

"Anybody who ain't," Pete said, pulling at the hackamore strap, "ain't worth knowing."

"How far back are you on the taxes?"

"Don't you worry 'bout it, Ray. There's plenty out there worse off than me."

Ray went to speak but thought better of it. Pete gave him a short look and then walked off toward the house.

"Maybe I'll nail that eavetrough back on the barn," Ray called out to him.

"Go see your sister," Pete said, still walking away. "You've put it off long enough."

He steered Pete's Ford pickup south, toward his old hometown. It took him a while to get used to the truck's handling. There was something wrong with the steering—a bad tie-rod, maybe, or the bushings gone in the control arm—and the vehicle had a habit of a jerking to the left every now and then. It took Ray a number of miles to develop the proper touch on the steering to counteract the motion. He doubted Pete was even aware of the problem; after spending so many years atop fidgety horses, he'd probably expect a pickup truck to buck a little.

The town hadn't changed, but when had it ever? He drove by the pickle factory on the way in and the pallet factory on the way out and not a whole lot in between. On Main Street he'd watched for familiar faces but saw no one he knew—at least no one he recognized. He couldn't be sure that the people he saw weren't acquaintances of old. Time and his own indifferent memory could have rendered them strangers.

It took him the better part of two hours to reach Mary's house on the north shore of Lake Erie. The place was tucked away on a rocky cove halfway between Port Dover and Long Point. ("About as close to nowhere as you can be, and still get regular mail," Mary liked to say.)

He hit the lakeshore road south of town and followed it west. The lake was high, pushed up against the shore by a considerable wind from the west. There were whitecaps skipping the surface like sailing ships at sea.

He found himself driving slower as he approached the house. He was not looking forward to arriving.

The yard was neatly trimmed, and the house had been painted since he'd last been there. There was a white Chrysler in the driveway, in front of the open garage. He parked alongside and sat there for a while. Before he got out, he looked at himself in the mirror.

He went in without knocking. Mary was in the kitchen, rolling pastry dough on the counter, a cigarette hanging from her lip, the long ash of which seemed in imminent danger of becoming part of the dough. She looked at him and smiled, and the act of smiling caused the ash to drop.

"How are you, Mary?"

"Well, I wouldn't say I'm winning, but I'm holding my own," his aunt said. She looked him over, taking inventory as he had himself minutes before. "It's good to see you, boy."

Elizabeth was sitting on a rock outcropping over the short bluff that overlooked the bay. Her hair was loose, whipping in the breeze, cutting across her eyes, catching in her mouth. When she saw him walking across the lawn, she smiled slowly and then looked away, back over the water.

"Hey, Sis."

She made no reply, just maintained the smile. He sat down beside her; when she didn't look at him he followed her gaze out over the lake.

"How're you doing?" he asked.

She reached for his hand, never turning her head. Her fingers in his palm were soft. After a moment he took his free hand and moved the hair away from her face. Finally, she looked at him.

"You know the *Bonneville* is out there," she said, and she pointed directly. "In eighty-five feet of water. She went down in a storm in 1847. Ninety people on board, all lost. Europeans mostly—Germans, Poles, headed for the West. Homesteaders."

Ray took a cigarette from his pocket, lit it one-handed, keeping her fingers in his palm. She smelled of mint, of evergreen.

"I think about them," she was saying. "It must be so peaceful there on the ship, their belongings all around them. Their families. Must be comforting, permanent. Safe." Her voice dropped. "They're talking of salvaging the ship, you know. For the coins, the artifacts. Canada and the States are arguing over ownership. I hope they argue forever. They should leave those people alone."

"Those people were fish food a long time ago, Sis."

Later, in the kitchen, Ray had a cup of coffee and a slice of pie, which did not, he noted, taste of cigarette ash. Mary sat across from him, flour in her hair, on her glasses.

"Jesus, Mary," Ray said. "What do you do out here all day long?"

"What does anybody do?" she replied. "I cook, I clean. I watch bad soap operas and smoke too much. Tuesdays, I play bingo. Fridays, I buy groceries and go to the legion for a beer or two. Once in a blue moon I go to the Savoy on a Saturday night and listen to the country-and-western band."

"You'll be taking up square dancing next."

"My point is, what I do is not any more or less significant than what anybody else does."

Ray turned toward the lake. "And Elizabeth?"

"She sits out there nearly every day. I kept waiting for her to get stronger, I kept looking for signs that she was getting better. She's not getting better, Ray. She hasn't been off the property for months."

"What's the doctor say?"

"Which one? They came and went, and they all said the same thing. There's no response, and without response, there's no treatment. They were rather . . . impatient with her."

Ray finished the pie, pushed back from the table, coffee cup in hand. She watched him quietly.

"Well, I guess I can understand that," he said. "I guess it's natural to just shut down. Maybe I'd be the same way."

"Bullshit." Mary got up, took the plate from the table, and put it in the sink. "Come with me."

They went into the sunroom. Elizabeth's paints were there. There was a watercolor on the easel, a blue-green portrait of the lake, the sky above cloudless, a washed-out blue. There were other paintings scattered about the room, leaning against the walls, sprawled on the floor, propped in corners. All were of the same scene; only the temperament of lake and sky distinguished one painting from another.

Ray walked around the room, examining each painting.

Mary stood by the bay window, looking out to where Elizabeth sat on the bluff.

"She's your sister, Ray, and I know you love her. We know where you've spent the past two years." She turned to him. "But do yourself a favor; don't try to understand why she is the way she is. Don't burden yourself with that on top of everything else."

An hour later Ray was drinking rye at the bar of the old Queens Hotel in town and talking to Bonnie, who was tending bar and had been tending bar when Ray used to drink there as a teenager. Her hair was blonder now and still in a rigid bouffant, as if she'd found a look she liked in 1969 and never strayed from it.

"Where the hell you been, Ray?"

"Here and there. You know."

"I thought I heard you were in jail."

"You know, I seem to recall something like that in my recent past."

"What was you in for?"

Ray emptied his glass, gestured for another as he considered the question. "I guess the judge was of the opinion that I didn't play well with others."

He was half in the bag when Steve Allman walked in, wearing work boots and coveralls and a Boot Hill Saloon cap. He ordered a draft and looked down the bar.

"Ray," he said. "When'd you get out?"

"Don't ask," Bonnie said. "He's pretty vague on the whole thing."

Steve brought his beer over, ordered another rye for Ray, who was to the point where he didn't need another rye.

"Good to see you," Steve said.

"Thanks for the drink. How you been?"

"Can't complain," Steve said in a voice that said he could. Ray decided to deflect the opportunity. He'd known Steve and his family for years, had worked one summer for Steve's father, combining oats and wheat, baling the straw afterward. Their farm was just a concession over from Pete Culpepper's, and Pete and Steve's father were old euchre buddies.

"How's your old man?"

"Well, he just retired."

"Really?" Ray paused to take a drink. "So you're running the farm?"

"Nope, he sold the farm. Never said a damn word to me. Came home one night and announced he sold it off. Machinery, livestock, everything."

"Doesn't sound like Ken."

"He sold it to Sonny Stanton."

Ray had the glass to his lips; he hesitated and then took a sip.

"Truth is, I been hoping you'd show up," Steve said then. "And not just me. Sonny's up to something."

Ray put the whiskey on the bar. "Yeah, well, Sonny's always up to something. If it wasn't for fucking up, he wouldn't know what to do with himself."

"He's set on buying up that whole concession; he's got better than half of it already."

"What's he want with it?"

"He's talking about building a huge co-op. Telling everybody how they're not getting fair price for their grain. Figures on growing seed corn, soybeans—says he's gonna put in dryers and enough storage to hold everybody's yield until the price is right."

Ray looked across the bar, to where Bonnie stood under her platinum helmet of hair. "Since when does Sonny give a damn about the farmers, or anything else?"

"He's lying, sure as God made little green apples," Steve said. "I figure he wants to develop it, build cheap houses."

"He'd have zoning problems," Ray said.

"You and I would have zoning problems," Steve said. "Not

Sonny; he's got too much money behind him." He drank off his beer and then signaled to Bonnie. "Anyway, we've been hoping you'd show. Sonny's playing some game; ask him a question six times, and he'll give you six different answers. But he ain't gonna pull that shit with you."

Ray looked unhappily at the drink on the bar. "I got no intention of tangling with Sonny Stanton again. Your dad wouldn't have sold if he didn't want to. I'm out on parole. All I want to do is find a job and lead a half-ass normal life. I have no intention of going within a mile of Sonny and that bunch."

Steve looked at Ray, and then he shrugged in resignation. "I guess it don't matter anyway. The money's gonna win in the end. I just hate to see all that good land get bulldozed."

"Me too," Ray said. "But you're right about the money."

Steve drank the beer and then wiped off his mustache. "You say you're looking for work?"

"Yep."

"I got into the roofing business after the old man sold out. I need a man. You look like you're in shape."

Ray left the Queens with a jag on and a new job. Driving home, he was neither happy nor not. Elizabeth was, in truth, no worse than he'd expected. She'd always maintained a detached relationship with life, as if it were something she just dabbled in.

Maybe that was true of everybody, though. Maybe they were all dabblers. The scholars and the poets and the judges and the jailers, the whiskey drinkers and the teetotalers, the rich and the poor. Hell, even the roofers. Well, he'd find out about that last part soon enough. Hauling shingles was a young man's game, but he'd no one but himself to blame. His career goals had pretty much been mothballed these past couple of years.

As far as the business with Sonny went, he'd just have to put it out of his mind.

. . .

The plan to put the business with Sonny out of his mind worked fine for about thirty minutes. Driving past the Parr farm, he saw a BMW roadster pulling out of the driveway, the man himself behind the wheel. Ray made a U-turn and went back as the roadster disappeared to the north. He hesitated and then drove up to the house.

Etta was in the backyard, taking wash from the clothesline. She turned at the sound of his step—he was still capable of surprising her. She was wearing jeans and a man's cotton shirt, faded pale blue. Her blond hair was short, but not too short. She wore no makeup, never had that he could recall, and there were faint lines around her eyes. She looked terrific.

The blue eyes didn't give him much as she went back to her work, filling the hamper and then lugging it to the back step. Setting it down, she turned to him.

"You want coffee? I can smell that whiskey from here."

"Sure." But when he stepped toward the house, she indicated the picnic table.

"We'll sit out here. Dad's inside."

"Fine."

"You know what I'm talking about."

She took the laundry in. Ray sat on top of the table, looked around. The field behind the barn was planted in corn, turning yellow at the tips. The barn itself had seen better days, better years. The cedar shakes were blown in patches from the roof; here and there a portion of tin had been nailed inexpertly over a hole. The Ford 9N was stranded in the orchard, one rear tire flat, the tractor in a forlorn list as a result.

Etta brought coffee, handed him a cup, then moved to sit on a lawn chair, keeping her distance in every way.

"How are you, Ray Dokes?"

"Never better."

"Where have I heard that before?"

She sipped at the coffee, watched as he fumbled in his

pocket for his cigarettes. When he produced the pack she walked over and took one. He lit both, and she retreated to her chair.

"This place is going to hell in a handbasket," he said.

"Well, you'd be the one to know about that particular destination." She inhaled and blew smoke above her head. "We're doing all right."

"How's Homer?"

"He's fine. Slowing down a little, I guess."

He took a first drink of coffee and realized that it was instant. She saw him look into the cup, and then—as if in rebuttal—she took a long sip from her own, watching him over the rim with her eyes narrowed.

He put the cup on the table and looked away. The lawn, he saw now, was half cut. There was a riding lawn mower stalled beside the house, its hood up. *Nothing Runs Like a Deere* advised the decal on the side.

"What was Sonny Stanton doing here?"

"Limping noticeably."

Her smile caught him unawares; he'd not known how much he'd wanted her to smile until after she'd done so. He felt defenseless in her presence, even more so now with the whiskey he'd drunk.

"Stopped to see Dad," she said then. "Sonny and Dad have become bosom buddies, it seems."

"Oh?"

"Sonny's trying to buy this place. For some reason he's trying to buy up the whole concession. He already owns a pretty good piece of it."

"I heard. What's Homer think about that?"

"My father has always been impressed by money. He likes the fancy cars and the talk. He thinks he likes Sonny because Sonny's telling him all manner of shit, no doubt. But my father won't sell this farm. And if he tried, I'd stop him."

Ray was watching her now, hoping that she would smile again and knowing that she wouldn't.

"Have you been painting, Etta?"

"No, I don't seem to have the time or . . ." She shrugged.

"Or what?"

"I don't know." She looked away.

"He's not safe to be around," he said after a moment.

"Sonny? I know that. But don't worry; he won't mess with me."

"Don't be so sure."

"He wouldn't dare. He knows who my friends are."

There was a sudden roar from the interior of the house, a man's voice calling her name. Etta stood, her expression one of resignation rather than alarm, then tossed the remainder of her coffee on the grass and started for the back door. Ray looked inquisitively toward the door for a moment, then slid from the table.

"You saying we're friends?" he asked.

"What do you think?" she said. "You shouldn't be driving, by the way. But I guess you can negotiate another mile to Pete Culpepper's. One of these days you're gonna have to start thinking about acting your age, Ray."

Pete was standing over the stove, drinking a beer and stirring a pot of chili, when Ray walked in. The smell of the chili and the unmistakable odor of sourdough biscuits filled the kitchen—the acrid bite of the peppers and spices afloat on the soft yeasty air of the sourdough. Ray was immediately famished. He tossed the truck keys on the table, walked over to look in the pot. The steam from the stew made his eyes run, cleared his sinuses. He crossed the room and sat at the table.

"That's got some heat to it."

"I ever tell you 'bout the rattlesnake chili we used to make down in El Paso?" Pete asked. "We'd find them big old diamondbacks, sunning themselves on the rocks, and pick 'em off with a .22. Cook 'em up with that local chili pepper, so hot you could light a cigar with it. You want a beer?"

"No." Ray had heard about the rattlesnake chili many times, although the locale had a habit of changing. "What were you doing in El Paso?"

Pete poured a little beer into the pot. "Working for a quarter-horse trainer, man was a great-nephew of Pat Garrett. That's no guff. His family had the gun that Garrett used to shoot the Kid with. Sold it to a dentist over in Austin for $125,000. It was the genuine article."

"It had better been, for that kind of dough."

Ray picked up a newspaper from the table, glanced at the headlines without interest. Pete watched him from his chili pot.

"How's your sister?"

"I don't know." Ray pushed the paper away. "She's not there, you want to know the truth. She's living inside her head, Pete. And I guess that's what she wants. Or maybe that's all she can do."

Ray was suddenly tired. He wasn't used to any of this—the hay baling, the driving, the drinking, the talking. He'd only gotten through the past two years by forcing himself to think of nothing. Now it seemed he had to think of everything at once. It occurred to him that his brain was out of shape.

Pete put the lid on the pot, grabbed a towel, and opened the oven door to pull out the tray of biscuits, plumped up like fat little puppies and sweet-smelling in the pan. He set the tray on the table in front of Ray.

"How's Etta?" he asked.

Ray looked up from the biscuits. "How do you know I saw Etta?"

Pete brought the chili over, set the pot on the newspaper so it wouldn't burn the arborite table he'd burned a hundred times before, then went into the cupboards for plates.

"You got that dopey look about you."

"I can have that without seeing Etta."

"But you did see her." Pete put down knives and forks, sat, and ladled out the stew.

"I guess I did. She's doin' all right."

"You needn't tell me that. She's tough as a cactus, that gal. Eat."

Ray rousted himself, took a biscuit and broke it open, dragged it through the chili on his plate. Pete got up and got another beer from the fridge.

"Homer there?" he asked.

"He was inside," Ray said. "I didn't see him. I heard him."

"I hear he ain't doin' too good."

"No?"

"That bunch down at the mercantile were goin' on about him having that Old-zimers disease." Pete uncapped the beer and flipped the lid onto the countertop. "Although I doubt he's any worse off than the dimwits that were tellin' it."

"Then that's why she's still there. Of course, she'd never let on. Told me he's doing okay. And it's called Alzheimer's disease."

"Not according to that bunch down at the mercantile."

Ray took another mouthful. "Why didn't you tell me about Sonny Stanton buying up the concession over there?"

Pete shrugged. "Maybe I was afraid you'd go riding off like the Lone Ranger."

"That what you were afraid of?"

"Maybe. What's Etta saying?"

"You know Etta; she thinks she can handle anything that comes along. The same with Homer being sick."

"There's lot of mule in that girl."

Ray sat chewing the hot chili thoughtfully. Thinking about Etta's smile. Those cornflower eyes, the slight disdain. "Yeah, well I guess she's bucking for saint."

"I'd say she's got a better chance than me or you."

4

Paulie was in the passenger seat of the Lincoln, Dean behind the wheel, driving like a lunatic as usual. They were running number 7 west of Brampton, headed for the Slamdance, doing 110 in a 50, Pearl Jam in the tape deck.

Paulie was wearing his porkpie hat, and every few seconds he would lean back, pushing the rear brim into the headrest, causing the front of the hat to pop up. Dean, watching with a peripheral eye, was growing agitated.

"Do you have to do that?" he asked.

"Nope," Paulie said, but he kept on doing it until the phone rang.

"Don't answer that," Dean ordered. "It'll be Jackson, sure as shit."

"So?" Paulie asked, the ringing phone in his hand.

Dean grabbed it away from him. "So? You think he wants to say hello? He's got some shit errand for us to run, like always. You wanna go in and look at pussy, or you wanna go play fetch for Jackson?"

Paulie knew that it didn't really matter what he wanted to do, so he remained silent. They walked out of the sunlight into the dark of the Slamdance, ordered a couple of beers, and then stood at the bar. A stunning blond woman announced as Misty was onstage, naked save for a creatively torn white T-shirt, the shirt flashing brilliantly under the black lights above. Misty's big finish was to "She Works Hard for the Money." Halfway through the song, the tattered shirt hit the floor, and it became immediately apparent that Misty's plastic surgeon had been infinitely more skilled than her dance teacher.

Dean turned to Tiny Montgomery, working the bar, and said, "Wow, where'd she come from?"

"Depends who's asking," Tiny replied, watching her with the jaded eye of a man who'd seen too many naked women. "Yesterday I heard her tell some dude she was from Vancouver; the day before it was New York. Saturday she was drawling like a Georgia peach, claiming she hailed from Savannah."

When Misty quit the stage she went into the back room and emerged ten minutes later, wearing tight jeans and a white tank top. She walked to the bar.

"Gimme an ice water," she told Tiny.

"Hi there," Dean said.

She gave him a quick look, her eyes flicking over him like a handicapper looking at a cheap runner, taking in the gelled hair, the gold chain around the neck, the inexpensive leather jacket.

"Hello," she said and looked past him.

"Buy you a drink?" Dean asked.

"Johnny Walker Blue," she said to Tiny at once, not even looking at Dean.

Tiny brought the Scotch neat and turned to Dean: "Twelve bucks." His great belly shook with mirth as he watched the look on Dean's face. But Dean was a trooper; he paid with a twenty and even left Tiny a dollar tip. Misty took the Scotch and smiled at him.

"So you're Misty?" Dean asked.

"Sure—why not?" she said.

"Where you from?"

She turned and looked at Paulie, who was shyly admiring the fabric of her tank top.

"California," she decided. "The Golden State."

"I'm Dino," Dean said. "This is Paulie."

When Paulie said hello he took his hat off, revealing jug ears and a spring-loaded cowlick. Misty nodded and watched out over the crowd, sipped at her Scotch.

"What d'you boys do?"

"We're in the thoroughbred business," Dean said.

Misty turned back to him. "Yeah? And what do you do in the thoroughbred business?"

"Well, I don't know about *Dino*," Paulie said. "But I shovel a lot of horse poop."

The three of them were sitting at a table and half pissed when Jackson Jones came in. Dean and Paulie watched as he stood just inside the door, waiting for his eyes to adjust to the darkness. Dean thought about the back door, knew at once there was no chance.

"Shoulda parked in the alley," he told Paulie.

Jackson didn't bother to sit down. He wouldn't, of course, not in a joint like this. He stood in his jeans and his boots and his faded blue shirt, and he looked at Dean without expression, the look that always pissed Dean off for that very reason. His voice, when he spoke, was as neutral as his look, and that pissed Dean off too.

"I been trying to get you," Jackson said. "Where's the cell?"

"In the car," Dean said. "We been here."

"What good is it if you don't have it with you?" Jackson asked.

"Battery's dead," Dean said. "So what good is it anyway? Say hi to Misty, Jackson."

"Hello, Misty," Jackson said. "You two better get your asses over to the house."

"Are you a genuine cowboy, Jackson?" Misty asked. "I never saw a black cowboy before."

"I'm a horseman," Jackson said.

When Jackson got back to the farm Sonny was on the porch, a Cohiba in his mouth, feet up on the railing, cane hooked over the arm of the wicker chair where he sat. Sonny was looking vacantly at the paddock across the lane, where Silver Dawn was grazing at some tufts of grass along the fencerow. The mare's stomach was large, even though she wouldn't foal for nearly three months. The sun was making the odd cameo appearance from the cloud cover, and when it did it threw specks of light across the gray of her withers, like blue sparks dancing in a bonfire. Sonny watched her and puffed on the Cuban.

Jackson parked the truck in front of the barn and sat there a moment, watching Sonny watch the pregnant mare. Sonny looked like shit, but then he usually did in the morning. He was wearing khaki pants—no matter the weather, he never wore shorts, self-conscious about the scars on his leg—and a short-sleeved shirt, which was unbuttoned to reveal his soft belly. He'd grown his dark blond hair long of late and had taken to treating it with some sort of styling gunk, which left it looking, to Jackson's eyes, more filthy than fashionable. Jackson himself was a meticulous groomer, and he couldn't understand why a good-looking man like Sonny would wear his hair like that or submit to the goatee that he was sporadically growing and then shaving away. It seemed to Jackson that Sonny was a man in search of an image.

Jackson decided he wasn't much in the mood for Sonny today, but he walked over anyway, stepped onto the porch, and leaned the palm of his hand against the post there.

Sonny continued to look past him. Jackson glanced out over the paved lane, which ran to the highway. The grass alongside the lane was plush and manicured, with flower beds planted every fifty feet, the flowers mostly dead with the autumn weather. The beds were Jackson's pet projects, a labor of love. There were rose gardens in front of the barns—pure white Nevadas and Snow Queens mixed with Robert le Diables and Henri Martins. As time-consuming as they were, Jackson looked upon his horticultural interests as therapy. The fact that he was the only one on the place who wasn't in particular need of therapy was another matter altogether.

"You know," Sonny said finally, "I got a good feeling about that silver mare. That Jimmy Buck is a good fucking stud. I think I've got a winner coming here. Maybe Queen's Plate." He glanced over. "Maybe the Derby even. I just hope she throws a colt."

But Jackson was looking at his rose bushes, thinking that he would have to get them ready for winter soon.

"What do you think?" Sonny asked impatiently.

Jackson was still looking at his roses. "I think I got too much to do than sit around talking about races that haven't been run by a horse that hasn't been born."

Sonny looked at him and smiled. "Jack, Jack . . . you got the weight of the whole world on your shoulders, don't you? When you gonna learn to relax?"

Jackson turned at the sound of the front door opening. "I figure you do enough relaxing around here for the both of us."

Earl Stanton walked out onto the porch then, burdened down by several pieces of mauve-colored luggage that was clearly not his own. He was wearing creased cotton pants and a pullover, the casual attire he'd adopted since remarrying. His gray hair was cropped short, and he was lean and angular; only the stiffness of his gait betrayed his years. A limo was parked in the yard, the trunk open, and he headed for it.

The owner of the baggage emerged a moment later. Gena was wearing tight capri pants and high-heeled mules. She had her shades perched atop her blond hair, and she was looking suspiciously younger than she had before she'd left for New York a month earlier. Her yappy miniature poodle was tucked under her arm. She showed Jackson the pained acknowledging smile she reserved for those in servitude and then, looking neither left nor right, stepped down from the porch and headed for the car. She somehow managed a goal line fumble, though, and soon the poodle was running around the yard, barking crazily like the inbred it was. Jackson watched as Earl chased the animal down, his face barely concealing the contempt in which he held the dog, and finally deposited the mutt back into the limo, where Gena was smoking a cigarette and shouting instructions.

Earl was breathing heavily when he came back to the porch to talk to Jackson. "Damn dog," he said in dismissal and then: "I still don't know about running the Flash in the Queen Anne. I want him tip-top for the Breeders'."

"He needs the work," Jackson said. "Horse has got to run."

"Ah, Jack," Sonny interjected, "he's just afraid we'll put the saddle on backward with him not around to show us."

Earl gave Sonny a sharp look, then turned back to Jackson. "Well, just make sure he's sound."

"I still can't figure you missing the race," Jackson said.

Earl grimaced as if he were passing a stone and indicated the limo. "Oh, she's got some big shindig happening down in the islands. Her fashion friends."

"Yeah, you wouldn't want to miss that, Earl."

"Shit," Earl said.

"Don't worry, Pop," Sonny said from the chair. "If the Flash breaks a leg, we'll just prop him up on crutches and stand him to stud."

This time Earl never even turned toward Sonny, who was still sitting in the wicker chair.

"Take care of my horse, Jack," Earl said, and he stuck out his hand. "And I'll see you in New York."

The limo pulled out of the yard as the Lincoln was driving in. Dean was wearing shades and trying hard to appear sober as he and Paulie piled out of the car. Sonny came down off the porch and limped over.

"Where you clowns been?"

"In town," Jackson said, and he looked at Dean to let him

know that he wouldn't rat them out. It wasn't out of friendship, though, Dean knew. To Jackson, they weren't even worthy of the effort.

"We were in the Slamdance," Dean told Sonny. "Drinking Scotch whiskey with an angel named Misty. A rack like Pammy Anderson. Right, Paulie?"

Paulie never said a word, just stood there, his eyes on the ground.

"I want you to take that roan up to the Double B in London to get her bred," Jackson said. "They're waiting for her."

"What stud?" Dean asked.

"River Ridge," Jackson said.

"Roy Gowling's got that good stallion just down the road," Dean said "You know the one, out of Sky Classic. You could breed her there."

Sonny smiled. "Lenny and Squiggy gonna take over the breeding around here?"

"No, and neither are you," Jackson said. "You two get that mare loaded and get her up to London. I'm driving in to Woodbine, to see to the Flash. Sonny, you can go sit on the porch and smoke your cigar and do whatever it is you do all day."

The roan mare bolted when they were loading her, slamming Dean against the trailer wall and then running off across the yard. Jackson, afraid that she would head for the highway, called to Paulie inside the barn. The mare was standing on the grass of the lawn, snorting loudly, her ears back, when Paulie came out. He began to talk to her, and as he approached her head seemed to drop a quarter inch with each step he took, and then her ears came forward. When he reached her she nuzzled him like a dog, and he took her by the halter and led her into the trailer without a hitch.

It was three o'clock by the time Dean and Paulie hit the 401, Dean behind the wheel of the Ford Crewcab, the single trailer behind. Paulie fell asleep before they reached Kitchener. Dean stopped for coffee at a BP station, checked to see that the cantankerous mare was still on her feet, then set out again.

Dean was getting plenty tired of his situation with his uncle Earl. Of course, Earl wasn't really his uncle. Dean's mother had been Earl's first cousin, and when Dean had had a little trouble with the law—stealing cars, selling grass; trumped-up charges in Dean's mind, despite the fact that he was guilty of them all—Earl had agreed to hire Dean as a kind of gofer. The judge always looked more favorably on a man who could attest to gainful employment, and Earl's generosity had kept Dean out of jail. Of course, for Dean it was mostly a case of out of the frying pan and into the fire. Maybe Earl did have a fine sense of familial responsibility, but he was getting some cheap labor out of the deal.

Paulie was another story. He *was* Earl's true nephew—his mother was Earl's sister. She'd never married and had died in Montreal in a flophouse with needle marks up both arms. Maybe it was foul play, and maybe it wasn't; apparently, she wasn't someone the cops cared enough about to investigate. Paulie never knew his father—knew nothing of the circumstances of his mother's union with the man. Whatever the circumstances, the result of that union led Dean to believe that the man was not the sharpest tool in the shed.

But Paulie had a way with horses that bordered on spooky, and he was a good man at the end of a shovel. Dean couldn't say the same for himself. He'd started out cleaning stables for the old man, then passed through a procession of menial jobs, proving himself to be ill-suited to each. Whenever he'd made an effort to assert himself, he'd been knocked back on his heels by Jackson or Sonny.

Now Dean was just spinning his wheels, baby-sitting Paulie and running whatever errands Jackson considered to be beneath his station. And Dean was getting sick of it. He was thirty years old, being treated like a teenager.

Paulie woke up a few miles east of London. It was near

dark now, and they were sandwiched in among the countless tractor trailers that crawled the 401 like caterpillars. Dean hated being in their midst; they stirred in him a raging claustrophobia never evident elsewhere. He had a need to see where he was going, to have a horizon to aim for. Otherwise, he feared that he was standing still.

"Why'd you tell that girl your name was Dino?" Paulie was asking now.

"What?"

"That girl Misty, at Slamdance. You told her your name was Dino."

Dean shrugged. "I like it. I might even change it, down at the courthouse. Dino is a cool name; it commands respect, you know. It's an Italian thing."

"You ain't Italian."

"It's a fucking attitude. You don't understand shit, Paulie. That's your problem."

Paulie yawned. "Least I know my name."

They reached the stables at shortly past eight. Dean got out and shook the stiffness from his joints. The place didn't measure up to the Stanton farm, but it was a pretty nice spread just the same. There were two barns, red with gray roofs, and a series of interconnecting paddocks that ran behind and to the east. The house itself was a two-story stucco, with porches across the front and one side.

There was an older guy waiting for them; he had a steel gray brush cut and long sideburns, and he said his name was Jim Burnside. Paulie thought that was pretty cool, having a name that fit the way you looked.

Paulie unloaded the mare, and they tucked her away in a stall in a small barn off the main building. Jim tossed in a sheaf of hay and filled a water pail.

"You guys sticking around?" he asked.

"When you gonna breed her?" Dean asked.

"Tomorrow morning, I'd guess," Jim said. "Have to wait for the boss. He likes to run the show himself. She might have to stay a couple days."

"Where's the stallion?"

"River Ridge? He's over to the other place. Can't have him around here, with the mares in season. He'd kick the fucking walls down."

"Well, we got no plans," Dean said.

"Then let's get a drink," Jim said.

There was a country-and-western bar in a mall a couple miles away. They sat at the bar, and Jim and Dean ordered rye and water, Paulie, a beer.

"How long you been with Stanton?" Jim asked.

"A while now," Dean told him. "I handle a lot of the breeding stock. I picked your stud River Ridge for this mare; I figure it's a good match."

Paulie snorted into his beer. Dean shot him a look.

"Paulie helps me out, with the loading and transport, that kind of thing," Dean said.

Paulie nodded. "You tell him, Dino," he said, and he slid off the stool, walked to a video machine along the wall. Dean watched him a moment, then signaled to the bartender: "Two more."

"So what's he like, Earl Stanton?" Jim asked, reaching real quick for the fresh drink. He was a thirsty man, it seemed.

"He's all right."

"He's sure been the big dog the past couple years, here and in the States both. That Jumping Jack Flash has gotta be the best four-year-old in North America. They got him at the home farm?"

"We got him at Woodbine right now. Running that big race on Sunday."

"Fucker can run. The old man can pick a horse."

Dean took a drink, turned to watch the waitress's ass as she walked past. He felt his anger come up. "Yeah, well it helps when you're sitting on half a billion dollars. You buy a hundred colts every spring; one of 'em's bound to be a keeper. Fucking nags are just a hobby to him. He makes all his dough with the electronics and the other shit. He could lose ten million a year on the horses, win a couple big races, and he's happy. Ten million's nothing to him; shit, I bet he's spent that much bailing his little boy out over the years."

"Sonny? Yeah, I heard some stories."

"Well, I'm betting they're all true. Sonny's got a real problem with women. Never convicted, though. They don't convict multimillionaires. You or me, we'd be dog meat."

"Spoiled rich kid, eh?"

"Yeah." Dean reached for his smokes, lit up. He was done with the subject. He turned to look at Paulie playing the machine along the wall. Simpleminded fuck, Dean thought. Must be nice, on a certain level. But then, where would he ever go, what would he ever have?

"What's the stud fee on River Ridge?" he asked, turning back.

"Fifty."

"Goddamn it," Dean said. "What a life. Do nothing but fuck; fifty grand a pop."

Jim laughed. "It's not like the horse gets the money."

"He gets the fucking."

"Why they breeding that mare this time of year, anyway?"

"I think they bred her in February, and she didn't catch." Dean shrugged. "Maybe the old man wants to see if she's barren. She's never foaled, that I know of."

"The Ridge will take care of her. He's damn near perfect in that area; that's why you're paying fifty grand."

"Fucking horse sperm's worth more than gold, you know that?" Dean said in wonderment. "What a racket."

They got a little drunk, and then Jim said they could sleep over at his place. They followed him out into the country, north of the town, where he lived in a tumble-down frame farmhouse, beside a weathered barn with half the windows broken or boarded up.

Paulie crashed on the couch right away, and Dean and Jim sat up and had another drink, sitting in the kitchen.

"You know," Jim said after a time, his voice thick with rye. "A man could make a lot of money with one of these top-notch studs. In a month, you could make enough to retire."

"How would you do it?" Dean asked.

"Well—there'd be some way. I mean, you got a product—it'd just be a matter of selling it. There's plenty of buyers out there. Guys who wouldn't ask questions."

"You know these guys?"

"You betcha I know 'em."

Sonny had watched the drama surrounding the loading of the roan mare from the house, waiting for the Percodan to gain the upper hand on his hangover. Five minutes after the trailer left the yard, he gathered his car keys and put on his coat. The mail was on the kitchen table; before he left the house he picked up the gas bill and put it in his inside pocket. Then he drove over to Holden County.

The farm was a fifty-acre piece, with a sugar bush at the back that produced maple syrup and a large vegetable garden in the field beside the house. When Sonny pulled up, the old man was in the field, picking the last of the season's tomatoes and placing them gently in a hamper basket. Sonny got out of the car and relit his cigar as he walked across the lawn. Passing the house, he could see the old woman inside, her head framed in the kitchen window. When Sonny waved, she didn't wave back.

The old man was wearing coveralls and a straw hat—like a farmer in a movie, Sonny thought—and he watched Sonny nervously as he approached.

"Hey there," Sonny said.

"Hello."

"Still got tomatoes, I see."

"Just about the end of them," the old man said, and he straightened up.

"Well, everything comes to an end," Sonny told him, and he smiled. He glanced at the house. "My man Rock tells me you're thinking of backing out of our deal."

"Well," the old man said slowly. "I've had second thoughts."

"But we had a deal."

"Well, there was nothing signed. I just been thinking—I don't know that I'm ready to retire. And the old girl doesn't think she wants to move after all."

Sonny walked along the row of plants. He stopped and turned over a large ripe tomato with the toe of his Topsider. "Now that's a shame," he said. "Because we had a deal." He crushed the tomato beneath his heel.

"See here," the old man protested.

"No, you see here." Sonny took the gas bill from his pocket and showed the back of the envelope to the old man. "This is from my lawyer. You're in breach of promise, Methuselah. I pay my lawyer a lot of money to make sure guys like you keep your word. And he tells me that all I have to do is sue your ass, and there's a good chance that I'll get this farm for nothing. So this is working out real good for me. I'm not so sure about you and the missus."

The old man stood silently, his eyes on the splattered tomato in the dirt, as if it was the source of his dismay. "There was nothing signed," he said again.

"You telling me your word is no good?" Sonny asked. "I thought that was a big deal to you people."

"You got a lot of nerve," the old man said, and he took a step toward Sonny. Sonny raised his cane instinctively. The man looked plenty strong in spite of his years.

"It's your choice," Sonny said, and he shrugged. "Maybe you should fight it in court. You got a good lawyer? My guy's a fucking maniac; I swear you could cut him with a chain saw and he wouldn't bleed. But you do what your conscience dictates."

Sonny turned and walked back across the field, taking care to step on as many tomatoes as he could. The old man watched as Sonny backed the BMW onto the lawn and then drove out of the driveway. Then he walked slowly to the house.

5

The Augustine auction was to begin at ten in the morning. Ray rode over with Pete Culpepper in the pickup, arriving at half past nine. It was to be a huge auction, with three auctioneers: one to handle the furniture, antiques, and other sundry household items; another for the machinery and the real estate; and a third for the livestock, which consisted of not only a dozen thoroughbreds but also a herd of Charolais cattle.

The horses were turned out in the paddock along the barn, and each wore a hackamore with a number on it for identification purposes. They were mostly broodmares, although there were a couple of geldings still running at Woodbine.

And the colt that had so recently become the apple of Pete's eye.

He was a good-looking horse, dark bay, tall, and not yet as big across the chest and shoulders as his configuration promised. He was standing away from the other horses, watching the crowd with wide intelligent eyes, his ears forward. Pete Culpepper was doing his best to study him while pretending not to.

"See anybody else looking at him?" he asked Ray after a while.

"Pete, there's two hundred people here. How the hell am I supposed to know where everybody's looking?"

"I just wish the sonofabitch didn't look so healthy," Pete said. "Too bad he wouldn't pick up a stone and limp a little."

"Want me to go kick him in the shin?"

Pete looked at Ray, thinking. "No, somebody's bound to see you."

The machinery and the cattle and the household items went on the block first. It would be after lunch before the horses and real estate went up. Pete and Ray found a place to stand in the sun along the barn wall and wait.

Sonny picked up Dan Rockwood, and the two of them drove out to the sale together. On the way they stopped at the village of Cook's Station, although it was hardly a village at all anymore, just an intersection of side roads, a cluster of buildings, a gas station, and the remains of the old train depot. Even the tracks were gone—pulled up a few years earlier and sold off for scrap. Rockwood—the Rock to his friends—motioned for Sonny to pull over when they arrived.

"This is what I was telling you about," he said. "Homer Parr's farm runs right up to the edge of the village. Now this is all zoned hamlet, which means residential building permits are a snap. Rubber stamp. This is the interesting part: the zoning runs the length of the concession—the whole of Parr's farm. Shit, he could sever as many lots as he wanted, make a fortune, if he knew about it."

"Why doesn't he know?" Sonny asked.

"Nobody knows. These villages were laid out 150 years ago, when the railroad went through. Back then, nobody knew whether a place like this would end up with a hundred people or a hundred thousand. So they'd designate anywhere from fifty acres to five thousand as being hamlet. Somebody would write it down in a dusty book somewhere, and that'd be it. I came across one like this north of Toronto—paid for my place in St. Barts."

Sonny had a cigar in his hand, and he used it to point at the bush lot, which separated the "town" from the country. "You're telling me I won't need rezoning."

"Not for Parr's farm," the Rock said. "And you already own the co-op on the other side of the concession. It's zoned commercial, which is perfect for you. After that, it's just a matter of persuading the board to let the whole concession go."

"And you know these people?"

"I deal with them all the time."

"And they can be had?"

"I didn't say that."

Sonny smiled. "No, you wouldn't—because if that were true, I wouldn't need you. Right?"

"I didn't say that either."

It was afternoon when they got to the Augustine farm. The sale was half over. Not that it mattered—Sonny wasn't interested in rocking chairs or antique crockery or hay balers or suckling calves. The only reason Sonny was there was the acreage.

He parked the BMW along the side road, and the two of them walked in. Sonny, as was his custom when dealing with the local farmers, was dressed the part, wearing jeans and a duck canvas jacket, a ball cap with a seed company logo on his head, work boots.

He and the Rock walked up the lane, stopped to give the house a look. It was a handsome two-story brick with leaded glass windows and a porch across the front and along one side; once Sonny owned it, he would have it torn down. They wandered over to the barns. There was a trailer there, owned by the auctioneer, where Sonny acquired a cardboard placard with a number to be used in the bidding. The woman who gave him the number told him that the farm would be on the block within the hour.

Sonny was leaning against a sugar maple in the yard when he was approached by a man with a bushy gray beard, wearing a plaid mackinaw and rubber boots caked with shit.

"You're Stanton?" the man asked.

Sonny smiled at the gruff manner. "I guess I am."

The man in the mackinaw obviously didn't know Sonny, but he'd already decided that Sonny was a stand-up guy. And it had nothing to do with Sonny's appearance, or his manner, or his reputation. It had everything to do with his money. It was a wonderful thing, Sonny thought; he'd recommend it to anyone who could swing it. Money can make an ugly woman presentable, a fat man thin, a moron a wit. And rumor had it that it made the world go round.

"They tell me you're gonna take on the wheat board," the man was saying.

"Isn't it about time somebody did?" Sonny asked.

"Anybody can say it."

"You're a farmer?" Sonny asked.

"My whole life."

"So you plant your corn, fertilize it, irrigate for it, harvest it, dry it, and store it. And yet they control it. That make sense to you?"

"Never has."

"Well then, you just watch. I'm gonna do something about it. This country can't get along without the farmer. The farmer's always known it; it's about time somebody informed the country."

The man nodded sagely into his beard as he moved away. Then the Rock walked over, a strange smile on his face. When Sonny looked at him he jerked his thumb over his shoulder in the direction of the paddock.

"What?" Sonny asked, looking.

"Along the wall," the Rock said.

Sonny looked, and after a moment he saw a grizzled old man in a cowboy hat, and standing beside the old man—sonofabitch—was Ray Dokes. Sonny's hand tightened on his cane when he saw Ray.

"Well, well," he said.

"Thought that might interest you," the Rock said.

"When'd he get out?"

"Don't know. But he's out."

"Then he's on parole," Sonny said. "They gave him five, fucking psychopath."

"What's he doin' here?"

Sonny looked across the yard as he considered the question. "I don't know. Maybe him and the old coot are here for the stock. Probably looking to steal one of those broodmares."

As if on cue the auctioneer announced that the bidding on the horses was about to begin. Sonny smiled.

"Come on," he said. "Keep an eye on that fucking Dokes. Don't let him near me."

"He won't pull anything, not if he's on parole," the Rock said. "But I'd be happy to break his goddamn neck."

They walked over to the railing of the paddock to watch the auction. The geldings went first. Sonny kept his eye on the pair across the corral—neither Dokes nor the old man made a move during the bidding. Then the colt came up, and the old man came forward immediately, his eyes bright, his step quick.

"Lookit this," Sonny said softly.

He looked at the bay colt and saw nothing special. Not that Sonny—around thoroughbreds most of his life—could claim to have an eye for horses or know much about them. The auctioneer began his spiel.

"—two-year-old out of Canfield Dancer and Lady Jane. In the interest of fair play we have to tell you that this colt did not run as a two-year-old as a result of a bowed tendon. This horse is being sold under the caveat buyer beware—"

Across the paddock Ray heard the auctioneer's warning, and he felt Pete's razor-sharp elbow dig into his ribs. The old man was thrilled with the auctioneer's caution. Ray held his sore ribs and looked at Pete—he was as giddy as a kid getting his first bicycle.

The price started at five grand, with three bidders joining in. The going was decidedly unenthusiastic; Ray saw right away that Pete was going to get his horse. The first bidder dropped out at seven thousand, and the second—a stout man in a beaver hat—quit when Pete went to eighty-five hundred. The auctioneer said the once, and he said the twice, and he had the gavel in the air.

"Eighty-five hundred and one," a voice called from the crowd.

Until that point the bid increments had been one hundred dollars. There was silence as the auctioneer sought out the new bidder. Ray followed his eyes, and then he saw Sonny Stanton, standing across the corral, cardboard number held high. Ray's stomach knotted.

"I'll be goddamned," he heard Pete say. And then: "Nine thousand!"

"Nine thousand and one!" Sonny said before the auctioneer could speak.

There was a large bald man with Sonny, and now he began to make his way toward Pete and Ray. He had gold hoops in each ear, and he wore a long leather coat that reached to his knees. Ray watched him cautiously.

"We've got nine thousand and one," the auctioneer was saying. Ray could tell by his tone that he was pissed at Sonny's bush-league bidding.

"Ninety-five hundred!" Pete called.

"Ninety-five and one!"

"You might as well forget it," Ray said then. He could see the veins in Pete's neck.

"Ten thousand," Pete said, but his voice was losing its timbre.

"Ten thousand and one!" Sonny was standing out from the crowd now, his number high above his head. People around him were watching in wonder. Some were smiling at the show.

The bald man had moved to within ten feet, and he had his back to the bidding, staring Ray down. Ray gave him a look, then turned away.

"How much money you got?" Pete asked him.

"Doesn't matter," Ray said. "It's over."

"I got a few hundred," Pete said desperately. "Can we make up a grand?"

"Probably, but it won't matter," Ray said. "You see what he's doing. It's over."

"Eleven thousand," Pete called out.

"Eleven thousand and one!"

And that was it. Ray could see that Pete's large gnarled hands were clenched into fists, and he knew he had to get him out of there. He pulled him gently, and when that didn't work he pushed him, not so gently, until finally Pete started to walk, his whole body shaking with rage. The bald man smiled when they passed.

"That's it, boys," he said. "Tails between the legs."

Ray kept his hand on Pete's shoulder and pushed on, refusing to look at the smiling man. He got Pete to the pickup, and then he got behind the wheel and drove them out of there.

When the Rock walked back around the paddock Sonny was in the process of selling the colt to the man in the beaver hat.

"Eight thousand?" the man was asking, confused.

"That's right," Sonny assured him.

"I'll get you a check," the man said, and he moved away.

"You just dropped three thousand dollars in about five minutes," the Rock said.

"Maybe so," Sonny said, and he turned to see Ray and the old man drive away. "But that was about as much fun as a man can have for three grand."

6

It was two weeks before Ray could get up in the morning without feeling as if his body was a seized piece of machinery. He had to oil his joints with coffee before he was loose enough to pull his socks on. He was surprised to find that he was in such sad physical shape, although he should have expected it. He hadn't worked out much in jail. He'd meant to, but in the end he'd found it boring, like everything else inside.

The roofing crew was working in a new subdivision of low-income housing, just north of Kitchener. Three hundred and forty-two houses, two-story duplexes, basic cookie-cutter design, tiny lots, the backyards not much bigger than a good-size automobile.

Ray had hitched to work the first couple of days, and then Steve Allman had let him have an old Coupe de Ville that had been sitting in the compound. The Caddy was dark blue; the radio worked, and the air didn't. The motor ran pretty well, smoked a little, but was quiet. Steve had let Ray have the car against wages.

They were getting paid by the square and could pretty much work their own hours. The crew was contracted to roof sixty of the houses in the subdivision. There were four men in the crew: Doc Randolph, Neil Mulvale, Ray, and Steve Allman. There was a kid whom everyone called Pottsy who cleaned up after the crew, ran for coffee, sometimes carried bundles.

Most days, Steve worked alongside his men, never came on

like a boss or a wheel of any kind. Ray had trouble keeping up with the others for the first few days, but nothing was mentioned of it. Everybody kept to their own pace.

Friday morning, Ray arrived on site at seven o'clock, barely light out. He finished a take-out coffee sitting in the Caddy and then got out, strapped his belt on, and walked to the next house in line. Doc was sitting on a bundle of shingles, looking sleepily across the open field to the north.

"Morning," Ray said.

"Ray."

"What're you doing?"

"Meditating."

"What're you meditating on?"

Doc stood up, shook off his lethargy like a wet dog after a swim. "I'm meditating on gettin' this motherfucker shingled, gettin' paid, and gettin' laid. That's what."

"Well, you're a spiritual sonofabitch, I'll give you that."

Ray walked to the truck, pulled down an extension ladder, propped it against the house, ran it up to the eave. Neil arrived, and the three of them spent the next half hour carrying bundles up to the roof. They were just starting to shingle when Pottsy showed up, driving his mother's Jetta.

"Where the fuck you been?" Neil asked.

"I had a late night," the kid said. "Went to see Urban Shocker in concert."

"Who?"

"They're this awesome rap group."

"Shit," Neil said.

It was a cool October day, a good day for working. Steve Allman was out pricing new jobs, and it was just the three of them shingling. The kid was dragging his ass, and Neil kept after him. By noon, when they quit for lunch, the house was a quarter finished.

They sat on the shingle pallets to eat. Pottsy hadn't brought a lunch, and he drove to the corner store and came back with Fritos and root beer.

"You kids and your health foods," Doc said.

Ray finished his sandwich and lay back on the pallet in the sun, stretching his back muscles. He was beginning to feel pretty good, making some money, getting in shape. Of course, just being able to come and go as he pleased was reason enough to feel good these days. What he might do with the rest of his life was another matter, something he was going to have to think about, but not today. Hell, he had houses to shingle.

"How can you listen to that rap shit?" he heard Neil ask the kid.

"How can you listen to country and western?" the kid asked back.

"Country and western is real music."

"Well, rap is my music," the kid said. "It's poetry; I can relate to it."

"Yeah," Neil said. "You're a white kid from Middleburg. You can relate."

"Urban Shocker is white."

"Shit, that's even worse," Neil said. "White kids pretending they're black. Everybody in the world wants to be something they're not. White kids wanna be black; black kids wanna be white. Poor folks wanna be rich."

"You wanna be smart," Doc added.

"Fuck you."

Doc laughed and looked at Pottsy. "You gotta listen to jazz, kid. Black, white, it doesn't matter. Jazz is the only original music ever to come out of North America. Ever."

"What about rock and roll?" Pottsy asked.

"Fuck rock and roll."

The kid finished his Frito lunch and walked over to throw the trash into the iron dumpster where he stowed the shingle remnants. Walking back, he looked at Ray, reclined on the shingles, eyes closed, hands clasped behind his head for a pillow.

"What about you, Ray? What do you listen to?"

"Depends on what you're doin'," Ray said without opening his eyes. "If you're traveling, listen to Hank Williams. If you're lonely, listen to Hank Williams. If you're having problems with a woman, then you better listen to Hank Williams. The rest of the time—well, I'd recommend Hank Williams."

Steve Allman drove in then, got out of the truck, took his tool belt from the back, put it on, and walked over. Ray raised himself to a sitting position.

"Steve," Doc said. "What kind of music you listen to at home?"

"I got one wife and four kids," Steve said. "The only thing I want to hear at home is silence."

They went back to work. Steve and Ray carried up a couple of lengths of valley and cut it to fit the dormers on the front of the house. They chalked the lines on the valley and then went back to shingling, each taking a dormer.

"You ever lay cedar shakes?" Steve asked after a time.

"Once or twice, when I was a kid," Ray said.

"I priced a place this morning," Steve said. "Old farmhouse in Caledon. Guy wants the original cedar roof. Figured you and I could do it next weekend."

"Sure."

When Ray got home from work, it was full dark and Pete Culpepper was gone. Ray took a cold beer from the fridge, filled the bathtub with water hot as he could stand it, and climbed in. He laid his head back against the porcelain, drank the beer, and let the water lubricate his muscles. He drank the beer so fast he had to get out after a few minutes and walk wet-footed into the kitchen for another.

The telephone began to ring, and he let it. It would be for Pete anyway. The phone rang maybe a dozen times—Pete didn't have an answering machine and wouldn't know how to operate one if he did—and then it quit. Ray leaned back, drank the second beer slowly, and willed his body and brain to relax.

When he got out, he put on clean jeans and a cotton shirt. In the kitchen he fried a steak and three eggs, ate standing up against the counter. Then he put the dishes in the sink and sat down at the kitchen table and wondered what to do.

It was Friday night, he had money in his pocket, and nothing that resembled responsibility to any thing or any person. There had been a time, in his younger days, when he wouldn't even have made it home after work, just headed straight for the bars. He'd had more energy then, he remembered, along with a huge capacity for getting himself into trouble. One had waned; with a little luck, and better judgment, maybe the other would as well.

He found Etta's number in the phone book, sat down, and looked at the phone on the wall for a long time. She would be home with Homer, he figured. Ray wondered if Homer really had Alzheimer's. Could be he was just getting old and forgetful. Maybe in time he'd forget about hating Ray's guts. He closed the phone book and grabbed his jacket from the peg inside the door and drove into town.

He had no intention of driving to the ballpark, but he drove there anyway. He saw the floods from two blocks away and knew that there was a game on. Home games were always played on Fridays. The ballpark was located on Canal Street, and it was built along the bank of the old feeder, in a valley of sorts. Ray parked up above, on the main street, which ran out of town. The teams were on the field, the game in the third inning when he arrived. He got out of the Caddy and sat on the hood, thinking he would watch a couple innings before he went down to see the guys.

He could see Bo Parker, sitting in the dugout, obviously not in the lineup. Pudge McIntyre was beside him, still managing the team, Ray guessed. Pudge was working over a wad of gum like it was the enemy, meaning he was still off the smokes.

There was a stringbean lefty on the mound for the home side. He had a wild windup, lifting his leg so high he almost kicked himself in the ear with his shoe, and then heaving himself forward in a jangle of arms and legs, releasing the ball from about three quarter. The movement was so herky-jerky that Ray wondered how the kid ever managed to throw strikes and then, watching for a bit, realized for the most part that he couldn't. The bases were full when Pudge walked out to talk to the kid the first time, and they were still full, with three runs scored and nobody out, when he pulled him a few minutes later.

Al Robins came in to relieve. When Ray was on the team the young guys used to joke that Al had three pitches: slow, slower, and slowest. Of course, what the kids couldn't understand was that a pitcher pitches with his brain, not his arm. Ray watched, smiling, as Al threw a total of four pitches, got a pop-up and a double-play ball, and walked off the field. Slow, slower, and slowest. Ray could see the guys kidding Al as he went into the dugout, and he knew what they were saying—ragging him about his age, his paunch, his lack of speed. The same things Ray might say when he went down to the field.

After another inning he got into the Caddy, sat there with the engine running for several minutes. Then he pulled out onto the street and headed out of town.

On the inside, all a man thinks about is getting out. Night and day, it's always there, like an unfulfilled promise—that always indistinct point of time somewhere in the distance when he is no longer in stir. It occupies a man's head when he's thinking about it, and it occupies his head when he isn't. The mental pursuit of that future moment is so powerful that he invariably forgets to consider the next question.

What to do when it finally happens.

Because being out with nothing to do and nowhere to go is not all that much different from being in. The difference between being inside and being out was that on the inside, a man always had a plan. And that was to get out. Being out robbed him of that objective, and it was in looking for a brand-new objective that he usually got himself in trouble.

Dean and Paulie were at the bar in the Slamdance. Dean drinking a vodka martini, Paulie, beneath his porkpie, nursing a beer, both transfixed by Misty strutting the stage. Dean was pissed at Tiny Montgomery; he'd asked Tiny for Grey Goose vodka—that's what Misty drank—and Tiny had told him he wouldn't know Grey Goose vodka from gray goose shit. So Dean, on his third drink, had yet to tip the big man. Tiny was taking his penance in stride; Dean wasn't much of a tipper in the best of humor.

Misty was into her finale when the door opened and a guy walked in, a guy Dean recognized but couldn't finger. The guy was late thirties, brown hair, thin. Wearing jeans and a leather jacket. When he came under the light of the bar Dean could see he had a slight hook in his nose and a thin scar across the point of his chin. His hands on the bar were large and calloused.

"Paulie, who's that dude?" Dean asked.

Paulie glanced over real quick, then went back to Misty, who was stark naked now, on a blanket on the floor, knees up, giving the boys on pervert row a reason to pay six bucks for a bottle of beer.

"I seen him before someplace," Paulie said.

Tiny Montgomery walked over to the man, and they shook hands across the bar, Tiny smiling broadly. He brought the man a beer, refused payment. They talked until a customer drew Tiny away. The man in the jacket took his beer to a corner table and sat with his back to the wall.

Misty finished up, gathered her clothes and her blanket,

and headed backstage. Paulie turned back to the bar and reached for his beer. He was thinking about asking Misty to go on a picnic.

Dean drank off his vodka, signaled to Tiny for another, and the big man brought it over. This time Dean tipped.

"Who's that guy you were talking to?" Dean asked.

"What guy?"

"In the leather jacket in the corner."

"Ray Dokes."

"Ray Dokes." Dean tried the name like he was sampling a drink. "How come I know him?"

"He's the guy," Paulie said. "I just remembered."

"What guy?"

"He's the guy put Sonny in the hospital for all them months," Paulie said.

"Sonofabitch," Dean said. "I thought he went to jail for that."

"He did," Tiny said. "That's why you haven't seen him around, genius."

Dean took his drink and turned around, leaned back with his elbows on the bar. Ray Dokes sat with his legs crossed, watching as a fresh dancer ascended the stage. The dancer was dressed as a cowgirl, with six-shooters, a red cowboy hat, and a bullwhip, which she cracked periodically over the heads of the patrons up front.

"He doesn't look so tough," Dean said.

"What's looks got to do with it?" Paulie asked.

"Shut the fuck up."

Misty came out of the back room, wearing a short tight skirt and boots, which meant she was still working. She cast an irritable eye about the room, as if she was looking for someone who wasn't there. When Dean waved to her, she rolled her eyes and walked over. She stepped between the two of them, and Paulie took the opportunity to smell her hair, her neck. She smelled, he decided, like a goddess.

"Johnny Walker Blue," she said to Tiny. She indicated Dean. "He's paying."

Misty smiled impatiently as Dean did as he was told. She'd been hanging with the two pretty steadily for the past week or so. Dean was an easy touch for drinks, and she had, just a couple days earlier, hit Paulie up for two hundred dollars, saying she needed the money to buy her son a pair of hockey skates. This in spite of the fact that Misty was taking home two grand a week and that her kid, who lived in Wisconsin with his father, was barely two years old and probably not all that interested in hockey.

Now Dean took a twenty from his pocket and offered it to her. "I want a table dance."

She shrugged. "We can go in the back."

"Not for me," Dean said. He looked at Paulie. "Watch—I'm gonna give this Dokes a treat." Then to Misty: "That guy in the corner. In the leather jacket. Tell him it's on Dean Caldwell."

"I thought your name was Dino," Misty said.

"It is," Dean said quickly. "But in certain circles, I'm known as Dean."

Misty glanced at Paulie. "What are you known as, in certain circles?"

"I'm always Paulie."

Ray was lighting a cigarette when he saw the blonde approaching, cutting through the crowd, the sway in her hips suggesting Monroe while the look in her eyes was all business. It took him a moment to realize that he was her target. Just as she arrived, the music ended. She sat down beside him, put her Scotch on the table.

"You're getting a lap dance."

"No thanks." Ray drew on his cigarette, watching her narrowly.

"Hey, it's paid for."

"By who?"

“Guy’s name is Dean Caldwell.” Misty crossed her legs, then turned toward the bar. “See the idiot at the bar with his mouth hanging open, wearing the hat? It’s the idiot beside him, with the spiked hair.”

Ray looked over. “I don’t know him.”

The music started up, and Misty got to her feet, moved in front of Ray. “I don’t care if you know him or not. He paid for a dance, and that’s what you’re getting.”

“Go away,” Ray told her sharply.

“Don’t fuck with me, man. I’m just doing my job.”

“Go dance for somebody else. If I want to see you naked, I’ll go sit up front with the wankers.”

Misty stared at him for a moment, gave him a look that told him she was this close to telling him to fuck off. But then she sat down.

“What’s your problem?” she asked.

“I don’t have a problem. You think you’re at a mixer?”

“You’re a miserable prick. What’re you doin’ here if that’s your attitude?”

“Minding my own business, for starters. I came in for a beer.”

“Who the fuck are you to look down your nose at me? I happen to have a B.A. in business from Yale.”

“Oh yeah? And I’m an astronaut.”

She took a drink of Scotch and glanced over to the bar, where Dean was watching her in puzzlement. Then she turned her chair around, regarded Ray, and told him, “I’m not giving the motherfucker his twenty back.”

Ray shrugged. “What do I care? I don’t even know them.”

“I thought they were your friends.”

“I’ve never seen them before. Don’t you know them?”

“They’re just a couple guys who hang out here. They claim they’re related to Earl Stanton, the billionaire.”

Ray had straightened in his chair now, and he was looking

in the direction of the bar. He glanced back at the woman for a moment. If it was some sort of power play, he had to wonder if she was in on it. He dismissed the thought, though; if she was involved, it would have been stupid to spill about the Stanton connection. And she didn't appear stupid. Ray got to his feet and walked directly to the bar. Dean had his back to him, ordering another round. Ray slammed him from behind, pinned him against the bar, felt inside Dean's jacket for a piece. Then he turned to Paulie, who was wearing a T-shirt, not hiding anything.

"Don't move," Ray said.

"What the fuck—" Dean said.

Finding no weapon, Ray turned Dean around, held him by the collar with one hand. "So what's the story here?" he asked. "You boys got a message from cousin Sonny?"

"You got it all wrong," Dean told him.

"I'll tell you what, asshole," Ray said. "Follow me out that door, and you'll have it all wrong."

He pushed Dean aside and walked out the door. Dean straightened his collar and gathered his dignity and then he turned to see Paulie watching him.

"It didn't appear to me as though that man wanted a treat," Paulie said, and then he ordered another beer.

Etta loaded the last of the whites into the washing machine and measured out the detergent. Before closing the lid, she glanced down at her own T-shirt, stained from the cereal Homer had tossed her way in a fit an hour earlier. She pulled the shirt over her head and placed it in the washer, closed the lid, and started the machine. There was a plaid work shirt hanging on the wall, just inside the back door; she took it from the hook and slipped it on. It smelled faintly of her father's pipe tobacco.

She walked back into the kitchen. Homer was sitting by

the window, rocking back and forth and watching a hummingbird as it searched fitfully for an autumn blossom. The second bowl of cereal sat soggy and untouched on the table. Etta considered another effort to get him to eat, then let it go. Homer would eat when he was ready.

Etta looked out the window and saw that the flag was up on the mailbox. She went out the front door and walked across the lawn to the road. The wind had come up overnight, stripping the large silver maples along the lane of their leaves and assorted small branches. The lawn was covered.

Etta flipped the red flag down and retrieved the mail from inside. There were several bills and the *Farmer's Monthly*. She glanced quickly through the pile, saw nothing encouraging, and started for the house. Her next-door neighbor drove by in her filthy white LeBaron, honking her horn like she just got it for Christmas. Etta waved over her shoulder and continued on across the leaf-strewn lawn.

When she went back into the house she saw that her father was no longer in the kitchen. Looking out the kitchen window, she saw him walking in the orchard. At least he'd put a jacket on.

Etta went into the pantry—her office—and sat down in front of the computer. She opened the envelopes one by one, keeping a running total in her head, then tossed them in a pile.

"Shit," she said.

After a moment, she turned on the computer and went on-line. She went into her bank account and checked her balance. Then she looked at the bills again, mentally aligned them in order of priority. Going off-line, she sat back and stared at the monitor until the screensaver appeared.

Zip-A-Dee-Doo-Dah, it advised.

Indeed.

She was still in the chair when Father Tim Regan walked in, wearing a windbreaker and carrying a brand-new Bible.

"I said hello!" he said.

Etta straightened with a start. She reached forward to turn the computer screen off, got to her feet. She wasn't thrilled to see the priest; his visits were growing more frequent. Etta had Mabel Anton to thank for that.

"Hi, Tim," she said. "I guess I was out of it."

"I guess you were."

"I need a coffee," she told him.

In the kitchen Etta took the bowl of sodden cereal from the table and dumped it in the garbage. She made a pot of coffee while Regan sat at the old pedestal table and watched her. The Bible was on the table. Once, turning to the fridge, she thought he was looking at her ass, but she couldn't be sure. Tim Regan was handsome, a boyish forty-one, and a charming man. There were people who thought that he was gay, but that was probably a preconceived stereotype more than anything. She'd never felt that he had any interest in sex at all. He'd never flirted with her.

When the coffee was ready she carried the pot to the table and brought out cups and cream.

"What are you doing in this neck of the woods?" she asked as she sat down.

Regan poured cream into his cup. "Just passing by. I thought I'd stop and see how things were going."

"Fine as frog's hair, as the old folks say."

"I just saw Homer. How's he doing?"

"Depends on what day it is. Did he speak to you?"

"He swore at me for parking on the lawn."

"Well, he's pretty much back to normal." She smiled at him, and they drank their coffee.

"So what're you really doing here?" she asked.

He shrugged. "I worry about him. And you, too. Especially when I see you sitting, staring at a blank computer screen. How are you making it?"

"I work three nights a week at the hospital in town. Nurse's aide, twelve-hour shifts. Mabel didn't tell you this?"

Regan smiled. "She told me. And that she comes in and looks after Homer."

"Must have been tough getting all that out of her."

"She has a good heart, Etta."

"She's a busybody, is what she is. She's decided to save my soul, and apparently she's signed you up to help."

"She cares about you. She thinks you're falling behind. Did your father pay the taxes?"

"You're as nosy as Mabel, padre. The taxes will be fully paid, thank you very much."

"Then you'll borrow the money to pay them." Regan hesitated, then pushed the new Bible toward her. "I brought you this. Thought I might see you and Homer at church."

"That what you thought?" she asked, smiling. She picked up the Bible. "And you think I'm in need of this?"

He shrugged. "Better to have it and not need it than the other way around."

She let go of the smile and looked away from him. Out the window, she could see Homer in the yard, making his way back to the house. He seemed unsteady on his feet.

"Sometimes he mistakes me for my mother," she said. "And when he does, he thinks he's entitled to his conjugal rights."

"Oh."

"Luckily, he's not that strong anymore. Or it could be a problem."

"But eventually he will be a problem. He can't be any help to you around here."

"Not a lot," she admitted. She looked at him. "Sonny Stanton's been bugging Dad to sell him the farm. Seems Sonny's bent on becoming a gentleman farmer. Although I doubt either word applies with him."

"Maybe you should consider the offer."

"No way. History is all I have left. This is where I make my stand."

Regan reached for his cup, found that it was empty. When he looked toward the pot she got up and poured another cup.

"Sonny Stanton," he said. "That's funny; Mabel mentioned that Ray Dokes is out."

"Tell me, padre, does Mabel have any inside information on the JFK assassination?"

"I couldn't say. Have you seen him?"

"JFK?"

"Ray Dokes."

"He stopped by the other day. Wasn't it in the newsletter?"

Regan shrugged and took a drink of coffee. "I've heard stories about the man. You two seem . . . an unlikely pair."

"What's going on here?" she asked. "You concerned about my welfare, or just looking for tales of true romance?"

"Maybe both." He smiled. "I'm a modern man."

Etta looked at him a moment, thinking that she'd like to tell the priest to go to hell. Though she'd probably lose her sitter if she did.

"All right. I'd just come home, what—three years ago. I was teaching art history at Sheridan College, and the job was losing its patina, if you will. Also, I'd just broken off with a guy who wasn't nearly as divorced as he'd led me to believe—gee, maybe that'll be next week's installment. Anyway, I decided to move back home for a while. I was teaching an art class at the Tompkins Gallery, and Ray's sister was one of my students. Ray started dropping in—he was still playing ball then—and next thing you know, I was going to watch him pitch, and we were going out for beers afterward, and we golfed a couple times, and then—well, you know all about the birds and the bees, right?"

Regan didn't bother to smile this time. "Why were you attracted to him?"

She leaned back in her chair and regarded him narrowly. She was torn between a feeling of resentment and a need to justify herself. "He is—" she heard herself say and then she hesitated. "I don't know what you've heard, but he is as good a man as I've ever known."

"Really."

"Really. Having said that, I should add that he is also—and you'll pardon my language here—a bit of a fuckup."

"I've heard that. Is that what made him so attractive?"

"Nice try, Oprah. No, that's what made him unattractive. I'm a pretty conventional person; I pay my parking tickets promptly, declare all income to the government, and only rarely cheat at solitaire. Ray, on the other hand, has very little regard for the law. Or authority in general."

"I've sort of gotten that impression. I mean, the man was in jail for attempted murder."

"That's what he was in for."

"And you have no problem with that?"

"From a moral standpoint I have absolutely no problem with what Ray did to Sonny Stanton. Our legal system sure as hell wasn't gonna take care of it." She paused. "But it was a stupid move. He spent two years in jail. And if you asked him today if he'd do it again, I'm betting he'd give you a big old Gary Cooper yup." She paused. "I just can't deal with that kind of . . . I don't know . . . recklessness."

"You're saying he's still reckless? Wouldn't you think that two years in jail might have changed him?"

"I think it's a pretty inherent trait."

"So he's not done with Sonny Stanton?"

Etta sighed in resignation. "Probably not," she said.

Regan was finishing his coffee. She hoped he didn't have designs on a third cup. She was through with pouring and through with talking. The next sitter she hired would be an atheist.

"How's Homer like him coming around?" Regan asked her.

"Homer hates Ray. Homer's a Sonny Stanton fan, believe it or not. To him, Ray's a criminal."

"Seems like you have a lot of things in your life that you could do without."

"You're really looking to recruit us, aren't you? One day Mabel brings you over for coffee cake—which she baked and passed off as mine, by the way—and the next you're looking to herd us into the flock."

"The Lord is your shepherd, not me."

"Yeah, so I hear."

"Maybe you should go back to the school," Regan suggested. "I'm sure you were a good teacher. Maybe you should do what you're good at."

"Are you saying I'm not good at this?"

"At beating your head against the wall? Nobody is."

Etta walked the priest to his car, said good-bye, and watched as he drove away. Homer was standing in the yard, and he hung back while Regan left.

It was a warm day, denying the month. Etta went into the garage and found a rake, walked out front, and began to gather up the leaves there. A moment later, Homer was at her side.

"I don't want that damn Johnson hanging around you," he said.

"That was Tim Regan, Dad," she told him. "He's the priest."

She stepped close to him, ostensibly to zip his jacket, but in truth to smell his breath. As she'd suspected, he'd been into the rye; she realized he would have a bottle, or perhaps two or three, stashed in the barn. Up to his old tricks. His medication, the doctor had emphasized, would be virtually useless if he continued to drink.

The doctors had decided that he was suffering from Wernicke's dementia. The good news was that it wasn't Alzheimer's; the bad news was that it might as well be. The doctor had put him on Aricept to combat the disease and Risperdal to calm him. It was a good bet that alcohol exacerbated his condition and quite possibly had a hand in initiating it. So now it was up to Etta to keep him out of the hooch. Along with everything else.

"He's a goddamn liar if he says he's a priest," she heard him say. "The Johnsons were all Baptists."

7

Jumping Jack Flash won the Queen Anne Stakes in a romp. The weather had warmed, and it was a sunny day at Woodbine; the track was fast and the crowd large and overly boisterous, as if its raucous holiday mood might somehow prolong the summerlike conditions. The two-year-olds were running now, and the veteran punters were even more optimistic than usual, hoping to stumble on a green colt whose speed the odds-makers had somehow overlooked.

Getting the big bay stallion to run wasn't a problem; getting him in the starting gate was. The horse was a nasty piece of work at his best, but he grew even more contentious when forced to do something. This day, Jackson had instructed the starters to try something different; he told them to leave the gate open as the horse approached, tricking him into thinking he was walking straight through. The plan worked. As soon as the stallion was in, the starters slammed the gates, back and front, closed.

Jockey Danny Hartsell kept the Flash quiet in the backstretch, holding him in with an effort, then let him go at the top of the stretch. The four-year-old took maybe twenty strides to run down the leaders, then coasted across the line to win by six lengths. Danny was grinning when he loped the bay over to Jackson in the winner's circle. He had a lot of horse left, and he told this to Jackson.

Jumping Jack Flash paid two dollars and twenty cents to win.

Jackson and Sonny posed beside the horse for the camera with Danny still in the irons, Sonny keeping the cane hidden behind him, as he did whenever he could, looking very clean and casual in his white Dockers and patterned golf shirt, his hair tied back. The congratulatory flowers arrived from some track official, and the Flash was ungracious in accepting the wreath; moments after the pictures were taken, the horse threw a tantrum, leaving Danny Hartsell sprawled in the infield. A couple of handlers grabbed the Flash before he could bolt for the barn and were dragged around the infield for their efforts. Sonny stood smiling at the whole spectacle like an indulgent father.

Dean and Paulie watched the race from the grandstand, Dean wearing his Armani knockoff, his shades, his Italian loafers, Paulie wearing his porkpie and a smile as big as a hubcap.

"The fuck you grinnin' about?" Dean asked.

Paulie held up his tote ticket. Dean took it.

"Twenty to win," he said. "That's great, Paulie. You get twenty-two bucks back."

"I know," Paulie said, still smiling.

Dean showed a handful of totes. "I had fifty to win on the filly. She comes in, I collect twenty-five *hundred*. I had her boxed with that gray, that woulda paid another grand. You won two fucking dollars."

"What'd you win?"

"Fuck you."

Paulie went to the wicket and cashed his ticket, bought french fries with his windfall. Dean left him sitting on a bench and went into the lounge for a drink. Big Billy Coon was sitting at the bar, racing form in front of him, cell phone at his elbow. Dean walked over and said hello.

"Scotch on the rocks," Dean said to the bartender. He gestured to Billy's glass. "Another here."

"Another club soda?" the bartender asked.

"Yeah," Billy said.

Dean slid onto a stool. "Whatcha, on the wagon, Billy?" he asked.

"I don't drink. Never have."

Billy wore a leather sports coat, black, and a bolo tie with a bear on the clasp. His hair was tied back in a ponytail, halfway down his back. And Big Billy Coon was *big*, six and a half feet tall, pushing maybe 280 pounds. His shoulders beneath the leather were massive and sloping.

"I thought you Indians loved your whiskey," Dean was saying.

"I'm a Mohawk. Indians come from India." He turned his eyes to Dean. "I don't know what they drink over there."

Dean raised his hands in mock surrender. "Hey, it was a little joke. Like, relax, man."

"I'm relaxed."

Billy was relaxed. His voice was soft and without seeming malice, although that surely was implied. Billy had about him a sense of calm that suggested an innate confidence approaching serenity. Underlying it all, though, was the feeling that it could all disappear in the flick of a switch and when that happened, surely mayhem would follow. However, this was all speculation on Dean's part—in truth, he had never seen the man angry.

"You see the Flash?" Dean asked.

"I saw him. The horse can run. Earl taking him to the Breeders'?"

"Yeah, we'll be taking him. Probably run him in the Classic. I mean, we could go for the mile, but why fuck around? He never raised a sweat today."

The cell phone rang, and Billy reached for it. Dean noticed that Billy had small wrists and hands, the fingers slender, the flesh soft. When Billy identified the caller, he gave Dean a look that indicated that the call would be private. Dean decided he would visit the gents'. Inside, he took a leak and then spent a good minute looking at himself in the mirror. The fake Armani was gray and hung on his skinny frame just right and looked like the real deal. He'd paid three hundred for it in Buffalo, at a discount place near the new arena. In the end it cost him five hundred because he'd bet a deuce on the Leafs over the Sabres that night. The Buds had been cruising, up two to zip late in the third, until Gilmour—that rat traitor—popped two goals in thirty-two seconds and the game ended in a tie. Dean lost the two hundred, but he did bring home the suit, and when you look at what a real Armani goes for, he figured he was still way ahead.

He spiked his hair now with his fingertips, turning his head, checking out the diamond stud in his left ear. He wondered how he'd look with a ponytail, like Billy Coon's. Of course, Sonny had a ponytail and Sonny was a creep. Maybe it was an Indian thing. Mohawk, whatever.

Back at the bar, Billy was off the phone and standing now, ready to leave. He drank the last of his soda and tucked the form under his arm. Dean reached for his Scotch, drank it off without sitting.

"I gotta get going," he said, wanting to convey the idea that he was leaving Billy, not the other way around. "I have to head down to the barn, check our horse out."

They walked out of the bar together, headed for the escalators.

"So, you have him?" Billy asked.

"At ten cents on the dollar? Not fucking likely."

"You don't bet him here," Billy said. "What are you—a mark? I had him at two to one."

Dean was doubtful. "How'd you do that?"

"The casino."

"I didn't see any tote board last time I was there."

"It's backroom," Billy said. "And it's futures. We had him posted a month ago at two to one. Come on, you gotta know that. Your boss is there three, four times a week."

"Who you talking about?"

"Sonny, who do you think? Hey, the cousins love Sonny over there. If there's a worse poker player in the world, Sonny should track him down. He might win a hand. Boy's got deep pockets, though."

"He ain't my fucking boss," Dean said. "I work for Earl."

"You work for Earl, you work for Sonny," Billy said simply. "You know it. But come on out sometime; I'll show you the setup."

Billy walked through the glass doors, heading for the parking lot. Dean watched him get into a new Navigator and drive off. Then he headed to the barn.

Jumping Jack Flash was still in the stall and the trailer backed up to the loading area. Jackson was making a show of running things, like always. Sonny was off to one side, talking to a good-looking woman in a blue blazer. Dean recognized her from one of the local television stations.

When Jackson spotted Dean he quit the others and walked over. "Where've you been, Dean?" he asked.

"Clubhouse," Dean said.

"We need help getting this horse loaded. You know that. If you're working, you can't be sitting in the clubhouse drinking whiskey."

"So what're we doing?"

"We're loading the horse," Jackson said simply.

There was a cameraman with a heavy video unit on his shoulder on the scene now. The woman in the blazer had a microphone in her hand, and she was about to interview Sonny. Dean saw Sonny toss his cane under the truck as he prepared for his close-up.

In the barn the Flash was still in a foul mood, turning circles in the stall, ears laid back, nostrils wide. Jackson went in cautiously, pushed the horse into a corner, managed to get a nylon lead on the hackamore. As he lead him out, though, the horse tried to rear. Jackson did a quick half hitch around the gate rail with the lead, pulling the horse's head down. The stallion began to back away, spooked by something—the opening in the stall, or the sunlight outside, or maybe just his own wrapped-too-tight self.

"Get in here," Jackson called outside to Dean.

Dean, who'd been watching Sonny spout horse-racing clichés to the reporter, reluctantly stepped inside, saw the big horse standing stiff-legged and obstinate, eyes just a shade off crazy. The horse was still wired from the run, and his muscled shoulders twitched and shuddered under the glistening red coat, adding to Dean's consternation.

"Where's Paulie?" he asked at once.

"At the other barn with the filly," Jackson said. "Come on."

Dean went in unhappily. He moved behind the stallion, and the horse spooked again, kicked out at Dean, and lunged for the stall door. Jackson tried to use it to his advantage; he shortened the lead and stayed with the horse's momentum, but the stallion slammed against him, nearly knocking him down, and jerked away again, back into the stall.

When Jackson recovered he saw that Dean was on the floor of the stall, his fake Armani smeared with real horseshit. Dean got up slowly, pissed off. The horse stood snorting in the corner, his eyes wide, ears laid back.

Then Paulie walked into the barn. He glanced at Jackson and then at Dean, and he went into the stall and spoke to the horse softly. The stallion released a guttural warning from deep in his throat, but Paulie kept coming, his voice low and easy, talking to the horse in the same voice he'd used to order fries a half hour earlier in the clubhouse. The horse's ears moved forward, and his head dropped maybe an inch. Paulie moved slowly to him, and then he took the lead and walked the horse out of the barn and into the waiting trailer. Dean stood in the doorway and watched.

Sonny had wrapped up his interview with the woman in

the blazer. She had removed her microphone, and they were standing by the trailer, watching the stallion load.

"So—I'll see you at the Breeders'?" Sonny suggested.

"I don't think the station has the budget," the woman said. She had shoulder-length brunette hair and eyes so green they had to be enhanced, Dean guessed, by colored contacts. She was stunning, but then all TV women were these days.

"Maybe you could make the trip on your own," Sonny said.

"How's that?"

"You could be my guest. We could head to New York a few days early, do the town." He stepped closer and lowered his voice, mindful that the cameraman was hovering. "I know New York City. What do you think?"

"What do I think?" she replied, and Sonny saw that the green eyes, real or not, were mocking him. "I think you've been standing too close to your horse. All that testosterone has clouded your thinking. Thanks for the interview."

Paulie walked back into the barn to find Dean standing in the corridor, looking down at the sorry state of his suit.

"Where the hell were you?" Dean demanded.

"At the other barn."

And then Sonny came in. Without warning, he struck Paulie across the shoulder with his cane.

"You two fucking jokers better start doing your jobs," he said.

Paulie hurried outside, holding his arm. Dean looked at Sonny and said, "You hit me with that cane, and I'm gonna shove it up your ass. I don't give a shit what you tell your old man."

Sonny wheeled and limped out. Dean walked the length of the barn, found a hose there and a sponge, and cleaned his suit as best he could. He was still seething when he went outside. Paulie was standing there, holding his shoulder. Every one else had gone.

"I was doing my job," Paulie said.

"It wasn't about that," Dean said. "It was about Sonny getting shot down by the babe from Sportsnet. You all right?"

"I guess."

They got into the Lincoln and went to the Slamdance. The place was crowded; they drank at the bar and watched the dancers. Dean was hoping to see Misty, but she wasn't there.

"I'm getting pretty sick of all this, Paulie."

"I thought you liked strippers."

"I'm not talking about strippers, fuck's sakes. I'm talking about Sonny and Jackson. Uncle Earl, too, you want to know the truth. You know how much money they're making? The purse today was $750,000. And that's just today. What do we get for falling in horseshit, getting whacked by Sonny? Fucking peanuts."

"Sonny just likes to yell."

Dean took a drink and watched two dancers on stage, French kissing, grinding against each other.

"Well, it's about time we got something for ourselves, Paulie," he said. "Some kind of profit participation. He runs that horse in the Breeders' Classic, the purse is four million. And that's nothing compared to when he puts him out to stud. Don't you think we should be entitled to a cut?"

"We should get some participation," Paulie agreed.

"Fucking right." Dean signaled to the bartender. "I'm gonna talk to Earl; I'll phone him in the Bahamas if I have to."

Tiny Montgomery was working the bar. He moved his bulk over, looked at them sullenly.

"Two more here," Dean said.

"Where you guys been?" Tiny asked.

"Why?"

Tiny looked up and down the bar. Dean noticed for the first time that the stools on either side of them were empty, even though the joint was full.

"Somebody's kinda rank," Tiny said then.

Paulie looked at Dean in alarm. Dean was staring at Tiny like he couldn't believe what he'd heard. Tiny was standing pat, eyebrows arched.

"I spend a lot of money in this place," Dean said.

"Maybe you oughta spend a little on soap and water," Tiny said, and he walked away.

Leaving the parking lot, Dean floored the Lincoln, fishtailing and spraying gravel all over the side wall of the Slamdance. He hit the street at full throttle, tires squealing, and headed uptown, Paulie holding on to the dash with both hands, watching the road ahead.

They went to Dean's apartment. Paulie sat on the leatherette couch and turned on the TV while Dean went into the bedroom to change. Paulie clicked through the channels, settled on a rerun of *The Simpsons.* The apartment was a mess, pizza boxes on the floor, empty bottles everywhere, stereo components strewn across the carpet. Paulie heard the shower running. He went into the kitchen, found a Coors Light in the fridge, walked back out to the couch. There was a *Playboy* on the coffee table; he picked it up and went straight to the centerfold, drank the weak beer, and alternated his attention between Miss October and Marge Simpson as he waited for Dean.

Dean came out of the bedroom, wearing jeans and a white dress shirt, carrying his suit. Paulie was still on the couch, sporting the beer, the magazine, and a hard-on. Dean picked up the phone and checked his messages.

"How much does a TV like this cost, Dean?" Paulie asked.

Dean looked over, receiver to his ear. "That's eight hundred bucks. Too rich for your blood, Paulie."

He punched the phone buttons and then hung up. "Shit," he said. "We gotta go out to the farm."

"What for?"

"Jackson left a message. But we're going to the dry cleaner's, first off. And while we're at the farm, maybe I'll ask some questions."

Paulie got to his feet, adjusting his pants to accommodate his condition. "What kind of questions?"

"Questions I shoulda asked a long time ago."

It was Sunday night. It took them the better part of an hour to find a dry cleaner that was open.

"Why don't you just wait 'til morning?" Paulie asked at one point.

"It can't wait," Dean said. "You know what kind of material this is?"

"What kind?"

"It's special Italian material," Dean decided. "It's gotta be cleaned right away."

They finally found a place open in a strip mall north of the city. Dean conducted a short interview with the owner, who was Korean, to ensure that the man possessed the expertise required to clean an Armani. Then they drove out to the farm.

Jackson was leaving the barn when they arrived. Dean parked in front of the house, and they got out. Sonny's BMW was parked on the lawn. Jackson walked over to the car.

"Sonny wants you to run his car over to the golf course," he said.

"Oh, wonderful," Dean said. "We were afraid you wanted us for something trivial. We want to talk to the old man, Jackson."

Jackson was walking away, finished with them. "Well, he should be back about April. If it won't wait 'til then, then I guess Sonny's your man."

He got into the pickup and drove off.

They drove Sonny's car out to Hidden Valley Golf and Country Club, Dean behind the wheel of the BMW and Paulie following in the Lincoln. They parked by the pro shop and got out. The clubhouse was huge and ostentatious, fashioned after an antebellum style, which seemed to appeal to the country club set.

"What's Sonny do out here all the time?" Paulie asked, looking at the pillars that supported the porch roof. "He doesn't play golf anymore."

"He hangs out with a bunch of guys just like him," Dean said. "They sit around smoking cigars and talking about sports and cars and all the women they've fucked. The kind of guys who'd rather talk about fucking than do it."

"It's a big place. How we gonna find Sonny?"

"Won't be hard."

Sonny was playing poker in the private dining room with a cluster of men, all smoking cigars and talking about sports and cars and all the women they'd fucked.

They were playing wild cards when Dean and Paulie walked in, and Sonny was down a couple hundred and about to drop another hundred by way of humping on a baby straight in a game where four of a kind was on the weak side. A big man with a shaved head and gold hoops in each ear won the hand with a straight flush. Dean knew the man to be a real estate developer named Rockwood. He called himself the Rock because he was an amateur bodybuilder who considered himself as hard as a rock. Dean had been in his presence several times and was of the opinion that he was also as smart as a rock.

When he lost the hand Sonny grabbed the cards and threw them into the air in a gesture of easy come, easy go. The cards fluttered about the room, and then Sonny noticed the two.

"You bring the car?"

"No, we're here to practice our putting," Dean told him.

"You better not have fucked with the stereo, like last time," Sonny said. Then: "Paulie, pick those cards up, will ya?"

Paulie did as he was told, gathered the cards, put them back on the table. The players watched him in amusement.

Dean stared at Sonny, and he returned the look, smiling around the Cohiba in his mouth.

There was a large Rottweiler sitting to the side of the Rock. The dog had a bandanna around its neck, and it was drooling on the Persian carpet. Paulie sat down at the next table and watched the dog. After a moment, the dog began to watch Paulie.

"You guys want to play a couple hands?" Sonny asked.

"We're leaving," Dean said. He'd decided to wait to talk to Earl about the profit sharing.

"I'll play." That was Paulie, grinning as he stood.

Sonny gave the others a look, nodding behind his cigar.

"You don't want to play, Paulie," Dean said sharply.

But Paulie was draping his jacket over a chair, taking his wallet from his pocket. "I like cards," he said.

Sonny and the boys were getting a big kick out of the whole scene, eyeballing one another, smiling into their drinks. Dean looked on angrily.

Sonny was shuffling the deck. "Kings and little ones, Paulie," he said. "You know the game?"

"I think so." Someone had given Paulie a glass of rye on the rocks.

"Paulie, you don't drink whiskey," Dean said.

"Would you relax?" Sonny said, and he dealt the cards.

Paulie won the first hand on five aces, the second with five queens, and the third with a royal flush. He took in roughly nine hundred dollars and then, drinking off his rye, announced to the table that he was out of the game. He unzipped his wallet, tucked his winnings carefully inside, and then pushed away from the table.

"What the fuck you mean you're out?" asked the Rock.

"I got enough to buy a new thirty-two-inch TV," Paulie said. "That's all I wanted."

"Sonny," the Rock said sharply. "What the fuck is this, man—a hit-and-run?"

Dean was laughing now. "Let's get outa here, Paulie."

"I have to go to the washroom first," Paulie said.

The Rock sat at the table and glowered as Paulie left the room. After a moment he got up and approached Dean. It appeared that the Rock bought his golf shirts a size too small; his biceps, already huge from lifting, looked even bigger under the thin double knit.

"That little fucker's not leaving," he told Dean.

"He can do what he wants," Dean said.

"He's got our money," the Rock said. "He stays in the game. End of conversation."

Dean looked past the Rock's massive shoulders and saw Paulie come back into the room and gather his jacket from the chair. Dean showed the Rock a grin and said: "Come on, you should be happy that all he wanted was a TV. What if he had his eye on a new Cadillac?"

"Yeah?" the Rock asked. "And what if I have my Rotty tear his fucking throat out?"

Dean looked past the Rock again, to where Paulie had the animal in question on the floor, the dog on its back, all four paws in the air, tongue lolling to one side as Paulie vigorously rubbed its belly.

"Sure, Rock," Dean said. "That oughta work."

8

When Ray walked outside Saturday morning Pete Culpepper was sitting on the porch, working on a plug of Redman and watching the sky like a man watching the dealer in a crooked card game. The morning was cool and clear, but there were clouds stacking up in the west and the wind was on the rise. Pete was watching the accumulation and occasionally spurting a stream of tobacco onto the tangled rose bushes along the porch, bushes planted years back by one of Pete's girlfriends, although Ray couldn't remember which one. It was probably no better than even money that Pete could.

"You 'bout ready?" Pete asked when Ray came out of the house.

"I'd like a little breakfast. Did you eat?"

"I had a cowboy's breakfast," Pete said.

A cowboy's breakfast, Ray knew, was a piss and a look around, and that alone told Ray that the old man was nervous. He wasn't one to miss a meal.

"Well, I gotta eat," Ray said. "Whoever it was said breakfast is the most important meal of the day probably wasn't talking about chewing tobacco."

They were on the road by nine, Pete behind the wheel of the pickup. They hit the QEW just east of Hamilton, skirting the city traffic. The rain began around St. Catharines, and when it did it came in a torrent. By the time they reached Fort Erie the ditches were running, and Pete was describing in detail what he would like to do with the weatherman's genitals.

The gelding Fast Market was in barn eleven. Pete had trailered him down on Monday and had been making the trip every day since, working him on the main track.

"What shoes you got on him?" Ray asked as they parked the truck.

"Put bars on him, just yesterday. I got calks if I need 'em," Pete said.

"Does he like the slop?"

"I don't know that it's got anything to do with liking it. All a horse knows is to run. How he runs in the muck depends on a lot of things, but mostly the trip."

They found the gelding calm and content in the barn. Pete gave him a handful of oats and then went to track down his rider. Ray got a brush from a shelf and began to curry the gelding's coat. The horse was as quiet as Pete's old hound as he worked; at one point Ray was certain the animal was asleep.

As Ray was finishing up, Pete came back, walking through the mud with a lanky brunette with dark eyes, wearing jeans and cowboy boots, a faded Nirvana T-shirt.

"This is Chrissie Nugent," Pete said. "Ray Dokes."

Chrissie Nugent wore dark eyeshadow and lipstick, and she looked to Ray like a wasted fashion model from the 1960s. Her eyes were rimmed with red, and she had a fuzzy look about her with which Ray was familiar. She was maybe twenty-five. She shook Ray's hand, then turned and hacked and spit in the mud.

"Chrissie was up when he won in July," Pete was saying. "Girl's been having a hell of a year, got near fifty wins. But she's fixin' to lose her bug."

Chrissie was in the stall with the horse now, her hands on his withers, talking softly to him, words Ray couldn't make out. Ray had never seen a jockey—male or female—wearing makeup before. But then he'd been away awhile.

When Chrissie came out she lit a cigarette and looked at Pete. "Anything I need to know? What about the hoof?"

"Ride the horse like he's sound," Pete told her. "I'd like to keep him middle of the pack 'til the stretch, but if this rain keeps up you might have to move him sooner. I wouldn't go wide with him. He gets a little lonely out there."

Chrissie nodded, looked at Ray a moment, then back to Pete. "That it?"

"That's it," Pete said. "The silks are in the pickup."

"Well, I don't have a mount 'til the fourth," Chrissie said. "I'm gonna go catch some sleep in my truck. I got a hangover that would kill a fucking Clydesdale."

They watched as she retrieved the silks from the truck and then walked away in the rain.

"Where'd you find her?" Ray asked.

"Turned around one day, and there she was," Pete said. "Gal's a comer; she's tougher than a boot sandwich, and she's a natural jock. Horses just plain relax around her. Ain't nothing you can teach. She's gonna be a great one if she doesn't kill herself. I think she's about half crazy."

"Well," Ray said, watching her walk in the tight jeans. "Half ain't as bad as whole."

They stood in the doorway of the barn and watched the rain come down. The lanes between the barns had turned to muck; the water ran off the tin roofs and pooled up on the ground below, sending rivulets along the lanes, racing for the lower ground.

Pete retrieved a bale of straw from the trailer and broke it up, tossed half in under the horse and spread the rest outside to keep the mud down outside the barn. Then he stepped back inside and had another long look at the sky.

"I guess I better change those shoes," he said at last. "I hate to bother that hoof two days running, but I got no choice with this weather."

Ray got the nail pullers from the trailer and removed the shoes from the gelding. The hoof that had been cracked looked sound enough, and he took extra care in pulling the nails from it. The gelding stood calmly as he worked, occasionally looking back at Ray as if checking to see that the job was being done right.

Pete Culpepper set to work shoeing the horse. Ray was in the way, so he decided to head over to the grandstand to have a look around. He walked between the rows of barns, trying to keep to the thin strip of grass alongside the lane, avoiding the mud. Luis Salvo loped by him, sitting a western saddle on a stout chestnut mare, the mare's hooves throwing mud in the air.

"Hey Raymond," he called. "You are free!"

"So they tell me. You riding today, Luis?"

"No more. I'm a fat mon, can't you see? Dese days I just exercise." He rode on, standing in the stirrups, easing the mare through the mire toward the track.

Ray walked around the west end of the grandstand and went inside. He was shocked when he walked in. The place was filled, wall to wall, with slot machines. It was carpeted, chandeliered, a cut-rate Vegas North. There were women in evening dresses, and it wasn't yet noon. Whether they were early for Saturday night or left over from Friday was anybody's guess. On closer inspection Ray decided they were leftovers. The place was bustling, and the bustling had nothing to do with thoroughbred racing. Ray stood on the scarlet carpet and looked in vain for a tote machine. Finally he walked to a kiosk, where a platinum blonde in cat's-eye glasses was serving juice and soft drinks.

"Where are the totes?" he asked.

"Clubhouse side," she told him. "You can't bet here."

"I can't bet here? What the hell happened to this place?"

She looked at him as if he'd just stumbled down from the hills. "What happened was, they either had to put in the slots or close the doors. I don't know where you've been, but the province has gone casino crazy. The government has finally found a surefire way to make money. They legalized gambling."

Ray looked around. "Look at this place."

"We couldn't fight 'em, so we had to join 'em," the blonde said. She gestured with both hands toward the people at the slot machines, slipping in coin after coin, going faster with each losing pull. "You know what it is, don't you?"

"What is it?"

"A tax on the stupid."

Ray left and walked over to the clubhouse. The wickets were just opening, and he walked up and placed the bets. Fast Market was listed at ten to one. Pete had given him twenty across the board, and he bet that first.

"Anything else?" the man behind the wicket asked.

Ray hesitated, thinking about Chrissie Nugent, her manner with the horse, her tough-guy pose under her hangover. He imagined her sleeping in her truck just now; no jingle-jangle nerves there, just the cockiness of her years and herself.

He bet a hundred to win on the gelding.

Back at the barn Pete had finished with the shoeing, and both man and horse were dozing off in the stall. When Ray got back he let them be, got into the truck, and turned on the radio. He lit a cigarette and slipped the match out the vent window.

He punched through the AM buttons, found a Buffalo talk show on which an enthusiastic hostess was endorsing capital punishment for homosexuality and other assorted crimes against humanity. She was of the belief that every word in the Bible was true, and when a caller asked what Noah did with the huge accumulation of manure on the Ark she called him a communist and hung up on him. The woman's voice possessed a hearty midwestern twang, and except for the fact that she was a raving lunatic she could have passed very easily for someone's kindly aunt. Ray turned the radio off.

The gelding was to run in the sixth race. After the fourth, Pete hooked a lead onto the horse's halter, and they followed as a walker led him over to the saddling barn. By the time they got there, the horses for the fifth race were already on the track. The rain had let up, but the track was sloppy and not likely to improve in the next twenty minutes.

"Better the slop than the mud," Pete said. "Least the slop don't stick."

They met Chrissie, wearing the Culpepper silks, as she was walking to the paddock. She had just raced, and there were traces of mud on her face and in her hair.

"How'd you do?" Pete asked Chrissie.

"Second last," she said, stopping. "Little filly was lugging in so bad it took all my strength just to keep her straight. Trainer said I didn't ride her right. Fuck him—if he can't train the horse, I can't ride it."

"I don't know that my horse wants to go in the slop," Pete said.

"Oh no, I like this old boy," Chrissie said, and she rubbed the gelding's nose. "He's sexy. He'll be in the bridle for me."

They heard the bugle for the fifth and then waited for the race to finish. Chrissie put her cap on and turned to walk into the paddock. She saw Ray watching her.

"I haven't seen you before," she said.

"I've been away."

"I kinda figured that, the way you been looking at me," she said.

The walker led the horse out for the paddock parade, and Pete followed. He gave Chrissie a leg up, and she and the other entries headed for the track. Ray and Pete watched for a moment, then went through the clubhouse and out to the track.

They made their way to the rail. Several people spoke to Pete, asking after his health, his horse's chances. Pete wasn't real talkative on either subject.

The horses were loaded in the gate. There had been two scratches—due to the track conditions, Pete speculated—and the field was down to eight. The route was seven furlongs.

"You make the bets?" Pete asked suddenly.

"I made them."

Fast Market, the gelding with the cracked hoof, and Chrissie Nugent, the bug girl with the hangover, came out of the five hole flying, took the lead at once, and headed straight for the rail. The lead was four lengths at the clubhouse turn, and in the stretch it was no contest. Chrissie never went to the whip, never needed to, stayed tight to the rail, hunched over the gelding's neck, her face tucked between his ears. From where he stood, Ray could have sworn she was joking with the animal.

Fast Market won by seven lengths. Chrissie ran the horse out to the first curve, then loped him back to the finish line. Ray was there with Pete Culpepper. Chrissie jumped down lightly, trying to hide a smile.

"So much for our strategy," Pete said.

"Hey, never let 'em kick mud in your face, that's my theory," Chrissie said.

Pete was looking at the hoof. When he straightened up, Ray could see that he was happy.

"Well, I got a mount in the seventh; thanks for the ride," Chrissie said. She walked past Ray and chucked the gelding under the jaw as she strode away. "See ya, handsome."

It took Ray a moment to realize she was talking to the horse.

Pete wasn't sure when he'd run the horse again, so they loaded him into the trailer and took him home. It was well past dark when they arrived back at the Culpepper farm.

They'd had a good day financially, with the purse and their winnings and they stopped at the Stevensville Hotel for chicken wings and a pitcher of beer.

Arriving home, Pete put the horse in the barn and gave him grain. Ray backed the trailer around behind the machinery shed and unhooked it, parked the truck, and went inside. Pete was sitting at the kitchen table, some paperwork scattered across the tabletop, along with his winnings and the check for the purse.

Ray put on a pot of coffee and sat down.

"Figuring on a new truck, Pete?"

"No, figuring how to fill a bushel basket with six quarts of potatoes."

"Today had to help."

"It didn't hurt none. That old gelding showed his blood today. Not enough to pay my taxes but—"

"You got your corn to come off yet," Ray said.

"It won't amount to much," Pete told him. "The spring was too wet and the summer too damn dry. Third dry summer in a row. Starting to remind me of Oklahoma back in the '30s."

"I somehow doubt you remember Oklahoma back in the '30s."

Pete looked over. "Thought you were making coffee."

When the coffee was ready Ray put the pot on the table, retrieved cups from the cupboard. Pete gathered up his paperwork and tucked it in a drawer beside the sink, then reached into a door just above and brought out a bottle of Cutty Sark. They cut the coffee with the Scotch and sat there at the table. Pete was tired, Ray could see. He had circles under his eyes, and his jowls were heavy with fatigue. Ray realized that he had no idea how old Pete was. Seventy, at least. Maybe seventy-five.

"Stick with the girl, and you might get a couple more wins out of the horse this fall," Ray said.

"I might at that," Pete agreed. "I'd breed that other mare in the new year if I had the jack. Horse throws a nice foal."

Ray sipped at his cup and watched the old man.

"I don't know," Pete said. "Maybe I should fold my cards, sell the place off. I never fancied these Canadian winters from the start, and the longer I get in the tooth, the less I like 'em."

"Where would you go?"

"West Texas, I guess. There's a woman there who I believe would still be agreeable to my company."

"You've been here—what—twenty-five years. And you figure this woman is still waiting on you? You must have quite an effect on the ladies, Mr. Culpepper."

Pete jumped to his feet, did a quick two-step around the kitchen.

"Now don't you doubt me, Raymond," he said. "There may be snow on the roof, but there's still fire down below."

Ray smiled, and he poured more coffee for them both, topped the cups off with the scotch again. Ten minutes later the old man was asleep in his chair. Ray sat in the scant light and finished his drink. It was midnight when he rousted Pete Culpepper and sent him off to bed.

Monday morning, Dean and Paulie headed back up to London to retrieve the impregnated mare. Paulie was waiting for Dean when he showed up, red-eyed and cranky, at the big farm. Jackson had the trailer hooked to the Ford pickup, ready to go.

"I'll get you the check," Jackson said, casting a bad eye on Dean before he went into the house.

"You're driving," Dean said to Paulie.

He'd been at the casino Sunday night, with Big Billy Coon and his bunch. In the back room. They'd bet the thoroughbreds out of Santa Anita, then played poker until first light. And they'd drank, everybody except Billy, that is. Billy's cousins—he seemed to have a never-ending supply of them—

had seemed overly interested in Dean's connection to Earl Stanton and the racehorse business.

It had been a long night, and everybody was pretty much drunk before it'd been half over. Some bad feelings had risen over the card game. Dean had gotten a little mouthy under the liquor; at one point he realized he was very close to a good old-fashioned shit kicking. He seemed to recall Billy Coon stepping in at some point and saving his ass from that eventuality. He had no recall of driving home.

When Jackson came down the front steps with the check, Dean and Paulie were already in the cab of the Ford, Paulie behind the wheel. Jackson handed the envelope over.

"Get a receipt," he told them.

"Yeah, we never done this before," Dean said.

"Just get it."

"We bringing the mare back here or the other farm?" Paulie asked.

Jackson looked to the house a moment. "Better bring her here," he said. "I'll see what Sonny wants."

"Where is he?" Dean asked.

"Well, it's not noon yet," Jackson said. "So my guess is he's still in bed."

Dean slept, and Paulie drove. That suited Paulie fine; it meant that he could poke along at his own speed and listen to the country station out of Kitchener. He set the cruise control, pulled his hat down low, and kicked back, watched the big Ford eat up the miles.

Paulie loved to drive, although Dean almost never let him behind the wheel. On the road, Paulie always imagined he was heading out on some great adventure, bound for greener pastures. Where those fertile fields might be he had no idea, but that didn't stop him from thinking about them. Somewhere where people took him seriously, where he had a piece of land to call his own. Maybe a few cows, some chickens in the yard. Maybe a woman like Misty waiting in the house, something good in the oven. Paulie doubted that Misty was much of a cook, though.

Dean was still sleeping when they pulled into the yard at the farm. The mare was in the corral, standing hipshot by the water trough, eyes half closed. The hired hand Jim Burnside came out of the barn when he heard them pull in. He wore a ball cap and carried a pitchfork. He removed the cap to wipe his brow with his sleeve, leaned the fork against the paddock fence.

Dean came to slowly, took a moment to figure out where he was. Paulie was already out of the truck, his foot on the bottom rail of the corral fence, regarding the mare.

"I'm supposed to get a check from you guys," Jim was saying.

Dean climbed out of the truck, took over.

"I'll need a receipt."

Jim took the envelope and walked up to the house. Dean walked over to where Paulie stood.

"Well, we better get her loaded," Paulie said.

"Let whatsisname Jimmy boy load her. It's his job."

"I thought it was our job."

"Our job is transport. And we're underpaid at that."

Jim came out with the receipt, handed it over to Dean, then he and Paulie put the mare in the trailer.

"Well, I hope she throws you boys a nice foal," Jim said, closing the door. "That stallion has a good record; he's got a colt making some noise down at Belmont. Two-year-old."

"Well, maybe we'll see him," Dean said. "We're thinking 'bout running Jumping Jack Flash in the Breeders' Classic. Just waiting to see how he came out of the Queen Anne's."

Paulie smiled. "Yeah, we're just waiting to see that."

Dean felt well enough to drive the return trip. Paulie was relegated to shotgun, where his dreams weren't as real, what with Dean's bragging and the radio blasting heavy metal. In truth Paulie liked Dean a lot better when he was sleeping.

When they hit the 401 Dean took the envelope from his pocket and opened it to have a look at the receipt. "Fifty grand," he said. "I thought he was bullshitting me before."

"That Jim's a pretty nice guy," Paulie said.

"He's a fucking drunk. You see the eyes on him?"

"Yeah, they look like yours."

"Fuck off." Dean turned the radio up. A mile down the road, though, the news came on, and Dean turned the volume down.

"What're you getting a week, Paulie?"

"Five hundred."

Five hundred dollars a week, Dean thought. Jesus wept. Dean was getting six and living in near poverty. Buying fake Armani suits, living in a cheap apartment. Driving his uncle's car, for Christ's sake.

"What're you getting?" Paulie asked.

"Same as you," Dean said at once.

"What—you thinking about asking for a raise?"

"I'm thinking about something. You got any idea how much money we're dealing with here? Shit, I bet Sonny goes through five grand a week in pocket change. Way he gambles."

"Yeah, well Sonny's got a lot of money."

"Sonny doesn't have two nickels to rub together. He's never worked a day in his life. It's all the old man's money. Where we gonna be in five years, Paulie?"

"I don't know about you, but I'd like to have a little place of my own."

"Be an awful small place on five hundred a week."

When they arrived back at the home farm Dean and Paulie knew right away that something was up. A couple of strange cars were parked in front of the house, stopped at odd angles as if they'd been parked in a hurry. Jackson, walking quickly from the barn to the house as they pulled up, never favored them with as much as a glance. Dean and Paulie got out of the truck, unloaded the mare, and put her in the corral behind the barn. When they walked out of the barn Jackson was coming across the yard, headed for his truck.

"Sonny wants to see you guys," he said.

"What's going on?" Dean asked.

"The old man's had a stroke," Jackson said, and he started the truck and drove out of the yard.

Sonny was in the kitchen, eating a ham sandwich at the table and drinking beer from a pilsner glass. He had his hair tied back in a ponytail. There were two men in suits in the dining room, speaking in hushed tones, papers strewn across the table in front of them. Dean sat down across from Sonny, folded his hands on the tabletop. Paulie stood inside the door.

"How bad is it?" Dean asked.

Sonny shrugged, his mouth full. "They're doing some tests," he said around the ham. "Right now he can't talk, and he's flat on his back."

"Where is he?"

"Still in the Bahamas. They're not gonna move him, not for a while, anyway."

"Is he gonna be all right?" Paulie asked.

"What the fuck I look like—a doctor?" Sonny asked. "Either he'll be all right or he won't. Maybe he'll be a veg, who knows? One way or the other, we're still in business. I'm taking over the horse operation. Which means Jackson is gonna answer to me, and you guys are gonna start pulling your weight. This isn't some halfway house for fucked-up relatives."

"If they start firing fucked-up relatives, won't you be the first to go?" Dean asked.

Sonny was drinking. He put the glass down slowly. "Don't fuck with me, Dean," he said. "As of today, I've got full authority. And you're gonna walk the straight and narrow, you and Bozo over by the door there. You think you're indispensable? You can drive a truck and shovel horseshit. I could train a couple of apes to do that."

Paulie was looking at the floor. Dean got to his feet.

"That what you wanted to tell us?" he asked.

"I wanted to tell you that things have changed," Sonny said. He pushed his plate away, leaned back in his chair.

The two lawyers appeared in the doorway then, side by side. For a moment Dean thought they might get stuck there, like two-thirds of the Stooges.

"Well?" Sonny said when they didn't speak.

"We'll need the medical records," the first lawyer said.

"Then get them," Sonny said, and he looked at Dean and Paulie. "You boys got something to do? I imagine Jackson's got stalls need shoveling."

It was dark when Dean and Paulie finished cleaning the stalls. They would have been done earlier if Dean had spent more time shoveling and less time leaning on his shovel, complaining about shoveling.

It helped that Paulie worked hard enough for the pair of them. When they were finished he was drenched in sweat. He ran the wheelbarrow outside, hosed it clean, did the same with the shovels. Back inside, Dean was smoking a cigarette, watching Jumping Jack Flash in his stall.

"Better not let Jackson catch you smoking in the barn," Paulie said.

"Fuck Jackson."

Paulie walked over, leaned his elbows on the top rail, and looked at the bay. The horse was standing smack in the middle of the stall, not looking at Paulie or Dean either, just staring off haughtily at nothing at all, as if nothing there was worthy of his gaze. His ears were straight up, and his jaw was set, the full jowls impressive. Every now and then the huge muscles in his forelegs would twitch under the copper skin.

"He's a beauty, isn't he?" Paulie said.

"A beauty?" Dean said. "You know what that motherfucker's gonna be worth if he wins the Classic?"

"I don't know. Thousands, I guess."

Dean snorted. "Try millions. As in twenty, thirty million. Shit, he'll be standing stud for a quarter mil a pop."

"You'd never know it to look at him," Paulie said. "He seems like just any other horse. Funny, isn't it?"

"What's funny is that Sonny's gonna own him if the old man dies," Dean said. "I'll tell you something else. Sonny is gonna find a way to get rid of us, Paulie."

"You really think so, Dean?"

Dean walked to the window to look at the house. "I got a feeling we're already gone."

9

Homer was lying on his bed, fully dressed, wide awake and scared. He couldn't get his thoughts straight today. Worse yet, he had no recollection of yesterday. The clock beside his bed said ten o'clock, but he couldn't remember if he'd had breakfast, or even been downstairs yet. He'd had a feeling for some time now that he was suffering a fever, and that as soon as the fever passed, his mind would clear.

He rolled over and looked at the wallpaper. He decided to play the Clear Springs course in his head; he thought if he could play the whole eighteen, his fever would pass. The first hole was a straight par four, 390 yards. Gotta watch that pine on the left off the tee; the green was bunkered front left, so the best approach was from the right anyway. Driver off the tee and then a five wood in. Chip and a putt for par. Second hole was a little dogleg left, hit a long iron out into the middle, and then it was just a flip in. Short was better than long, the green running up the hill. On the third hole he hit his drive into the right rough, and then he started thinking about the spring plowing and he couldn't get his mind back to the course. After a while he went back to the first tee and started over.

Etta was vacuuming when Homer came down the stairs, his eyes wet. He sat unsteadily in the big chair by the bay window and looked out over the fallow field to the north. When Etta shut the vacuum down she heard the hammering from the barn. Homer heard it too, and he turned toward her.

"That'll be the Monroe brothers," he said. "Come to put up the chicken house."

Etta went into the kitchen to look out the window. From there she could see an extension ladder against the front wall of the barn. At the bottom of the ladder was Ray Dokes's Cadillac, and at the top of the ladder was Ray Dokes. When she turned around, her father was watching her expectantly from the other room.

"It's the Monroe brothers," she said. "Come to put up the chicken house."

Etta took her jacket from a chair and went outside. It was a cool morning, and she buttoned the coat as she walked across the lawn. She stopped a few feet from the barn and watched him a moment.

Ray had pried a metal patch from the roof and was fixing the hole beneath properly with cedar shingles.

"What do you think you're doing?"

He replied without looking down, like he knew she was there. "What do I *think* I'm doing? I *know* what I'm doing."

"Must be a strange feeling, for you."

He turned to look at her. "Well, I'm gonna try not to analyze it too much."

"Who asked you to fix my barn roof?"

He slipped a shingle into place, drove home two nails as he pondered the question. "Maybe I'm a Samaritan. Didn't you ever read the good book?"

She went back inside, and Ray went back to work. There was maybe a dozen tin patches nailed here and there over the roof. He removed them one by one, tossed the tin down to the yard below, and reshingled the bad spots in the roof. It took him all morning. The day warmed as the sun climbed high, and soon he was down to his shirtsleeves.

By noon he was on the back side of the barn, out of sight of the house, finishing up. He'd heard a vehicle pull in the driveway thirty minutes earlier, heard a door slam when someone got out. He patched the last hole. It was pure luck and not good management that he ran out of shingles at just about the same time he ran out of places to fix.

He climbed down and put his tools in the trunk of the Caddy. Then he took down the ladder and stowed it in the barn where he'd found it. When he walked up to the house Etta was sitting in the backyard with a man, the pair of them lounging in the sun, drinking coffee. Etta wearing a cotton dress, sleeveless, the sun splaying across the freckles on her brown arms. The man was maybe forty, dark haired, and he wore a windbreaker and khaki pants. He was a handsome bastard, Ray couldn't help but notice.

"Are you finished your good deeds for the day, Mr. Dokes?" Etta asked.

"I could drink a cup of that coffee while I'm being made fun of," Ray said, talking to her, but looking at the guy in the windbreaker.

There was an extra cup on the picnic table beside the carafe of coffee.

"This is Tim Regan," Etta said as she poured. "This is Ray Dokes, Tim. Mr. Dokes is auditioning for the role of hired hand."

Regan got to his feet and shook Ray's hand. When Ray sat down with his coffee Regan remained standing.

"I was just leaving," he explained.

"You don't have to leave on my account," Ray said.

"Tim knows that," Etta said. "He has to get back to work."

"What do you do?" Ray asked.

"Tim's in the salvage business," Etta said.

Regan laughed. "You might say that. I'll see you later, Etta."

Ray watched as he got into his car and drove down the

driveway. When he turned back to Etta, she was looking at him with amusement.

"I say something funny?" he asked.

"You're funnier when you don't speak," she said. "What do I owe you for the barn?"

"Nothing."

"Come on. At least let me pay you for your materials."

"They were left over from a job I did. Boss let me have 'em."

"Well, thank the boss for me. Are you hungry?"

"I could eat something."

They went into the house. Homer was upstairs in his room; when she looked in on him he was lying on his side in bed, looking at the wallpaper. She thought she heard him mumbling to himself. If he knew she was there, he never let on.

In the kitchen Etta set out bread and cold meats, lettuce, and mustard. There was a new Bible on the table, and Ray picked it up. It was the same edition he'd been given in prison.

"I was joking when I asked if you'd ever read the good book," he said as he set it aside. "You should close in the north end of that barn. You're missing some boards there."

"I know," she said. "There's a lot I should do around here."

She sat sideways in the chair and nibbled at her sandwich without interest. Ray ate his lunch and tried not to look at her legs.

There was pumpkin pie for dessert. Etta cut a piece for Ray only.

"You on a diet for your new boyfriend?" Ray asked.

She smiled. "Yeah, that's it."

"You shouldn't be. You're too thin. How do you know this guy anyway?"

"Tim? I met him a while ago, through a friend. He gave me that Bible, matter of fact."

"So he's a Bible thumper?"

"Something like that."

"And he's in salvage?"

"Yup."

"He must be in the business end," Ray said pointedly. "He's got pretty soft hands for somebody in salvage."

He finished his pie and leaned back, lit a cigarette. He offered the pack to her, but she passed. He blew smoke into the air, and then he heard Homer's voice: "What the hell is he doing here?"

Homer was standing in the doorway to the living room. His pants were unbuckled—presumably he was going to or coming from the bathroom. His eyes were narrow, his fists bunched.

"Hello, Homer," Ray said.

"You're not welcome here. Get the hell out."

"Dad," Etta said.

"Goddamn hoodlum—get out of my house," Homer said.

"Come on, Dad," Etta said. "You promised I could have a hoodlum over if I was good."

She stood up and moved him into the living room. Ray could hear her talking to him in there, and then he heard footsteps ascending the stairs. A minute later she was back, helping herself to one of his cigarettes.

"Fine time for him to recognize somebody."

"What are you gonna do?" he asked after a moment.

"What am I gonna do about what?"

"You can't live like this. You'll turn into some sad old spinster."

"And you'll be what—the lonely old bachelor? Hey, maybe we can fix up the barn and put on a production of *The Glass Menagerie.*"

Ray took a drink of coffee and changed the subject. "You're broke, aren't you?"

"You think I'm gonna discuss my financial affairs with the hired hand? Are all you roofers this presumptuous?"

"You're broke."

"Maybe I am. What I don't know is how that might affect you, Mr. Dokes."

"It doesn't affect me. It just seems there's a lot of that going around. I thought this was a rich country." He took a drink of coffee. "I couldn't care less how you live your life. Who you spend time with."

"Well, that's good to know." She was smiling with her eyes, but not with her mouth.

"Sonny been back?"

"Yes, sir. His father had a stroke, did you know that?"

"No."

"Well, he did. And Sonny's got power of attorney, or so he claims. You think he was the big frog in the puddle before, well, look out."

"He's still pushing Homer to sell?"

"Yeah, but very gently. Sonny seems to have developed some diplomacy of late. Which makes him a little bit scarier, if anything. A fucking monster with tact."

"I don't like you even talking to him."

"I don't like talking to him, Ray. But short of calling the cops, how do I keep him off my farm?"

"You could call me."

"Yeah? Did you like jail that much?"

He looked away from her. She stood up then, went over and put her hand lightly on the back of his neck.

"I'm not going to deal with Sonny Stanton," she promised. "And neither is Homer. I'd set a match to the place first. And don't worry about my finances, Ray."

"I told you—it doesn't matter to me."

"Yes, it does. And I'm glad it does. But you have to have a little faith." She saw his eyes go to the Bible. "I'm talking secular here. You should try it sometime, cowboy. Believe me, it'll make your life a whole lot easier."

"That something else you got from your boyfriend?"

"Tim? Naw, he's more in the nonsecular vein. And did I say he was my boyfriend?"

"You didn't say he wasn't."

She walked him to the car, thanked him again for the roof. Driving away, he watched her in the rearview, walking easily across the lawn, barefoot in the faded summer dress.

Ray headed south on the side road and thought about the concept of secular faith. What she couldn't understand was that certain things were unavailable to certain people. It frustrated him that she'd never been able to understand that about him. Of course, it was her inability to understand it that made her so at ease in the world.

Thinking about the concept of secular faith made him thirsty. He drove past the Slamdance, thought about the two slugs he'd encountered last time he'd been there, and kept going. A couple of blocks along, he turned back. He'd drink where he wanted.

The place wasn't busy, this early in the day. Tiny Montgomery was behind the bar. Ray ordered a beer and sat himself on a stool. A weary-looking blonde with bad implants was moving slowly on the stage, looking like she'd rather be somewhere else.

"So what're you up to, Ray?" Tiny asked.

"I don't know, Tiny," Ray said. "Spinning my wheels."

"Where you living?"

"Out at Pete Culpepper's spread."

The waitress came to the counter. Tiny supplied her with a couple Caesars and a draft, deposited the cash in the register. "Pete still in the thoroughbred business?"

"About half ass," Ray said.

"Aw, you gotta be rich to play that game these days," Tiny said. "I haven't even been to the track in years. I quit my gambling about the same time I quit drinking. One was no fun without the other, and they were both about to kill me."

"Speaking of the track, who were those two guys in here last week, tried to buy me a lap dance? The woman said they were some kin to Earl Stanton."

Tiny took a moment to think back. "Oh, Dean and Paulie," he said. "Yeah, they're nephews or cousins or something. They're just flunkies for the stable. Paulie's a good kid, you get to know him. Dean's your basic ten-cent wise guy."

"I thought maybe they were working for Sonny, looking to catch me alone."

"They got no more use for Sonny than you do, if that's possible. It was probably just Dean, trying to make friends. He's a bit of a rounder, one of these guys who works real hard at being lazy."

Ray drank from his beer and took a look around the room. The blonde finished up, and she departed the stage like a man caught cheating at cards.

"Well, he's barking up the wrong tree if he thinks I'm some kind of outlaw," Ray said. "I'm just a working man these days. I don't have enough energy to get myself into trouble. And I figure that's a good thing."

"So you're walking the line," Tiny said.

"I'm walking it. Straight and narrow."

A new dancer walked out on stage. She was slightly built, but she could actually dance. She started off to a song by Madonna, whom she favored. The boys in the front row perked up right away.

"You ever think about the old days, Ray?" Tiny asked. "High school football?"

"Sometimes, I guess."

"When we played football, that's all I cared about. Even now, I play those games over and over again in my head. I swear I can remember every play." He hesitated, as if maybe he'd revealed too much. "Thing is, that was the best time of my life. I never once gave a thought to where I'd be twenty years later. And look where I am."

"You're making a living, Tiny. Taking care of business."

"I guess I am," Tiny said resignedly. "And you're walking the line."

Ray took a long pull on his beer and watched the material girl for a moment. "You know the problem with walking the line?"

"What's the problem?"

"There's no surprises, Tiny. You got that line in front of you, far as you can see, and that's it. I used to like to get surprised once in a while."

"You will be again."

"Yeah—when?"

"You can't know that. It'd ruin the surprise."

When Ray finished the second beer he decided to go. As he pushed the glass away and shook his head at Tiny to indicate he was done the front door opened and Jackson Jones walked in. He stood in the entranceway and looked with squinted eyes about the room. It was apparent he hadn't stopped by for a drink. After a moment he walked to the bar and spoke to Tiny.

"Dean and Paulie been in?" he asked.

"Haven't seen them," Tiny said.

Jackson shook his head. "I swear those two could get lost in a shoe box."

When he turned to go he saw Ray, and surprise flickered across his face. He hesitated, then said, "Ray."

"Hello, Jack."

Jackson took a moment to decide on something. Then he looked back to Tiny. "Rye and water. And another beer for Ray."

Ray nodded his agreement, and Jackson sat down beside him at the bar and watched as Tiny brought the drinks.

"How you doing, Jack?" Ray asked.

"Good."

"How's the thoroughbred business?"

"We're having a real good year." Jackson took a sip of whiskey. His hands, Ray noticed, were huge, the fingers long and square at the tips. "We're running this four-year-old in the Breeders' Classic."

"That's what I heard. I hear he's quite a horse."

"The best I ever trained. He was an expensive colt; the old man paid damn near a million for him. But he's one that's gonna pay off, just on running alone. Then, if he's a good stud—"

"That's gravy."

"That's gravy," Jackson agreed. "What're you doing, Ray—still playing ball?"

"I'm a roofer these days."

"Oh, yeah?" Jackson paused a moment. "Sonny know you're out?"

"Yep." Ray took a drink of beer and set the glass on the bar. "I saw him at an auction sale over at the town line."

"Right. Sonny's buying up a lot of farmland. God only knows why."

"I'm done with him, Jack."

Jackson nodded. "You got a raw deal, Ray. Everybody knows it. But Sonny's just Sonny, and that's not ever gonna change."

"Yup. Sonny's just Sonny, and everybody figures they got to live with it. You too, Jack."

"You asking me why?"

Ray shrugged. "Not my business."

Jackson drank off his rye and signaled for another. "I'll tell you a story, Ray. Happened twenty years ago. Sonny was what, fifteen or sixteen—no, he had to be sixteen because he was driving this new Corvette the old man bought him. Anyway, he was in a big golf tournament, some junior championship. And Earl was supposed to be there, to watch his boy. Well, Earl forgot all about it, of course, and he spent the day at the electronics plant. Sonny wins the tournament, and he brings this big trophy home and throws it in the driveway and runs it over about ten times with his car. Pissed at the old man, you see?"

"Sounds like Sonny."

"Well, that's nothing. I've never told anybody the rest of the story. Earl was just new to racing then. He had a two-year-old he bought at the Kentucky sales, paid a hundred grand, which was a lot of money back then. Good-looking colt out of Northern Dancer. Same night as the golf tournament, somebody took a steel pipe to that colt, damn near killed the animal. I found the pipe a few weeks later, stashed in some hay bales in the mow. That horse was never worth a dime after that."

"That's a sad story," Ray admitted. "But you know what I know, Jack. Nothing you say about Sonny is gonna surprise me."

Jackson took his fresh drink and had a sip. There was genuine sadness in his eyes. "He was sixteen years old, Ray. Sixteen."

Sonny played cards at the club until midnight, when the last of the players, facing work in the morning, begged off and headed home. Sonny, who didn't have to work tomorrow, or any other morrow, got into his car and headed for the casino. There was little traffic, and he ran the BMW up to 160 on the thruway, punching the radio stations with one hand as he drove.

Inside he dropped a quick two hundred on the slots and then made his way to the back room, where Big Billy Coon was sitting behind a desk with a skinny guy in a black suit. The guy looked Indian, Pakistani maybe. There was nobody else in the room.

"Hey Billy," Sonny said. "Where is everybody?"

"Slow night. Mondays," Billy told him. "Grab yourself a drink."

There was a full bar at the far end of the room. Sonny walked over and helped himself to a vodka and tonic. Billy looked at Sonny, then at the skinny guy and nodded his head. When Sonny came back he sat down at the poker table, put his feet up, flashing his thousand-dollar Tony Llamas.

"This is Raul," Billy said. "Sonny Stanton. Sonny's in the thoroughbred business."

"Oh?" Raul said.

Sonny shrugged off his own importance like a pretty girl deflecting a compliment and took a long drink of vodka. Raul walked over and sat down at the poker table. Billy got up from the desk then and went to the bar for a coke.

"So you're an owner?" Raul asked.

"He owns the horse that's gonna win the Classic next month," Billy Coon said and he joined the two of them at the poker table.

"You got an early line on that yet?" Sonny asked.

"Yup," Billy said. "You can get four to one on Jumping Jack Flash right now. Horse will be two to one the day of the race. Maybe not even that."

"I don't know," Sonny said. "There's a couple of hot horses from Europe running."

"Bet 'em then," Billy said. "I can get you ten, fifteen to one on both those nags. You should load up on 'em. Except we both know they aren't gonna win."

Sonny smiled and had another drink. "How long can I get four to one?"

"Today. Maybe tomorrow, maybe not."

"Okay," Sonny said. "Give me ten grand on the nose."

"You got it," Billy said. "I've been looking to introduce you to Raul here. He's an investor. What's going on with that piece of land you got in Holden County?"

"I still got a couple of farms to buy," Sonny said.

"That's not what I asked."

"No?"

"What're you gonna do with the land?"

"Become a farmer."

"No, you're not." Billy looked at Raul. "Sonny's got a secret."

Raul appeared disinterested. "What's his secret?"

"Nobody knows; that's what makes it a secret," Billy said. "One day he's gonna build a broodmare operation; the next it's a subdivision. Then I hear he's looking to put in a casino. That one's kinda tricky, though. The government doesn't let just anybody build a casino. You have to be charity minded. Or an honest-to-goodness Injun. I don't figure Sonny here fits either profile."

"Maybe that's why I'm being so nice to you," Sonny said.

"Hey, we've got a casino," Billy said. "You figure we need another? Besides, that's not exactly the rez you're buying up. I don't think you're looking to build a gambling palace."

"In a way, I am," Sonny said.

"Yeah?"

"I'm gonna build a racetrack," Sonny said, and then he smiled. "Among other things."

Billy had the pop halfway to his mouth. He stopped, put the can on the table. "Bullshit," he said.

Sonny just showed his Sonny grin and recrossed his snakeskin boots on the tabletop. Raul watched him.

"You can't just build a racetrack," Billy said.

"Why not?" Sonny asked. "They think they got a fucking monopoly. Says who? I'm gonna build a world-class track, Billy, and that's not all. I'm gonna build a golf course on the back of the concession that'll put Glen Abbey to shame. They'll play the Open there. And then I'll build a couple hundred homes in the middle of it all, price 'em from a million up. That concession is a beautiful piece of land; it's got forest, streams, hills. I'm gonna build a fucking showplace."

"You're buying farmland," Billy said. "You're gonna have zoning problems."

"There's no such thing as zoning problems," Sonny said.

"Come on, Billy, you're not that naive. I got two farms to go. Some stubborn old squarehead who I'm about to close on, and this senile old fart who's got a foxy blond daughter who's too smart for her own good. But I have it on good authority that they're hurting financially. I'm looking forward to making her squirm."

"You looking for investors?" Raul asked.

Sonny had a long look at Raul, then deliberately got up and went to the bar for a refill. When he returned he picked up a deck of cards and began to shuffle absently.

"I don't know that I need outside investment," he said. "Stanton Stables is a pretty solvent enterprise. But I may have something open, for the right partner. I like these futures, Billy. The Ontario Jockey Club doesn't offer them."

"Officially, neither do I," Billy said.

"But we could, under the right umbrella."

Big Billy Coon shrugged. Sonny looked at him in annoyance—goddamn Indian, you never knew what he was thinking. When he looked at Raul, he got the same stare. Indians—east or west—were all the same, it seemed.

"Where you from?" Sonny asked.

"Sri Lanka."

Sonny didn't have a clue where Sri Lanka was, but he assumed it was over there somewhere.

"They got racehorses over there?" he asked.

"They sure do."

"That where you got your money?"

"No," Raul said.

10

The lawyers arrived at ten o'clock, as scheduled. Jackson, unloading feed at the barn, saw them pull up together, mount the steps in their eight-hundred-dollar suits, briefcases tucked under their arms, an air of gravity and purpose and importance hanging over them.

The first lawyer rang the bell and waited. After a moment the second lawyer knocked on the door, and they waited again. Jackson left the feed truck and, cutting a wide circle so as to remain out of sight, walked around and entered the house through the back door.

He went up the back staircase. Sonny was still in bed, as Jackson had known he would be. The blinds were shut tight, and the room was as dark as night.

"Sonny! For Christ's sake, the lawyers are here."

Jackson walked over and opened the louvered blinds, zebra-striping the bedsheets with the morning sun. Sonny kicked his legs under the sheet and raised his head. He squinted red-eyed at Jackson, as if he didn't recognize him. The smell of alcohol and sweat hung in the room. When Sonny swung his legs out, Jackson could see the thick raised scars from the operations on his right knee. Sonny reached for his cane and then turned to look at the clock on the nightstand.

"Shit," he said. "I'll be down in a minute. Tell Marla to make some coffee."

"She's off today."

"Shit," Sonny said again. "Okay, I'll be right down. Tell 'em a story, Jackson. Tell 'em I was up all night with a sick mare."

"Sure," Jackson said, and he left.

He let the lawyers in and led them into the dining room. They placed their briefcases on the heavy oak table and then sat and opened them and began to spread papers about the tabletop.

"He'll be down in a minute," Jackson said.

"Is there a problem?" the first lawyer asked.

"He's been out all night drinking," Jackson told them, and he went to make coffee.

Sonny arrived at the same time as the coffee. He was leaning heavily on his cane as he came down the stairs, and Jackson suspected that his knee was giving him at least as much pain as his hangover. He was wearing jeans and a golf shirt with a Hilton Head logo above the pocket. His eyes were red and puffy, his hair tousled.

"I'm sorry, but I was up half the night," Sonny said when he walked in.

"Jackson told us," the second lawyer said.

Sonny, approaching from behind the two attorneys, gave Jackson a conspiratorial wink, then he took a seat at the head of the table.

"Well, I got grain to unload," Jackson said. "Unless you want me here."

"No, no," Sonny said. "You tend to the feed; I'll be along to help when we finish here."

Jackson nodded as he left. He'd known Sonny for more than twenty years and had never in that time seen him lift anything heavier than a bottle of Glenlivet.

Sonny poured himself a cup of coffee and took a large drink, burning his mouth. He'd swallowed a couple of Demerol before coming downstairs, and he was waiting for the drug to kick in. Maybe the caffeine would jump-start it.

"So what's up, guys?" he asked while he waited.

"You've got a cash problem, Sonny," the first lawyer said.

"Yeah, right."

"It's not a joke. Everything's been frozen."

"How the fuck can that happen? I have power of attorney," Sonny said.

"That might not be true," the second lawyer said cautiously. "Some new paperwork has shown up, with another law firm. It looks as if Gena might have power of attorney."

Sonny felt his stomach turn over, and he thought he might throw up his drugs. "You better not be telling me that. That fucking skank has a prenup; there's no way she can pull this off. We settled all that before he married her."

"First of all, Sonny, a prenuptial agreement is a pretty iffy proposition under the best of circumstances," the first lawyer said. "Secondly, these other papers have been filed in the Bahamas. For the here and now, it doesn't matter a hell of a lot whether or not they're valid. You might prove that they're not, but you could be in court for years doing it. And the money would be frozen the whole time." He hesitated. "The best thing that could happen right now would be if your father came around."

Sonny poured cream in his coffee to cool it and had another drink. The Demerol was hitting him already, thanks to an empty stomach. But it was hard on the heels of his anger, that familiar uncontrollable feeling that he was being used.

"Then we gotta get him home," Sonny said. "Who knows what they're doing to him down there. She's probably got some fucking voodoo man sticking pins in him."

"Why don't you fly his doctor down, see if he can be moved?" the second lawyer said. "You're right; things would be a lot easier to monitor if he was home."

"Have I got enough money for a plane ticket?" Sonny asked sarcastically.

"You're not broke, Sonny," the first lawyer said. "You just

have to stop spending money like you've been. Buying all these farms. You're seriously overdrawn at the bank. Ordinarily that wouldn't be a problem. But until this is straightened out, it is. You have no access to the old man's money, Sonny. Do you understand that?"

Sonny fell into a sulk. The lawyers exchanged glances, then each looked at his watch at precisely the same moment. Sonny saw, and it infuriated him further.

"Just sit there," he said. "You're still getting paid, aren't you?"

"We're still getting paid," the first lawyer agreed.

"Then sit there," Sonny said. "Wait a minute—what about the money we got coming in?"

"What money would that be?" the second lawyer asked. It was his turn for sarcasm.

"Thoroughbred money," Sonny said. "Purses, stud fees, whatever."

The lawyers looked at each other for a moment. The hesitation was all that Sonny required. He'd always been adroit at twisting rules. Indeed, before he lost most of the use of his right leg, he'd been famous on the golf course as a cheat of astonishing imagination.

"Think about it," he said. "We've got a huge overhead in this horse operation. Anything coming in should go back into the business. How else we gonna pay the bills?"

"You might be able to make that argument," the first lawyer said.

In his head, Sonny had already made it. He could foresee a dozen ways to potentially turn this to his favor. There was enough diversity and ambiguity in the thoroughbred end of things—the feeding, the training, transport, vet bills—that he could get pretty creative with the bookkeeping.

"Let me put it another way," Sonny said. "You tell my wicked stepmother that either that's the way it works, or I sell every nag we got. Have her explain that to the old man when he wakes up."

When the lawyers had packed up the papers—which might as well have been props for all the attention they'd received—Sonny walked them to the front door. On the porch the two had attempted to initiate small talk about racehorses and the weather, and Sonny had closed the door on them in midsentence. He went into the kitchen and mixed a Bloody Mary and drank it looking out the rear window, watching the broodmares in the back paddock. When the drink was done he mixed another, and then he went out to the barn. It was a cold morning, and halfway across the yard he wished he'd grabbed a jacket.

He found Jackson in the tack room, drinking coffee and reading the morning paper. The tack room served as an office of sorts for Jackson. There was a desk and a couple of chairs, a filing cabinet in the corner. There was a small electric heater on top of the cabinet, and the room was cosy. On the walls, above the saddles and halters and blankets, were pictures of various Stanton horses over the years. There was a large picture of Jackson and Earl Stanton, posing with Supernova minutes after the colt had won the Queen's Plate ten years back. Sonny could be seen just over the horse's haunches. In the old man's shadow, even then.

Jackson looked at him impatiently over the sports section of the *Post*. Sonny picked a copy of *Thoroughbred Magazine* off a chair and tossed it onto the desk, then sat down. He took a large drink of the Bloody Mary. Everything was flowing together now—the Demerol, the caffeine, and the vodka—and his mind was functioning again, click-clacking along like a train on a track.

"Gena's trying to take charge," he told Jackson.

"I figured that when I saw the look on that lawyer's face," Jackson said. "Man looks like he hasn't taken a shit in a week."

"Tell me something, Jack. We gonna win the Classic?"

"I believe we are." Jackson indicated the various periodicals on the desk. "Just about every handicapper in North America thinks so, too. Why?"

"We're off the mother tit, at least for the time being. But any money we make through the stable is ours to run the operation."

Jackson nodded slightly.

"What's our take if we win it?" Sonny asked.

"The purse is five million," Jackson said, wondering why Sonny, given his gambling jones, had never mastered common mathematics. "Winner gets 52 percent of that. Place or show is nothing to sneeze at, either."

"Place or show, my ass. What else is there out there? I'm gonna need some working capital, Jackson. I got outside investments. Anything at Woodbine?"

When Jackson never inquired about the other investments, Sonny had to assume that he knew about him buying up the property in Holden County. But of course Jackson would know. In spite of his laid-back pose, it was pretty obvious that Jackson never missed a trick. It was his nature, and it was also why Sonny didn't trust him as far as he could toss him.

"We've got a couple two-year-olds running, but that's about it," Jackson said. "The old man never planned anything else this year."

"What about Fort Erie?"

Jackson took a moment to thumb through a magazine on the desk, checking out the racing schedules. Sonny finished his drink and leaned back, his hands behind his head, and looked at the ceiling. The panic he'd felt earlier had passed.

"There's a two-year-old stakes race next weekend," Jackson said, his tone reluctant. "A hundred-thousand-dollar claimer."

"We could run that big chestnut colt," Sonny said at once. "He'd win it easily."

"He'd be dropping down. We'd lose him on the claim."

"Even better. If we lose him, we get the purse and the claim price. Double bubble. That's the risk you take when you run in a claimer."

"It's a stupid risk. Running a quarter-million-dollar colt in a hundred-thousand-dollar race."

"We got plenty of horses, Jack."

"It's not just that. Though I do hate the thought of losing that colt—I got a feeling he's gonna be a hell of a three-year-old. But it's not just that."

"What is it?"

"The old man never liked to drop horses down just to win a race. He figured it wasn't fair to the smaller owners."

"Gee willickers, Jack—I never thought of that. Fuck the small owners."

Jackson tossed the schedule onto the desk and got to his feet. He took his jacket down from a hook on the wall and put it on. He looked at Sonny.

"I guess that's your philosophy in life," he said as he walked around behind Sonny, opened the door. "I'm just saying the old man wouldn't like it. That's not the way he operates."

"Have you seen the old man today, Jack?" Sonny said, asking over his shoulder, still sitting in the chair. "Have you?"

Jackson made no reply.

"I didn't think so. Ship that colt down to the Fort. Let's make some money."

Etta's shift ended at seven in the morning, but her replacement had called and said she'd be fifteen minutes late. Either her estimate or her watch was wrong; she showed at the hospital at seven-thirty.

"I'm sorry," her replacement said when she finally arrived. She was young and vivacious, always talking about her lively social life. She was apparently a karaoke singer of some renown in the bars of Kitchener and Guelph, and it was this distinction that led her to regard herself as a celebrity of sorts.

"It's all right," Etta said.

"Oh well, it's not like you had anything important going on," her replacement said.

"Just my life," Etta said, and she left.

She stopped for coffee for herself and donuts for Homer on the way out of town. It began to rain as she drove. She turned the wipers on and was reminded at once that the wiper blade was missing on the driver's side of the Taurus. It had been gone for weeks; each time it rained, she cursed herself for not having it replaced. Of course when it wasn't raining, she never thought about it.

After a few miles, she had to pull over to wipe the windshield with a cloth from beneath the seat. Not that it would help much; the rain fell steadily. As she finished wiping the glass Ray Dokes came upon her from the opposite direction. He pulled over to the shoulder of the road and powered the window down. He was wearing his work clothes; his Tigers' cap, pulled low over his eyes, was splattered with raindrops.

"What are you doing here?" she asked.

"Well, I'm not standing out in the rain," he said. "You got trouble?"

"I've got no wiper on this side. I keep forgetting to fix it."

Ray shut the Caddy off and got out, walked around and opened the trunk. There was a toolbox inside; he retrieved a slot screwdriver and walked over to the Taurus.

"You're soaked; get in the car," he said.

"Don't tell me what to do," she said, but she got back in.

Ray crossed over to the passenger side of the Taurus and with the screwdriver began to remove the wiper there. Etta watched from inside. He had his collar up, and rain dripped from the brim of his ball cap. He needed a shave, she saw, and he looked wonderful.

As she watched him in the rain she was reminded of the night they got caught in a downpour on the pier at Port Maitland. They'd just finished dinner—along with a couple of bottles of red wine—and had gone for a walk along the pier afterward. In the lee of the lighthouse they had begun to kiss, and in her memory it seemed as if in an instant they went from kissing to making love on a bed of their discarded clothes. When the skies opened they were both drenched at once, but they carried on gamely, laughing crazily, breathlessly, before pulling on their wet clothes and dashing for the car.

"Shit," she said now, sitting in the car. She'd exorcized those memories a long time ago. It was the rain, she decided. The goddamn rain.

Ray brought the good blade around and slid it onto the arm on the driver's side. Etta rolled her window down.

"Why didn't I think of that?" she asked.

"You want me to answer that?"

"No," she decided. "What are you doing out here?"

"Heading home. We got rained out at work."

"Oh." She hesitated. "Well, I'm just getting off work myself."

"I figured that when I saw the nurse's getup. I'm getting wet. I'll see ya, Etta."

"Hey," she said as Ray walked away. "Thanks."

He raised his hand and kept walking back to his car. She waved as he drove away, but he wasn't looking. She sat there along the side of the road for a time, watching the rain as it fell.

When Etta got home Mabel was watching Regis on TV, and Homer was nowhere to be seen. Mabel Anton was a heavyset woman in her fifties, and she wore her usual uniform, matching sweatpants and sweatshirt, pink running shoes. On occasion she would wear a like-colored baseball cap with a white pompom on top.

"I'm sorry I'm late, Mabel," Etta said when she arrived.

"It's all right."

"Where's Dad?"

"Went back to bed."

"Good, maybe he'll let me have a nap."

"Not right now. . . . Feel a little chilly in here?"

"Is the heat off?"

"The furnace made a loud noise and then quit about an hour ago. I called my brother-in-law; he's coming to have a look. Should be here by now, in fact."

"Great."

"I'll wait. See if I can get you the family discount. The old man will be screaming for his breakfast, but let him if he can't fry an egg."

Etta drank her take-out coffee, and she and Mabel watched Regis Philbin talk to Charles Grodin. Mabel was quiet until a commercial break.

"Has Father Tim been to see you?" she asked.

"As a matter of fact, he has," Etta said. "More than once. I assume you sent him."

"I did not."

"Right. Why this mission to hook me up with your church?"

"Because you have no direction. You are rudderless."

"I am rudderless? Yikes."

"Don't make fun. You were sleeping with a married man. That's a sin."

"I really wish you would let that drop."

"You're the one who told me about it."

"That was before I knew you were a nut."

Mabel shot her a dark look. "You'd better decide where your life is going, Etta. You've been a failure at everything you've done."

"Gee, thanks."

"Go ahead and mock. It's the one thing you're good at. But you listen to Father Tim. He's a very wise man."

"I'm not sure how wise he is, but I find him kinda sexy, you know."

"Etta! Father Tim is a priest. Priests have no interest in sex."

Etta looked at her closely. "You've never actually read a newspaper, have you, Mabel?"

When the repairman showed, fifteen minutes later, he seemed to be in a hurry. He went into the basement, had a look at the old furnace, administered its last rites, and then gave Etta an estimate of four thousand dollars to replace it.

So much for the family discount.

After he and Mabel had gone, Etta sat at the table a long while, resisting the urge to lay her head on the cool surface and go to sleep. When it seemed that she could no longer stay awake she got up and went upstairs to change her clothes. She threw her scrubs in the hamper and pulled on jeans and a wool sweater.

She walked outside. The rain had stopped. The sky to the west was growing brighter, offering at least a promise of sunshine. The few remaining leaves on the maples and the ash in the yard dripped sporadically around her. She stood in the yard and took stock of that to which she and Homer could claim ownership. It occurred to her that there must be something on the old place they could sell. She walked to the barn, pulled open the large doors, and walked inside. There was an old milking machine, ancient harness, pitchforks, shovels, buckets, tools of various types and vintages. Nothing to make a buyer's pulse quicken.

As she walked back outside, her eyes fell on the Ford tractor in the orchard. After glancing around futilely for a better idea, she went over to have a look. Then she went into the machine shed and found a tire pump and a tool box. There was a pair of coveralls hanging on a peg inside the door, and she put them on.

Before going back to the orchard she went into the house and saw that Homer was now in front of the TV, his head tilted to the side as if in great curiosity. She watched him for a moment, and then, carrying her tools, she went back to the tractor.

Using the old hand pump, she worked for twenty minutes to pump air into the deflated back tire. Even then it was only half inflated, but she figured it would do for the moment. She found a spark-plug socket in the tool box and removed the plugs, cleaned them with a wire brush, looked to see that the gap was all right—pure speculation on her part—and then replaced them in the engine block. With an oil can she lubricated the carburetor and linkage. The gas tank was empty. She retrieved the can of lawn-mower gas from the shed and emptied it into the tractor. The battery was dead, of course; she doubted the tractor had moved in more than a year.

She drove her Taurus through the long grass into the orchard, spinning the tires briefly as she bounced through the shallow ditch in the lane beside the barn. She pulled up beside the tractor and then connected the old booster cables from the shed from one battery to the other.

Sitting on the tractor, she turned the key and bumped the starter switch. The engine turned over at once, whirring rapidly. But it did not start. She tried for maybe ten minutes, adjusting the throttle and the choke. Finally, she gave up.

Both hands on the wheel, she watched the clouds overhead as they raced across the unsettled sky. Something caught her peripheral vision, and she looked toward the house to see Homer standing in the backyard, a pitching wedge in his hand. She was glad for a moment to see that he was out and about and wanting to hit golf balls, but as she watched she saw the look on his face and then realized that he was staring at the wedge because he had no idea what it was.

She was suddenly weary to the bone. She sat motionless for a moment, and then she began to pound on the dash of the tractor with her fists.

"Goddamn it! Why are you doing this to me?"

She managed to cut her knuckle on the sharp edge of the dash. She sucked at the blood a moment, then on impulse hit the starter button again. The tractor roared to life, coughing and sputtering, then evening out. Etta listened to the engine and gave a quick look skyward. She offered no acknowledgment, though. She was still pissed off.

Driving around to the front yard, she parked the tractor beneath the large ash trees there. In the shed she found a For Sale sign her father had painted on a square of plywood years earlier and had used numerous times to sell off a series of junk-heap vehicles he'd owned. She hosed the sign off and then carried it out and propped it against the front wheel of the tractor. Then she stepped back to have a look. She gave the half-inflated rear tire a kick.

"That's a good tractor," she heard her father say.

When she turned he was standing along the driveway, the pitching wedge still in his hand.

"That's what they say," she said.

"I got one just like it at home," he told her.

11

Dean and Paulie were to be at Woodbine at nine, and they showed at half past. Jackson was on the track, walking out the horse that they were about to transport. The colt was a dark gray two-year-old, long and lanky like a standardbred.

"Just once, you could be on time," Jackson said as they got out of the car.

"Hey, it's only nine-thirty," Dean said. "This is the earliest we've been late yet."

Paulie held his tongue. The reason they were late was that Dean had still been in bed when Paulie had shown up at his place at eight o'clock. Paulie had gotten him up, but Dean was irritable from lack of sleep. There were a number of stereo components, new in boxes, scattered about the apartment. Paulie looked them over while Dean was in the shower.

"Where'd you get all the stereos?" he asked when Dean came out of the bathroom.

"I'm a fucking Sears outlet, what do ya think?"

Paulie had sat in the kitchen patiently and waited until Dean shaved and then decided what to wear. Apparently, Dean felt he needed just the right outfit to deliver a horse to Fort Erie.

"Turn the colt over to Erskine," Jackson said to them when the animal was loaded. "Barn nine. And don't dawdle down there. Get back to the farm; there's plenty to do with the old man sick."

"Yup," Dean said.

"And don't be driving like a maniac. The horse is pretty green."

"We'll be careful," Paulie said.

"Yeah," Jackson said without conviction. "You guys better get your shit together. We gotta ship the Flash down to New York City next week. Sonny's not big on you two to begin with."

"Not like you, eh?" Dean said.

"Just do your job," Jackson said. "That too much to ask?"

Even with the traffic, they made it to the Fort in two hours. Erskine was waiting for them, and they got the colt settled in a stall without a problem. Erskine had other horses to see to, and he left them there. Dean and Paulie stood by the trailer and watched the activities around the barns for a moment. There was a card starting at one o'clock, and the place was busy.

"What do you think, Paulie?" Dean asked. "We could stick around and bet some of these soupbones."

"Jackson said to get back."

"Jackson said, Jackson said," Dean mocked. "One of these days Jackson's gonna get something he doesn't want." And then he saw Ray Dokes, leaning against the hood of a pickup, the next barn over.

"Look who it is," Dean said. "Come on."

Ray saw the pair approaching from between the barns, the dark-haired one wearing dress pants and a turtleneck and the other trailing in his porkpie hat.

"Shit," Ray said.

Pete Culpepper came out of the stall, where he'd been checking the gelding Fast Market's hoof. He watched the two approach.

"Now who's that?" he asked.

"The two I told you about. From the Slamdance," Ray said.

"Hey, Raymond—how's it going?" the dark-haired one said, and he stuck his hand out. "Like, we got our signals crossed at the Slamdance the other day. I wasn't trying to pull nothing on you. Sonny Stanton can kiss my ass, you want to know the truth. I'm Dean Caldwell; this is Paulie."

Dean turned to Pete then, introduced himself all over again. Pete reluctantly said his own name. Ray looked at the kid in the hat and nodded. The kid smiled and ducked his head. He was wearing jeans and work boots. The boots were scuffed, and the toes were worn through, revealing the steel plates beneath.

"This your horse?" Dean said, barely glancing at the gelding. "Good-looking horse. What's he—three-year-old?"

"He's nine," Pete said.

"Yeah?" Dean said. "Well, I'm with Stanton Stables; don't know if you knew that. We just brought a colt down. Two-year-old I've been working with, he's running the stakes race next weekend."

"Well, that's good to hear," Pete said, and he looked at Ray. "It's real nice to know that you big-time operators are supporting the small tracks."

"How big's your stable?" Dean wanted to know. Horseman to horseman.

"I got this gelding and a couple broodmares," Pete said. "That's how big it is."

Ray smiled as Pete spit a wad of Redman in the dirt, narrowly missing Dean's shiny black shoes. Paulie had moved over to the stall, was looking at the gelding. Dean turned back to Ray.

"Well, we got to be going. I just wanted to straighten out that little misunderstanding. I know all about Sonny, and let's just leave it at that. What're you doing these days?"

"I'm in the roofing business," Ray told him.

"Roofing business, huh?" Dean said, and he smiled pointlessly at Paulie. "Well, from time to time, I come across an opportunity that might interest you. You know, a chance to make a quick buck."

Pete went back inside to finish cleaning the gelding's feet.

Paulie moved closer to watch. He put his hand on the gelding's neck, and the horse turned his head and nuzzled Paulie's cheek. Then he lifted his nose suddenly, as if by purpose, and knocked Paulie's hat off. Paulie laughed, and even the horse appeared to be grinning as he pushed his nose into Paulie's shoulder.

"What's his name?" Paulie asked as he picked up his hat.

"Fast Market," Pete said, and he looked the kid over. "You in the thoroughbred business too?"

"We just do odd jobs, really," Paulie said. "Dean, he always likes to make a big deal of things. This here's a nice horse. He's sure got a soft nose."

"The roofing business keeps me pretty busy," Ray was telling Dean outside the stall.

"I'll keep you in mind just the same," Dean said. "I'll stand you to a drink next time at the Slamdance."

Ray nodded and didn't say anything.

"Let's go, Paulie," Dean said then. "We gotta get back to the farm. We're breaking some young horses."

Paulie looked at Pete and shook his head slightly. Pete looked out at Dean, and then he smiled at Paulie.

"You gonna race your horse today?" Paulie asked.

"Yes, sir, first race."

"Well, I hope he wins, Mr. Culpepper."

Dean came closer. "I'm gonna put some money on that horse. I like his configuration, you know that?"

They left then, Dean leading the way and Paulie dragging along behind, turning back every so often to look at the gelding. After a moment Pete came out of the stall, the hoof pick in his hand.

"That's who you told me about?"

"That's them. You figure they're the brains behind Stanton Stables?"

Pete snorted. "The kid seemed all right. Polite, and you could tell he likes horses."

"What about the other one? The one who likes that gelding's configuration?"

"We got a saying back home," Pete said, and he watched as the pair departed. "That boy's all hat and no cattle."

When they got back to the pickup Dean climbed in and fired it up. Paulie got in reluctantly.

"I thought we were gonna bet on Mr. Culpepper's horse," he said.

Dean snorted. "I wouldn't risk a dime on that broken-down nag. Shit, I don't think I'd cut him up and feed him to my dog."

"I never knew you had a dog, Dean. What kind is he?"

"Shut the fuck up, Paulie."

By the time they reached the Falls, Dean had decided that they'd done enough work for the day. He thought he'd play some blackjack. They went down Clifton Hill and parked the truck and trailer illegally on a side street.

The place was full, as it usually was, with high rollers and tourists and nickel-and-dimers. A large percentage of the bettors were Asian. The only spots open for blackjack were at the hundred-dollar tables. Dean had to wait to get a spot at a cheaper table. He played some roulette and complained while he waited: "Fucking Orientals. Why don't they go back where they came from?"

"Where did they come from, Dean?"

"Where?" Dean repeated. "Well, from the Orient, where do you think?"

Paulie spent ten dollars on the quarter slots and then quit. "I'm gonna go look at the Falls," he told Dean.

"Yeah, maybe they changed since the last time we were here."

"I doubt that. How long we gonna be here?"

"I don't know; couple hours. I'll see you later."

Paulie walked out of the casino and wandered over to the

big bridge just down the street. He liked to watch the rainbows above the escarpment, how they constantly appeared and then disappeared into the mist. Paulie leaned on the railing and watched the spectrum over the cascading water, and from time to time he would turn back toward the blinking neon behind him, and he wondered why anyone would think they needed all those lights next to something that was advertised as one of the world's great wonders. Paulie often thought that the Falls must have been an amazing thing before human beings found out about them.

After a while he walked to a Wendy's and had a burger and fries. At three o'clock he was sitting on a bench in front of the casino, talking to one of the limo drivers there.

"How come you're not gambling?" the man asked. "Shoot your wad?"

"I'm just waiting for my cousin."

"So he's the gambler?"

"He sure thinks he is."

Finally, Paulie went in to get Dean. On a whim, he bought five dollars' worth of tokens, hit a jackpot on his first pull at a slot, and won four hundred dollars. He cashed in and then saw Dean coming through the crowd, looking glum.

"Let's get the fuck out of here," he said.

The truck had a fifty-dollar parking citation on the windshield. Dean tore it up and threw it in the street, and they drove away.

On the drive home Dean was silent, and Paulie never mentioned his windfall at the slots. He knew better than that.

Pete Culpepper was waiting for Chrissie at the saddling barn, standing in front of the stall, his hat low on his head, his eyes narrow beneath the brim. Inside the stall, Fast Market was already bridled. Ray Dokes was leaning with his back to the paddock fence, the Culpepper silks under his arm.

She arrived in the backseat of a cab. They watched as she

got out at the gate, paid the driver, and made her way toward them.

"It's the first race," Pete said.

"I know. I had truck trouble," Chrissie said.

"Well, let's get moving," Pete said, and he spit tobacco in the dirt.

Chrissie turned toward Ray, who was watching her as he lit a cigarette. "The fuck you lookin' at?" she demanded.

"What kind of truck trouble?" he asked.

"Like, the kind where I can't find it," she said. "Gimme the fucking silks."

Ray offered them over. When she was near, he could see her eyes and smell the alcohol on her. "How you feeling?" he asked.

"Fuck you."

He smiled. "I bet you're a joy to wake up to when you're like this."

She jerked the clothes from his hand and stomped off into the jockeys' room to change and to weigh in.

Fast Market was sound as a new dollar now, and he ran like it. She had him in second coming into the stretch, and he was hardly breathing. The leader was a bay mare, Juan Romano up, and the mare was tight to the rail, but she could be had, Chrissie knew. With a furlong to go, she moved the gelding outside and just touched him on the shoulder with the whip. He jumped under her hand, and Chrissie knew at once she had enough horse; she laid her hand on his neck and watched the mare drop back to her. Her head was feeling better with every stride.

Juan Romano turned his head toward them, and then suddenly the mare lurched into the gelding's path, barely clipping the horse's front shoulder with her hip. Chrissie felt the gelding stumble, and then the front left hoof caught the right and he went down. Chrissie went over the horse's neck, hit the dirt headfirst, felt the gelding roll over her. Her face was mashed into the track, and her nostrils filled with dirt.

At the rail Pete and Ray had watched as the gelding made his move in the stretch. They saw that the bay mare was done and there was nothing behind coming on. Ray turned to see Pete smiling, and then he saw Pete's eyes widen, and he turned back in time to see Fast Market go down, and Chrissie disappear underneath.

Ray jumped the fence and ran across the track. He had to wait for the trailers to pass him, and by the time he reached her, Chrissie was on her feet. Her face was covered in dirt, and her nose was bleeding. There were tears streaming down her cheeks, and when he tried to grab her, she pushed him away.

"Are you all right?" he asked.

But she pulled away from him and began to run to the gelding, who was limping along the rail near the finish line, moving on three legs, favoring the left front.

Pete Culpepper was on the track now, too, trotting stiff-legged across the dirt. Chrissie caught the gelding by the reins.

"I'm sorry, I'm sorry . . . ," she said over and over. Ray couldn't tell if she was speaking to the horse or to Pete.

She held the horse's head still while Pete knelt in the dirt and had a look at the leg, running his hands gently down each side of the shin, feeling for the source of the pain. Then he ran his hand up the leg to the shoulder, felt there too.

"I don't know," he said when he stood up. "I don't know."

Chrissie was watching him, the side of her face pressed tightly against the gelding's cheek, her arm beneath the horse's neck, keeping him still.

"Are you okay?" Ray asked her.

When she turned toward him, she saw Juan Romano loping the mare back to the finish, standing in the irons and grinning like he'd just invented winning. Chrissie let go of Fast Market's reins and headed to the finish line. When

Romano jumped down from his mount, she decked him with a hard right hand.

"You fucking asshole," she said. "You wanna win like that?"

Ray moved over, thinking to protect her. There was no need, though; Romano got to his feet at once, but he clearly wanted no part of Chrissie. Bleeding from the mouth, he retreated behind the horse's owner, a heavy blond woman with a Lhasa apso in her arms and a jangle of gold jewelry around her wrinkled neck.

"My horse jumped," Romano said.

"You're a fucking liar," Chrissie said. "You better hope my horse is all right."

"Watch your language," the fat blond woman said. "It was an accident."

"Fuck you and your little dog too," Chrissie said, and she walked away.

They led Fast Market back to the barn. Limping from her fall, Chrissie kept her hand on the horse's withers as they walked. Inside the stall, they pulled the saddle and bridle off and rubbed the gelding down, and then they waited for the vet to come. The horse had a scrape on his shoulder. Pete got some clean cloths in the truck, and he wiped the scrape down with witch hazel before spreading some salve over it.

Ray took one of the cloths and gave it to Chrissie. "Clean yourself up," he told her.

Ray watched as she used the hose to wash the dirt from her face and arms. Her nose had stopped bleeding now, and he could see that her upper lip was cut. It looked as if she'd pushed a tooth through it.

"You're gonna need some stitches," he told her, but she ignored him.

The vet finally showed and examined the horse exactly the same way Pete had. The only difference was about seven years' education, Ray figured. Even at that, he doubted the man knew more than Pete Culpepper about the species at hand.

"Well, he's going to need an X ray," the vet said, still kneeling.

"I figured that," Pete said.

"If it's a break, it's not a bad one," the vet went on. "The bone is intact, but any kind of fracture is bad, you know what I mean. This is not a young horse. I don't know how far you want to go with him."

Pete nodded. "I'll take him up home. See to him there."

The vet shrugged and left them to their own decisions. They loaded the gelding into the trailer, mindful of the bad leg. When they closed the tailgate, Chrissie was gone.

"Didn't even say good-bye," Ray said.

They loaded the tack and the feed into the truck. Pete left a check for the vet at the office. Getting into the truck to leave, they saw Chrissie walking between the barns, dressed in her street clothes. They waited by the truck.

"I'm going with you," she said.

"Why would you do that?" Pete asked.

"It's my fault," she said. "I wasn't so hungover, it never woulda happened."

"I figured you punched out Juan Romano because it was his fault," Ray said.

"Oh, he bumped me all right, the motherfucker," Chrissie said. "But if I'd have been sober, I'd've seen it coming."

When they got back to the farm, they installed the horse in the barn, and then Pete went in to call Ben Houston. Ray and Chrissie stayed with the horse, Chrissie in the stall, cleaning the dirt from his tail and mane. She continued to fuss over the animal as she'd never fussed over a human, Ray suspected.

"Either way, he won't run again," Ray said.

"I don't care about that. Long as they don't have to put him down."

"You still need stitches," he told her.

"What am I—some fucking fashion model?"

She moved around the horse, the curry comb in her hand, and as she brushed him out she maintained a steady conversation with the animal, her voice low and soothing.

"You must've had a rough night last night," Ray said.

"That's it, that's it," she was saying to the horse. Then: "Last night was nothing. I'll tell you my life story sometime."

"You will?"

"No, I won't," she said. "Take it easy now," she said to the horse.

Ben Houston arrived and X-rayed the gelding's leg right in the stall. Ray wouldn't have thought it possible. Ben developed the pictures in the cube van he'd arrived in and then brought them into the barn. He was wearing what appeared to be his fly-fishing outfit. He'd just come back from the Grand River when he got Pete's call, and he looked like he'd stepped out of an ad for *Field and Stream.*

"You're not hoping to run him again?" he said to Pete when he came back with the X rays.

"No, I'd just like to save the animal," Pete said.

"Well, he's got a hairline fracture in his tibia," Ben said.

Ray looked into the stall to see Chrissie watching the vet, her eyes narrow and judgmental, as if she was only prepared to accept Ben's prognosis if it was good.

"What's the horse's disposition?" Ben asked then.

"He's pretty quiet," Pete said.

"I thought so," Ben said. "Well, we can try him with a walking cast. Keep him in the stall for three or four weeks. He's gotta stay quiet. He'll keep the weight off it himself so long as it's hurting him, and that's good. You just don't want him in a situation where he might spook and throw his weight on it. Outside in the corral, or something like that."

Chrissie was watching Pete, and it seemed she was holding her breath. Then Pete nodded his head and said, "Let's do it."

It was ten o'clock when Ben Houston finished. He'd given the gelding a shot of painkiller to keep him settled while he applied the cast, and the horse was practically asleep when he left. Chrissie was in the stall yet. Ray watched as she knelt and gave the finished cast on the horse's leg a critical once-over.

"I could use a drink," Pete said.

They convinced Chrissie that the gelding would be all right on his own, and went into the house. Pete opened a bottle of rum, Morgan's dark. They drank it with Coke and ice.

"You, know," Pete said, sipping at his drink. "I had a three-year-old colt at Greenwood, back when they still ran the flats there. Broke his front leg in the backstretch and still won the race by seven lengths."

Ray looked doubtfully at the old man and then over at Chrissie, who was watching Pete over the brim of her glass.

"Now, you sure his leg was broken?" Ray asked.

"Well, it was a bad sprain anyway," Pete said, and he took off his hat and tossed it in the corner.

After the first drink Chrissie had a good look at herself; she was still wearing the stale clothes from the night before, and there was dirt from the track in her hair and in her ears and pretty much everywhere else dirt could find a place to stick. She asked Pete if she could use the bathtub, adding, "I don't have any clean clothes."

"You ain't much smaller than me," Pete said. "I expect I got something you can wear."

She was in the tub a long time. Pete had another rum and then said he thought he'd turn in. He looked tired, Ray thought. He'd looked tired a lot lately, but then he'd had kind of a rough day.

The woman in the tub was singing to herself, songs Ray couldn't recognize, hip-hop or dance, some crap like that. Her voice was terrible; Ray was surprised the hound wasn't howling in protest. He poured himself another drink and decided to go check on the horse.

The night was starless and the moon not yet up. Ray didn't bother to turn the porch light on, crossed the barnyard in the pitch blackness, the rum running easily through his veins and through his head.

The gelding was sleeping, leaning three-legged against the side of the stall. Ray set his glass of rum on the top rail and watched the horse's shallow breathing. The animal had had a hard day, but he'd come through it. The gelding had character and a heart as big as a washtub. He was never destined to be anything more than a ten-thousand-dollar claimer, but that didn't change the fact that he had heart. It was something you couldn't take from him.

Ray heard the clang of a tin bucket being kicked and Chrissie cursing loudly. She came into the barn a moment later, hopping on one foot, rubbing her shin with her hand.

"Can you make a little more noise?" Ray asked. "You got a horn you want to blow?"

"Ever hear of turning on a fucking light?"

She was wearing blue jeans and a plaid shirt, each a couple of sizes too big for her. She sat down on a bale of straw inside the door and lifted the pant leg of Pete Culpepper's Wranglers and had a look at her leg. There wasn't a mark that Ray could see. But it was an attractive leg, he was moved to admit.

She tugged the pant leg into place and walked over to have a look at the gelding, took Ray's drink without asking, and had a long pull on it. Her hair was still damp from the bath, and she smelled of Ivory soap. Her lip was swollen from the cut there, but up close Ray could see that it wasn't as bad as he'd thought. She took another drink and then handed the glass over to him.

"He nodded right off," she said of the horse.

"Yeah," Ray said. "The drugs help. He might sleep through the night, providing we go easy on the bucket kicking and such."

She turned to him, leaned against the stall gate. "You don't like me very much, do you?"

"That's not true," he told her. "I like you just fine."

"You don't act like it."

"Well, sometimes I don't know how to act. Or so I've been told."

He took a drink and then handed the glass over to her. It was nearly empty, and she finished it off.

"I figured you were pissed at me today when I showed up the way I did," she said.

Ray shrugged, nodded toward the house. "I was afraid you were gonna let him down."

"Yeah? And what's he to you?"

"He's my friend."

She set the empty glass on the rail and gingerly touched her forefinger to her lip. Her eyes were soft brown, and they never seemed to be still. Even when she was looking at him, they seemed to be moving constantly, from his eyes to his mouth, his chin to his forehead.

"He's your friend," she said. "And is that something important to you?"

"These days, it's about the only thing that is."

She nodded slowly. "I've never had that many friends."

"I don't know that quantity is the main objective."

"I guess not."

She walked over to the corner, where Pete kept his western saddle and other tack. The saddle was a deep brown, of tooled leather and raised stitching, and the cantle and horn were pronounced after the Mexican style. She ran her hand over the leather and then pulled down a couple of blankets from a shelf above the saddle and walked back with them.

"I'm gonna sleep out here," she told him.

"There's plenty room in the house," Ray said.

"I'd like to stay with the horse if it's all right. If he wakes up in pain and gets to stomping around, I can settle him maybe. I've slept in plenty of barns. I had a Shetland pony when I was a kid, and my dad used to let me sleep in the stall."

Ray looked at her in the hand-me-downs and smiled. "I figured you'd be going out on the town in those duds."

She folded the blankets over the top of the stall wall and turned back to him. "It's not about the clothes. Figured a guy like you would know that."

Suddenly she stepped close, in her boots almost as tall as him, and she put her hand behind his neck and breathed of him a moment, a curious thing. When he kissed her, he could taste the rum and smell the soap. He kissed her carefully, mindful of the cut on her lip. She turned her head for a better vantage point, slipped her tongue quickly in and then out of his mouth. He put his arms around her and pulled her to him. She was sinewy and strong, and her heart was beating quickly. After several moments she stepped back from him and reached for the blankets.

"I hope you know you're not getting any head," she told him bluntly. "I got an awful lip on me after that horse rolled me over."

"You had an awful lip on you before that horse rolled you over," he said.

But he followed her into the stall.

12

Early Monday morning Jackson trailered Jumping Jack Flash from Woodbine, where he'd been working, to the home farm, where he would get him ready to ship to New York City. The horse had put on a few pounds since the Queen Anne Stakes, and Jackson wanted to monitor his diet. He suspected that the grooms and exercise riders at Woodbine had been spoiling the celebrated steed.

At the farm he put him in the front stall in the main barn. There were a couple of mares in season in the other barn, and Jackson was afraid that the stallion would hurt himself trying to get at them if he was left out in the paddock.

Sonny showed up midmorning, having been gone all night. Jackson wanted to talk to him about shipping the horse, but Sonny got out of his car and limped straight into the house. Jackson didn't see him again for the rest of the day.

Dean and Paulie arrived at noon. Jackson was in the tack room, heating soup on an electric grill. He looked at the pair when they walked in. Paulie wore jeans and a sweatshirt, work boots on his feet, that goofy hat. Dean was decked out in dark dress pants with a crease and a silky-looking shirt, black pointed-toe shoes. Jackson went back to stirring his soup.

"What's up, Jackson?" Dean asked.

"What do you mean?"

"Well, what you got for us today?"

Jackson took a handful of crackers and crumbled them

into his soup. "What the hell does it matter what I got for you? You never do anything you're asked anyway."

"What's that supposed to mean?" Dean asked.

"I told you to drop that gray at Fort Erie and then get your asses back here. You show up a day and a half later."

"It wasn't our fault," Dean said.

"No?"

"It wasn't our fault they built that big casino in the Falls." Dean laughed. "We couldn't get by it, Jack."

"That's real funny, Dean," Jackson said, and he sat down with his lunch. "You're gonna laugh yourself right out of a job."

"We're sorry, Jackson," Paulie said. "We screwed up."

"I believe you're sorry, Paulie," Jackson said. "And I doubt it was you that screwed up. It's just that I'm to the point where I can't depend on you anymore."

He blew on a spoonful of soup, tried it carefully on his tongue. Dean gave Paulie a look, rolling his eyes like a smart-ass kid in the principal's office. Paulie, hands stuffed in his pockets, turned and looked out into the barn, saw the stallion there.

"When did you bring the Flash home?" he asked.

"This morning," Jackson said around the soup.

"I guess we'll be taking him to New York," Dean said.

"That's where the race is," Jackson said.

"We'll need some expense money for that trip," Dean said. "We're a little underpaid as it is, Jackson."

"If you spent half as much time proving your worth as you did complaining about your worth, you might be worth something," Jackson said. "Maybe," he added. And then: "Paulie, I want you to run that Massey tractor over to Bertle's in Middletown. The hydraulics are acting up again; they might have to replace the pump."

"Okay," Paulie said.

"Dean, you can pick him up. Then I want you to head over

to the other place and start gutting the old barn. I want everything out of there. I'm gonna pour new concrete for the floor, and then we're gonna build some stalls along the south side. I want it ready for the new year, when those mares start to foal."

In the doorway Dean stiffened up. He was already chafing under the comments regarding his worth, and the prospect of spending the afternoon tearing rotten boards out of a barn didn't improve his disposition any.

"I'm not exactly dressed for construction," he told Jackson.

"It ain't *con*struction; it's *de*struction," Jackson said. "Maybe you should start dressing like a man who works for a living. Half the time you look like a damn pimp."

"We can't all dress like we're one of the Village People," Dean said. "I don't feel like tearing apart barns or being your gofer, Jackson. What reason do I have to stay with Stanton Stables if that's all I'm ever gonna do?"

"This isn't exactly the time to start talking about your future with the company," Jackson said. "Nothing's gonna change so long as the old man's laid up. If I was you, I'd try to make myself useful in the meantime. You think you've been pulling your weight, Dean?"

"You gonna tell me Sonny's been pulling his weight?" Dean demanded.

"What's Sonny got to do with it?" Jackson asked. "You seem to have it in your head that you're somehow on an equal footing with Sonny around here. Well, you're not. Sonny's about as useless as tits on a boar hog, but he's the old man's son, and that's something you're never gonna be. Now you're gonna have to learn to accept that or hit the road, Dean. The fact of the matter is, we don't have enough money right now to pay you to fuck the dog."

"But Sonny can piss it away at the casino."

"What did I just say?" Jackson asked. "Sonny has got nothing to do with you."

Jackson finished his soup and pushed the bowl away, wiped

his mouth with a piece of paper towel. He looked at the tabletop a moment.

"Paulie, head over to Bertle's with that tractor. It'll take you longer than Dean to get there."

Jackson waited until Paulie had gone. "I know what Sonny's up to," he said. "I know he spends time at the casino."

"I'm talking about the back room, Jack," Dean said. "Big Billy Coon and the boys are tapping Sonny like he's the mother lode. They got fucking totes back there, you know that? Futures, too. All under the table. You can bet any race in North America. Not to mention the poker."

Jackson got to his feet and walked out of the office. He went to the open door of the barn and looked toward the house. Dean hung back and watched. After a minute they heard the tractor roar to life and then saw Paulie head down the driveway in the big diesel.

"You sure about Sonny and that bunch?" Jackson asked Dean.

"Yeah."

"Shit."

Dean picked Paulie up at the Massey dealership, and then they headed out to the other farm, stopping first at the Colonel's for a bucket of crispy chicken and the beer store for a twelve-pack.

The farm was one concession south of the home farm. There was a large frame farmhouse, with a full porch across the front and down one side. The house had green shutters and roof, and it was where Jackson had lived since Earl Stanton hired him twenty-three years earlier.

There were two barns. The one was only a couple of years old, and it housed the yearlings and two-year-olds until they were ready to be broke. The second barn, the original, was older, and it was built completely of wood. It had been sitting vacant for some time.

Paulie went straight to work when they arrived. Using a

crowbar and sledgehammer, he broke up the stalls and carried the pieces out back, where he stacked them on the old manure pile. The wood was full of dry rot, and the work was dirty, and the air was soon filled with dust. Paulie wished he'd thought to bring along a dust mask. After a few minutes he removed his T-shirt and tied it over his mouth and nose.

Dean ate most of the chicken and drank half the beer. Then he had a nap.

Paulie worked away all afternoon. As usual, he didn't mind that Dean was loafing. He'd rather work alone in silence. As he cleared the old barn out, he returned to his dream, pretending that the barn was his, and that he was fixing it up for himself. He'd have a rabbit hutch in the corner and maybe a chicken coop for laying hens. A couple of stalls for horses and a stanchion for a Jersey milk cow. Paulie'd never milked a cow, but he figured he could learn. And he'd have a goat; he liked goats because of their eyes, their rectangular pupils. There'd be fresh hay in the mow and grain for the horses and a good dog for a pal. A yellow tomcat to keep the rats and mice out of the feed.

It would be nice to have a place of his own.

Late in the afternoon, Dean woke up and helped Paulie carry the last of the debris outside. Then they swept the place clean and dumped the sweepings on the pile in the barnyard. When they were finished they leaned the tools against the wall just inside the door and then opened a couple of beers. Dean surveyed the scene.

"Well, I'd like to see that sonofabitch Jackson say we didn't earn our money today," he said. "Right, Paulie?"

Paulie looked over and tried to decide just where among his imaginary horses and rabbits and chickens and dogs he might find a place for someone like Dean. He was still contemplating the question when they finished the beer and headed for home.

· · ·

Jackson went into town after lunch. He had a dentist's appointment at two o'clock, and what was scheduled as a routine checkup became a painful root canal. Leaving the clinic, his cheek puffed with cotton like a squirrel hoarding acorns, he walked over to the bank and checked out the company accounts. Taking the statements back to the farm, he passed the rest of the afternoon paying bills and attempting to make sense of the paperwork.

It was dark when he finally left the barn. The lights were on in the house now, and he walked over, entered through the kitchen door. The freezing was gone from his jaw, and the tooth hurt worse than before.

Sonny was in the dining room, eating a thick steak and french fries. He was wearing sweatpants and a polo shirt. Jackson pulled out a chair and sat down across from him.

"Hey, Jackson," Sonny said, his mouth full. "You bring our horse home?"

"What's going on with you and Billy Coon?"

"What?"

"Answer the question."

"I asked you if you brought the stud home," Sonny said sharply.

"Why don't you look in the barn?" Jackson asked. "It's the big red building across the way. Now answer the question."

"What the fuck's it to you? You got a problem with Billy Coon?"

"I don't know Billy Coon. It's you I got a problem with. I got the statements from the bank. Looks like you've been writing some sizable checks on the business account. Some of them are down payments for the farms you've been buying. But not all of them."

"Poker debts, Jack. Sometimes you win; sometimes you lose."

"Well, if that's the case, I guess you must be due to win, Sonny. Looks like you're down about seventy grand the past two months. How'd you plan on explaining that to the old man?"

"That's not for you to worry about, Jack."

Jackson shrugged his indifference. "You're right. But I'm telling you right now, stay out of that account, Sonny. We've got enough cash problems with the old man out of commission. We don't need to be pissing money up against the wall just because you don't have enough fucking brains to fold a pair of eights."

Sonny pushed his meal away from him, tried a look on Jackson that he liked to think was threatening. "Don't tell me what to do, Jack," he warned. And then: "Jesus Christ! What the fuck's got into you today?"

Jackson got up from the table and headed for the door. "What's got into me?" he asked, turning back. "I got a spoiled rich kid spending money like a drunken sailor. I got Dean, who won't do a lick of work but figures he should be on the board of directors. I got an overweight horse who acts like a goddamn movie star and who's about to run in the biggest race on the planet, and I got a molar that feels like somebody's poking it with a hot stick. Now I'm going home, Sonny, and if I don't have a better day tomorrow, I swear I might decide to geld *you*, just out of pure fucking meanness."

Sonny, for his part, couldn't say he was sorry to see Jackson go. His appetite was gone now; he poured himself a glass of vodka, dropped in a couple of ice cubes. He sat at the table and considered firing him. There were a couple of problems with that, though. One, he didn't know if he had the authority. And two, if he fired Jackson, who was going to do the work around here?

There would come a time when he could give Jackson his walking papers. Once he bought the Parr farm, he'd have the whole piece sewn up and he could get on with the development, including the new track. When that happened he'd sell off the whole racing operation, every damn horse. He couldn't exactly be running horses on his own track anyway; it wouldn't look right and might even be illegal.

Of course, the old man wouldn't go for selling off the breeding stock, but Sonny was counting on him doing the right thing and dying by then anyway. Sonny could then pay off Gena, that scheming cunt, sell off Stanton Stables in its entirety, and fire Jackson's black ass in the process. He could see it all happening simultaneously, like the scene at the end of *The Godfather* when Al Pacino settles everybody's hash at once. Sonny could imagine it, with the music playing in the background, and him sitting here in the big house, above it all.

It was going to take some time, though. The main thing right now was getting enough cash together to carry on until the situation with the old man righted itself. He had the race in Fort Erie on the weekend, then the Stanton Stakes at Woodbine, where they were running the Irish horse Rather Rambunctious, and where the purse was a quarter million. And then the big one at Belmont. If they won all three, there'd be plenty of cash to see him through until the other matter was resolved. And they had the horses to win all three.

He drank off the vodka and decided to drive into town. He showered and shaved and put on clean jeans and a shirt. He twisted his knee pulling on his cowboy boots, and the pain shot up his leg, forcing him to lie on the bed for a few minutes until it passed. When he got up he took two Demerol. He was going to have to let them operate on the knee again.

That was another score he was going to have to settle.

It was a cool night, and there was a slight drizzle falling as he drove. He considered calling Susie but then dismissed the idea. He was behind two months on the alimony, for one thing, and he'd also heard that Susie had a new boyfriend who was some sort of martial arts freak. The guy was supposedly upset with some bullshit Susie'd told him about Sonny smacking her around when they were married. She was like a broken record with that stuff. She never got around to mentioning that she was living in a $500,000 house, compliments of Sonny. Not bad for an ex-Argo cheerleader with a high school education.

Thinking about Susie just pissed him off. He'd only married her because he suspected she was going out with the Argo running back, a hotshot from Arkansas who'd been the runner-up for the Heisman Trophy and who'd come to Toronto to play when his agent couldn't wring enough bonus money out of the Rams. Of course, it turned out that Susie wasn't dating the guy; Sonny'd got married for no reason at all. Just his luck. The hotshot played one year in Toronto and then headed for New York, where he played half a season for the Jets, broke his leg in three places, retired, and was now the host of some lame reality TV show. Sonny got a nine-month marriage and an eternity of alimony payments.

Thinking about Susie got Sonny to thinking about strippers—to Sonny, cheerleaders were just strippers with no nerve—and he drove over to the Slamdance to see if any of the boys from the golf course were there.

Inside, he sat at the end of the bar and ordered a Heineken from the bartender. The place was mostly full, but in the darkness Sonny couldn't spot anybody from the links. He drank his beer and watched the action on the stage, where a dark-haired women in flimsy Egyptian attire was charming what appeared to be a mechanical snake. The snake's prospects were predictably good, and the boys around the stage were loving this little slice of high culture.

Sonny sipped at his beer, and when his eyes adjusted to the dark he noticed Dean and Paulie, sitting against the wall with a blond woman in a tight white dress. Sonny bought another beer and headed over, the two bottles in one hand and his cane in the other.

Paulie was watching the snake charmer on the stage, wondering if the snake was real and if it was, how it could breathe.

Dean was leaning in to the blonde, who was a pretty impressive piece in a synthetic *Baywatch* sort of way, Sonny thought.

When Dean saw Sonny his eyes went flat as creek water, but Sonny just smiled and pulled up a chair to sit down. He hooked his cane over the chair's arm.

"Hey, boys," he said.

"Hi, Sonny," Paulie said. "I didn't know you were here."

"Imagine that," Sonny said. "You're usually right on top of things, Paulie. You gonna introduce me to your friend, Dean?"

The blonde looked at Sonny with disinterest.

"This is Misty," Dean said unhappily.

Misty showed a slight disdainful smile, then looked away. Sonny leaned over and extended his hand.

"Sonny Stanton," he said.

Misty ignored the hand. "Yeah, I been hearing about you."

Sonny, undeterred, shifted to his good-old-boy persona. "I knew the boys were spending a lot of time here, but until this moment I didn't know the reason why. They may not be the sharpest lads around, but they've got good taste in women. I'll give 'em that."

Misty looked at Dean. "You're right; he's a load."

Sonny turned and made a big production of signaling the waitress, even though she wasn't looking their way. Dean sat back in his chair and crossed his arms. The snake lady was finished now, and Paulie turned back to the table and placed his beer in front of him.

"What's with the cane?" Misty asked Sonny.

"Oh, I used to rodeo," Sonny told her without hesitation. "Got into a tussle one night with a fifteen-hundred-pound Brahma bull. I was a little out of my weight class."

"Where was that, Sonny?" Dean asked.

"Calgary," Sonny said at once. "During the Stampede. Three years ago."

Misty laughed. "Does anybody believe this shit?"

"I thought you hurt your leg at the golf course," Paulie said.

"Yeah, you *thought*," Sonny said. "Now that's where you get into trouble, Paulie. Thinking. You weren't put on this earth to think. You just wear your funny hat and watch the lady on the stage with the fake snake, and you'll be okay."

Dean saw Paulie's face flush. Paulie glanced over to Misty, but she was still watching Sonny, her eyes cold.

"Tell me something," she said to Sonny as she stood up. "Did you become an asshole because you're rich, or did you become rich because you're an asshole?"

"Works both ways, baby," Sonny said.

"I gotta go dance," she said.

Sonny was smiling yet, watching her walk, then he turned and got the waitress's attention, circled his hand to indicate a round.

"So what did you guys do to Jackson today?" he asked. "Shit in his cornflakes?"

"We didn't do nothing," Dean said. "We were out at the other place all day, working on the old barn."

"You didn't see Jackson?"

"Yeah, we saw him," Paulie said. His face was still red.

"He said you were about as useless as tits on a boar hog, Sonny," Dean added.

"That so? And what'd you say?"

"Well, you know Jackson," Dean said. "When he's right, he's right."

The waitress brought the beers. Sonny, with the woman gone and nobody to impress, paid for his and left the other two to pay for their own. A moment later Misty came onstage and began to dance.

"So what you guys got going with Miss Implants here?" Sonny asked. "You dicking her or what?"

"None of your fucking business," Dean said.

Sonny smiled. "Maybe I'll expand my business to include her. She looks to me like she could suck the stripe off a skunk."

"Maybe she's a nice person, Sonny," Paulie said.

Sonny took a long drink of beer and then adjusted his chair to get a better look at the stage. Misty, removing her top, was looking straight at him, contempt in her eyes. Sonny rubbed the neck of the beer bottle across his chin and leered.

"That your poker face, Sonny?" Dean asked. "No wonder you're such a lousy card player."

"You fucking guys are pathetic," Sonny said. "I have no idea why I even keep you around."

13

Chrissie received a seven-day suspension for the roundhouse right she'd landed on Juan Romano's mug. It probably would have been longer, but there'd been an inquiry on the race and the track officials had ruled that Romano had fouled Chrissie's mount and he was disqualified from the win. That didn't help Pete Culpepper's wallet any; Fast Market never actually finished the race and therefore didn't qualify for any purse money.

Chrissie hung around the farm for the week and helped Pete out when she could, kept an eye on the horse the rest of the time. Not that the gelding needed much tending to; he took to the cast pretty well, kept the weight off the leg as Ben Houston had suggested he would. It looked as if the leg would knit.

"So what are you gonna do with him?" Chrissie asked one day after she and Pete had turned the two mares out into the corral and had just finished shoveling out the stalls. The pile of warm horse manure in the barnyard sat steaming in the cold morning air.

Pete hung his shovel on a wooden peg that jutted out from the main support beam in the barn, and he bit the end from a plug of Redman as he looked at the gelding in his stall.

"I don't rightly know," he said. "He ain't as high-strung as most thoroughbreds; I guess he might make a good pleasure horse for somebody. Providing that leg heals proper."

"He won't fetch much of a price as a trail horse," Chrissie said. She was still in the stall, leaning on the shovel, her chin on her hand.

"I expect not. A thousand, fifteen hundred maybe. A week ago I might've got eight or ten thousand for him. But that's the racing game."

"Well . . . that's my fault," Chrissie said.

"I want you to stop that talk," Pete told her. "You got fouled. Hell, even the commission backs that up. Otherwise, you'd have got a month for slugging Romano."

"I'm still not done with him."

"Oh yes you are. You can't carry grudges in this game. It'll just end up backfiring on you. You made your point, and now you just gotta let it go."

"Maybe."

"No maybe about it. And I'm not just talking on the racing business here. It's the same in life. You carry grudges around with you, and they'll just eat you up. Half the time the person you're grudgin' against don't even know it. You better learn to let things go."

Chrissie cleaned a bit of manure off her boot with her shovel, then scooped it up and tossed it outside. When she came out of the stall she pulled her gloves off and stuffed them in her hip pocket.

"What are you, Mr. Culpepper—some cowboy philosopher today?"

"I ain't no philosopher. I'm just somebody who's been around about three times as many years as you. I'd be pretty goddamn dumb if I hadn't learned something in all that time."

"Well, if you're so much smarter than me, then tell me what you're gonna do now. Can we get one of those mares ready to run?"

"One of those mares is in foal."

"I can see that. What about the other?"

"Those mares are all done running. I was hoping to get that bay bred in the new year. She throws a nice foal. But I don't know what I'm gonna be able to afford when it comes to a stud."

"So you're done racing for the year?"

"I expect I am. Unless a runner falls out of the sky."

They walked up to the house and had some lunch. Pete made an omelette with ham and onions and green peppers. When it had became apparent that Chrissie intended to stick around awhile, Pete's first thought had been that she would come in handy at mealtimes. As it turned out, the woman could barely open a can of beans. She could do anything Pete could in the barn and in the fields, but putting her in the kitchen was like cinching a saddle on a milk cow.

"Didn't your mother ever teach you how to cook?" Pete had asked.

"My mother left when I was still wearing diapers."

"What about your dad?"

"My old man couldn't boil water if he had the recipe right in front of him."

As they were eating their eggs, they heard a roar out in the yard. Pete got up and went to the window in time to see Bob Miller's big corn harvester humping past the barn and heading down the lane.

"They've come to take my corn off," Pete said when he came back to the table.

After lunch they climbed into the pickup and drove back to the east field in front of the bush, where the combine was working. One of Bob's sons—they were twins, and Pete could never tell the one from the other—showed up, driving the five-ton grain truck. When Bob stopped to unload the combine's hopper for the first time, Pete walked over.

"How's it look?" Pete asked, meaning the yield.

Bob shrugged. "With the drought and all, probably about what you expected."

"I guess," Pete said.

"The price might scare you."

"Oh?"

"It's down under three bucks. It'll probably go up after January, if you wanted to sit on it."

"I got no place to store it. If I wait, whatever I gain on the price, I'll lose on the storage."

"Yup."

Bob put the machine in gear and went back to work. When the truck's hopper was full, Bob's son drove it away. Five minutes later, his twin brother showed up with a second truck. Seeing him climb down from the cab, Chrissie did a double take. Pete laughed and told her they were twins, and then they watched as the harvester pulled up and dumped its load into the truck.

"I ever tell you about the old farmer had two horses he couldn't tell apart?" Pete asked as the combine circled to go back to work.

"No, you didn't," Chrissie said.

"This old farmer had two horses he couldn't tell apart," Pete began. "Workhorses. So one day he decided to clip the top of the one's ear off. So he did, and that was fine; he could tell 'em apart. But then the other horse got his ear caught in a threshing machine and clipped it just identical to the first horse. So the farmer decided to bob the first horse's tail, and that solved his problem. But then the second horse backed into a hay mower and cut his tail off the exact same as the first. So he's back to the same old problem. Right?"

"Right."

"So you know what finally happened?"

"The white horse died."

Pete fell sullen. "You heard it before."

"I heard it before. It's an old joke, Mr. Culpepper."

Pete nodded and held his pout for a moment, and then he smiled. "It's a good one though, isn't it?"

"It is, you know."

They watched the harvester for a while, and then they went back to the house. Pete allowed that he was feeling tired. While he went in the house for a nap, Chrissie saddled the bay mare and took her for a few laps around the hay field out front. The mare was eager enough, but she was out of shape and a few years past anything that might resemble racing condition. Chrissie gave her an easy work, then took her into the barn for a brushing. She'd been rolling in the barnyard and had about ten pounds of dirt on her hide. When Chrissie had her cleaned up, she turned her back outside.

She and Pete were sitting on the front porch, having a whiskey and soda, when the Millers finally finished the combining. The boy drove the grain truck out of the lane and down the side road to the highway without stopping. Bob came along a few minutes later. He turned the combine off in front of the house and walked over to the porch. When Pete asked if he wanted a rye, he said yes.

"You caught up then?" Pete asked when he came out with the drink.

"Hell, no," Bob said. "Doing all this custom work, and I haven't touched my own yet. Need another week or ten days of dry weather." He took a drink and then looked at Chrissie. "So who's this—your daughter, Pete?"

"Sorry—I forgot my manners," Pete said. "This here's Chrissie."

"I'm not his daughter," Chrissie answered.

"Oh."

Bob's tone, and the whiskey, were just enough to set her off.

"I'm not that, either," Chrissie said. "Get your mind out of the fucking gutter."

Pete Culpepper was smiling. "She's just a friend, Bob. She's a jockey at the Fort. She's got a little rough on her."

"To hell with you both," Chrissie said, and she got to her feet. "I'm gonna go see to my gelding."

"*Your* gelding?" Pete said as she walked away.

Bob sipped at the whiskey and propped his feet up on the railing. "Ain't she a corker," he said.

"You oughta see her when she gets her back up."

The sun was dropping beneath the horizon and the

temperature dipping fast with its disappearance. The cars on the highway, a half mile away, had their lights on already.

"So what do you want me to do with your corn?" Bob asked.

"Sell it," Pete told him.

Bob nodded. "How's the horse business?"

"Well, I only had the one runner left, and he broke his leg."

"That's not good."

"No. I'm about to the point where I gotta make some sort of decision. It's always been a rich man's game and now more so than ever. I might be about at the end of my run here. Thinkin' I should head back south."

"What would you do with the place?"

"I couldn't say for sure. I got Ray Dokes staying with me. I don't know, but maybe he'd be interested in buying me out."

"Ray Dokes is out of jail?"

"Well, he wouldn't be staying with me if he wasn't."

"Aren't you nervous having him around? Do you trust him?"

"Like the sun comin' up."

"I don't think I would. Not after what he pulled on Sonny Stanton."

Pete took a long drink of rye. "Sonny Stanton should thank Ray."

"Why's that?"

"Because if it was me, I'd have killed the sonofabitch."

When Bob finished his whiskey he declined the offer of another and set out on the combine. He had thirty acres on the town line he wanted to get off before he quit for the day.

Ray came up the driveway in the Caddy as Pete was picking up the glasses to go inside. Ray parked behind Pete's pickup and came up the steps.

"Having a party?" he asked.

"Bob Miller was here, took off the corn," Pete said by way of explanation.

Ray followed him inside, put his lunch pail on the table.

He sat on the bench inside the back door and pulled off his work boots. Pete put the rye away and then went about making a pot of coffee.

"Where's Chrissie?" Ray asked, and before he was done asking it she walked through the door.

"Hey," she said to him.

"Hey, yourself," Ray said. "How's the gelding today?"

"He's doing real good. I think he's kinda full of himself, like he's the center of attention with his fancy cast and all. Those old broodmares will be wanting one next."

She sat down at the table and propped the heel of her right boot on her left knee. She reached for Ray's cigarettes and helped herself to one.

"So, what's for supper?" she asked.

"That all you think about—eating?" Pete asked. "You're gonna have trouble making the weight when you go back."

"I never put on a pound," she told him. "Got something to do with my metabolism, or so I been told. Anyway, what's for supper?"

"Well, I thawed some hamburger; I thought I might make a meatloaf, unless you were thinking of whipping something up," Pete said.

"You'll end up in the hospital, the both of you, if I whip something up," Chrissie said. "Meatloaf sounds good to me."

Pete carried his coffee to the counter, where he began to fix the meal. Chrissie got a cup from the cupboard and poured herself some coffee.

"How'd the corn look?" Ray asked.

"Well, they won't be writing me up in the *Farmer's Monthly*," Pete said. "The price isn't gonna be much, either, from what Bob says. I guess I'll be a couple of dollars ahead of not planting it at all."

Ray nodded. He didn't need any more elaborate explanation than that. Chrissie watched the two in silence. When she caught Ray's eye he looked away. She splashed a little milk in her coffee and sipped at it. Ray looked at her again, and she watched him over the rim, saying nothing.

After they ate, Ray had a shower and a shave and then came out wearing clean clothes and smelling like Pete Culpepper's aftershave. Pete and Chrissie were playing checkers at the kitchen table, and Pete was up three games to none.

"Old bastard's cheating," Chrissie said.

"How can you cheat at checkers?" Pete asked.

"If I knew how you were doing it, I'd stop you."

Ray carried his lunch pail to the kitchen sink and took the thermos from inside and rinsed it clean under the tap. Then he lit a cigarette and leaned against the kitchen counter and watched the game. Pete won again, and Chrissie gave up.

"I was thinking I might drive into town for a drink," Ray said. "You two up to it?"

"Not me," Pete said. "I think I'll turn in early. I want to plow that corn ground tomorrow, before we get wet weather and I have to leave it 'til spring."

"I'll go," Chrissie said.

She lit a joint on the drive into town and offered it over to Ray, who declined. She took a couple of heavy pulls on it, then pinched it off with her forefinger and thumb and put it back in her shirt pocket. She was wearing her black jeans and one of Pete's cotton work shirts. She looked good in the old man's duds, but to Ray's eyes she'd never looked anything but good.

They went to the Tap. It had been a country-and-western joint when Ray had been a kid. He and his friends used to go there and get into fights with the local crowd. One Saturday night Ray and two of his friends had ridden their dirt bikes into the place, causing a general uproar and a lot of broken glasses and bruised knuckles.

Ray and Chrissie sat at a booth across the room from the bar. The waitress was short and covered with more tattoos than a fleet of sailors. They declined menus and ordered beer.

The band was playing Merle Haggard.

"I guess this isn't exactly your kind of music," Ray said as they waited for their beer.

"Hey, I know every word to 'Okie from Muskokee,'" Chrissie said. "My dad was a country freak; he played mandolin in a band called the Grand River Ramblers."

The waitress brought two mugs of draft, and Chrissie insisted on paying.

"So you gonna dance with me or not?" she asked.

"Or not."

"I figured that."

Ray took a drink of beer and then leaned back and had a glance around the room. There was nobody there that he recognized. Glancing toward the bar, he caught a glimpse of himself and Chrissie in the mirror. A perfectly normal couple, out having a beer.

"So what's the story on Pete—he's broke, isn't he?" Chrissie asked.

"I don't know that he's broke," Ray said. "He's had a stretch of bad luck, that's all. He'll be all right."

"I wish I could help him out. I like the old guy."

"He's a good man."

"So what can I do to help him?"

"There's nothing you can do to help him. He wouldn't let you if you could."

"You cowboys are all the same."

"Pete's the cowboy."

"Oh no. You are too; you just don't know it."

"Is that a good thing or a bad thing?"

"It's both," Chrissie decided after a moment. "Doesn't matter; you're stuck with it either way. What'd you think—you were just some normal guy?"

Which made Ray look in the mirror again. The couple was still there, but the image had somehow changed.

"I guess not," he admitted. "What about you?"

"Shit. I wouldn't know normal if it came up and bit me on the ass."

Homer started the new medication on Saturday, and by Tuesday afternoon he was feeling well enough to go to the golf course and play nine holes. Harvey Jones picked him up and told Etta he'd have him home by supper.

Etta had worked the night before, and she was happy to have the house to herself for a change. She did some vacuuming and washed the bedclothes and cleaned out the fridge. Then she changed and drove into town to the bank. She spent a discouraging half hour with the manager and then bought a take-out coffee and headed out of town. As she drove she began to consider Father Regan's advice to go back to teaching. She'd always suspected that at some point she would do just that, but that point had been rather indistinct, a dot on the horizon. She knew that she couldn't run the farm and teach at the same time.

She hadn't counted on Homer getting sick. He'd always been a bull of a man—not particularly ambitious or admirable or even responsible—but a strong physical presence. His weaknesses in other areas, however, had left him with an inordinate amount of debt, and now that debt had fallen into her lap like a lead weight.

Something else she hadn't counted on.

On the way home she stopped at Pete Culpepper's place. Driving down the lane, she saw Ray standing along the corral, his arms resting over the top rail. He turned when he heard the car tires on the gravel driveway. If he was surprised—or pleased, or anything else—to see her, he didn't show it.

She pulled up and got out and opened the trunk. There were two glass gallon jugs of apple cider inside. She lifted them out and carried them over to Ray and set them down.

"What's this?" he asked.

"Appreciation for roof repair," she said.

As she spoke a dark-haired woman came around the corner of the barn and into the corral, riding a bay mare at an easy lope. She came close to the fence where they stood and then at the last moment veered the animal off. The woman sat the western saddle like she was born to it. She took the mare around the corral once at a canter, then slowed to a walk. Etta watched her for a moment. She was a pretty girl. Etta raised her sunglasses briefly to give her the once-over, or rather to let Ray know she was giving her the once-over. She glanced at Ray before she let the shades drop back into place.

"Pete not around?" she asked.

"He went in to the bank," Ray said. "He'll want to make applejack out of that cider."

"You can do what you want with it."

Etta walked over and turned her back to the corral, leaned against the rail there. She made a pretense of looking out over the pasture field, but in truth she was looking at him. He was leaner than when she'd last seen him. He needed a haircut, and he had a couple days' growth on his cheeks, partly concealing the fresh scar on his chin—the scar he'd received in jail, how she had no idea, but she was sure that it involved him standing up for something or somebody, railing against some slight that another man might have had sense enough to let alone. His hands where they hung over the fence rail were calloused and marked with small cuts here and there.

"Still in the roofing business?" she asked.

"Yup," he said, looking at her. "How're you doing, Etta? I see you got the old tractor for sale."

"I haven't had any buyers yet." She gestured toward the corral. "So who's Annie Oakley?"

"Name's Chrissie Nugent. She's a jock at Fort Erie, rides for Pete when he's got a horse to run."

"What's she do the rest of the time?"

"Here she comes," Ray said. "Why don't you ask her?"

Etta turned to see Chrissie leading the bay by the reins to

where they stood. She was long-legged and loose in her jeans and her boots, and she was watching Etta openly as she approached. When she got to them she gave the reins a half hitch around the top rail and then stepped back to unfasten the cinch on the saddle. Ray introduced the two women, and Chrissie offered her hand over the fence rail.

"It's dirty," she said. "I hope you don't mind."

"I don't mind a little dirt," Etta said, shaking hands.

Chrissie pulled the saddle from the mare and set it and the blanket on the fence. Then she climbed through the rails, and, outside the corral now, she hoisted the saddle to her shoulder and carried it into the barn. When she passed Ray, Etta saw her run her hand across his back.

Ray shot a glance at Etta and then decided that it would be a good time to kneel down to have a better look at the cider.

"This is all right," he said. "Been a long while since I've had fresh cider."

"Right," she said. "Well, I better be going. Say hi to Pete for me.'

"He should be back any time," Ray said, straightening up. "Why don't you stick around, say hello yourself?"

"No, it looks like you're busy."

"I'm not doin' a damn thing. Why would you say that?"

"Well, you've got fat horses and pretty girls to tend to. Why aren't you working anyway?"

"We're between jobs; we start a new subdivision Monday. . . . I told you, she's a jock who rides for Pete."

"Only you could turn up a jockey who just happens to be a pretty girl, Ray."

He tried not to smile. "I'm just fortunate, I guess."

Chrissie came out of the barn then, carrying a nylon halter in her hand. Going back through the corral, she saw the cider on the ground. Her eyes lit up. "Where that come from?"

"Etta brought it," Ray said.

Chrissie slipped the bridle from the mare and looped it

over a fence post. Then she put the halter on and took the horse by the ring underneath. Ray opened the gate.

"So what are you—an apple farmer?" she asked as she led the mare out the gate and past Etta.

"Yeah, I'm an apple farmer," Etta said. "I have to go."

Chrissie smiled and led the mare into the barn. Ray followed Etta to her car. She got inside and tried to close the door, but he held it open.

"Everything okay, Etta?"

"Everything's fine," she told him.

"You seem a little stressed."

"Now what would you know about that, Ray?"

He shrugged. "Is everything okay at the farm?"

"Everything's fine at the farm."

"Okay."

"Okay." She started the engine, reached for the door again.

"Annie Oakley wasn't a horsewoman," he told her then.

"What?"

"She was a sharpshooter."

"Well, that's good to know, Ray. I'll be sure to make a note of that when I get home."

She made a U-turn and drove away, spinning her tires in the gravel. Ray was aware that Chrissie had come up behind him, in fact had probably heard the last exchange.

"That the one?" Chrissie asked after a moment.

"That the one what?" he asked.

"The one you're thinking about when you're fucking me?"

14

Before leaving for New York City, Jackson had to tend to his rose bushes. He'd be gone at least a week, maybe ten days, and there might be cold weather, snow even, before he got back.

The blooms were long gone, but the plants still required work. He'd already covered the beds with a mulch made from horse manure—he had a ready supply of that—and wood chips and a fertilizer mix. Now he pruned the bushes back and then wrapped them in burlap, securing the wrappings with binder twine. Then he used a square-mouth garden shovel to heap the mulch around the roots to protect them from the elements. He had to hurry the job, and it irked him; he hadn't intended to leave until later in the week, but his plans had changed, rather abruptly, the day before.

Sonny's car was parked half on the grass and half on the driveway. The driver's door had been hanging open when Jackson arrived, and he'd closed it before the interior light killed the battery. Sonny hadn't shown his face yet, but then it was only ten o'clock. When Jackson was done with his plants he leaned the shovel against the barn wall and then made a trip over to the other farm to pick up the double horse trailer.

Back at the home farm Dean and Paulie were standing in the yard, Dean drinking a take-out coffee and yawning, Paulie looking at the rose bushes in wonder.

"It's like they got little parkas on," he was saying when Jackson got out of the truck.

"Come on," Jackson said. "You can help me load the Flash."

With Paulie there to quiet him, the big stallion went into the trailer without incident. Then they loaded an older dapple gelding as well for a companion horse. Not that the stallion was much for companionship, but Jackson reasoned that the other horse might help to keep him quiet. He didn't want to tranquilize the animal, which was why they weren't flying him to New York City.

When Jackson went into his office for the paperwork that he would need for the border, Dean followed him.

"We got to talk about money," Dean said. "We're gonna need a credit card, Jackson."

"What're you gonna need a credit card for?" Jackson asked.

"Expenses, for fuck's sake. Motels, gasoline, food—little things like that, Jackson. How else we gonna get this horse to New York?"

"You don't need a credit card."

"Why not?"

"Because you're not going to New York," Jackson told him. "I am."

Paulie came in then. "I filled that twenty-gallon water tank," he said. "That gonna be enough?"

"That's good, Paulie," Jackson said. "Thanks."

"We're not going to New York," Dean said.

"We're not?" Paulie asked.

"I'm taking him down myself," Jackson said. "I want you guys over at the other farm; you can help put in those new stalls."

"This sucks, Jackson," Dean told him.

Jackson tucked the papers inside his jacket and walked around the desk. He stepped close to Dean, looked down at him. "Why does it suck, Dean?"

"We're supposed to trailer the horse to the Belmont," Dean said. "Why the change all of a sudden? We're good enough to drive these other nags all over Ontario, but we're not good enough to take this horse to New York?"

"Sonny and I decided last night that I would do it," Jackson said. "I'm the trainer."

"Fucking Sonny . . ."

Jackson shrugged and walked outside. Dean looked at Paulie, who was worrying a hangnail with his teeth. Paulie was not too upset with the news; in truth he hadn't been looking forward to a long drive with Dean. And big cities scared him. Hamilton scared him, and it was a small city.

"You got nothing to say?" Dean asked and then left without waiting to find out.

Jackson was putting his bag into the cab of the truck when Dean came up behind him.

"I'm not building fucking stalls for Sonny," Dean said.

"Suit yourself, Dean. I'm sure you got plenty of options. Maybe IBM's looking for a new CEO."

Jackson popped the hood of the Ford, checked the oil and coolant. Dean stood by, fuming. He was looking for an argument, and all Jackson wanted to do was talk shit.

"Why don't I go with you, Jackson?" Dean asked when Paulie came out of the barn. "You'll need a hand."

"I was gonna take anybody, I'd take Paulie. He pulls his weight. But I'm not taking anybody."

"Shit," Dean said. "Well, I'm not building fucking stalls for Sonny."

"I guess you will if I tell you to," he heard Sonny say.

They turned to see him coming across the yard, leaning on his cane. His eyes were puffy slits, and his hair was flying every which way.

"What're you doing up so early, Sonny? You shit the bed?" Dean asked.

"You're a funny guy, Dean," Sonny said. "So what's your problem today?"

"My problem is I thought I'd be taking this horse to New York," Dean said.

"You thought I was gonna let you take my ten-million-dollar racehorse on a road trip to New York City," Sonny said. "That's a hoot. You oughta be on the comedy circuit. How about you grab your retarded cousin over there and get to building stalls, like Jackson told you."

"I didn't hire on to build stalls," Dean said.

"No, you hired on to piss and moan," Sonny said.

"Would you two stop this crap?" Jackson suggested.

Paulie was standing by the trailer, looking at the ground. Dean hesitated, glanced at Jackson, then looked back at Sonny and smiled.

"Shoulda been at the Slamdance last night, Jackson," he said. "Sonny boy was telling my girl Misty how he fucked up his knee riding this mean old Brahma bull at the Calgary Stampede. What was the name of that bull, Sonny? Oh, that's right—that mean old bull was named Ray Dokes, wasn't it?"

Sonny was turning away, and now he spun back. "You're done, Dean. Write him a check, Jackson. One more fucking word, Dean, and you won't even get that. Write them both a check, Jackson, and then get him and that other fucking moron off the property."

Sonny stood his ground a moment longer, and Jackson thought he might reconsider.

"Do it now, Jackson," Sonny said, and he turned and got into his car and drove off.

Jackson looked at Dean in disgust. "You dumb sonofabitch," he said.

He went into the office and came back with the ledger that contained the checkbook. He opened the ledger on the hood of the truck.

"I'll talk to him about you, Paulie," he said. "But you brought this on yourself, Dean. You had to go out of your way to aggravate him." Jackson was angry now. "What the hell did you expect? You never did a lick of work around here anyway. You're always whining about wanting respect. Well, you gotta show it to get it."

As Jackson made to write the check, Dean walked over and picked up the garden shovel from the rose garden. When Jackson turned, Dean hit him above the ear with the shovel. Jackson hit the ground with a thud like a bag of grain makes when thrown from a wagon. Dean took a stance to deliver another blow, but the big man was motionless on the ground. His scalp was ripped open, and soon the blood was running in thin rivulets across the dirt on the ground.

"Jesus," Paulie said.

"Come on," Dean said, and he tossed the shovel aside. He opened the truck door.

"What are you doing?" Paulie asked.

"We've just been fired," Dean said. "That suits me just fine. But I'm taking this horse for severance."

"Jesus, Dean."

"What—you feeling loyal to Sonny all of a sudden? He holds you in such high regard."

Paulie walked over and kneeled in the dirt beside Jackson. He was relieved to see that the big man was breathing. "We can't leave him like this," he said. "He could be bad hurt."

Dean thought about it. "He'll be all right. But you're right, we can't leave him here. Get that gelding out of the trailer, Paulie."

With Paulie helping reluctantly, they put the dapple gelding back in the barn and then carried Jackson into the trailer. He was even heavier than he looked, and it was all they could do to lift him. Dean got a length of nylon rope from the tack room and bound Jackson's hands behind his back, tied the rope to the railing in the trailer. He found the stallion's papers in Jackson's coat pocket, and then he gagged Jackson with a rag. He and Paulie carried a dozen bales of hay into the trailer and stacked them around Jackson's prone form.

"He's bleeding pretty good still," Paulie said.

"Fuck him," Dean said. He walked over to the spot where

Jackson had gone down and with his shoe covered the blood with dirt. "Let's get going."

"Where?"

"I got a plan."

Dean and Paulie took the highway north, sticking to the speed limit. Dean was quiet as he drove, his hands fidgeting on the steering wheel, his eyes constantly looking at the mirrors. Paulie watched him; he'd seen Dean nervous before, but he'd never known him to be quiet.

"I'm worried about Jackson," Paulie said. They were in the village of Dundurn, idling at the lone traffic light.

"He's all right," Dean said. "Black guys got harder heads than other people. It's been proved. That's why all the good boxers are black these days. You can't hurt 'em."

"Why don't we drop him at a hospital?"

"No fucking way. The longer he's out, the better chance we got of getting away. Don't worry about Jackson being knocked out, Paulie. When he comes to—that's when you better start worryin'."

After traveling north for maybe half an hour, Dean suddenly pulled over and then turned the rig around.

"What're we doing?" Paulie asked.

"I changed my mind," Dean said. "I'm heading for the border."

"Then what?"

"Don't you worry about it."

"I thought you said you had a plan."

"I do. I've got a beauty, Paulie."

Paulie fell silent and leaned against the passenger door. He was troubled by the image of Jackson lying in the dirt, his head split open like a cantaloupe. He was troubled by the stolen horse in the trailer.

He was particularly troubled by the fact that Dean had a

plan. In the years he'd known Dean, there had been a lot of brilliant plans. Try as he might, Paulie couldn't remember a single one working out.

They hit Highway 3 outside of Simcoe and headed east, reaching the border by midafternoon. They gassed up in Fort Erie. Dean got the key from the attendant and went to use the restroom. As soon as he was gone Paulie went into the trailer. Jackson was still unconscious, but his eyelids were fluttering and he seemed about to come around. Paulie removed the gag from his mouth. He wanted to give Jackson a drink of water, but he couldn't figure how to do that when Jackson was still out. He decided to wait until they stopped for gas again.

They crossed the Niagara River at the Peace Bridge on the outskirts of Buffalo. As they approached American customs Dean had the horse's papers ready. "Let's hope they don't check the trailer too close," he said.

It was a slow day at customs. The border guard was eating a slice of pizza when they pulled up. He straightened in his chair and wiped his mouth when they stopped. "Citizenship?"

"Canadian," Dean said.

The guard jerked his head toward Paulie.

"Him, too," Dean said.

"Let him speak for himself," the guard said.

"Canadian," Paulie said. His voice was high, ready to break.

"What're you guys hauling?"

Dean handed the papers over. "We've got a thoroughbred we're taking to New York City. Belmont Race Track," he added.

The guard looked at the papers and then got up reluctantly and put his coat on. He came out of the booth and gestured for Dean to get out of the truck. He was short, with a big gut and an untrimmed mustache. He carried a large-caliber pistol on his belt, slung low like a cowboy in a movie, and he had a walk that supported the image.

He and Dean moved around behind the trailer. Paulie got out too, holding his breath and wishing he'd walked away at the gas station in Fort Erie, but knowing that he couldn't have, not while Jackson was in the trailer.

"Open it," the guard said.

Dean unlatched the trailer and swung the door open. The guard stepped forward to have a look. Jumping Jack Flash took exception to the invasion of his privacy and unleashed a kick that missed the guard's shaggy mustache by maybe a quarter inch. The fat guard hit the pavement and actually reached for his gun.

"You sonofabitch—" he said. He caught himself then, climbed quickly to his feet, and had a look around to see if anyone had seen him go down. Dean closed the gate at once.

"He's a little ornery," Dean said.

"I see that," the guard said, and he made a show of inspecting the horse's papers. "These look to be in order."

"Oh, he's had all his shots and whatever," Dean said, enjoying this now. "You wanna have another look?"

"No!" the guard said immediately. "You're holding the line up."

Dean looked; there was no line to hold up. The guard handed the papers over and went back to his booth, his dignity and the nation's security intact.

They left customs and took the ramp to the thruway. Paulie saw a sign that read: 90 East New York City. Dean took the next ramp and headed west.

By dark they were clear of Cleveland and heading south on 71 across Ohio. They skirted around Columbus and then took 62 south. At nine o'clock they stopped at a fish-and-chips joint in Hillsboro and got takeout, ate in the truck as they drove. In spite of his anxiety, or maybe because of it, Paulie fell asleep against the passenger door. He dreamed he was on a train, traveling through a precarious mountain pass.

When he woke up they were stopped on a gravel road beside a running stream that glinted in the moonlight. Dean was sitting silently behind the wheel, smoking a cigarette. Paulie watched the running water, which looked cold and clear in the faint light.

"Where are we?" he asked after a while.

"Kentucky."

"Kentucky," Paulie repeated, and he took another look out the window. He'd never been to Kentucky before. "What are we doing here?"

"Getting rid of Jackson, for one thing."

Jackson was conscious enough by now to describe in detail what Dean's future would hold. Dean stuck the rag back in his mouth, and then they dragged him out of the trailer and pushed him down the creek bank. He rolled along the grass and stopped a few feet from the running stream. He turned his head toward them, and in the moonlight Paulie could see his eyes, burning like they could set the truck afire.

They drove back out to the highway, and then they headed back north. Fired by cup after cup of take-out coffee, Dean drove all night. They reached Detroit as the sun was coming up. They crossed back into Canada—Dean showed the customs agent the horse's papers and told him that he'd raced the animal in Saginaw the day before—and headed back east.

They were at Jim Burnside's farm before noon. Jim was nowhere in sight. They put the stallion in the barn, gave him hay and water. Then they went into the house—the door was unlocked—and they both found old couches and lay down. Paulie was asleep at once. Dean was fatigued to the point that his vision was blurred, but he couldn't put his mind to rest.

In the past twenty-four hours he'd been fired from his job, stolen a champion racehorse, kidnaped the horse's trainer, driven all the way around Lake Erie, with detours across Ohio and into Kentucky, and ended up not all that far from where he'd started.

After a day like that, it was only natural for a man to toss and turn a little.

. . .

Chrissie's suspension was up on a Saturday. She procured four mounts over the phone for Sunday's card, and on Sunday morning she and Ray and Pete Culpepper headed for Fort Erie in Ray's Cadillac. It was clear and cold, and the day had arrived with a heavy frost on the grass, which didn't burn off until midmorning. Winter seemed close for the first time that fall.

"You gonna behave yourself today?" Pete asked on the drive down.

"Depends on everybody else," Chrissie said. "I just go with the flow."

"The hell you do," Pete said.

When they got to the track Chrissie went to find the trainer for her first mount. Pete and Ray were lounging near the barns when one of the grooms came over and told them that Jumping Jack Flash was missing.

"What do you mean—missing?" Pete asked.

"Jackson Jones left yesterday with him, heading for Belmont. He never showed up, and nobody's heard from him."

"Well, I'll be a sonofabitch," Pete said.

"They're thinking maybe foul play."

Chrissie won her first race but finished out of the money in the other three. Afterward she sat and had a beer with Pete and Ray in barn eleven.

"I got mounts the rest of the week, and I'll be working horses in the morning," she said. "Guess I'll go see if my apartment's still there. My pickup's still over the border; my girlfriend's gonna take me to get it."

She looked at Ray when she said this, and he drank his beer and looked back.

"All the jocks are talking about Jumping Jack Flash," she went on. "They said Sonny Stanton pitched a fit when he heard the horse was missing. Got about half drunk and went down to the cop shop and started yelling for something to happen. One of the cops slapped him across the head, and now Sonny's talking about suing the police department. The riders are getting a big kick out of it."

"I bet they are," Pete said. "Wonder where that damn horse is."

"One theory is the trainer kidnapped him," Chrissie said.

"Jackson Jones never kidnapped that horse," Ray said. "But I don't know what Sonny's going on about. They'll have him insured from here to next Sunday."

He finished his beer and stood up. It was dark outside now and darker yet in the stall where they sat. Ray took his ball cap off and adjusted the crease in the bill. He put it back on, and then he put his collar up. Finally, he looked at Chrissie. After a moment she got up and walked over to him.

"I guess I'll see you whenever," Ray said.

She put her arms around his neck and kissed him on the mouth. "I guess so," she said.

Pete and Ray started out for home. Driving through Stevensville, they decided to stop at the hotel there for chicken wings and a game of eight ball. Ray went to the bar for a pitcher of beer, and Pete racked the balls.

Ray won the first two games and then scratched on the eight ball in the third. Then Pete ran off three games in a row. The waitress came with their wings, and they left off the pool game and sat down to eat. They had a second pitcher of beer with their food.

"So what the hell are you gonna do?" Pete asked.

"About what?"

"About your life. I was thinking maybe you should buy my farm."

"With what?"

"You don't need money to buy things nowadays," Pete told him. "All you gotta do is sign your name."

"And what're you gonna do?"

"I told you. I'm fixin' to head back to Texas. I don't feel

like starting up again with any young horses. Besides I got no money to breed those mares if I wanted to."

Ray took a wing from the basket and took a bite. He wished to hell that Pete Culpepper hadn't brought up the subject of what he intended to do with his life. It was a subject he'd avoided quite nicely so far. In fact it was something he prided himself on.

"So what do you think?" Pete asked.

"I don't know."

"I figured maybe you and Chrissie could set up there."

"What the hell—how many beers have you had?"

"Same as you."

"Then how come you're the only one talking nonsense? What—you turning into Cupid in your old age?"

"I ain't no Cupid. I just thought . . . never mind. What the hell do you intend to do, then? Go back to pitching baseball?"

"My baseball days are done. Doesn't mean I'm looking to become Pa Kettle."

"It was just a thought. Forget I even mentioned it."

"I already have."

They finished their meal in silence. Ray paid the bill, and they started for home. It was raining lightly.

"You like her, don't you?" he said to Pete in the car.

"Chrissie? If I was younger, I'd fight you for her," Pete said, and in the light Ray couldn't tell if he was joking or not.

They reached the QEW and were heading west now. The rain continued, heavier now, and Ray had to turn his wipers up a notch.

"Well, what is it about her that you like so much?"

"For one, she don't take any shit from anybody."

"No, she doesn't."

Pete lit a cigarette and slipped the match out the vent. He was still smoking those nonfilters; Ray couldn't figure how he did it.

"But then, she's not Etta."

"No, she's not," Ray said. "I don't know, Pete. Sometimes I think that not even Etta is Etta."

Pete looked over. "You're a mixed-up sonofabitch, aren't you?"

"I figured you knew that."

After the incident at the police station Sonny spent the day at the golf course, boozing in the clubhouse. He went through a number of drinking companions, guys either waiting to tee off or having a drink after their rounds. The drunker Sonny got, the wilder his imagination grew with regard to the fate of his racehorse. And in every scenario Jackson was the villain.

"He's been planning this for a while," Sonny told the bartender at one point. "Give me another beer here. That's why he insisted on hauling the horse to New York himself." This in spite of the fact that it had been Sonny's idea.

"I wouldn't doubt he's on his way to Europe right now," he said to Dick Manwar. He had moved on to gin at this point.

"I knew something was up all along," he told the Hutchinsons as they had their dinner, seared halibut in a pear sauce. "But I couldn't watch everybody at once. With my dad sick, I was running the whole operation."

By ten o'clock he was in the game room, drunk on brandy. When his cell phone rang it took him several seconds to remember how to turn it on.

Jackson was on the other end. "That you, Sonny?"

"Jackson!" Sonny shouted, and then he stalled, not knowing if he was angry, happy, or confused to hear the voice. Confusion seemed to be his strong suit, and he went with it. "Where are you?"

"Maysville . . . Kentucky."

"I want you to bring my horse back, Jackson. No questions asked."

"I don't have the horse, Sonny."

"I don't care what . . . did you just say you were in Kentucky?"

"That's what I said. Listen to me, Sonny. Are you drunk?"

"No. I've had maybe three beers."

"Dean and Paulie took the horse, Sonny."

"What? I fired them."

"Why do you think they took the horse? Jesus Christ. I'm heading to Louisville to catch a flight. I'll see you in the morning."

The line went dead in Sonny's ear. He looked vacantly around the room a moment. "Jackson. I knew he would never be involved in anything like this."

The bartender drove Sonny home, left him sitting on the front porch in the cold. Sonny's eyes were glazed, and his tongue was thick in his mouth.

"You want a drink?" Sonny asked.

"No. Go to bed, Sonny."

"Fuck that. I'm going into town. Where's my car keys?"

"They're in your pocket, Sonny. But they're not gonna do you a lot of good—your car's at the golf course."

Jackson showed up at the home farm at eleven the next morning, having flown from Louisville to Buffalo to Toronto. Sonny was in the kitchen, drinking coffee and feeling sorry for himself. Jackson came right from the airport. His head was wrapped in a gauze bandage, and he had a headache that threatened to knock him off his feet.

"You look like I feel," he said to Sonny.

"Tell me about it."

Jackson sat down. "Well, I don't know what the hell they're up to. But I guess they're in Kentucky somewhere. Thoroughbred country."

"Christ, do they think they can sell the horse?" Sonny asked.

"First of all, it's not they. Paulie's just along for the ride. Probably because you treat him like shit. This is Dean all the way. I've been giving it some thought; I don't figure he's looking to sell the horse. Even Dean knows he could never pull it off. But he's always been real interested in the breeding end of things. Always asking how much a certain stallion brings at stud. My guess is—if Dean's got a plan at all—he's looking to set up a stud service on wheels."

"Come on," Sonny said. "No reputable breeder's gonna touch that."

"I doubt Dean's gonna set his sights on reputable breeders," Jackson said.

"I called the broker. The old man had him insured for twelve million. In case Dean panics and puts a bullet in him, leaves him in a ditch somewhere."

"Like he did me?"

"That what happened to your head?"

"Thanks for noticing, Sonny. I had some old sawbones in Kentucky stitch me together like he was fixing a football. What did the cops say?"

"Fucking OPP. I'd have a lot more confidence in the cops finding Dean and Paulie if I thought for a moment that they were smarter than Dean and Paulie."

"Well, we're gonna need more than the provincials in on this. Especially if the horse is in the States. We might need Dudley Do-right himself before this is done. I'm gonna go make some calls."

Jackson got to his feet. Sonny stood up hesitantly, not having a clue what to do.

"How'd the chestnut do at Fort Erie?" Jackson asked.

"We won. I deposited the check already."

"Did we lose the colt?"

"Well . . . yeah."

"That's just fucking great, Sonny."

"Oh, and I entered Rather Rambunctious in the Stanton Stakes. He should romp."

Jackson looked at him, clearly angered. "Why would you do that? You know your father never ran a horse in that race."

"And why the fuck not?"

"Because he figured it wouldn't look good, winning his own race." Jackson stood back and gave Sonny a long look. "You know, Sonny, it's too bad the folks who say the acorn never falls too far from the tree never got a chance to meet you."

Jackson left, and Sonny sat back down. He poured more coffee and sat back and rubbed his temples with his palms. At least Jackson was back. For all his lip, he would take care of things. Sonny'd been in charge for exactly two days, and the pressure had been too much. For this, he blamed his father. The old man had never given him any responsibility, had never trusted him with anything. No wonder he wasn't prepared when it all suddenly landed in his lap. It was his father's fault he was the way he was. And Sonny was man enough to admit it.

He started thinking about breakfast, and then he started thinking about a drink instead of breakfast. He was leaning toward the more liquid of the two options when the phone rang.

It was Dan Rockwood. "You find your horse yet?"

"No. Have you heard anything?"

"Yeah. I heard he's in Kentucky; I heard he's in Europe; I heard he's in five thousand cans of Alpo dog food."

"You're a big fucking help."

"Maybe I am. I'm down at the clubhouse. You should get your ass down here."

"I got no time to fuck around today."

"You better make time for this."

Sonny got dressed and walked outside, only to remember that his car wasn't there. He went into Jackson's office to ask for a ride, but Jackson was waiting for the cops and he told Sonny to find his own ride. Jackson was sitting in his office with a garden shovel across his lap. Sonny didn't ask why. He phoned for a cab.

When Sonny got to the country club the Rock was on the putting green, a dozen balls at his feet. Sonny had taken some Percodan before leaving the house, and his head was beginning to clear now. He'd stopped at McDonald's for a Happy Meal and a shake. He was feeling back on top when he got out of the taxi and walked over to the Rock, who knocked his last couple of putts past the hole and then looked up.

"Guess who's inside at the bar, hitting the sauce."

"Who?" Sonny asked.

"Homer Parr."

15

Jim Burnside stood in the walkway between the stalls and looked at the great bay stallion in front of him. The horse had his ears back and his nostrils wide and his head in the air, as if he was offended to be here in this dilapidated barn, with its broken windows and patched roofs and makeshift stalls. Jumping Jack Flash was accustomed to better digs than this.

Dean stood to one side, his arms draped over the top stall rail, ready to jump back if the cantankerous stud decided to come after him. Paulie had found a litter of kittens, no more than a month old, and he was watching them as they played in the straw at the bottom of the mow chute, tumbling and falling over one another, attacking with mock ferociousness.

Jim had been standing there for maybe five minutes without saying anything. And for about four and half minutes Dean had been antsy as hell. Finally, Jim walked over to the broken window beside the barnyard door, hacked, and spat out into the yard. Then he walked back, his eyes on Dean, and he asked, "What do you intend to do with him?"

"Breed some mares, what do you think?"

"How do you figure to pull that off?"

"Hey, you're the one told me if you had a top stud for a month you could make enough to retire. Didn't I get you a top stud?"

"Yeah, well that was late at night I told you that. Sometimes the rye gets the better of me."

"I thought you had the connections."

"Jesus Christ, man. You stoled one of the best and most famous thoroughbreds in the world. What do you think you're gonna do? Put an ad in the paper? Jumping Jack Flash, standing stud at Jim Burnside's truck farm? Bring your broodmares, one and all?"

"No, that's not what I figured."

"Then what?"

Dean drew himself up. "We're gonna use artificial semination," he said. "We're gonna collect his whatdya call it—sperm—and we're gonna sell it that way."

"They don't do that with thoroughbreds," Jim explained.

"They don't, but they can. And you know what else? You can freeze it. I been reading up on it. You know, if you got a cow you want to breed to some champion bull who's been dead for ten years, you can do it. 'Cause they got his stuff frozen, up in Guelph or someplace. And you just put in your order, and they unthaw it and there you go."

Paulie, on his knees in the straw, had his hat in his hand, and he was filling the hat with squirming kittens. Each time he put one in, another would climb out.

"I still don't see how you can work it," Jim was saying.

"Easy," Dean said. "We collect the horse's stuff every day for, say, a month. And we freeze it. Then we give the horse back, on the condition they don't press charges. And they won't. Jackson will be so happy to get the nag back, he'll agree to anything."

"What're you gonna do with all this frozen semen?"

"That's where you come in," Dean said. "You know these small owners. What's this horse gonna go for when he stands stud. A hundred grand a pop?"

"At least," Jim said.

"Right. Now these little guys aren't gonna be able to touch that. But what if we tell 'em they can breed their mares to this horse for say—five grand?" Dean paused, looked for some sign of recognition on Jim's face. "They're gonna be throwing money at us, Jim."

"How you gonna talk a vet into doing it?"

"I don't need a vet. I can do it. I told you, I been studying up on this. All you need is a big syringe and a rubber glove. And the beauty is, you only need a few drops of the stuff. One drop has got like millions of them little eggs swimming around in there. That means we could have enough of this stuff to keep us going for years. I figure a gallon will make us millionaires. And not just here. Think about Kentucky, California, Florida."

Jim walked over to a grain bin and scooped out a small measure of oats with a battered tin bucket. He came back to the stall and offered the grain to the horse, who cleaned it up in seconds, then pushed his nose roughly against Jim's arm, demanding more.

"I don't know," Jim said at last. "I'm taking an awful risk."

"A loser looks at the risk," Dean said sagely. "A winner looks at the gain."

"How you gonna get that stuff out of the horse?" Paulie interjected. He stood up and put his hat back on.

Dean shot him a look, and Paulie shrugged his innocence.

"Well, I'm gonna fix some lunch," Jim said. "I have to think about this."

He turned and walked out of the barn, stepping carefully over the barn cats. Dean watched his back, looking for some sign, but there was nothing there that he could interpret one way or the other. He turned to Paulie, who was scratching a spot between the stallion's eyes, the horse nodding in pleasure. Anybody else, the horse would take a chunk out of him.

"What do you think about our boy Jim?" Dean asked.

"Jim's a good guy."

"I don't give a shit about that. I need to know if he's on

board or not. Is he really fixing lunch, or is he up there dropping a dime on us?"

"How *are* you gonna get the stuff from the horse, Dean?"

"I'm still working on that."

When they went in, Jim had a pot of beans on the stove and was stirring the pot with a big wooden spoon. There was water set to boil in an electric kettle. The kitchen was messy and smelled faintly of garbage that hadn't been carried out.

They sat at the table and ate the beans with slices of unbuttered bread and drank instant coffee. The walls of the kitchen were covered with pinups from the *Toronto Sun*. There were a number of empty Five Star whiskey bottles by the back door.

"We gotta do something with that horse trailer," Dean said, watching Jim. "Even where it is behind the barn, you can see it from the side road."

Jim kept at his beans. There was sauce in his mustache.

"I figure I should give you some money up front," Dean continued. "You know—for good faith."

That got Jim's attention. He wiped his plate clean with a piece of bread and then leaned back in his chair to drink his coffee, his eyes on Dean now. "Yeah?"

"I was thinking five grand," Dean said.

Jim nodded carefully, like the figure was at least worthy of consideration. Paulie stopped eating long enough to give Dean a glance. He never would have guessed Dean to have that kind of money on hand.

"Five grand to keep, whether things work out or not?" Jim asked. Real nonchalant, looking into his coffee cup and talking like he was thinking about something else.

"Either way," Dean said. "I have to go pick it up, though. I'll need to use your truck. I can't be driving that Stanton truck all over the countryside."

After a moment's more consideration, Jim got up and carried his plate to the sink, already piled high with dirty dishes. "You can run the trailer back to the bush," he said. "It'll be out of sight there."

Dean and Paulie parked the horse trailer in a thicket of Scotch pines, deep in the bush lot. When they got back to the house Dean hid the Ford behind the barn.

"Make sure that horse's got water," Dean said to Paulie.

"Where you going?"

"I have to go round up five thousand dollars for Jimbo."

"How you gonna do that?"

"Well, Paulie. You know how sometimes I just make things up as I go along?"

"Yeah?"

"This is one of those times."

The roofing crew worked until after dark in the cold evening air, trying to get the last house shingled before the rain, which was promised for the next few days. Steve pulled the truck around and parked the front wheels on some stacked pallets to gain elevation, and then he shone the headlights on the roof. He and Ray finished the ridge cap shortly after nine o'clock; then they packed up the tools and headed for home.

"That's it 'til they get the survey over in Bolton ready," Steve said.

"Well, let me know," Ray told him, and they parted company.

The long day's labor and the cool weather had stiffened the muscles in Ray's back. He needed a hot tub and a cold drink. Approaching the Slamdance, he decided to reverse the order and pulled into the parking lot.

Tiny Montgomery was working the bar. Ray ordered a dark rum and coke and then told Tiny to make it a double. His lower back felt like someone had twisted a knife in it. Sipping the drink, he turned on the barstool and looked around the room. The usual suspects surrounded the stage; Ray was happy to see no one he knew. He didn't much feel like conversation.

Tiny walked over during a lull in the bar business, a cup of coffee in his beefy hand. "Ain't that a corker about that horse of Stanton's?"

"Yeah. Tough break for Sonny."

"Right. That fucking Dean, he's got more balls than I ever figured. More balls than brains, way I see it. Rumor has it they're in Kentucky."

"I heard."

"What do you suppose they're gonna do with the horse?"

"I don't know," Ray said. "But if it was me, I'd set the horse free and run for the hills. If Jackson Jones gets hold of Dean, he'll be the newest gelding in the barn."

A waitress came up with an order, and Tiny moved to serve her. Ray drank off the rum and left. Outside he got into his car and started the engine. Almost immediately there was a rap on the passenger window, and the door opened. Dean Caldwell looked in.

"Ray, it's just me. Got a minute?"

Ray looked over in surprise as Dean closed the door. Dean shot a quick look over his shoulder, a clandestine move out of a spy movie. Ray was inclined to smile in spite of the pain in his back.

"Well, if it ain't the world-famous horse rustler," he said.

"Don't be nervous," Dean began.

"Why would I be nervous?"

"Well . . . I just want to talk a minute. I got a proposition for you."

Ray lit a cigarette and put the match in the ashtray. "I thought you were supposed to be in Kentucky."

Dean grinned like a kid who'd just tied his shoes for the first time. "That's what you're supposed to think. The cops too. If they figure I'm down in the States, they won't be looking for me here. I'm not as dumb as you think."

"Be something if you were. What do you want with me?"

"I got to raise some money. Quick. I got a business proposition for you and your buddy, Pete whatshisname."

"Culpepper, that's his name."

"All right. He said he's got a couple of broodmares, right?"

"That's right."

"Well, how would he like to breed those mares to the best four-year-old in the country?" Dean paused dramatically, then tossed in the kicker. "For twenty-five hundred apiece? What would the old boy say to that?"

"He'd pass."

"Yeah, right." But then Dean saw that Ray was serious. "What do you mean, he'd pass?"

"It's not your horse. Pete Culpepper wouldn't go near it. And you couldn't register it if you wanted to."

"Who cares about that? It's the blood that matters. You can say you bred the mares to any horse you wanted. You can say you bred 'em to that nag you were running at the Fort."

"That gelding?"

"Oh, he was a gelding?"

Ray turned in his seat and had a look at Dean, in his leather jacket and his pleated pants, his spiked hair. Ray could say one thing: if you had to pick a horse rustler out of a crowd, it wouldn't be Dean.

"Why are you bothering me with this?" he asked.

"I told you," Dean said. "I had a proposition for your buddy."

"Then bother him with it."

Dean looked over his shoulder again. He'd been expecting a different reaction from Ray Dokes. In light of what he'd done, he'd been expecting a measure of respect. Instead he was getting a look that told him it was time to get out of the car.

"I thought you might want in on this," he said then.

"Why?"

"Well . . . because it's Sonny's horse. I know there's bad

blood between you and Sonny. I thought you might like to stick it up his ass."

"I'm on parole. I have to stay away from things like . . . grand theft thoroughbred. As for what went down between Sonny and me, that's none of your fucking business. That's been settled as good as it's gonna be. And if it wasn't, it's highly unlikely I'd be enlisting your help anyway."

He dropped his cigarette out the window and then started the car. He looked at Dean again.

Dean ran his hand over his chin nervously. "Now what? You gonna rat me out?"

Ray hadn't really given the matter any consideration. His mind, for the most part, was still on the pain in his lower back and the notion that he was at least temporarily out of work. He didn't wish to disappoint Dean any further, but the fact was that the nickel-and-dime horse thief was pretty low on his priority list right now.

"You gonna hurt the animal?" he decided to ask.

"No way," Dean said at once. "Christ, Paulie would kill me if I tried."

Ray nodded. "I'll stay out of it. If you were as smart as you pretend to be, you'd hand the horse over to Jackson Jones, but that's none of my business. You want to put a bee in Sonny's bonnet, you go ahead and do it."

Dean nodded and opened the car door.

Ray had a thought. "You're not gonna try and set up a stud service, are you?" he asked. "How you gonna keep that quiet?"

"That's not what I got in mind," Dean said. "This is a one-time offer, 'cause I need some cash."

"Then what do you figure to do with the animal?"

"I'm gonna give him back. But first I'm gonna pull enough semen out of him to make me a rich man. Ever hear of artificial semination?"

Ray managed not to laugh out loud. He put the car into gear, and Dean got out.

"You're a crazy sonofabitch, I'll give you that," Ray said, and he drove away. When he looked in the rearview, Dean was standing in the parking lot, looking like he didn't quite know which way to turn.

When Ray got up the next morning Pete was already gone. There was a pot of coffee simmering on the stove, and Ray could smell bacon. There were dirty dishes in the sink. The newspaper was on the kitchen table, unopened. Ray poured himself a cup of coffee and sat down to read the news.

On the back page of the front section there was an update on the status of the missing thoroughbred Jumping Jack Flash. Apparently, the police in Kentucky were pursuing some very promising leads. The FBI was now involved, as were the RCMP, and it occurred to Ray that it was only a matter of time before Scotland Yard and Interpol were called in.

Ray put the paper aside and sat back to drink his coffee, thinking about the trees that would be saved if you took all the bullshit out of the paper and just printed things that were known to be true.

He was frying eggs when he heard the truck pull up outside. A minute later Pete walked in, carrying the mail. He poured himself some coffee and sat down to open some letters. Ray slid the eggs from the pan, buttered a couple slices of toast, and came over to the table to eat.

"You using the truck this morning?" he asked Pete.

"Nope."

"I was thinking about taking some pine boards over to Etta's and closing the end of that barn in, before the snow flies."

"Where you gonna get the pine?"

"Down to the co-op, I guess."

"I got a dozen or so boards in the old machine shed, sixteen footers. She's welcome to that."

"You'll need 'em around here."

"No, I won't." Pete tossed the mail aside and got up. "And I don't intend to haul 'em to West Texas."

Ray gave him a look.

"I got the vet bill for the gelding's leg, my tax bill, and my check for the corn all at once," Pete said. "The money from the corn don't cover the vet and the taxes. I've about made up my mind, Ray. I'm selling out and headin' south."

Ray dipped the corner of his toast into the yolk of the fried egg, looked at it for a moment.

"I can help you out with some money, Pete."

"It's not the money. Besides, you ain't even working now. No, it's time I pushed on. I'd like to spend my last years in a place where I knew I never had to shovel snow."

He grabbed his jacket and his Stetson and walked out the door. Through the window over the sink Ray could see him head for the corral and stop there and drape his arms on the top rail. Ray finished his breakfast and then washed the dishes in the sink and put them away. He took some paper towels and wiped out the old cast-iron frying pan and hung it on a hook above the gas range. When he finished cleaning up, Pete was still standing there, leaning on the fence.

Ray got the keys and backed the pickup around to the machine shed, and Pete helped him load the lumber in the back. Ray packed his tools in the cab and then drove over to the Parr farm. There was no traffic on the side road, and he drove slowly, taking note of the season and its hold on the countryside. The leaves from the hardwoods were mostly on the ground, roadside markets offered little other than pumpkins and squash and onions, fresh-cut firewood was stacked neatly along garages and sheds, and the cattle—Holsteins and Herefords and Angus and Charolais—were down to the last of the summer graze. People were raking leaves and putting up storm windows and fixing leaky roofs.

Aside from the odd satellite dish and the newer vehicles, a man could drive down this road and not even guess what decade it was, let alone the year. It seemed to Ray that it was right to be that way.

At Etta's the tractor was still parked on the front lawn, the For Sale sign propped against the tire. It was a cool morning, and he could see smoke rising from the chimney of the house as he drove up the lane.

He parked by the barn and got out and set up to work. He'd forgotten to bring along sawhorses; luckily he found a pair in the old smokehouse by the orchard. They were worn and a little wobbly legged, but they would serve their purpose.

When he'd stacked the pine boards on the horses and ran an extension cord from the barn, he heard his name and turned to see Etta walking over the frosted grass of the yard. She was wearing jeans and a man's canvas jacket, her hands thrust in its pockets. He could see her breath in the air.

"Good morning, Mr. Dokes," she was saying.

"Morning."

Huddled in the coat, she walked to the lumber pile, looked at it and at the tools on the tailgate of the pickup truck and at Ray, who was sharpening a lead pencil with his pocketknife.

"And what selfless deeds would you be turning today?" she asked.

"Sounds like you got a bit of an attitude," he said in reply.

"Does it?"

"Yeah, it does. I got some time on my hands. Figured I'd replace those broken boards on the end of the barn."

"That what you figured?"

"Yup."

She sat down on the lumber, and for the briefest of moments Ray thought that she was going to cry.

"You're gonna have to find some other damsel to rescue," she told him. "The place is going on the market first of the week."

"Why?"

"Because my sainted father got drunk at the golf course

two nights ago and lost twenty-five thousand dollars to Sonny Stanton in a card game."

Ray put his knife away and tucked the pencil behind his ear. He sat down on the edge of the tailgate. "You better explain how something like that could happen."

"Before I could explain it, I'd have to understand it myself," she said. "But apparently there were plenty of witnesses—Sonny's gang, no doubt—and everything was on the up-and-up."

"Homer's not competent—how could it be on the up-and-up?"

"In the eyes of the law, Homer is competent. Because I never went after power of attorney. I should have, but I kept putting it off, I guess because I knew when I did I would be admitting that he is . . ." She let the sentence trail off.

"Okay. But you better get a lawyer now. This thing's got an awful smell about it."

"You figure I've got enough money to fight Sonny in court?"

Ray lit a cigarette, glanced at Etta, and then handed it over to her and lit another for himself. He looked up at the broken and rotten boards in the north end of the barn. One was hanging by a single nail, and in the slight morning breeze it swung, hingelike, back and forth, banging softly against the barn wall.

"What's this about the market?" he asked.

"If I'm gonna sell, I'd rather sell the place to a stranger than to Sonny. Then I can pay him off. There's something else: my father has two other mortgages on the place that I never knew about. The total is about forty thousand."

"You put the place on the market, and Sonny'll buy it. Get one of his buddies to put in the offer. How you gonna know?"

"Aw shit, I never thought of that." She looked at him. "Do you have to be so damn smart?"

"First time you've ever accused me of that."

She drew on the cigarette, squinting against the smoke. He saw now that her hair was slightly damp, as if she'd just stepped out of the shower. Her eyes flickered on him a moment and then looked away.

"Got any rich relatives about to kick off?" he asked.

She smiled. "Nah, but there's a dirt-poor one up at the house that I thought about killing. What was he thinking? Hell, he couldn't play cards when he was lucid."

She let the smile go and stood up and took one last drag on her smoke before she dropped it to the ground. She pulled her collar up. "Maybe it's just time to leave. Maybe we have no control over these things. It's just the way it's meant to be."

"I don't know if anything's the way it's meant to be."

She smiled at Ray. "Whatever the case, you'd be advised to find another barn to fix. Or better yet, a warm place to sit inside."

"Well, this is the only barn I know of that needs fixing. You haven't lost it yet, Etta."

"You gonna fix it for Sonny Stanton?"

"No, but I'll fix it for you."

She went back to the house then, and Ray got down to work. After a few minutes Etta came back out, wearing coveralls and carrying an old leather carpenter's apron. She was wearing a red ball cap, and it took Ray, on the ladder, a moment to realize it was his old cap, from when he played for London. He'd forgotten he'd given it to her.

"You want to cut or nail?"

"I'll cut," she said. "I'm not much on heights."

Ray called down a measurement, and she marked the length of board, squared and cut it with the circular saw. Ray watched; it wasn't a perfect cut, but it wasn't a bad cut. She handed the pine up, and he slid it into place and started a nail.

"So where's Annie Oakley these days?"

"I don't know Annie Oakley," he told her, mumbling, with a half-dozen nails in his mouth. "If you're talking about

Chrissie, she's down in Fort Erie, racing. She might be up at the first of the week. I'll bring her by for tea if you want."

"Don't bother."

Ray nailed the board to secure it, then took another measurement. "Where's your salvage man?"

"Busy salvaging."

"Maybe he's with Chrissie."

Etta laughed as she picked up the saw. "Now I doubt that."

Shortly before noon Etta went into the house and came back fifteen minutes later with lunch. They ate in the barn, in the old milk house. They had homemade soup and thick slices of fresh bread; apparently, Etta had been baking earlier. There was a fresh pot of coffee and a couple of Macintosh apples.

They sat and ate their lunch on the old bench that used to hold the milk cans, back in the days when Etta's grandfather had one of the best dairy herds in the county. The herd that Homer sold off, cow by cow, over a period of maybe eighteen months. In the end there were no cows, no milk quota, and—Homer being Homer—no money.

When the soup and the bread were gone she asked him for a cigarette, and they both lit up. Ray got up and walked to the cottage door, which led outside to the barnyard, and opened the top half. The air smelled of autumn—wood smoke and overripe apples and decaying leaves. There were clouds piling up to the west, and the wind was threatening.

"We might be just in time," he said. "There's some weather coming."

When she made no comment he turned to see her looking at him. Sitting on the bench, her legs crossed, leaning forward with her elbow on her knee, eyes narrowed. Her expression never changed even as he watched her, and after a moment he looked away. He cast his eye over the field behind the barn.

"So what're you gonna do?" he asked.

She didn't reply for a long time, and that made him uncomfortable too.

"I don't know," she said at last. "Maybe these things happen for a reason. Maybe it's time I faced facts. I could move into town, go back to teaching. What do I need a farm for anyway? I'm no farmer."

As Ray looked out over the field he realized suddenly that there was a doe standing along the fence line, her head up, nose sniffing the wind. He reasoned she'd been standing there all along and in her camouflage had fooled his eye. As he watched she dropped her head to pick at whatever meager grazing was left in the field.

"I hear the words coming out of your mouth," Ray said. He turned and looked at her. "But I don't see it in your eyes."

"It could be that I don't mind leaving," she said. "Maybe I'd just feel better about it if it was my idea. I guess in the end, it's the same old question. Do I listen to my brain or to my heart?" She looked up at him and smiled. "This heart of mine has gotten me into trouble before."

Ray turned toward the door again, flicked his cigarette out into the mud.

"There's a doe standing along the fence line out here," he said. "She must be awful used to people, coming this close."

"You've always been good at changing the subject," Etta said sharply, and she got to her feet. "That doe coming so close means she doesn't know a damn thing about people. If she did, she'd turn and hightail it out of here."

They finished the repairs by late afternoon. The temperature had dropped again by then, and the storm clouds had moved in. The first raindrops hit as they were packing up the tools. Etta had been quiet for most of the afternoon, and when she'd asked Ray if he wanted to stay for supper, he'd hesitated and then said no, not wanting to rankle Homer again.

When he got back to the farm Pete Culpepper was sitting by the space heater, wearing his hat and his slippers and drinking rum and Coke, the hound settled at his feet. Ray poured himself a shot and then sat down.

"You get it closed in?" Pete asked.

"Yup."

"Good thing. This could turn to snow tonight."

"It might at that."

There were papers scattered over the kitchen table. It appeared that Pete had been considering his finances. The hound got to his feet and made his way over to Ray, looking for attention. Ray obliged, reaching down to scratch the animal's ears.

"How's Etta?" Pete asked. "Did you thank her for the cider?"

Ray gestured to the kitchen table. "Etta's got the same problems you do. She's about ready to sell out, too."

Pete got up stiffly and went to the counter for another drink. Ray watched him quietly. He absently left off petting the hound for a moment, and the dog nuzzled him for more. Pete poured more rum than Coke, came back, and sat.

"You really heading for Texas?" Ray asked.

"Yes, sir."

"Where in Texas?"

"Southwest. Not far from Pecos, right on the Pecos River."

"Nice country?"

"Maybe not so green as here, but good country. You don't see snow, most years. If you do, just light a fire and sit tight, and it's gone in a day or two."

Ray fell silent again.

"You thinkin' about coming along?" Pete asked.

"I'm thinkin' about it."

Pete pulled his chair closer to the heater. He took off his hat and placed it on the floor and then ran his hand through his wiry hair. "Might do you some good to get away from here for a spell."

"That's what I've been thinking."

"What about your parole?"

"I don't know. If I had a job down there, it might be okay. Or I could just go."

"Tell 'em you're working for Pete Culpepper," Pete said, smiling.

Ray nodded and drank off his rum. He got up and went for another, disappointing the hound to the point that he walked over and flopped down behind the heater and was immediately asleep.

"What about the farm, Pete?"

"I could just put it on the market and tell 'em where to reach me when it sells. Lot of it's gonna go for back taxes anyway."

Ray poured his drink and leaned with his back against the counter. "When did you figure?"

"Well, if I see any snow this year, I'd like it to be in my rearview mirror."

16

Saturday morning, Jackson was working the gray, Rather Rambunctious, at Woodbine, prepping the horse for the upcoming Stanton Stakes. Against his better judgment. It was just an hour past sunup, and there was a light mist suspended over the turf. Jackson had Tommy Fallon on the gray, and he worked five furlongs in just over fifty-seven seconds. Jackson watched from the infield rail, stopwatch in hand.

When Tommy brought the horse back to where Jackson stood, he was grinning, standing in the stirrups, one hand on the horse's mane. He stopped, and the horse settled right down, blowing a little but calm. In spite of his name he had an even temper.

"In the bridle today, Jack," Tommy said. "What'd he do?"

"Fifty-seven two," Jackson said.

"I figured about that. He's ready to rumble."

"Well, I don't want him too ready. He's still got a week to go."

"Hell, you could feed this horse beer and pizza all week, and he'd still win the Stanton by ten lengths. There's nothing in that field that can touch him."

"I guess we'll see next Sunday. I'll walk him off, Tommy."

Tommy jumped down, and Jackson held the reins as the exercise rider slipped the saddle from the gray.

"I'll tell you one thing, Jack," Tommy said. "This here horse is a pleasure to ride. Compared to that Jack Flash. Shit, I'd rather go grizzly bear hunting with a pocketknife than gallop that mean old bugger. Any news on him?"

"None," Jackson said, and Tommy knew that Jackson wasn't going to talk about the stolen horse. He pulled the bridle off and replaced it with a halter. "Thanks, Tommy."

Jackson tied a blanket on the horse and then walked him off on the main track for fifteen minutes, before leading him back to the barn. He brushed the horse down, and then he fed him a cup of grain and a sheaf of alfalfa and made sure he had sufficient water.

It was nearly noon when he left the main barn and started the walk to the parking lot. Tommy Fallon was standing along the paddock, talking to a man in a fedora. Tommy called Jackson over to introduce him to the man in the hat, a writer for a newspaper Jackson didn't know. Jackson talked politely about nothing for a few minutes and continued on his way to the lot.

Which is where he saw Sonny, cruising between the rows of parked cars in the BMW, his shades on, slumped behind the wheel like a surly teenager. Jackson cursed Tommy Fallon. If Tommy hadn't called him over, he'd have been gone before Sonny showed.

Sonny was looking for Jackson. By way of doing that, he was cruising the parking lot at Woodbine, nursing a Bloody Mary and waiting for Jackson to emerge from the track. When he saw Jackson finally come out, he powered the window down and beckoned him with a look rather than a word. Even from thirty feet he could tell Jackson was pissed off.

"What's up?" he said, approaching the car.

"I'm just headed to the casino to watch the Breeders' on the simulcast," Sonny said. "Get in a minute, will ya?"

Jackson hesitated, then walked around and got in the passenger side.

"How'd he look today?" Sonny asked.

"The gray? He's ready."

"We need that race, Jackson. For more reasons than just the purse. We gotta show the world that Stanton Stables is still in the game, whatever happens to the Flash. This race is important."

"So you don't care about the purse?"

"Oh, I'll cash the check, don't get me wrong. I got irons in the fire you don't even know about. Heard anything from Kentucky?"

"Yeah, I think they got Barney Fife on the case. I doubt they're even in Kentucky. Dean isn't the smartest guy in the world, but he's not the dumbest, either. Why would he dump me in Kentucky if that's where he figured to take the horse? He was just fooling the hounds, if you ask me."

"So where are they?"

"Who knows? Maybe they headed for Florida. Or California. If we knew what they were up to, we might make a better guess where they went. They haven't asked for ransom—why the hell not?"

"Maybe they're not after ransom."

"What else is there?" Jackson asked. "It's not like you could sell the animal. Be like selling the *Mona Lisa*."

Sonny took a drink from the glass on the console. "What's the insurance company saying?"

"Nothing," Jackson said. "And that's all they're gonna say for now. They're not about to pay off a claim on a horse that's just missing. If the animal turns up dead, then they'll pay. Otherwise, they could make us wait a long time."

Sonny set the drink down carelessly, spilled the juice over the seat. He removed his sunglasses and looked at Jackson. "We paid the fucking premiums," he said angrily. "They owe us twelve million dollars, and they'll fucking well pay or I'll drag them into court and sue their asses for twice that."

"The insurance company isn't afraid of you, Sonny. And don't be so quick after the twelve million. We want the horse back. He turns out to be a good stud, he'll be worth ten times that before he's done. That's always been your problem, Sonny. Everything with you is short term."

"Don't tell me what my problem is, Jackson. It was your job to get the horse to New York City, where he was gonna win the Classic this afternoon. How'd you make out? Hey, maybe that's where the nag is. Maybe Dean and Paulie hauled him down to the Belmont; Paulie's gonna ride him in the Classic. Watch for him on the TV; Paulie'll be wearing that stupid hat."

Jackson opened the car door and then looked back at Sonny. "You get enough booze and painkillers in you, and you get awful stupid, Sonny. You have fun with Big Billy Coon and the boys. I'm sure there's nothing they like better than to see a stupid rich boy walk through the door."

He walked to his pickup and drove away without looking back. Sonny sat nursing his Bloody Mary as he watched Jackson pull out onto the highway and head south.

"Just keep pushing," he said out loud.

Big Billy Coon was having a private party for the simulcast. There were maybe fifty people in the back room; there were three poker games in session, a blackjack table with a hundred-dollar minimum, and, of course, the totes. Billy had set the odds early in the week and was keeping with them. The wagers wouldn't alter the payoffs as they would at the track or the OTBs. But it worked both ways; a horse bet at even money stayed there even if the odds at the track went up. And there was no money returned on a scratch.

Sonny said hello to Billy and then proceeded immediately to one of the poker games and found himself a seat. They were playing Texas Hold 'Em. Sonny bought five hundred dollars' worth of chips and looked at the other players.

"Gents, you ain't gonna like this," he said.

The races from Belmont started at one in the afternoon. Sonny played poker until then, but his confident mood fell as quickly as his bankroll. There was a bad vibe in the place, although he couldn't really pinpoint its origin. It had been his experience with natives that they were silent to the point of surliness when interacting with whites they didn't know. Sonny, with his mouth and his money and his pharmaceuticals, didn't help matters any. He was soon holding forth on his expertise in all matters regarding horse racing, while denigrating any opinion offered by the others. The quiet Indians grew quieter.

Sonny's superior understanding of the racing game was hardly in evidence once the card started. There were eight races, the Classic being the last, and Sonny had his picks for each race scribbled across the form he'd brought with him. He bet ten thousand a race for the first seven and lost them all. Then he bet twenty-five thousand in the Classic, on a horse from Ireland, a lanky standardbred-looking roan who had made considerable noise in Europe over the summer and who was off at seven to one. Sonny was betting on a marker, and he needed the last race to get even.

"This is the race Stanton Stables was gonna win," Sonny announced to the room as the Classic was about to begin. "Motherfuckers hadn't stole my horse."

The Irish horse finished tenth in a field of twelve. Sonny'd turned his attention back to the poker game before the race was even over. He was drinking Scotch now and growing resigned to the fact that it was not his lucky day. Losing ninety-five thousand dollars in four hours could have that effect on a man. Finally, he tossed his cards and got to his feet, looking at Billy Coon and smiling through his pain.

"Well, I got a hot date," he said. "I'll be in next week."

"You'll be in next week for what?" Billy asked.

"To settle up."

Billy smiled. "I'd prefer you settle up right now."

"Come on. It's close to a hundred large. I don't have it on me."

"Wouldn't that be something to consider before you bet it?"

"You know who I am," Sonny said sharply.

"What does that mean?" Billy asked. "That you want special consideration?"

The quiet Indians at the poker game saw Sonny swallow, saw his Adam's apple working as he dropped his tone, leaned into Billy, and asked, "Can we go outside and talk about this?"

"You gonna tell me a different story outside than you're telling me in here?" Billy wanted to know. "I'll tell you what, Sonny. Why don't you tell me the outside story in here?"

Now everybody was watching: the poker players and the blackjack players, the drinkers and the punters and the hangers-on. They were all watching Sonny, and Sonny was this close to crawling, and even though he'd crawled before—most notably at the golf course three years ago—he'd never crawled with this kind of hostile audience before.

He looked into Big Billy Coon's black eyes. "Billy," he said.

"What?"

"Come on, Billy. Please."

"What's that?" Billy asked, his voice rising.

It took Sonny a moment longer to get it. "Please, Billy."

Billy Coon laughed and clapped Sonny on the shoulder, and then he took the remote from the bar and began scrolling through the channels on the big screen. Sonny hesitated, and then he turned and walked out.

Once outside, he moved across the parking lot as fast as he could without actually breaking into a run. He was still shaking when he got behind the wheel. He watched in the mirror as he started the BMW. Billy Coon might send the cousins after him even yet.

He finally began to relax when he reached the 401. When the concern for his personal safety passed, though, he remembered that he'd just lost a hundred grand—a hundred grand that he couldn't lay his hands on just now. It could be a problem; he doubted that Billy Coon was as forgiving as the bank. It seemed that everything was turning against him of late.

It was early evening, and the Slamdance was slow. Sonny

ordered a Bloody Mary from the woman behind the bar, and she brought it. He put his Gold American Express card down in front of him. When he finished his second drink he ordered a third, and then Misty came out of the back room, wearing a tight navy-blue dress that barely covered her ass. She looked at Sonny, recognized him, and pointedly sat down at the far end of the bar.

"Ice water," she said to the bartender.

Sonny tapped his credit card on the bar. "I'll buy you a drink."

"Johnny Walker Blue," she told the bartender.

She sat there and drank his Scotch, but she didn't talk to him and didn't even look at him. Sonny smiled to himself, and he worked on his vodka, and after a while he bought her another Scotch.

"Where you from?" Sonny asked at some point.

She looked at him, but she said nothing.

So they sat and they drank, and people came and went and Sonny bought more drinks on the credit card, and then finally he asked again where she was from. This time, she looked over.

"Two hundred for an hour," she said. "Five for the night."

Which sounded reasonable enough to Sonny, after the day he'd had.

Dean stood in the stall, hands deep in his pockets, and he looked at the thoroughbred Jumping Jack Flash in frustration. Paulie was holding on to the horse's halter, and the horse was leaning into Paulie but looking calmly at Dean. Jim Burnside was outside the stall, and he was looking at Dean too, but not all that calmly.

"I thought you said you studied up on this," he said.

"I studied up about the part about seminating the mares," Dean said. "I never read nothing about getting the stuff out of the stud. Goddamn book never said nothing about getting the stuff out of the stud."

"What did you figure to do?" Jim said.

"I figured you just, you know—jack him off," Dean said.

"Then get to jacking."

"I *tried* that," Dean said. "I can't even find it, for Christ's sake. How you gonna jack him off if he doesn't have a hard-on?"

Paulie stood scratching the horse's ears, and every now and then the horse chortled his appreciation. "Maybe we should forget about it, Dean," Paulie said.

"We're not gonna fucking forget about it," Dean said. "Give me that picture again."

"The picture ain't gonna do anything," Jim said.

"Give it to me."

Jim handed the print over. It was a picture of a broodmare from a farm in Kentucky that Dean had cut out of a breeder's magazine and then taken into the Kinko's in town and had blown up. Sort of an equine Betty Grable.

Dean showed the print to the stallion, who looked at the picture then dropped his head to pick at the bedding beneath his feet. Dean looked underneath the horse to see if anything was happening there, and when there wasn't he tried to show the animal the picture again. This time, the horse swung his head toward Dean and showed his teeth. Dean scrambled for the gate and let himself out.

"Jesus, Paulie!" he said. "Hang on to him."

The horse settled at once, and Paulie took him by the halter and ran his hand down his withers. Dean watched the bay in stony silence for a moment, then turned to Jim and said, "We're gonna need a mare."

Jim was gone all morning. Dean smoked cigarettes and watched as Paulie cleaned out the stallion's stall and threw in fresh bedding and brushed the horse down and combed the tangles out of his mane and tail. The stallion stood stock-still while Paulie worked on him.

"How come that fucking horse likes you so much?" Dean asked.

"I don't know," Paulie said. "I guess he knows I like him."

"He's a fucking horse, Paulie."

"Yup."

"He's a dumb animal. How can he know anything?"

"I think he knows he doesn't like you."

"Well, fuck him. People like him are always looking down their nose at people like me."

Paulie turned away from his brushing. "What?"

"Forget it."

Paulie finished his grooming; then he found a hoof pick and cleaned the stallion's feet out. He had an apple in his pocket, and he broke it in half and gave the horse one piece and bit into the other himself.

"We done here?" Dean asked.

"Yeah, we're done," Paulie said, and he looked at the horse, and the horse looked back at Paulie as if he knew what Paulie was thinking.

"Then let's go in the house and have a coffee," Dean said. "I thought Jim'd be back by now."

They sat in the dirty kitchen and waited for the water to boil. Jim had a woodstove in the living room. It had been stoked earlier in the morning, but now it was all but out. Paulie carried in some wood from the back porch and got the fire going again while Dean sat at the kitchen table and smoked. Then they made instant coffee.

"He brings me a mare in season, and we'll be all right," Dean said.

"I don't know."

"What don't you know?" Dean demanded.

Paulie sipped tentatively at the hot coffee. "I think maybe

we should quit this, Dean. If we took the Flash back now, they might go easy on us. We haven't really done anything wrong. Well, except for you hitting Jackson with the shovel like you did."

"Yeah, you think Jackson's gonna go easy on me? We'll let the horse go when we've done what we set out to do."

"I don't think he's gonna let you do it."

"He'll let me. First thing he's gotta learn is that I'm a lot smarter than him. The sooner he figures that out, the better. I thought he'd of come to it by now, but he's a dumb motherfucker. I don't care what his bloodlines are—that horse is dumb."

"I don't know that he's all that dumb."

"You think he's smarter than me?"

Paulie tried the coffee again, and then he looked at Dean. "I think the best you could hope for would be a tie."

They heard Jim pull in as they were finishing their coffee. The truck shut off, and a moment later Jim walked in the door. Paulie was rinsing the cups in the sink.

"Well?" Dean asked.

"I got you a mare. Buddy of mine races standardbreds at Flamboro. He's got this older mare just come in heat. I got her in the trailer."

"Should do the trick," Dean said.

"I had to promise him a thousand bucks," Jim said. "He was pretty suspicious."

He stumbled over the amount, and Dean knew he was lying but he let it go.

"He'll get it," Dean said, "when we do."

The mare did the trick all right. Jumping Jack Flash had only to sniff her presence in the yard, and he was fully and quite visibly prepared. They'd tied him to the stall before bringing the mare in; he snapped the nylon lead like it was a piece of licorice and began to batter the stall boards with wild kicks, first with the front feet and then the back. Paulie managed to get hold of the halter and hooked a length of steel chain from a support post to the horse. As soon as he stepped back the stallion jerked his head back and ripped the hitching ring out of the wood.

Jim walked the mare all the way around to the other side of the house, out of range of the stallion's nose, he hoped. With the horse settled somewhat, Dean climbed into the stall, a bucket in his hand.

"Get hold of the sonofabitch," he said to Paulie.

Paulie took the bay by the halter and managed to control the horse's head, at least to a point.

"Jesus, look at the cock on him," Dean said.

He knelt down carefully. Paulie talked softly to the horse and stroked his nose. When Dean tried to do the same underneath, the stallion exploded; he was so fired up that he ejaculated immediately and then broke free from Paulie, kicking and bucking madly, lashing out at Dean.

Dean scrambled on his hands and knees out of the stall. The horse's ejaculate was pretty much everywhere but in the bucket: on the bedding, on the stall boards, on Dean's jacket, and in his hair.

With Dean out of reach, Paulie grabbed hold of the halter once again. Jim walked in and took in the scene.

"Holy shit," he said.

Dean looked down at himself. He took a glob of semen from his coat and flicked it into the bucket. In the stall the horse was shaking from his effort. Paulie was talking to him softly and checking his legs for damage.

"Well," Dean said uncertainly. "At least we know we can do it."

"Yeah?" Jim asked.

"I think maybe we should take a break," Dean said. "Give the animal some time to recover, you know what I mean."

"Maybe I should put the mare back in the trailer," Jim said. "For the time being."

"I'll give you a hand," Dean said. He was anxious to be away from the horse. "I could use a drink," he mentioned as he followed Jim out of the barn.

Paulie stayed in the stall with the horse. After a while the animal quieted enough that Paulie let him go, and he walked over to sit on the edge of the manger. He sat looking at the big horse and thought about what they were doing. It wasn't right; he knew that. And even if it wasn't Paulie's idea, it might as well be, because without Paulie they'd never get close enough to the animal to do anything.

"I'm sorry about all this," he said.

The stallion watched him, his legs still trembling slightly. Then he came over and pushed the water bucket with his nose. The bucket had spilled in the commotion. Paulie took it to the tap along the front wall of the barn and filled it and then put it in the stall with the horse.

The horse was drinking from the pail when Paulie walked out of the barn and across the field to the road. He put his collar up and started walking, heading east. When a station wagon approached, Paulie stuck out his thumb.

17

Chrissie won the last race of the season at Fort Erie, aboard an aging mare named Along the Vale, a three-length victory over a less than stellar field of horses. The mare was owned by a dentist from St. Catharines and her husband, and it was the animal's first win of the year after a dozen tries. Chrissie had a drink with the couple afterward in the clubhouse, and they were thrilled with the victory and her riding of the mare, even though the purse of six grand was probably a quarter of what they'd spent in maintenance over the season.

"Where do you go now?" the dentist asked. She was drinking gin and tonic, and her husband—an affable, compliant type who wore a toupee and such a consistent look of bliss that Chrissie was convinced he was perpetually stoned—had a light beer. Chrissie had a rye and water.

"Try to pick up some mounts at Woodbine," Chrissie said. "They run another month."

"Then what?"

"Christ, I don't know."

"Do you have a boyfriend?"

"I don't know that either."

She went to the Eddy with some of the riders and had a couple beers, but she was feeling restless and out of place. She'd never really fit in with the other jocks, and they were even more wary of her since the day in September when she'd slugged Juan Romano, even though deep down they would probably all agree that the sonofabitch had deserved it.

The season was over, and all the jocks were talking about what had happened throughout the year. Chrissie had never been as interested in what had happened as she was in what might happen next.

She left a full glass of beer on the table and walked out the door and got into her truck and headed for Holden County, pushing eighty miles an hour on the QEW and singing along with Janis Joplin on the radio. When she got to Pete Culpepper's place, Pete was standing in the kitchen, putting his coat on.

"Hey," Pete said when he saw her. "How you doin'?"

"Feelin' nearly faded as my jeans," she said.

"What?"

"Aw, just a song in my head."

Chrissie was looking around the house, even though she'd seen that Ray's car was gone. "I just stopped by to have a look at the gelding."

Pete smiled. "He's out to the barn; that's where we been keepin' him."

"I know where he is, smart ass."

Pete walked out with her, and they looked in on the horse. Pete had been spoiling him since the injury, and he was looking fat and happy, with his hide grown fuzzy with the cold weather. He came over to Chrissie at once and pushed his nose over the stall to sniff her. She took him by the hackamore and bit his ear lightly, then she looked at Pete.

"You goin' somewhere?" Chrissie asked.

"I gotta meet this real estate guy at the Tap."

"What do you need him for?"

"I'm selling out," he told her. "Headin' back to Texas."

"Yeah?" Chrissie looked around the barn. "What're you asking?"

"You interested?"

She thought about it. "Nah, I can't get tied down."

She picked a bundle of hay from the manger and offered it

to the gelding, but he wasn't interested in foliage. He had his mind on carrots or sugar cubes. He'd been spoiled for sure.

"Ray around?"

"I haven't seen him all day. I don't know where he's at."

She rubbed the horse's cheek with the palm of her hand. "So what's his story anyway?"

"You better ask him that."

"He doesn't say a hell of a lot."

"Look who's talking," Pete said, smiling. "Ray's just wound a little tight right now. Trying to figure out his place in the world, maybe. He has to get used to being out."

"Out?" She turned to him. "He was in jail?"

"Aw, shit. I figured he told you that much. Goddamn, I got a big mouth." He hesitated, looking at her. "Well, I better tell you the story now, or you'll think he robbed the bank at Winnemucca."

"You better."

Pete looked at his watch. "Come on, let's have a drink. That realtor can wait. He's working for me; I ain't working for him."

They sat at the kitchen table, and Pete poured bourbon and water for them both. Pete's old hound came over and placed his head in Chrissie's lap, and she scratched him beneath the chin while Pete told the story.

"Ray's got a sister, Elizabeth," Pete began, "and she's got some problems. Mental problems, I guess you'd say. She's kinda withdrawn. But she's real smart at some things, and she's pretty as a day-old foal. She's a painter and a good one, or so I heard. She was taking a class that Etta was teaching—did you meet Etta?"

"I met her. She's not real big on me."

"I bet she ain't," Pete said, smiling. "Well, Elizabeth was taking this painting class at this gallery where Etta worked. Which is how Etta and Ray met up, if you wanna know." Pete paused and took a drink. "Now, you know Sonny Stanton?"

"Just by name. I've never laid eyes on the man."

"Well, by chance Sonny stumbles into the gallery one day, and he meets Elizabeth. There's a couple things you need to know about Sonny Stanton: One, he's got a bad reputation with women. And two, his whole life, he ain't ever really heard the word no. He starts dropping in on Elizabeth, and he starts hearing it. One day he shows up, and I guess he's drunk and maybe drugged up, and the woman who runs the gallery isn't there. Sonny puts a move on Elizabeth, and she tells him no. And then . . . well, it was a bad situation."

Chrissie looked at him a long moment. "He raped her," she said flatly.

"That's what he did. And he beat her up. Pretty bad."

"Jesus Christ."

"That's right. The cops don't even charge Sonny, 'cause the only witness is Elizabeth and she can't testify. She had her problems before this happened, but after this there's just not much left of her, not enough to put on a witness stand anyway."

"So Sonny gets away with it?"

"I wouldn't say that. Ray caught up with Sonny the next day at the country club. Sonny was out on the course. Ray gave him a beating like you never seen. He beat Sonny with his own golf clubs; every time he'd break a club, he'd start in with another. He punctured one of Sonny's lungs; he broke a vertebra in Sonny's neck; he pretty much demolished Sonny's knees, the one in particular. He beat him all the way from the course to the parking lot. The only reason Sonny's alive today is that about a half dozen of them boys in polyester pants got hold of Ray and wrestled him down."

"You don't have to tell me the rest. Ray goes to jail, and Sonny doesn't."

"When was the last time you saw a billionaire's kid go to jail? Sonny's gang kicked up a fuss with the authorities and told a bunch of damn lies, and Ray gets convicted of attempted murder. He had a record—he was a bit of a hothead when he was younger—and they give him five years in the pen. He did two and then got parole."

"Wow," Chrissie said when Pete had finished. "How long's he been out?"

"Just a few weeks."

"So that means I was probably . . . the first woman he was with?"

"I expect that's true, yeah."

She grinned. "Well, that explains a few things."

"I don't need to hear any more about that." Pete finished his drink and got to his feet. "So there you are. I expect you have a right to know. Another thing: it may seem like it's over, but I'm not too sure. Ray carries things around like a damn packrat. Half the time I don't know what he's thinking."

"Well, neither do I."

"I gotta go meet this man. You can hang around here if you like."

Pete left, and Chrissie sat at the table and finished her drink and scratched the old hound's nose. From time to time the dog would release an involuntary moan of pleasure.

"God, you're easy," Chrissie said.

She drove into town. Aimlessly, not knowing where she would find Ray or if she wanted to right now. She needed some time to digest what Pete had just told her.

A few miles down the road, though, she spotted the Caddy at a bar called the Slamdance. She knew it wasn't her kind of place, but she parked and went in anyway. He was sitting at the corner of the bar with a full beer in front of him. When he saw her he smiled, and she knew it was all right, her being there. She walked over and leaned into him and bit his ear, the same as she'd bit Pete's gelding, then she sat down. The bartender was big and burly; she asked him for a beer.

"I'm not staying long," she said, looking at the dancer on the stage. "I didn't figure you for a gawker, anyway."

Ray indicated the bartender. "Tiny's an old buddy. I'm here for the conversation."

"Sure, sure. I just stopped to say hello. I was out at the farm, looking at the horse."

Tiny brought the beer, and Ray paid for it.

"Pete's talking about selling out," she said, the glass to her lips.

"I know."

"What do you think about that?"

"I don't know. He's talked about it before. And it's usually this time of year. He's got a thing about snow."

"Well, he's off to meet the real estate man today."

"He is?"

The door opened, and the room flooded with sunlight, and out of the sunlight walked an attractive blond woman. She was wearing oversized sunglasses and a ball cap, a leather coat, and jeans. She stood at the end of the bar and gestured to Tiny, who stopped at the cash register and took out an envelope before he walked over.

She moved under the dim light, and then Chrissie saw that her upper lip was swollen and she had a bruise on her cheek that she'd tried to cover with makeup. Tiny handed her the envelope, and then he gave Ray a look as he moved away. The blonde tried to read the numbers on the check but had to finally remove the shades. Her right eye was purple-black and swollen almost shut.

"What happened to you?" Ray asked.

"Nothing."

"Doesn't look like nothing to me."

"Why don't you mind your own fucking business," she suggested, and then she saw Chrissie watching her. "What's that bitch's problem?"

"Go fuck yourself," Chrissie said.

The blonde pushed the shades back on and walked out. Tiny came over then. Ray looked at him.

"Sonny," Tiny said.

Chrissie saw the muscles in Ray's jaw tighten. "What happened?" he asked.

"She took him for a roll." Tiny shrugged. "Sonny didn't have the cash. She flipped out, and he beat her up. Surprise, surprise."

"She go to the cops?"

"Nope. I figure she's got her own reasons for that. Like maybe warrants in her real name, 'cause I doubt it's really Misty."

Ray sat staring at the full beer before him on the bar.

"Don't let it in your head, man," Tiny said. "She's a nasty piece of work, that chick. Probably deserved it."

Ray stood up angrily. He pushed the beer off the bar, and then he walked out. The beer mug smashed on the floor. Tiny watched as Ray left, and then he bent down to pick up the broken shards of glass and in doing so managed to tear a gash in his index finger.

"Shit," he said.

Chrissie looked at him. "Cut yourself?"

"I'm fucking bleeding, aren't I?"

"Oh well," Chrissie said as she stood up. "You probably deserved it."

Bo Parker was living in a subdivision along the Grand River on the outskirts of Paris. The area was newly developed and the landscaping minimal. Some lawns had been sodded; most were patches of bare dirt with the odd tuft of grass peeping through, struggling to gain a foothold before winter arrived. The only trees in view were freshly planted saplings whose chances of survival looked a little iffy to Ray's eyes.

Bo's house was a split level in a cul-de-sac maybe five hundred yards from the river. The house was of yellow brick, and its design was similar to all the other houses on the street but not identical. This nod to individuality had undoubtedly been a selling point.

Ray parked in the driveway, behind a Jeep and a Lumina, shut off the engine and got out, and walked to the front door and rang the bell.

It had been over three years since he'd seen Bo up close, and when Bo opened the door he smiled his open smile and looked at Ray the way he used to when Ray had pitched a good game. Bo had his hair cropped short, and he was thicker than ever across the chest. He wore a full beard.

"Hey, buddy," he said.

Jen was in the kitchen, putting dishes in the dishwasher. The house smelled of newness: new paint, drywall, cupboards, carpet, appliances. Even the dog, chewing the corner of the doormat, was just a pup.

Jen looked at Ray, and while it didn't seem that she was happy to see him, it didn't really seem that she was unhappy either. She said hello, and then Bo said that they would go into the basement to the rec room.

The room was sparsely furnished—apparently the upstairs got priority in the furniture department—but there were assorted chairs and an old couch and a big-screen TV and a stereo. Bo went to a bar fridge behind a corner bar and brought out two bottles of beer.

"How the fuck are you?" he said to Ray.

"Never better."

"I heard you were out. I thought you'd come by eventually." Bo poured his beer into a glass. "It's real good to see you, Ray."

Ray took a drink and then looked at the bottle. "You drinking light beer?"

"Jen's got me on a diet. You know how it is."

"Actually, I don't." Ray smiled nevertheless. "How was your season?"

"Aw, what season? I never got a hundred at-bats. This kid from Michigan caught most of the time. I just backed up. Hard to get your stroke when you're only batting five times a week. The kid hit .360, so I couldn't complain."

"No, I guess not."

"We never really got it going. Finished third, but we were twelve back. You know the story: the whole team could hit .360, but if you don't have the pitching, forget it. We coulda used you, buddy."

"Those days are done."

"You could throw next year. Shit, you could throw relief."

"No." Ray shook his head. "I saw you hit the home run against Toronto."

"You were there? Why didn't you come to the dugout?"

"I thought about it but . . ." Ray paused. "I'd just got out, you know. I watched a few times from the highway. Half the guys I didn't even know."

"Shit, I'm on the team, and I don't know half of 'em. Kids, man. They all got tattoos and pierced ears."

Ray looked around. "So it looks like you got yourself suburbanized, Bo. You're doing a real *Ozzie and Harriet* number here."

"You bet. I figured it was that time in my life when I should just go ass over teakettle in debt. You know the amazing thing, Ray? How easy it is to borrow money. Sit down and sign away your soul, and they just throw it at you, man. And if you ever find out you don't have enough, hell, they throw more at you. It's called restructuring your debt."

Ray smiled and then got to his feet and walked over to a trophy case behind the bar. There were various team photos, awards, trophies in Bo's name for baseball, golf, hockey.

"So what are you doin', Ray?"

"Shingling roofs for Steve Allman."

Ray reached out and took down a picture from the wall. It was the team picture from the year they won the championship. He and Bo were standing side by side in the back row, arms folded, grinning like pigs in a rhubarb patch. Ray was wearing a straggly beard in the photo, and he looked fifteen years younger. The picture was only seven years old. He'd won sixteen games that year and lost just three. His ERA had been under two.

He put the picture back. When he turned, Bo was looking at him quietly, his beer propped between his legs.

"Shingling," Bo said after a moment. "No wonder you look in shape."

"I don't know what kind of shape I'm in these days, Bo."

"What's that supposed to mean?"

"I don't know." Ray came back and sat down. "I'm thinking 'bout maybe going to Texas."

"What's in Texas?"

"I'll let you know when I get there." Ray took a drink of beer, and then he looked about the room for a long moment. "So what's it like?" he asked quietly.

"What's what like?"

Ray made a gesture with his palm. "This."

"I don't know, I guess it's like anything else in life. Sometimes it seems like you spend all your time compromising. Other times, it's pretty damn good. Why—you thinkin' about trying it?"

"No. I don't have the parts."

"Shit, everybody feels like that, going in. It's like being a starting pitcher. You're nervous as hell 'til you throw that first pitch. Then you're okay."

"Unless you get knocked out of the box in the first inning."

Bo nodded slowly. "What's on your mind, buddy?"

There were soft steps on the stairs, and then a little girl came into the room. She was five or six, and she carried a curly haired doll in her hands. She wore denim overalls, and she had a Band-Aid on her forehead above her nose. She walked a wide circle around Bo, watching him and then Ray carefully.

"Daddy, you still mad at me?"

"Yup."

The little girl moved over in front of the TV, made a pretense of studying the set even though it was off. She gave Ray a glance, then looked away.

"Daddy, can I have a hug?"

"No."

"Why not?"

"Because you're bad news," Bo told her.

The little girl turned to look at her father then, her expression a perfect blend of contrition and exasperation. Then she shifted her eyes toward Ray without moving her head.

"Hi."

"Hello," Ray said.

"What's your name?"

"Ray. What's yours?"

"Mud," Bo said.

"It is not!" she said. "My name is Ashley."

"Hi, Ashley."

"Tell Ray what you did today," Bo said.

"No." She stared at her father defiantly.

"All right," Bo said. "I'll tell him. Ashley and her mother went shopping this morning, and Ashley decided that she doesn't have to wear her seat belt anymore. Because Ashley's the smartest person in the world. They're in the mall parking lot, and some guy pulls out in front of them. Now Jen doesn't know that Ashley's unfastened her belt; Jen hits the brake, and Ashley goes face-first into the dash. That's where she got the Band-Aid. Isn't that about the way it went, Ashley?"

She continued to stare at him as he finished; then she looked at Ray again, her face blank. "I'm going back upstairs," she said.

"Good," Bo said.

"I don't want to be around you," she said.

"Good."

"You don't love me."

"Good-bye," Bo said, and she started walking to the stairs. "Hey," he said then.

"What?"

"Come here."

And she turned and ran to him at once, climbed into his lap, and put her arms around his neck. Ray watched as Bo returned the hug, his eyes closed for the moment, his face buried in her blond hair.

"You gonna smarten up?" he asked her.

"Are you?" she said, and then: "Yes, I will smarten up." She patted his cheek with her small hand, then went back upstairs.

Bo looked over to see Ray watching him. He shrugged. "That's what it's like."

It was dark when Ray left. Jen had made sandwiches, and he and Bo had watched golf on the TV; then Bo had taken him into the garage and shown him his new snowblower and his table saw and his router, although Bo wasn't quite sure what a router did; and then he'd walked him around the estate, the whole half acre, and shown him where his vegetable garden would be and the swing set he'd put up for Ashley.

When he left, Jen had given him a hug, and Ashley had solemnly shook his hand. He drove back to the city under darkness. On the highway he watched the center line and wondered what the hell he would do. It had never seemed to him that the things available to other people were available to him. And going to Texas wasn't going to change that. All the things that were unavailable to him here were going to be unavailable to him in Texas. But maybe Pete Culpepper was right; it was best he get away from here for a while for other reasons.

No sooner had he thought about Pete than he saw Pete's pickup, parked at the Tap. Ray turned around at the Dairy Queen and went back and parked alongside. Pete was at the end of the bar, drinking draft ale and talking to Reese Wycliff, the realtor. Ray settled in beside Pete and ordered a beer for himself and another for Pete. Ray was of the opinion that Wycliff was a hustler and a slickster and as such could buy his own drinks.

Ray drank his beer while Pete talked to Wycliff. There was a country band setting up for the evening's performance, and Ray watched as they carried in their amps and their instruments.

After a few minutes he saw Pete shake hands with the realtor and the realtor take his leave. Pete pushed his empty glass away and picked up the full one. He gestured with the glass to Ray and then had a drink of the ale.

"The sign goes up tomorrow," he said.

Ray nodded and looked at the pudgy bartender, who was standing in front of the TV with the remote in his hand, looking for some sporting event or another. He finally settled on women's golf, which was probably not his first choice, but it was better than no golf at all.

"Where you been?" Pete asked.

"Went to see Bo Parker. Guy I used to play ball with."

"Yeah?"

"Yeah."

Pete drank from his glass, wiped the foam from his whiskered upper lip with the back of his hand. So that was it, Ray thought. His old friend was really heading back to Texas.

"Whatever brought you to these parts anyway?" Ray asked. And then: "How come I never asked you that before?"

"I don't know the answer to the second part," Pete said. "But the first part's easy, and it's not gonna surprise you. It was a woman."

"I thought you had a good woman down in West Texas."

"Having a good woman and knowing you have a good woman ain't always the same thing. There's always a woman around the corner who looks a little bit better. Because she's new, and you don't know all the little things about her that'll eventually take the mystery out of it. And you're new to her, and she thinks you're the greatest thing since barbed wire fencing."

"Who was this wonderful woman?"

Pete waved her identity away with his hand. "Doesn't matter, coulda been anybody. What mattered was, next thing I knew, I was in Ontario; she was gone off with some guy I'm sure she figured was the greatest thing since barbed wire fencing, and I was over at Woodbine, exercising thoroughbreds and trying to earn a dollar."

"They can be cantankerous creatures."

"Thoroughbreds?"

"Women."

Pete signaled to the bartender and indicated another round. He waited until the draft came and he'd paid for them. Then he said: "Woodbine's where I met your father, Ray. And you too, though I doubt you remember it; you were still in short pants."

"I remember. And I was wearing long pants. You were the first person I ever saw wearing a cowboy hat who wasn't in the movies or on television. I remember my old man telling me that you were the real deal."

"Your dad was a good man."

"I never got to know him well enough to make that judgment."

"Then you're gonna have to take my word for it." Pete got down stiffly from the stool. "I gotta take a leak."

When he was gone Ray lit a cigarette and took a long drink of beer, and he thought about his father, or rather he thought about how little he knew of the man.

Bobby Dokes painted barns for a living, but that really wasn't what he considered living. He drank, and he shot pool, and he played poker, and he loved the ponies, forever talking about getting a stake together and buying a thoroughbred. He probably wasn't much of a husband, but when Ray's mother fell sick his father quit all his rambling and gambling and stayed by her side for the last year of her life. But when she died at the age of thirty-one, he went back to his old ways with a vengeance, out of grief or time lost or whatever. Ray was four at the time, and he only heard about this later, from his aunts and cousins and his mother's father.

Elizabeth went to live with Mary then, while Ray stayed with his father in the rented house on Locke Street. When Ray was big enough to run the compressor and haul the air lines and clean the spray guns, his father began to take him along on painting jobs. The first night he'd ever spent at Pete Culpepper's farm was after they'd painted Pete's barn and his old man and Pete had gotten into the rye to the point that the old man couldn't drive. Ray was maybe twelve and pretty much taken with the Texas cowboy. After that he would ride his bicycle the ten miles to the farm a couple of times a week to help out with the haying or the horses or just to sit around and shoot the breeze with Pete. In those days, Pete always had one girlfriend or another hanging around; sometimes they were nice to Ray, and sometimes they looked upon his presence as competition for Pete's attention and tried to drive him off. One even attempted to initiate him to the world of sex, but Ray had declined, partially out of respect for Pete and partially because the woman smelled, for some reason, like pickles. He found out later that she worked at the Bick's plant in town.

The summer Ray was thirteen, his peewee team was playing a tournament in Owen Sound and had made it to the finals. Ray was to pitch the championship game. His father, shooting pool in the old Royal Hotel in Milton, somehow heard of it and decided to drive up for the game. He was drunk when he left the bar and dead before he'd gone twenty miles, rolling his Chevy flatbed, with the compressors and hoses and ladders aboard, into a ravine just outside of town.

After the funeral it was decided that Ray would go to live with his father's sister. Ray wasn't thrilled with the arrangement, and apparently neither was his aunt. When, after a month, he packed up his few belongings and moved out to Pete Culpepper's farm, nobody said a word in protest.

Ray drank his beer and sat and watched as the singer for the band did a sound check. The man was tall and lean, like a country singer should be, and he wore sideburns and a black cowboy hat and brand-new bluejeans.

Ray had another drink, and then he looked down the bar and directly into the face of the kid Paulie. He was wearing his porkpie hat and absently fingering the ashtray on the bar as he waited for some service. He must have just walked in. His eyes were downcast; he looked like a man who'd just lost his best bird dog.

The bartender brought over a bottle of Molson's, set it down, and took Paulie's money. After working the cash register he picked up the phone there and punched in a number. Paulie took a short sip from his bottle and then directed his attention to the TV.

Pete came back from the gents', unabashedly zippering his fly as he crossed the room, and sat back down. He took a drink of ale, and then Ray tapped his forearm with the back of his hand and gestured down the bar.

"We got a horse thief in our midst."

"I'll be damned," Pete said when he looked.

"The bartender gave him a beer, and then he made a phone call."

"You don't say." Pete took another drink of ale and then looked at Ray, who was sitting with his hands flat on the bar, his eyes dark and contemplative on the bartender.

In less than fifteen minutes the back door opened, and the bald man who'd taunted them at the auction sale entered. He looked at the bartender, and the bartender nodded toward Paulie. The man came at Paulie from behind, put him in a hammerlock before Paulie could move, and hustled him out the back door.

Pete looked at Ray and saw the angry resignation on his face. They drank off their beer, and as they got to their feet, the bartender approached.

"You guys had enough?"

"Enough of you, you fat fucking rat," Ray said.

Sonny was out there, of course, in the back corner of the parking lot, against a rough wooden fence that separated the bar's property from the residential area beyond. The bald man had both of Paulie's arms twisted up behind his back, and Sonny had his cane in both hands and was working Paulie over pretty good with it, screaming that he wanted to know the whereabouts of his horse. Paulie's hat was lying on the ground by his feet. He had his head turned away from the blows, and blood was running down his face, but he wasn't saying a word.

Ray approached the bald man from the side and hit him on the temple as hard as he could with an overhand right. The big man let go of Paulie, and Paulie fell to the ground. The big man stayed on his feet, and he turned on Ray in a rage, his small pig eyes marked by surprise born of arrogance and then pure malice. Out of the corner of his eye Ray could see Sonny scrambling for his car.

"Where'd you get the balls?" the man asked, and he came on.

His first punch clipped Ray's forehead, and Ray lost his temper then and stepped inside the big man's advance and clubbed him with a half-dozen right hands, turning his shoulder into each punch, driving the big man back against the fence, breaking his nose, and knocking him down in the dirt. He would've hit him some more if Sonny hadn't stopped him by screaming his name.

When he turned, Sonny was standing maybe fifteen feet

away and had an automatic pistol pointed at Ray. Sonny's chemical grin scared Ray a hell of a lot more than the gun. Ray put his arms out slowly to the sides.

"I knew it'd come to this," Sonny said, his voice thin and reedy with nerves, the pistol actually shaking in his grip.

Ray saw Sonny's fingers twitch on the gun, and he knew he had to move. His eyes went to the fence, gauging the height. He was ready to leap when he heard Pete Culpepper's voice: "Take the kid and get in the car, Ray."

When Ray turned back, he saw Pete standing at Sonny's side. Pete had a handful of Sonny's ponytail in his left fist, and he had the muzzle of his double-action Colt .44 pressed against Sonny's temple.

Sonny had a pained, frightened look on his face, and he was squinting in deference to the gun barrel against his head.

"Put the gun on the ground," Pete told him. Sonny went to drop it. "Place it on the ground," Pete snapped. "You want it to go off, you fool?"

Ray put Sonny's gun in his pocket and Paulie in his car. As he drove off, Ray could see Sonny and the bald man standing in the parking lot. Sonny was fuming, and the bald man was bleeding, and neither would look at the other. Ray smiled—he guessed that each was holding the other responsible for their predicament.

A couple of Ollies with no Stan to blame.

Ray drove Paulie to the hospital, and Pete followed in the pickup. The first person they saw when they walked into the emergency ward was Etta.

"Oh, my God," she said when she saw Paulie's face. "What happened?"

"Sonny beat him with a cane," Ray told her.

There was no doctor on duty, and they had to wait until one was summoned. Etta took Paulie into an examining room, where she and a nurse cleaned him up and took stock of his injuries. Pete and Ray sat in the waiting room and looked without interest at the magazines and waited for the doctor.

"Texas is looking better all the time," Ray said.

When the doctor arrived Pete decided that there was no point in the two of them sticking around. After he left, Etta came out and sat with Ray while the doctor and the nurse tended to Paulie.

"How's he look?" Ray asked.

"He's gonna need twenty-five, thirty stitches. How do you know this kid?"

"I don't."

Etta reached over and took Ray's right hand and looked at the skinned knuckles.

"He's crying in there," she said. "He kept saying it's all his fault; he stole Sonny's horse."

"I don't know whose fault it is, but it's not his."

"He said Sonny pulled a gun on you."

He looked at her and shook his head. She watched his eyes for a moment, but he looked away, and then she let go of his hand and left the room. She came back with alcohol and gauze and some Band-Aids, and she cleaned the cuts on his knuckles and dressed them.

"You don't need to be getting involved with Sonny again."

"I know," he told her.

"Just stay clear of him."

"I couldn't figure out a way to do that tonight, Etta."

She glanced toward the examining room, where Paulie's face was being stitched back together.

"Okay," she said. "But from now on, just let him go. Sonny Stanton's gonna have to answer for himself one day. And when he does, it'll be to a higher authority than you, Ray."

"Sounds like you've been reading your new Bible. But I'm not so sure about that."

"I know you're not."

Ray held up his right hand and examined the repair job. He flexed his fingers and felt the joints stiffening already.

"What about you?" he said. "You gonna take your own advice? You gonna let him have his way?"

"To hell with the farm." She realized she was making the decision as she spoke. "In the end he'll win out anyway. It's all about money. If he wants it bad enough, he'll get it. I'm tired of the whole damn thing."

"Being tired of it is not a good enough reason to let him win."

"I don't want anything else to happen that's gonna encourage trouble between you and Sonny. His money will win that one too, and you'll end up back in jail. Or dead, if he's playing with guns now."

Ray got to his feet and walked across the room. He took his cigarettes from his pocket and put one in his mouth, but when he turned back to her she shook her head and he put it away. He stood there watching her for a moment, in her green scrubs, her blue eyes steady on his.

"Pete's headin' back to Texas," he told her. "I been thinking about tagging along."

"I think you should."

He nodded, and he didn't ask her why she thought that. He thought that he knew, and if he was wrong he'd rather not know he was wrong. He reached into his coat pocket and pulled out Sonny's little automatic and handed it to her.

"Can you get rid of this for me?" he asked. "Sonny maybe went to the cops, like last time. I'm on parole—I get pulled over with this on me, I'm right back in stir."

She took it without hesitation. He watched her eyes for a moment. He was hoping for a smile or something, he wasn't sure what. Something to tell him that things were the way they were because there was no other way for them to be.

"So Sonny wins—you can live with that?" he asked.

She looked away, and he could see that she wasn't any

happier with the notion than he was. But when she turned back, her eyes were clear and her voice was even. "This isn't about what I can live with, Ray. It's about what you can live without."

Ray took Paulie home with him to Pete Culpepper's spread. Stitched up, Paulie's face didn't look nearly as bad as Ray would have thought. There was a sizable gash across his left cheekbone and another above his left eye; other than that he had a few bruises and minor cuts. He'd be sore as hell in the morning, but it could have been a lot worse. No doubt it would have been a lot worse.

"You feeling all right?" Ray asked as they left the hospital lot.

"Yeah, not too bad," Paulie told him.

Ray drove the back roads out of town, not knowing if the cops would be out for him, or if Sonny had rounded up a posse. It was a moonlit night, and as he drove he could see the cattle grazing in the fields and the stark, leafless limbs of the trees along the road silhouetted against the sky. He smoked a cigarette and offered one to Paulie, who declined.

"I'm really sorry," Paulie said.

"Don't be sorry."

"I'm glad Sonny didn't shoot you."

"Hey, me too."

When they got to the farm Pete was already in bed and asleep. Ray opened a bottle of rum, and he and Paulie sat in the kitchen and had a drink. The hound got up when they came in, and he walked directly to Paulie and lay down at his feet.

"What were you doing in town?" Ray asked.

"I left Dean and them," Paulie said, looking into his glass, his eyes heavy. "I just didn't like it."

"They still got the horse, I assume."

"Yup."

"How's Dean making out collecting semen?"

Paulie looked at Ray and smiled. "Not too good."

"I bet." Ray smiled back at Paulie.

"Who was the guy with you?" Paulie asked after a time. "The guy with the gun?"

"That was Pete Culpepper. You met him at Fort Erie."

"He looked like a cowboy."

"That's what he is."

After the first drink Ray made another, but pretty soon Paulie's eyes started to flutter shut. Ray made him up a bed on the couch, and Paulie lay down and was asleep in a heartbeat. The hound lay down on the floor beside the couch and went to sleep too.

Ray took his drink out onto the porch and sat in one of the old ladderbacks, his boots up on the porch railing. The night was warmer than recent nights, and he saw now that it had clouded over since they'd driven home. There was a smudge of light in the clouds where the moon had gone to hide, and the air was heavy with the promise of more rain.

Well, the weatherman could do whatever he damn well pleased. This time next week, he and Pete Culpepper would be sitting on another porch in West Texas, drinking bourbon and branch water. Maybe eating some of that rattlesnake chili Pete liked to brag on.

Tonight had cinched it. Let Sonny have his way; let him use his money and his deceit and his nasty disposition to get what he wanted. In the end it wouldn't make him happy because Sonny didn't have it in him to be happy.

And if Etta was resigned to Sonny taking her farm, then let him have that too. Sonny was always going to get what Sonny wanted. He had his money, and he had his lawyers. So he could smack his women around and get away with it, and he could beat on kids like Paulie and get away with that, too. Well, let him. Ray didn't give a hoot in hell anymore.

"Goddamn it," he said out loud.

He came down off the porch and walked through the darkness to the barn. Inside, the bay was sleeping on her feet, but the other mare was restless, circling in her stall. The gelding was awake, and he came to Ray when he walked over to the stall.

Ray looked at the horse, and he thought of all the times he'd spent here, and of the conversations he'd had here with Pete Culpepper, and of how all that would be ending in a few more days. And he thought of how this gelding and the two mares would be sold off and he wouldn't see them anymore, but that it didn't matter because they were just horses anyway. And things like horses and this farm and Etta's farm didn't matter because they were just things, and you could get on fine without them.

The gelding took a half step forward and pushed his velvet nose against Ray's cheek, and Ray breathed in the sweet horse smell of him.

"Hey buddy," he said, and then he heard the pregnant mare in the next stall grunt heavily and begin to stomp. When Ray looked, she began to circle once more; then she made to lie down but at the last second got back to her feet.

"Shit," Ray said, wondering why he hadn't picked up on the signs earlier.

He went into the stall, and by the time he got the mare on her side he knew she was in trouble. Her breath was coming in sharp gasps, and she was struggling mightily with the contractions. Ray found a roll of friction tape on a shelf and gave the mare's tail a few quick wraps to keep it out of the way. Then he knelt in the straw and had a look. The baby's nose was visible so he knew it wasn't a breach, but the foal wasn't moving at all and appeared to be stalled in the birth canal. Ray thought for a moment to run for Pete, but he knew there was no time. After all, it had been Pete who had taught him that a foal locked in the uterus could be lost in a matter of minutes.

Ray rolled up his sleeves and reached into the uterus, clearing the placenta as best he could from the foal's nose. He couldn't determine if it was breathing or not.

The mare's left hind leg was in the air, and she was in a constant state of push, but nothing was happening. Ray reached in farther and found one front leg and straightened it out along the foal's nose. The other seemed to be twisted sideways and pushed out at an angle from the foal's body. It wouldn't move, and after a moment he felt the cord wrapped around it. The mare was crying out in pain now, and her leg was kicking dangerously near Ray's head. The foal's nostrils were still and its eyes closed, and Ray feared it was already dead. He pulled his jackknife from his pocket and unclasped the smaller of the blades, then went up into the birth canal again. Working blindly, he fumbled with the cord, unable to pull it loose enough to cut it.

There was no movement from the foal, and the mare's kicking grew less fervent. Ray was suddenly afraid he would lose them both. He turned the blade of the knife sideways and slid it along the foal's leg, felt it cut the skin there, but pushed it farther until he felt it under the cord; then he twisted the blade upward and felt the cord separate as the leg came free. Grabbing both legs now, he dug his heels in on either side of the mare and began to pull. Sweat was running down his forehead and into his eyes, and the mare kicked wildly. Ray continued to pull, his shoulders strained, his boots digging for traction in the straw. His eyes were on the foal's shoulders, where they were stalled in the uterus, and he pulled and he cursed and he hoped and he yelled and then he prayed.

And finally, the foal came, moving just a fraction at first and then sliding along steadily until it was completely out. Ray lay the newborn in the straw and knelt over it and cleared its mouth and nose, and as he did the foal suddenly snorted to life, shaking its small head and sucking at the air, kicking out wildly with its small, soft hooves. Ray felt the tension go out of the mare, and he sat back in the straw and ran his sleeve across his forehead. The foal was a filly, he saw now, dark brown and nearly black. The cut on her foreleg was bleeding but minor.

A moment later the mare, in spite of her exhaustion, began craning her neck. Ray slid his arms beneath the new filly and moved her up onto the straw where the mare could nuzzle her.

Ray's breath was coming in gasps, and he had placenta and blood on his clothes. He sat back in the straw, trying to catch his breath, and watched the two. As he watched, the filly decided she would stand. She got halfway up on wobbly knees, and then she fell, but she tried again immediately.

"Whoa now," Ray said. "You're in an awful hurry."

But she kept at it. Finally, Ray got on his knees and took her in his arms and stood her up, held her there until she got her feet underneath her and could manage on her own. When he moved back she stayed on her feet, knees knocking, legs trembling, looking at him with eyes that were seeing everything for the first time.

And Ray sat in the straw, and he looked back at her in the faint light.

After a while he got up and walked out of the barn and hooked Pete's truck up to the trailer, and then he went into the house and shook the kid Paulie awake.

"Wake up," he said. "We're going for a drive."

18

"And that's your story," Jackson said, and it wasn't a question.

They were in Jackson's kitchen, the three of them. Jackson at the table, elbows on the arms of his chair, fingers bridged in front of his face. Sonny sitting across from him, indignant and defiant. The Rock standing just inside the door, his face all lumpy and his nose pushed to one side like somebody who had just had the shit kicked out of him.

"That's it," Sonny said, maintaining his pose.

There were apples in a bowl on the table. Jackson picked one up and cut a wedge out of it with a paring knife. He chewed carefully on the fruit, all the while watching the two men across the room. Then he cut another wedge.

"Paulie shows up, and instead of calling me or calling the cops, you decide to handle it yourself," he said to Sonny.

"Why not? It was Paulie. I was just asking him a few questions, and I would've got some answers too if that fucking Dokes hadn't shown up."

"Why would Ray concern himself with it?" Jackson asked. "He wouldn't even know Paulie." Jackson cut another wedge. "Unless you guys were doing more than asking questions."

"Well, you weren't there, Jackson. Were you?"

"If I was, then we might know where the horse is by now. But I can probably guess what happened. I know what Ray's like. And you know it better than anybody, Sonny." He glanced over at the bald man. "By the looks of your face, you're in on the secret too now."

"I got sucker punched," the Rock said.

"You tough guys are always getting sucker punched," Jackson said. He put the last piece of apple in his mouth. "Well, Sonny—now what?"

"I guess we have to find Dokes."

"I don't see Ray getting involved in this," Jackson said. "He's on parole, for one thing. I got a feeling he was just saving Paulie's bacon. You say the old guy pulled a gun on you?"

"Motherfucker's gonna answer for that," Sonny said.

"Looking at the two of you, I wouldn't have thought it necessary," Jackson said. He gave Sonny a long look. "I just got this feeling you're not telling me everything. Where's your .38, Sonny? Still in the glove box?"

"No," Sonny said, but he hesitated. "I sold it."

"You sold it, did you?" Jackson said, and he got to his feet. "You just keep fucking up, see where it gets you. I gotta get some sleep, I have to work that gray in the morning; we got a race to win on Sunday. You happen to run across Paulie, or Dean, give me a call. Unless you and the punching bag here want to have another go at it yourselves."

Sonny fell quiet as they drove back north. The Rock, his battered face sullen, looked over at him in the dim light.

"That's a mouthy fucking nigger you got working for you," the Rock said.

"Think I don't know it?" Sonny said. "Don't worry, he's on his way out."

"He's lucky I didn't knock him out."

"Don't do that. He's gotta get that horse ready to run. I'm gonna need that purse to get straight with Big Billy Coon and to pay that bitch over in Holden County. I need Jackson Jones—for the time being."

"What about the other?"

"I gotta find Paulie again." Sonny shrugged. "He's not the sharpest knife in the drawer; he'll be around."

The Rock touched his fingertips tenderly to the lump above his eye. "I guess we shoulda called the cops."

"The law is the last fucking thing I want in on this."

"Why not?"

"I don't want the horse back. Not now. Think about it. He missed the Breeders'—that was the big one. *Maybe* he'll win some races next year. *Maybe* he'll be a successful stud. I got cash problems, I don't need a bunch of maybes. And alive, that's all that nag is—a big fucking maybe. But dead, he's worth twelve million dollars, and I mean now."

"So what're you gonna do?"

"I find out where the animal's stashed, and I send a guy in there at night to . . . initiate my insurance claim. It's a huge racket in North America. Show horses, mostly. They take an extension cord with a couple of alligator clips. Hook one clip to the horse's lip and the other to its asshole and plug it in. Looks like the horse dies of natural causes, so the insurance company has to pay."

"You're gonna kill your own horse?"

"I guess I'm gonna have to." Sonny laughed. "I can't depend on those fuckups to get it done."

Sonny was tired as he drove home; twice he nodded off and woke up to find himself headed for the ditch. He'd dropped the Rock at the country club, which is where they'd started out.

On the way up the driveway to the farmhouse, he saw a rusted half-ton parked by the front porch. There was a man standing by the tailgate. Sonny pulled the BMW alongside and got out warily.

"Hey, Sonny," the man said. He was older, and he had gray sideburns.

"Who are you?"

"Jim Burnside," the man said. "We've met a couple times.

I'm a stable hand for the Double B. I help out with the breeding and that."

"Fascinating," Sonny said, and he walked past the man and started up the steps.

"I know where your horse is, Sonny."

Inside the house Sonny sat the man at the kitchen table and brought out a bottle of rye. Sonny was no longer tired. Jim Burnside liked his whiskey with ice and not much water. Sonny could have sworn that he'd never seen the man before, but they could have met. Sonny met a lot of people.

"You looking for ransom?" Sonny asked.

"No, sir," Jim said. "I'd just like to see you get your horse back."

Sonny nodded and pushed the bottle closer to Jim. And he waited.

"Of course, I thought there might be some kind of appreciation," Jim said.

"How much appreciation?"

"I don't know—maybe ten thousand? The horse is worth a lot of money."

"You got it." Sonny watched Jim's reaction, and he knew the old man was cursing himself for not starting higher.

Jim took a drink of rye. "All right," he said softly.

"Where's the horse?" Sonny asked.

"I got a little truck farm, this side of London. 'Bout an hour and a half from here. The horse is okay; they ain't harmed him any."

Sonny stood and went into a drawer and brought out a sheet of paper and a pencil. "Draw me a map," he ordered.

Jim hesitated a moment.

"You'll get your money when I get my horse," Sonny told him emphatically.

Jim drew the map, including details such as oak trees and culverts and grain silos. Sonny watched impatiently.

"Just give me the goddamn road and the number," he said at last.

Jim finished his masterpiece and then pushed it across the table to Sonny, who glanced at it and then put it in his shirt pocket.

"Who's there?" he asked.

"Just me and Dean Caldwell."

"All right. I'm gonna get some sleep; I've had a long day. I'll be there around noon tomorrow, me and Jackson Jones. I'll have your ten grand, and you'll get it when we get the horse. Okay?"

"Okay."

"I'm going to bed," Sonny said again, dismissing the man this time. "Take the bottle if you want."

Jim looked at the bottle, and then he looked at Sonny. After a moment he picked it up and put it in his coat pocket.

Sonny stood in the front room and watched the battered pickup make its way down the driveway. He turned the possibilities over in his head and knew that he had no choice in the matter. He was going to have to move on this tonight, and that meant he was going to have to handle it himself. For someone who was bone-tired and who didn't like to get his hands dirty even when rested, it was not a welcome consideration.

He went into the upstairs bathroom and found a bottle of methamphetamines and took two with a glass of water. Then he went out to the main barn, where Jackson kept a workshop off the tack room. Sonny found a heavy extension cord and cut off the receptacle end. He dug through Jackson's junk drawers until he found an electrical test lead. He cut the alligator clips from the lead and attached them to the extension by twisting the ends together and then wrapping them with tape. Sonny was not mechanically inclined; it was a clumsy job but would have to do.

By the time he walked back to the house the speed was taking effect. He wasn't a big fan of the stuff; he preferred the nod he got from Demerol or Percodan, but tonight he needed the up, not the down. He took a half bottle of orange juice from the fridge, filled it with vodka, and then walked out to his car. It was four in the morning.

Whatever his feelings about the meth, there was nothing like it for driving. He sipped at the vodka mix and headed for the 401. He turned the radio up loud so he didn't have to think about anything. Sonny found life a lot easier to handle when he didn't have to think about anything.

He burned the miles to London and found the farm without any problem. He drove by once, saw the rusted pickup in the driveway, then turned around and drove by again. The house was a white frame story and a half with a missing front porch, and it was dark. It was maybe a hundred yards from the barn. He parked a quarter mile down the road, killed the engine and the lights, and got out. He slung the extension cord over his shoulder and pulled on a pair of leather gloves. As he walked he began to hope that he would find the horse asleep. Given the animal's temperament, it could be tough attaching the wires otherwise.

He entered the barn on the east end, the door away from the farmhouse. Inside it was pitch-black, and he thought too late that he should have brought a flashlight. He had no choice but to risk turning on a light. He pulled the gloves off and set them down along with the cord, and then he fumbled along the wall, the odor of hay and bedding and horse manure strong in his nostrils, until he found a switch. A single overhead bulb came on, and he turned.

The barn was empty.

He walked back outside. There was a machine shed off the north end of the barn, and he had a look inside and found it empty as well. There were no other outbuildings. He walked around the perimeter of the house in the darkness and discovered a lone horse in the pasture field at the west end of the farm. He had hope for a moment, but when he got closer to the animal he saw it was a scrawny standardbred. Sonny walked back to the barn and had another look inside. The one stall had fresh bedding in it, and a bucket of water in the manger. There was a pile of horseshit in the bedding.

He walked back outside. If Jumping Jack Flash was on the premises, he must have been in the house, sleeping in one of the beds.

19

Ray woke up to the sound of Pete Culpepper banging around in the kitchen downstairs. It was dawn, but not a minute past. Ray had been in bed for maybe an hour, and he lay there in the gray light for a time. By the time he got downstairs, the coffee was made and the smell of sourdough was beginning to creep from the oven.

Ray made it to the barn just a minute or so after Pete. When Pete looked at him, Ray offered a smile that was not returned.

"Looks like we had a busy night," Pete said. "I wasn't aware I was running a bed-and-breakfast."

"I figured I'd better bring the kid back here. You know, for safekeeping."

"You know damn well I ain't talking about the kid."

"Well, that little foal just showed up on her own. I didn't have anything to do with that."

"You know damn well I'm not talking about the filly, neither. I'm talking about that big bay stallion in the back stall. The one I expect you're planning to return to Stanton straightaway."

"That's exactly what I plan to do."

"Good."

"But not straightaway."

Ray walked over to Fast Market's stall and put his hand out. The gelding came over to see if there was something in the hand for him.

"You know Sonny's running that big gray of his in the Stanton Stakes on the weekend," Ray said.

"I heard."

"Well," Ray said slowly, rubbing the gelding's forehead. "I figure this old horse of yours has got one last race in him, Pete."

"You figure my old horse with the broken leg has got one last race in him?"

Ray turned. "I'm gonna beat Sonny in that stakes race, Pete."

"How you figurin' on doing that?"

"I'm gonna beat him with his own horse."

Back at the house, they cooked up ham and eggs to go with the biscuits and coffee. Pete never said anything about Ray's plan until they were done eating and having a second cup of coffee at the kitchen table.

"We'll load that stud in the trailer and run him on over to Stanton's this morning," Pete said then.

"I'll take him back on Monday."

"You listen to me. It ain't ethical, it ain't possible, and goddamnit, it ain't right. That horse is stolen property, Ray."

Ray had anticipated this conversation but wished he was having it on more than an hour's sleep. He had no choice in the matter.

"First of all, I think we should forget about any ethical considerations where Sonny Stanton is involved," he said. "You saw his ethics in action in the parking lot last night. If you want another look, then check out the kid's face on the couch in there. Sonny's horse is gonna win that race, Pete; everybody knows it. The old man would never even run his own horse in the race; you know that to be true too. But that horse we got in the barn will beat Sonny's gray running backward. And the only person we're hurting is Sonny. The purse is a quarter million; the winner gets what—$130,000 or $140,000. Pay off what you owe on this place, for one thing."

"I don't care about this place. I'm headin' to Texas, and I thought you were comin' with me."

"Maybe I am. But I'm gonna do this first."

Pete butted his cigarette and raised his cup to his mouth. "This is all about you and Sonny," he said after he drank. "You can pretend it's about this farm or the kid in there, but it's just you and Sonny. Jesus Christ, you already did two years in jail for him."

"Not for him. For Elizabeth."

"Two years is two years; don't matter who it's for. You get this out of your head. It's a bad idea, Ray."

Ray got up and went to the counter for more coffee. His brain was fuzzy from lack of sleep, and he was beginning to worry that maybe Pete Culpepper was right, that maybe the whole thing had been a bad idea from the get-go. Another flash of midnight brilliance that didn't play too well in the harsh morning light.

"Sonny's holding a note on Etta's place," Ray said, and he came back to the table and sat down. "He chiseled Homer in a poker game."

Pete stared at him. "How come I never knew this?"

Ray shrugged. "I don't know. Maybe I was afraid you'd go riding off like the Lone Ranger."

"That sounds familiar. How the hell did Sonny pull that?"

"Shit, I don't know. You know Sonny. Doesn't matter how it happened, just that it did. Etta needs forty thousand dollars, and she needs it now."

He looked at Pete over the rim of his cup, and he thought he saw in the old man's eyes a tiny shim of reconsideration. Ray lit a cigarette and watched as Pete turned in his chair to gaze out the kitchen window toward the barn. He shook his head and looked back at Ray.

"How would you ever pull it off?"

"That gelding of yours may not have world-class speed, but he's a good-looking horse. He's about the same size as the stud, and he's jowly like a stallion. The only difference is the color; we gotta make that bay look like a chestnut. And we'll have to be fast on our feet when it comes to the ID. Remember, it doesn't have to be perfect; nobody at Woodbine knows what your horse looks like anyway."

Pete, thinking about it, shook his head again. "What about Etta? What makes you think she's gonna take the money when she finds out where it came from?"

"I'm hoping she'll go us one better. I'm gonna ask her to help us."

"Good luck with that. I guess I don't have to ask about a jockey."

"That one might take some convincing, too."

"Looks like you got your work cut out for you."

"Yeah, and right now I need some sleep. I'm a little lightheaded to be facing either of those women right now. I might forget which one is which." He got to his feet. "That stallion still gonna be here when I get up?"

Pete Culpepper glanced toward the barn again. Ray stood there waiting for him to say something, and when he didn't Ray went back upstairs and went to bed.

When he woke up it was midafternoon. He lay awake in bed for a time, leafing through the Bible he'd been given in prison, looking for something to bolster his case. When he got up he had a shower and put on clean jeans and a sweatshirt. He shaved and brushed his teeth, and then he went downstairs.

Pete was at the kitchen table reading the paper, drinking coffee, and smoking a cigarette, or rather allowing a cigarette to burn in the ashtray by his elbow. Pete had a habit of lighting cigarettes and never smoking them.

"Where's Paulie?" Ray asked.

"Out to the barn," Pete said. He glanced up. "With your horse."

Ray nodded at the news. "How is the animal?"

"About as affable as a damn scorpion. I went in the stall to spread some fresh straw, and the sumbitch took a kick at me, near took my head off. Funny thing is, the kid goes in, and the animal's like a lapdog. I never seen anything like it."

"It was the same last night when we took him," Ray said. "I think we better keep the kid around 'til this is done."

"I think we better keep him around anyway," Pete said. "He runs into Sonny again, he might not get off so easy."

Ray drank a cup of coffee and drove over to Etta's. She was in the kitchen, making dinner for Homer, who was sitting at the table, watching her prepare the macaroni and cheese. When Homer turned toward him, Ray braced himself, but the old man never said a word. It took Ray a moment to realize that Homer didn't recognize him at all; his eyes were vacant.

Etta took one look at Ray, and he could see that she knew something was up. But then she could always read him. She put a plate in front of Homer and made sure that he began to eat. Then she walked over to Ray and said, "Something on your mind?"

"Can we go in the front room?"

They sat by the bay window, Etta on the couch and Ray in the big overstuffed chair—Homer's chair. Ray looked out the big window. The Ford tractor was still parked on the front yard, the For Sale sign propped against the wheel.

"No bites on the tractor?" Ray said.

"No," she said. Then, remembering: "Oh, Mabel's husband offered me five hundred dollars. But I'm not giving it away."

"I'll give you forty grand for it."

"Sure." She smiled and waited for him to smile back. "Okay, what's going on?"

"I'll give you forty grand for the tractor."

"You said that."

He told her his plan, or at least as much as he'd figured out so far. While he talked she sat and looked out the bay window.

Occasionally, when the scheme grew a little too unlikely, she would glance over at him. At one point Homer began to ramble in the kitchen. She let him, and in a moment he stopped.

When Ray finished, he waited for her to say something. She turned to look at him, and then she smiled in the manner of someone who'd just been told a joke. "I think you should go to Texas," she said.

"You been talking to Pete?"

"No. But I can see him giving you the same advice. It's the sensible thing."

"I'm not exactly famous for doing the sensible thing."

"Hope you're not looking for an argument on that."

She shook her head then and got to her feet and walked across the room. She glanced into the kitchen, and then she walked to the staircase and sat down on the lower step. She looked at him evenly and said: "You're like a goddamn ten-year-old. You just need to be in trouble."

"I don't plan on getting into trouble with this. If I thought that, I'd leave it alone."

"Like hell you would. You have a need for this, Ray. You gotta have a windmill to tilt at, or you get bored. You haven't been out of jail for two months, and you're set to do something that's gonna get you thrown back inside."

Ray, sitting in the chair, looked out at the yard. It was growing dark already; to him it seemed like morning still.

"I was hoping I could talk you into this," he said after a moment.

"Why is that so important?"

"I don't know. Maybe there's a part of me that knows that it's wrong, and if I can get you involved that'll make it right. Because you're usually right, Etta," he said without a hint of sarcasm.

"So if I say no, you'll forget about thc whole thing?"

"Maybe." He stood up and half-smiled. "But I wouldn't bet on it," he added.

"Neither would I."

He walked over to where she sat on the stairs. She stood up, stepped on the first tread so she was as tall as him, looked him in the eye. He returned the look.

"I don't want him to take this place from you, Etta. He's gonna get away with it, like always."

"Maybe not. I hired a lawyer yesterday. We're gonna challenge Dad's marker to Sonny in court."

"And Sonny'll bring in half a dozen of his boys to testify that's it's legit."

"Maybe."

"And you're gonna spend money on a lawyer that you can't afford."

She sighed. "Maybe."

He reached out and brushed her hair back from her forehead with his fingertips. Then he turned and walked to the back door. She stepped down and followed. In the doorway he turned back to her, his hands in his coat pockets, and he played his hole card.

"To me, Sonny's like those money changers in the temple," he said. "Remember, Jesus had to go in there and kick some ass. It was the Book of Mark, if memory serves."

"Been reading the Bible today, Ray?"

"I might have glanced at it," he said and then left.

Etta crossed the room and watched out the kitchen window as he drove down the driveway and onto the side road. Behind her, Homer had finished what he was going to finish of his macaroni.

"What do you do with a guy like that, Dad?" she asked without turning. "Steals me a horse and then tells me that Jesus says it's okay."

Dean got back to the farm at a little past ten in the morning. He'd spent the night with the waitress from the Dorchester Tavern, and over the past twelve hours he'd drank too much and ate too much and invested way too much time and money in a fruitless effort to get laid. When he got out of the truck Jim was standing in the doorway of the barn, leaning against the jamb. He was in the shadow of the awning, and he was giving Dean a look that appeared to be somewhere between huge disappointment and just plain pissed off.

"What'd you do with him?" Jim demanded.

"What'd I do with who?"

"The goddamn horse."

Dean pushed past Jim and went into the barn to find the horse gone. Jim was following, and Dean turned on him: "What the hell's going on?"

"You tell me."

"You think I took him out of here?" Dean asked. "Why the fuck would I do that?"

"I don't know. Why did you?"

Dean turned to look at the empty stall, his mind working. "Go back to the bush, Jim. That horse trailer's still sitting there where Paulie and I left it." He paused. "Shit, you don't think Paulie—"

Jim jumped at the suggestion. "Well, it wasn't me, and it wasn't you."

Dean wasn't convinced. He opened the stall door and had a closer look inside. Then he walked over to the exterior door on the east end of the barn and opened it and stepped outside. There were hoof prints scuffed in the dirt there.

"They took him out here," he said.

When he came back in he saw something on the bench just inside the door. "What the hell's this?"

There was an extension cord and a pair of leather gloves on the bench. Dean picked them up and showed them to Jim, who was still standing by the stall, looking inside as if he thought the stallion might somehow reappear by magic.

"This stuff belong to you?"

Jim walked over. The extension cord had its wires stripped

back, and there were alligator clips on the ends. "Jesus," he said when he saw it. "They killed the horse."

"They didn't kill the fucking horse," Dean said. "What—you think they killed him and then dragged him out of here?" He looked at the extension cord again. "But they were sure as hell gonna kill him. They musta changed their minds."

"You think Paulie?"

"Paulie wouldn't step on a bug," Dean said. "Lookit these gloves, read what it says. One hundred percent calfskin, made in Italy. These aren't work gloves. These are a rich boy's gloves."

He handed the gloves over to Jim, and then he took a long look around the barn, sniffing the air as if it might give him a clue. There was no getting around it. There was only one person who would benefit by killing the horse. There was only one person he knew who was capable of killing the horse. And there was only one person who would wear hundred-dollar Italian leather gloves to do it.

"Sonny was here," he said. "Sure as shit."

Jim was growing nervous. On the one hand, he wanted it to have been Sonny, because if it wasn't, then Sonny was going to show up at noon, looking for a horse they didn't have and exposing Jim's double cross. On the other hand, if it was Sonny, Dean was going to want to know how he knew where to come.

"That fucking Paulie rolled over on us," Jim said. "Probably went to Sonny and made a deal."

Dean nodded absently and walked back to the doorway and looked outside. It didn't add up. He turned back to Jim, and he held the extension cord out for display.

"Sonny came here to kill the horse," Dean said. "For the insurance. That part I get; it's what Sonny would do. What I don't get is why he changed his mind."

"Maybe Paulie talked him out of it," Jim said, working Paulie's name into the conversation again.

"Paulie wouldn't have anything to do with this," Dean

said, indicating the cord again. "Not for a minute and not for a million dollars. I doubt he was even here."

"Sonofabitch gave us up, though, didn't he?"

"I guess so. That fucking Sonny is up to something, though. Otherwise he'd have shown up here with Jackson Jones and a couple carloads of cops, lights flashing. Hell, he'd call the newspapers. You know something—I bet Jackson don't even know Sonny's got the horse. What the fuck is he up to?"

"Maybe he still figures to kill him. He just didn't want to do it here."

"Why not? If he does it here, it looks like we did it. No, he's got something else in mind. That's the problem with Sonny—you never know what the fuck he's gonna do."

Dean turned and walked out of the barn, heading for the truck. Jim followed at a distance. Now that he'd convinced Dean that Paulie was the rat, Jim was back to thinking about how he was going to profit from all this. The possibility seemed a little iffy, now that they no longer actually *had* the horse. Sonny sure as hell wasn't going to honor his offer of the ten grand, not after sneaking in here in the dead of night and stealing the nag. It seemed to Jim that you couldn't trust anybody these days.

"Where you going?" he asked Dean when they were outside.

"I'm gonna take a drive," Dean said. "That fucking Sonny's about to pull a fast one, and I gotta figure out how. Remember, if he does kill the horse, we're the ones gonna get blamed for it."

Dean got into the truck and powered down the window.

"Yeah, well—you remember you owe me five grand," Jim told him.

Jim was standing by the door of the truck, trying to look defiant and hard done by, like he was the only one in the whole situation holding up his end. Dean gave him a look like he had two heads, and then drove off without a word.

. . .

In general, people had little respect for Dean's intelligence. And while there were times when Dean didn't do a hell of a lot to refute the notion, the truth of the matter was, given enough time and enough information, Dean's powers of deduction were as good as most.

By the time he'd driven a couple of miles he knew that Paulie wasn't the rat. Even though Paulie might have been concerned about the horse's safety, he wasn't the one who rolled over. Dean knew this because he knew that Paulie would never go to Sonny. Paulie hated Sonny as much as anybody. If Paulie was worried about the horse, he'd have gone to Jackson. Jackson had always treated Paulie decently, like a human being.

So if Paulie wasn't the rat, then Jim Burnside was. Which is why he was so anxious to tar and feather Paulie. Shit, he'd probably helped Sonny load the horse in the trailer. Sonny had paid him off and been gone. Dean wondered what Jim had gotten for the double cross.

He drove around north of the city, keeping to the side roads. He was nervous driving the Stanton Stables truck so close to the scene of the crime, even though he'd painted over the logos on the doors. As he drove he listened to the radio, catching as many newscasts as he could. There was nothing about the missing horse turning up.

He went to the casino and parked around back, beside the black Navigator. Big Billy Coon was in the back room, sitting behind the bar and watching a tape of a heavyweight fight from Las Vegas.

When Billy saw Dean, he smiled and said, "Look at you, walking round, bold as day."

"Hey, Billy."

"Get yourself a beer."

Dean went to the cooler and grabbed a Corona. It seemed

to him that Billy was being awful friendly for some reason. He'd been unsure whether to come; he knew that Sonny spent time here and that Sonny and Billy were acquainted, were maybe even good friends. He opened the beer and went to sit at the bar.

"Stole any good horses lately?" Billy asked.

"Just the one."

"Crazy bastard. What the hell you gonna do with him?"

"I don't have him anymore. Sonny's got him back."

"Hell, I never heard anything about it."

"You're not gonna hear anything about it. Sonny found out where I had him stashed and stole him back in the middle of the night. I got a feeling he hasn't told anybody. If he did, it'd be on the news. He's up to something, Billy."

"He always is."

"He been here?"

"Breeders' Cup, he spent the day here. Never had a winner, dropped ninety-five grand on the ponies and more at cards. The ninety-five he still owes," Billy added.

"He ran a tab on a hundred grand?"

"Yup, and his leash is getting shorter every day. He's got that gray Rather Rambunctious running in the stakes race on Sunday. He should romp—they're dropping him down—and Sonny better pay me out of the purse, or I'm gonna send a couple of the cousins over to his place to cut his balls off and bring 'em to me. I'll pickle 'em and put 'em in a jar above the bar here. Just a little reminder for folks who might find themselves delinquent in their debts."

Dean took a long drink of the beer and had a look above the bar. There were indeed jars of pickled meats there. Dean decided he didn't want to know the nature of the contents.

"What do you suppose he's doing with that horse, Dean?"

"I'll be goddamned if I know," Dean said. "That's the problem with a guy like Sonny. His brain doesn't work like a normal person's. There's no telling what he's gonna do. The only thing you can count on is that it'll be fucked up when he does it."

Sonny woke up feeling like Elvis must've felt most mornings. It had been daylight when he'd returned from the Burnside farm, and he had still been flying from the speed in his system. He'd attempted to counter it with Demerol and vodka and finally fell asleep at about nine. The cocktail mix, however, was messing with his head this afternoon. He took more Demerol when he got up, and then went downstairs and ate a bowl of Frosted Flakes. Now he was sitting in the kitchen, looking out the window to the barn, where he knew Jackson was at work, and trying to decide whether he should tell Jackson about Jim Burnside's visit, and about his own early morning excursion to the Burnside farm.

He was inclined not to mention any of it. Jackson would be sure to tell him that he'd fucked up again, just as he had with Paulie. As if Jackson's presence would have changed anything this time. Even Jackson couldn't pull a horse out of thin air. Besides, nothing had changed with regard to the situation. Sonny was of the opinion that Dean had somehow been spooked—maybe Jim got cold feet and tipped him off—and moved the stallion before Sonny had arrived. After all, there'd been no sign of the truck and the horse trailer at the farm.

He had the option of sending the cops to the Burnside farm to see what they could get out of the old piss-tank, if he was still around. He began to warm up to the idea. Jim Burnside was a leaky vessel, Sonny suspected, and he would spill whatever he knew, if properly persuaded.

But when he was having his first vodka and tonic he suddenly remembered that he'd left the extension cord in Burnside's barn and that decided it as far as Jackson or the cops were concerned. If the cord turned up, with the alligator clips, they would know exactly what Sonny had been planning.

There was nothing to do but pretend the whole incident

had not happened. Maybe Dean would do the right thing and kill the goddamn horse himself.

The mail was on the table. Glancing through it, he spotted a letter from a lawyer in town, a name he didn't recognize. He opened it; it was notice that Etta Parr was fighting his note on her father's farm. Sonny felt his anger rise.

He pulled his jacket on and walked out to the barn. Jackson was in his office, and he was looking at a printout of Sunday's Woodbine entries. The bandage was gone from his head, and Sonny could see the arc of stitches above his left ear.

"How's the gray looking?" Sonny asked.

"He'll win," Jackson said. He was still pissed and didn't bother to look up.

"What's in the field?" Sonny asked.

Jackson tossed the papers across the desk. "Just six horses," he said. "Four trainers pulled their mounts, probably 'cause we're running the gray. We can expect some comments about that."

"Fuck 'em," Sonny said, looking at the sheet.

"You talk to the cops?"

"No."

"Why not, Sonny?"

"Why would I talk to the cops?"

Jackson gave him a look. "You saw Paulie last night. If Paulie's in the area, then Dean's in the area. If Dean's in the area, then maybe—just maybe—the horse is in the area. And everybody beating the bushes down in Kentucky can go home to a big ol' heaping plate of opossum and collard greens. None of this occurred to you, Sonny?"

"It's not like we know where Dean is. Or Paulie either."

"I was thinking maybe that's where the cops would come in handy." Jackson's voice was heavy with sarcasm, his eyes on Sonny like he was looking at a stray dog that had just pissed on his pant leg.

"They haven't been much good to us so far," Sonny said.

"Never mind. I'll call them myself."

"I'll do it," Sonny said quickly. "Matter of fact, I'll stop by the station on my way to town. You gonna work the gray today?"

"I breezed him this morning. You work horses in the morning, Sonny."

Sonny drove into the city. He didn't stop at the police station. The more he thought about it, the more he was convinced he didn't want the horse back. And the longer the horse was in the hands of those idiots, the better the chances he wouldn't make it through alive.

He went to the track and drank a half-dozen Bloody Marys in the lounge, watching the races on the screen and telling everybody who would listen that his big gray was going to win the Stanton Stakes. He presently found himself drinking alone, and he left.

Driving back out of the city, he stopped at the country club for a drink in the bar. The place was largely empty. The pins had been pulled earlier that week and the course shut down. The clubhouse would stay open over the course of the winter as a service to the members, but with no golfers, business was greatly reduced.

There was no one there to get drunk with, so Sonny left after a couple of drinks. In the car he popped another Demerol and started for home, then decided to drive out to Holden County to have a look at his acquisitions there.

He really had no intention of stopping at Etta Parr's place until he found himself pulling into the driveway. Sometimes it seemed that he had no real control over his actions, that his muscles simply took over from his brain. When it happened he quite often found himself in trouble, and when he did Sonny always rationalized that it was not his fault because he really wasn't in charge.

It was nearly dark as he coasted up to the house and parked behind the Taurus in the driveway. The house lights were on.

. . .

Etta was getting ready to go to work. She heard the car approaching, and she knew it was too early for Mabel. She thought for a moment that Ray had returned. Maybe he'd found a passage in the good book that advocated the fixing of horse races. She turned on the porch light, and when she looked out the window she saw Sonny getting out of his car. Watching him walk, she realized at once he was wasted.

Homer was in the living room, and she went quickly past him and up the stairs and into her room. She unlocked the top drawer of the old rolltop and found the little automatic and slipped it into the pocket of her jacket.

By the time she got downstairs Sonny was already in the house, standing in the doorway to the living room and looking at Homer.

After a moment Homer turned toward him. "Sonny!" he shouted. "My old buddy—come on in!"

"Homer, would you shut up," Etta said sharply as she walked past him. "He's not your old buddy."

Sonny looked wired and cocky, his eyes drooped with fatigue or booze or whatever. Etta was incensed that he would walk right in.

"What can I do for you?" she asked.

"Etta, what're you doing hiring a lawyer? You gotta be smarter than that."

"Sonny! Want a drink?" Homer was grinning.

"Homer, would you stop," Etta said. "You better leave," she told Sonny.

"Listen, I'll tear up the note," Sonny said, slurring the first word. "You'll end up losing the place anyway. Sell it to me outright. I'll forgive whatever's owed, give you a good price." He stumbled over the last word as well.

"I'm not dealing with you," Etta said. "I'll take a bath on the place before I sell to you."

"I'd like to see you take a bath, Etta. When's this gonna happen?"

"You'll be leaving now, Sonny."

She stepped past him, toward the door, hoping he would follow her lead. He stood his ground and looked again at Homer.

"What do you need all this land for anyway?" he asked. "You're no farmer, and that idiot over there can't tie his shoes."

"You're sick," she said. "Are you even aware of that?"

She saw him stiffen, but he turned and walked to the door. She followed, anxious to usher him out. He moved slowly, insolently, making a show of taking in the contents of the room. He turned back to her at the door and smiled, looking to see if he was out of Homer's sight. Suddenly, his hand was on her throat.

"Don't ever talk to me like that," he said, his voice cheery and light, as if he was imparting an amiable bit of advice. His breath was terrible.

Etta gripped his wrist with her left hand and at the same time slipped her right hand onto the pistol in her pocket. "Get your hand off me," she said, trying to control her tone, in spite of the fear.

Sonny increased the pressure for a second, cutting off her wind. "Why don't you call your boyfriend?"

"What?"

"Where's Dokes? Come on, Etta. You think this is about you? I could care less about you and this shit-hole. But your man Ray is gonna answer for what he did."

"I don't see him. I have no idea where he is."

"Now don't you lie to me." Sonny released his grip. His voice remained light. "You might piss me off, and I'm not a lot of fun when I'm pissed off. Ask Ray's sister, although I think she kinda liked it. Hard to tell with a retard."

When he was gone she pulled the gun from her pocket and looked at it. She had no idea how to shoot the thing. But she was very curious about the fact that she had been willing to try.

She had to work that night, another twelve-hour shift. She left Homer with Mabel and drove into town. She told Mabel to lock the doors and not open them to anyone. She was still shaking as she drove, nearly an hour after he'd left. What if he'd have shown up an hour later, with Etta gone? She doubted Mabel was a match for Sonny.

It was a quiet night at the hospital. There was an emergency cesarean early on, and then nothing until eleven o'clock when two young hockey players came in, both bleeding freely from cuts on their faces. They'd duked it out on the ice and then been driven by their respective trainers to the hospital for repairs. They were loud and obnoxious, the pair of them, all testosterone boast and bad judgment. After Doctor Wan, who'd performed the cesarean, stitched up their wounds, they began to yap at each other in the reception area and then ended up in another fistfight in the parking lot. Both had their stitches ripped open. After the fight they traipsed back inside for more treatment. Doctor Wan went ballistic at the prospect; it took Etta and the reception nurse fifteen minutes to convince him to stitch them up again. By this time, both players were sitting side by side in the waiting room, looking sheepish and talking about going for a beer.

When Etta got off in the morning, she drove over to the parish and was relieved to see Tim Regan's car in the parking lot. She found him in the rectory, drinking coffee and poring over some papers, the nature of which appeared, to Etta's eye, to be more financial than spiritual.

"Well, Miss Nightingale," Tim said when he saw her outfit.

"Hi, Tim," Etta said, and she sat down. She indicated the ledger. "Trying to figure out how the church can buy my farm?"

"The church has more interest in your soul than your acreage, Etta."

"Then I'll sell 'em both to you," Etta said. "Give you a good deal, padre. Two for one. How can you say no?"

Regan closed the ledger and leaned back in his chair and clasped his hands together behind his neck. He wore jeans and a ribbed sweater. He hadn't shaved, and he looked more like a weekend sportsman than a priest.

"How's it going, Etta?"

"Oh, you know," she said easily. "Good days and bad. How about you?"

"Life is good," he said simply.

"Oh, did I mention that I almost shot a man last night?"

Regan came forward in his chair, bringing his hands down on the desk. He waited in vain for some indication of jocularity. "Maybe you'd better tell me about it."

"Sonny Stanton showed up on my doorstep, fired up on liquor and pharmaceuticals. Advising me that he was in the catbird's seat and that I'd be wise to sell to him, rather than look for a buyer elsewhere. He called my father names, and then we ended up by the back door with his grimy hand around my throat. I had my hand on a gun in my pocket, and I was thinking real seriously about busting one of the commandments, Tim. The big one."

"Why do you have a gun?"

"I've been dating Charlton Heston. Shouldn't you be more concerned with the fact that I was thinking about using it?"

"I am. I'm also concerned that he's walking into your house like this. Did you call the police?"

"No. What're they gonna do—give him a stern talking-to like they did when he raped Elizabeth?"

"There are laws to protect you, Etta."

"I don't have a lot of faith in them."

"Lack of faith seems to be your problem these days."

"Lack of money is my problem these days. I don't want him to end up with the place, Tim. Especially after last night. And if I sell it to somebody else, he'll just step in and buy it from them. Plus, I'll still have to pay him the forty thousand I owe. But if I sell it to the church, then you won't sell to him.

He'll be screwed. Even Sonny Stanton has gotta back down from the Catholic Church."

He listened to her discourse, his eyes on the desktop. There was fatigue in her voice, and an urgency that she was trying hard to disguise. When he looked up she was watching him with feigned optimism.

"Etta," he said. "This just isn't something the church is involved in. You must know that."

She brushed off his apology and got to her feet. "Well, I thought maybe you could have a chat with . . . the powers that be."

"I speak to Him every day."

"Yeah?" She got to her feet and pointed to the paperwork on the table. "What do you and the big guy do to pass the time these days—crunch a few numbers?"

"That's not fair, Etta."

"You let me know when you find something that is," she said, and she left.

20

Paulie leaned against the section of rail fence that separated the bean field from the bush lot and watched Chrissie ride Jumping Jack Flash. The field belonged to Pete's neighbor to the west, and it had been recently harvested; the leaves left behind provided a cushion underfoot, and while it wasn't the ideal track for working a horse, it was the best they could do under the circumstances. It wasn't like they could take the animal to Woodbine and run him for the whole world to see.

The horse had been idle since the kidnaping, and he was revved up and ready to run. Chrissie had held him in at first, loping him around the perimeter of the field, and then finally ran him flat-out for a distance she guessed to be about six furlongs.

Paulie stood along the fence and watched. He was wearing an old Stetson given to him by Pete Culpepper. The hat had seen many years, and there was a hole in the crease on the crown, and it was maybe half a size too big for Paulie's head, coming to rest on his ears. Paulie had been real attached to the hat he'd lost in the parking lot, but he was already partial to the Stetson.

After running the horse out, Chrissie cantered him back to the fencerow where Paulie stood. The horse was still full of energy, prancing sideways and snorting, fighting the bit. Paulie took him by the bridle and talked to him, and he settled.

Chrissie crossed her leg over the saddle and patted the bay's neck.

"Oh, Paulie," she said. "I never had a horse like this under me. This motherfucker can fly. I never even put the pedal down."

"We better walk him out," Paulie said.

She jumped down and removed the saddle while Paulie slipped the bridle off and replaced it with a nylon hackamore. Then they started back for the barn through the bush, where a lane had been cut for snowmobilers and dirt bikers, Chrissie carrying the saddle, Paulie leading the horse by the halter.

Ray had tracked down Chrissie at Woodbine, where she'd been picking up a few mounts for the big boys. When he'd approached her with the scheme to fix a race, she'd turned him down immediately, was actually pissed that he would suggest it.

When he'd mentioned that it was Sonny Stanton who would get screwed, she'd changed her mind.

Now she and Paulie and the bay stallion made their way through the trees, with the leaves underfoot and the bare branches of the hardwoods overhead. The sky was overcast and gray, a typical November day, but there was no wind and the temperature was mild. As they walked the horse continually nuzzled at Paulie's pocket, looking for a treat, but Pete had warned Paulie not to spoil the animal before the race.

"One thing about him," Paulie remembered as they walked. "He hates to go into the starting gate. You have to trick him: open the gate so he thinks he can go right through; then when he's in, slam 'em both shut, front and back."

"I've seen that before," Chrissie said.

"Well, that's what you gotta do."

They came out of the bush and onto the lane that led back to the barn and Pete Culpepper's house. The lane was bordered by split-rail fences, and the grass underfoot was soft and tangled. There was a pond along the edge of the bush, and as they passed, a half-dozen mallards burst forth from the reedy shore, squawking loudly as they flew off.

"So do you think he can win?" Paulie asked.

Chrissie snorted. "They'd have to stick a rocket up that gray's ass for him to beat this horse. And there's nothing else in the race."

"I hope you're right."

Chrissie looked at Paulie's face, at the black eye and the stitches that surrounded it. Ray had told her about the incident behind the Tap. She'd spent most of the past two days with the kid and the horse; Chrissie had always had a special rapport with animals, but she'd never seen anyone who could put a horse at ease like Paulie. The stallion was like a damn snapping turtle with anybody who got close to him. All Paulie had to do was speak to the animal, and he quieted down like he'd been drugged.

"We'll win the race," she told him. "It's the rest of it I'm not too sure about. I don't know if anybody's ever pulled something like this off before."

"But if they did and never got caught, you'd never know. Ray seems like a pretty smart guy."

"Ray's a pretty determined guy. As far as him being smart, I guess we're gonna find out about that."

When they got back to the barn Ray was in the stall with the gelding Fast Market. He had a large pair of tin snips in his hand, and he was cutting the cast from the horse's leg. The gelding was standing patiently under the task, his shoulder close along the wall of the stall. When Paulie and Chrissie passed with the stallion, the horse threw his head in the air and showed his teeth to the gelding, but Paulie kept him straight and led him into the stall at the back of the barn. Paulie rubbed him down with an old blanket and began to brush him out.

Chrissie watched for a moment, and then she came back and leaned over the top rail of the gelding's stall and looked in.

"How'd he run?" Ray asked.

"Like Seabiscuit," Chrissie said. "You sure that cast is ready to come off?"

"I hope so. We're gonna need this horse on Sunday."

"What you gonna need him for?"

"Well, that's part of the overall plan."

Ray was cutting with one hand now, while clumsily pulling the cast away from the leg with the other, mindful of catching the horse's leg with the snips. Chrissie opened the stall door and went inside to help.

"Why don't you tell me the overall plan?" she asked.

"I would," Ray said. "But I'm afraid you might cut and run."

"I don't cut and run, cowboy."

She grabbed the fiberglass with both hands and pulled it apart while Ray cut. They had the cast off in a couple minutes. The leg was foul smelling, and Ray went into the house for a bucket of warm water and a quart of rubbing alcohol. He and Chrissie cleaned the horse's leg and then rubbed him down with the alcohol.

"Well, let's take him outside and let him walk," Ray said.

Paulie was finished with the stallion now, and he followed them outside to the corral. He and Ray leaned on the fence and watched as Chrissie walked the gelding slowly around the enclosure. The horse was uneasy putting weight on the leg.

"He's got a limp for sure," Chrissie said.

"That's good," Ray said. "I want him to favor it."

"You do?"

"Yup."

"I suppose that's part of the overall plan?"

"Yup."

They heard a vehicle and turned to see Pete Culpepper coming down the driveway in his pickup. He parked in front of the house and then got out and walked over. He was wearing an old pair of dress pants and a blue suit coat over a denim shirt, his good Stetson. Dressed up, for Pete.

"Is he sound?" he said, looking at the gelding.

"Sound enough, I hope," Ray said. "How'd you make out?"

"Do I look like a crazy old man?" Pete asked by way of reply.

Ray stole a quick glance at the others, who were watching Pete warily.

"Why would you ask that?" Ray said.

"I want to know if I look like a crazy old man," Pete said. "Because when I went to Woodbine and entered my nine-year-old gelding in the Stanton Stakes, everybody there looked at me like I was a crazy old man."

Ray was lighting a cigarette, and he grinned around the smoke. "I bet they did."

"The part that worries me is they might be right," Pete said.

"Well, I could tell you that you aren't any crazier than the rest of us, but that probably wouldn't give you much consolation," Ray said.

"Not one bit."

Pete pushed his hat back with his thumb and put his foot on the bottom rail of the corral. Ray watched as Paulie copied the old man's moves precisely, looking over slyly to see if he had the hat just right.

Chrissie walked the gelding over to the far side of the corral and back again. The animal wasn't favoring the leg so much that he seemed to be in actual pain, Ray decided. The joint would be stiff from the cast, and the animal was just naturally cautious about it.

"I guess we can put him back inside," Ray said.

Paulie went and opened the barn door for Chrissie, and they both went inside with the horse.

"So there was no problem?" Ray asked. "Other than the question of your sanity?"

"I had to pay a supplement for late entry," Pete said.

"How much?"

"Five thousand."

"Where the hell'd you get five grand? Oh—the ten you got from that acre piece?"

"I gave that back." Pete took a half plug of Redman from his pocket and bit off a chaw. He turned toward the barn for a moment, then spit in the dirt. "Chrissie put it up."

"Jesus." Ray hung his forearms over the top rail. "I don't know about this, Pete. I've always been real willing to fuck up my own life, but I never liked to drag other people into it. If this blows up in our faces, there's gonna be a lot of people in a lot of trouble."

"Well, we ain't quittin' now, Ray." Pete nodded toward the barn. "That Paulie—he's a damn good kid. You see the change in him already? Hell, he even walks different. When he first got here, he'd walk into a room like he was apologizing for something. And now he don't. All I did was give him an old hat, and he thinks I'm the second coming. He's been told his whole life he ain't worth nothin', by people like Sonny Stanton. Calling him down and hitting on him. His whole life. Now maybe I done a few things I shouldn't have done, and maybe you done a few things you shouldn't have done, and maybe when the last steer is branded we ain't much better than Sonny. But I gotta believe we're a little bit better than Sonny, and I'd like to show that kid that it's so. I'd like to show him that the Sonny Stantons in the world don't always come out on top."

It was a long speech for Pete Culpepper. When it was done Ray looked at his old friend a moment, and then he flicked his cigarette into the dirt. "I wouldn't mind knowing that myself," he said.

When Chrissie came out of the barn she was carrying a short length of hemp rope in her hand, and with it she was showing Paulie how to make a hackamore. Paulie hung on her every word like it was the gospel, and when she was finished she pulled the rigging apart and let him have a try. Then she walked over to Ray and asked, "What's next, boss?"

"Next we have to figure how to change that bay into a chestnut," Ray said. "We can use Pete's bay mare as a guinea pig; she's about the same color as the stud."

"How you gonna do it?" Chrissie asked.

"I was hoping you could tell me," Ray said. "I've noticed that women like to color their hair."

"This is my natural color, if that's what you're getting at," Chrissie said. "I dyed my hair once, in high school. It was purple."

"I can't see us fooling a lot of people with a purple horse," Pete said.

"I'll go to the drugstore after lunch and see what they got in a chestnut brown," Chrissie said. "We are gonna eat lunch, aren't we?"

They went into the house, and Pete cooked up hamburgers and fried potatoes, and the four of them sat at the kitchen table to eat. Pete hung his hat on a peg inside the back door when he came in, and Paulie was halfway through his first hamburger before he noticed, and then he got up and hung his hat alongside. When they were finished eating, Pete made a pot of coffee, and they all had a cup.

"There's one thing nobody's mentioned," Pete said. "How you gonna pass that stallion off as a gelding. And don't tell me we're gonna geld the sonofabitch."

"Might improve his disposition if we did," Ray said. "But no, we're not gonna geld him. I figure he's doing us a favor, and that'd be a hell of a way to repay a favor. The thing is, when it comes to *cajones,* a horse isn't like an Aberdeen bull. You have to get pretty close to see 'em. I figure we braid his tail up, maybe weight it down some so he can't swing it, and we'll just take our chances. And he's a nasty piece of work; nobody's gonna want to get too close behind him. And when he's on the track, the plan is for him to be moving so fast that nobody'll get a look at anything."

"What about afterward, in the winner's circle?" Chrissie asked.

"That's gonna take some fancy footwork," Ray said.

"Because Sonny and Jackson Jones are both gonna be there," Pete said. "Before and after."

"I'm guessing Sonny will be in the bar," Ray said. "Jackson will watch the race from the clubhouse, with the high hats. But you're right; Jackson knows that horse better than anybody, and he'll be tough to con. We have to get out of there before he gets close."

"What about afterward?" Chrissie said. "The grooms and the hot walkers are gonna see something; you're never gonna keep this quiet."

"Monday, we tell Jackson he gets his horse back, safe and sound, if there's no questions asked," Ray said. "He'll do it to get the horse back. And Jackson's word is good."

"What about Sonny?" Pete asked. "You gonna trust his word if he finds out?"

"Not on your nelly."

Ray looked at Paulie across the table. Paulie was watching Chrissie at the counter, pouring more coffee. Pete was right; the kid seemed more at home on the farm each day.

"What if Sonny was in on it?" Ray asked.

"Yeah, we'll just call him up," Chrissie said.

Ray sat there thinking. "What if somebody else called him up?"

Ray dropped Chrissie off at the drugstore in the mall, and then he drove over to ask Tiny Montgomery where he might find Misty. Tiny sent him to the Ramada but said he didn't know if she was still around. She'd only been at the club once since her encounter with Sonny, and that had been to get her pay.

"Hard to say where you might find her," Tiny said as Ray left.

Ray thought about it as he drove across town, heading for the Ramada. Finding her would be the first problem.

Convincing her would be the second.

After Ray and Chrissie had left, Paulie gathered up the dishes and ran the sink full of water and set to washing them. Pete finished his coffee and then came over, dumped his cup in the dishwater, and then took up a dish towel and began to dry.

"I see you got a For Sale sign out front," Paulie said.

"Yup," Pete said. "You in the market?"

"No. I don't have any money. It's sure a nice farm, though."

They finished up the dishes and then sat at the table while Pete had a cigarette and Paulie patted the Walker hound. It was a warm day, and there was no reason to have the space heater on. After a moment Pete went over and shut it off.

"Looks like I'm heading to Texas when this is over," he said when he sat back down. "Ain't really fair to drag that hound all that way at his age. Would you consider taking him?"

"I'd like to, but I don't have anyplace for him," Paulie said.

"Where do you live, anyway?" Pete asked.

"I just got a room at a motel."

"You live in a motel?"

"Yeah, just a room."

Pete put out his smoke in the ashtray. Paulie had hold of the loose skin at the scruff on the hound's neck and was shaking it gently, and the hound had his eyes closed and his neck arched.

"How old are you, Paulie?"

"Twenty-three."

Pete leaned back and looked out the window. The two broodmares and the new foal were moving along the fencerow in front of the barn, the mares walking single file, heading for some spot near the lane, where there was grazing or maybe something else altogether, something that would be of interest to broodmares only. The foal was full of piss and vinegar, kicking her heels and running back and forth, circling her mother, her head high. Less than a week old, and she was as confident as a cock rooster. Pete watched the horses, and he tried to recall being twenty-three.

He liked to tell stories about his wild youth—about the panhandle and oil derricks and flat-head Fords. Flush Fridays and busted flat Mondays. Pretty Texas girls in thin summer dresses. The problem was, he couldn't remember what was truth and what was made up anymore. It was a hell of a thing when a man couldn't distinguish between what he'd lived and what he'd invented.

"Maybe I'll bring that mare up to the corral for Ray," he heard Paulie say, and he turned to see him standing at the door, the Stetson in his hand.

"Yeah," Pete said. "Take a pail of grain, she'll come right to you."

"Okay," Paulie said, and he opened the door.

"Paulie, why do you suppose Sonny is the way he is?"

"I don't know. My mother used to say that it just seemed like the devil had a lot more interest in Sonny than he did in other people."

Paulie walked out onto the porch, and the hound followed him. After a few moments Pete saw him walking into the pasture field, a grain bucket in his hand, the animal still on his heels. It was the first time in a year the old dog had ventured that far from the house. Pete Culpepper sat at the kitchen table, watching the two crossing the field and trying to remember what it was like when he was twenty-three.

Sonny was in the den, watching the PGA on the satellite, when the phone rang. He set the clicker down, reached for the phone with one hand and his drink with the other. He said hello, watching the television.

"Sonny Stanton?"

"You got him."

"This is Detective Frank Harmer," the voice said. "Metro police."

Sonny's hand froze on his drink. "Is this about my horse?" he asked.

"No, it's not about your horse. We've had a complaint lodged against you by a young woman. She claims you assaulted her."

Sonny's heart jumped in his throat. He took a drink, tried to keep his tone nonchalant. "Who is this woman?"

"She's a dancer at a club. That's all the information you get for now. Do you have anything to say about this?"

"Yeah—I never assaulted anybody."

There was a short silence. "Listen, Sonny. I know your father."

"What's your name again?"

"Detective Frank Harmer."

Sonny had never heard of the man. "You say you know Dad?"

"I've known him for twenty-five years. Now, there's going to be a warrant issued for your arrest. I can stall it for twenty-four hours. If you can get in touch with this woman before then and settle this, maybe we can avoid a bad situation. You've had problems in this area before. Do you know what I'm saying?"

Sonny was staring at the set, and as he watched, Sergio Garcia sank a forty-foot putt for eagle, then leaped in the air and ran across the green, pumping his fist. Sonny took another drink and then set his glass down.

"This allegation is complete nonsense," he said into the phone. "Let me talk to the woman."

"You've got twenty-four hours."

Pete hung the phone up and looked across the room at Ray, who was leaning against the counter and watching him expectantly. Chrissie and Paulie were sitting at the table, also looking on.

Pete just shrugged his shoulders. "Wait and see," he said.

"Who's Frank Harmer?" Ray asked.

"A good old Texas lawman from the days of yore," Pete said.

"Does he know you're using his name?" Chrissie asked.

"He's dead," Pete told her.

"So are we," Chrissie told him, "if we get found out."

There was a cold wind off the lake and a buildup of dark clouds over the green hills of Pennsylvania on the far shore. Etta parked in the driveway and got out of the car and was hit with the frigid air. Pulling her jacket around her, she hurried to the house. It had been unseasonably warm at her place.

In the kitchen, Mary greeted her with a hug and told her to sit down for coffee. Etta sat at the old wooden table. There was the smell of baking in the air, but then there always was. Today it held the promise of cinnamon and brown sugar.

"We haven't seen you for a while," Mary said. The coffee had been brewed, and she poured two cups.

"I'm sorry about that," Etta said. "There's been a lot going on."

Mary sat down. "I'll have some buns in about ten minutes."

"Coffee's fine," Etta said. And then: "How is she?"

Mary offered a look that suggested she was growing weary of the question.

"I'm sorry," Etta said. "Am I supposed to stop asking?"

Mary sipped at her coffee, then left the cup on the table as she got up to have a look in the oven. She used an oven mitt to pull a pan halfway out, then slid it back and closed the oven door. She sat down again, apparently satisfied that things were progressing as they should.

"Ray was here."

"Today?" Etta asked in surprise.

"Last week."

"Oh."

"Have you seen him?"

"Oh, I've seen him. He's about to get himself in shit."

Elizabeth was sitting in the studio, wearing shapeless cotton pants and a heavy pullover and looking out the French doors. The room faced the lake, and the windows were inexpertly sealed, allowing the cold drafts to penetrate. She turned at the sound of Etta entering and smiled when she saw her.

"Hey," Etta said.

When she moved closer she saw Elizabeth tense up, and she backed away at once, knowing that physical contact was not always welcome. Etta pulled a chair up and sat down. The paintings of the lake were scattered about the room; there must have been fifty of them in all. Etta looked from one to another, hoping to find some diverse subject matter and knowing in her heart that she wouldn't. There was a half-finished canvas on the easel.

"You've been busy," she said.

"Not really," Elizabeth said. She was looking out over the water again. "You've been gone a long time."

"I guess."

Elizabeth smiled as if they had shared a joke, and she continued to watch out the window. In spite of the wind the surface of the bay was flat, with the occasional ripple skipping across the water like a series of flat stones.

"Ray was here," Elizabeth said.

"So I keep hearing."

"I think I've disappointed him."

"You know that's not true."

"He expects me to be as strong as him." The slight sad smile never left Elizabeth's face.

"It's not about strength. It's about happiness. I think he would like for you to be happy."

"Happiness." After a moment Elizabeth turned her head toward Etta. "What does Ray know about happiness?"

"Well, you know your brother. I'm not convinced he believes it's available to him. He's his own version of Robin Hood—he believes he can give it to other people."

Elizabeth's smile was genuine this time. "Hooray for Robin Hood."

Etta looked out over the lake and saw a man in a small aluminum punt heading out into the bay. The man appeared to be elderly, and he pulled stiffly at the oars, heading for a yellow buoy a couple hundred yards from the rock point that marked the west edge of the inlet.

When he reached the buoy the man tied the boat to it and then bent over the side of the punt and pulled up an iron anchor to which was attached a plastic water line and foot valve. The man unfastened the anchor and put it and the buoy in the boat and then tied the water line to the bow. Etta watched as he started back for shore, the punt pulsing slowly forward with each stroke of the oars. The water line formed a wide arc on the surface and followed him along.

"Have you been painting?" she heard Elizabeth ask.

"Not really."

"How long has it been?"

"A long time. I haven't painted since . . . it's been a long time."

"You haven't painted since I was raped," Elizabeth said matter-of-factly. "Isn't it strange that I still paint and you don't?"

"I don't know that I would call this painting, what you do," Etta said, looking about the studio. "You may have fallen into a bit of a rut, kid."

"You can only paint what you feel. If you're honest, anyway. Every time I sit at the easel I start a different painting, and every time I paint the same scene. My hands are no longer connected to my brain. I want to be me, and yet I can't be."

She stopped talking and was now watching the man in the aluminum punt. She was still smiling the wan smile but there were tears in her eyes.

"Do you know what I mean?" Elizabeth asked Etta.

"Not really."

"He didn't leave enough of me to live my life."

Etta left with that and a half-dozen apple cinnamon buns. Following the lake road, she drove slowly until her eyes dried and her anger settled into something more manageable, resentment maybe. When she reached the highway she went into a convenience store and bought her first pack of cigarettes in ten years.

She headed back north, smoking and punching the radio buttons in search of something that might improve her mood. Maybe Coltrane would help. Or Cohen. Hell, she'd give old Spike Jones a try if she could find him on the dial.

She wondered what it would be like to feel at peace with the world. She'd long held the suspicion that she was missing out on one extraordinary truth just around the corner. So she had kept turning corners, only to find more.

It was around one such corner that she'd found Ray. And while he was not the truth she'd been seeking, he was indeed one of the things she'd been missing. Not that he'd been looking for the same. With Ray, it was never a matter of spiritual enlightenment or a quest for one shining moment. His motives were a lot simpler than that. In fact, he was a lot simpler than that. With him it was all instinct, and that was one of the things she admired about him. It was also the thing that drove her crazy.

It was midafternoon and sunny when Etta pulled into the driveway at Pete Culpepper's place. She drove up beside Pete's pickup, parked, and got out. There was a crowd in the corral off the end of the barn. Pete was sitting on a wooden chair just outside the barn door; he had a western saddle on a stand in front of him and he was working oil into the leather with a cloth. Ray was standing beside him, leaning against the wall. Paulie stood at the head of a bay horse, and the jockey Chrissie was kneeling down beside the animal's flank, which was splotched here and there with various shades and shapes of brown. On the ground there were two buckets of water and several packages of hair-color kits from the drugstore, all opened and scattered about. A chestnut horse was standing to one side, tethered to a post, watching the proceedings. All six of them looked up as Etta walked over.

"That horse named Joseph?" she asked.

"Who the fuck would call a mare Joseph?" Chrissie demanded.

"Well, it's got a coat of many colors."

Etta ducked down and slipped through the railing into the corral. When she straightened up, Ray was smiling at her. She shrugged just a little, holding his eyes, and then she looked at Pete and said hello.

"Nice to see you, Etta."

She turned to the kid Paulie and said hello. She saw that he was healing nicely, what she could see of him under the oversized hat. Then she walked over and gave the various dye jobs on the mare a close scrutiny. Chrissie was staring at her like she might throw a punch. After looking at the mare, Etta turned to her and said, "I've forgotten your name."

"Well, it ain't Annie Oakley," Chrissie said.

Etta smiled at that, and she nodded toward the gelding. "That the color you're going for?"

Ray walked over then, thinking he might have to get between the two women. "We're not having a lot of luck. Horse hair is different than human hair."

"Gee, do you think?" Etta asked. "Do the people at Clairol know about this?"

She walked around the other side of the mare, where her flank was still a fresh canvas, and had a long look. Then she glanced over at the gelding.

"The race is tomorrow?"

"Yup."

"What's the weather?"

"Cool but sunny, that's what they're saying," Ray said. "Why?"

Etta took another look at the mare. "I'll be back."

She got into her car and drove off. Chrissie stood by the fence, her bottom lip pushed out just a little.

Ray regarded her a moment and decided to change the subject. "You make arrangements for the track pony?"

"Yup. Cost me a hundred bucks, but it's done."

"Good," Ray said. He stood in the corral, thinking. "This deck could use another joker. Paulie, any chance to get a message to Dean?"

Paulie squinted across the corral, his tongue between his teeth as he considered the question. "He doesn't like me to say it, but he calls his mom a lot."

"Why don't we give that a try?" Ray said.

"Sure."

Ray turned back to Chrissie, who was still sulking.

"What the hell does she figure on doing?" she demanded. "She thinks she's pretty goddamn smart."

She turned to glare at Pete Culpepper. Pete looked at her and then at the mare with the twelve or thirteen splotches of different shades of brown on her flanks and at the packages of ladies' hair coloring on the ground. He got to his feet and put the cloth on the saddle he'd been oiling.

"I'll fetch a bottle," he said.

The bottle was half empty by the time Etta came back, and they would open a second before she was through. She backed the Taurus up near the corral fence and unlocked the trunk, and they all watched as she took out various powders and water bottles and misters. Then she crawled through the rails into the corral and had a hard look at the gelding, who looked back at her like he was the only one there who knew what she was about to do. Turning to Ray now, she said, "I'm gonna need a table of some sort out here, and some warm water."

Ray hauled an old harvest table out of the shed while Paulie went to the house for the water. Etta set everything up on the table and then walked to the mare and ran her hand over the horse's hide.

"Just what're you fixin' to do, ma'am?" Pete asked the question, but it could have come from any of them.

"Well, first I'm gonna mist the animal," Etta said, her hand still on the mare. "Then I'll combine some burnt sienna, some alizarin crimson, maybe a touch of umber. Mix it good and then just sift it over the horse."

"Speak English," Chrissie said.

Etta looked over, and she smiled. "I'm gonna paint him."

It was nearly dark by the time Etta got the color close to what she wanted. Chrissie pulled her horns in a little and helped out, mainly with keeping the mare still, allowing Etta to experiment. Paulie pulled another chair out of the barn, and he and Pete sat side by side in the sun along the barn wall. Ray knelt in the dirt along the wall beside them, drawing pictures in the dust with a stick.

"Why did you ask about the weather?" he asked at one point.

"I was worried it might rain. This is water-based paint," Etta said. "I just thought you'd want your horse to finish the race the same color that he started."

"That would be nice," Ray agreed.

She went back to her mixing. "How you gonna make the switch?" she asked.

"Well, we got a plan," Ray said.

"Is it gonna work?"

"Ask me Monday."

Pete poured himself another drink and began to mutter into his glass.

"What is it?" Ray asked after a while.

"I'm still worried about Sonny."

"Sonny'll be in the bar."

"Maybe he will, and maybe he won't," Pete said. "He could damn well show up at the paddock. He likes to make a show. And even Sonny's gonna recognize his own horse."

Ray fell silent. Etta, mixing powders together, looked over at him. Then she glanced at Paulie, his battered face beneath the hat. She thought about Sonny's hand on her throat, Elizabeth's sad and resigned face.

"I'll take care of Sonny," she said.

Pete looked at her. "How do you figure to do that?"

Etta stood up from her work and looked at him. "I'll take care of him, Pete."

When she got the color close Ray walked over and untied the gelding and led him next to the mare for a closer comparison. Etta stood back and had a look, then shook her head and went back to the mix. While she was working she gave the gathering in the corral the once-over.

"Quite a gang you've assembled, Mr. Culpepper," she said.

"You betcha," Pete said. "Old Jesse James himself would cut a wide swath around this bunch."

About the time Etta was finishing up, the stallion in the barn began to snort and whinny and soon after that kick the walls of his stall. Paulie went in and fed him some grain and watered him, and he settled for a bit but started up again. Etta got the mix the way she wanted it, and then she packed up her paints and put them in the barn.

"I'll do the racehorse in the morning," she said. "I'll have to go into town for more paint. This is a bigger canvas than I'm used to."

The mare was getting antsy now, sidestepping around the

enclosure, bumping into Etta, nearly knocking her down. Then the horse in the barn started up again. Pete got to his feet and took the mare by the halter and then called Paulie over to hold her quiet while he walked around behind her. After a moment he looked at Ray.

Ray watched him, and then he looked over to Chrissie, and she smiled. Ray turned back to Pete, and after a moment Pete shrugged his shoulders and nodded his head.

"Well, Paulie," Ray said then. "Tell that stud of yours to splash on a little Old Spice. Looks like he's got himself a date."

21

Saturday afternoon, Sonny caught the last two races at Woodbine and picked up a form for Sunday's card. He had the winner in the last race—a five-furlong sprint for untried two-year-olds—and he won eight hundred dollars on a hundred-dollar bet. He cashed and then walked down to the barns.

Jackson was there. He'd run a little charcoal filly in the last race, and now he was checking in on Rather Rambunctious before he headed for home. Sonny walked into the barn as Jackson was having a look at the horse's feet. His jacket was hanging on the stall door.

"Hope you didn't blow your allowance on that filly," Sonny said.

"I don't bet," Jackson said. He didn't bother to look up. If he was surprised at Sonny's presence, he didn't let on.

"I had the winner," Sonny said then. "A little seven-to-one action. I had him two hundred to win." Sonny couldn't help lying even when he didn't need to.

Jackson straightened up and walked out of the stall. Sonny showed him Sunday's racing form. "See this?"

"No."

"They got him at three to two, the fuckers. Hard to make money at three to two."

"That's what you get when you drop him down," Jackson said.

Sonny was still looking at the form. "You got Juan Romano on him? What happened to Danny Hartsell?"

"Gone to California for the winter."

"So much for loyalty."

Sonny recognized all the horses in the race except for the gelding out of the three hole. The horse was listed at ninety-nine to one, off the board.

"What's this?" he said, reading. "This number three horse, it says he's *nine* years old. Fast Market, by some outfit called Pecos River. This a misprint?"

"It's not a misprint," Jackson said, putting his coat on.

"What the fuck is this?" Sonny said.

"Some horse, been running at Fort Erie. I don't know what they're thinking, but the race is open."

"The horse is nine years old."

"Not against the law to dream, Sonny," Jackson said, and he left.

Sonny looked at his watch and then walked outside and got into his car and drove to the golf course. He parked at the far end of the lot and waited. If she showed with muscle, he would hightail it to the highway.

Misty came alone, driving a newer-model Jag convertible. She parked by the restaurant and got out; she was wearing jeans and a heavy sweater, sunglasses. She looked around and then walked inside. Sonny waited a few minutes to see if anybody else would show; then he walked over and followed her inside.

She was sitting at a table in the corner, a cup of coffee before her. When he approached she took her glasses off to reveal the bruises on her face, the cut above her eye.

"Sit down," she said.

Sonny looked around nervously before he sat. The waiter approached, and Sonny waved him off. He looked at Misty, and she looked back at him.

"You want to talk—then talk," she said.

"I just think we can work this out without involving the cops."

"I've already involved the cops."

"I'm aware of that."

"I coulda handled this differently. Believe me, if I wanted your fucking legs broken, you'd be in a cast by now. But from what I hear, you've been beat up before for being an asshole, and it didn't do any good."

"Listen, I am genuinely sorry—"

"No, you're not, and I don't give a fuck either way. I can't dance with my face like this. And guess what? There's no workman's comp for getting smacked around by some fucking moron in a hotel room. So you're costing me money."

"What do you want?"

"First of all, you're gonna pay me five grand for lost wages. Yes or no?"

Sonny shrugged. "Sure."

"Leave it at the bar at the Slamdance, and I mean today. Secondly, you're gonna make a bet for me."

"What?"

"I hear the odds are locked at Billy Coon's casino, some backroom deal. That right?"

"Could be."

"I want to bet a horse at Woodbine tomorrow. A horse called Fast Market."

Sonny looked at her for a moment. "You're outa your mind," he decided. "What's going on here? Why that horse?"

"The jockey is an old friend of mine. She says they been exercising this nag in some swimming pool and it's worked miracles. She says it's gonna win."

"What's the jock's name?"

"Chrissie Nugent. I knew her in New Orleans."

Sonny was trying not to smile. "Never heard of her. And she's telling you this horse is gonna win."

"A thousand on the nose."

"What?" Sonny eyes registered his surprise. "You gotta be kidding me."

"I got no reason to kid you. I don't even wanna be in your presence, you fucking creep. It's a thousand—that's why I don't wanna bet it at the track; it'd knock the odds to shit. Now, you gonna make the bet, or do I go back to Plan A?"

Sonny raised his hands in surrender. "Where's the grand?"

"In your pocket, asshole," she said. "And don't think about *not* making the bet 'cause you think the horse can't win. I want the ticket from Billy Coon's in my hand before the race goes off. I'll meet you at Woodbine, tomorrow afternoon. In the clubhouse lounge."

"Wait a fucking minute. What about the cops?"

"You hold up your end, and you won't hear from the cops." Misty smiled. "I guarantee it."

Sonny watched her leave, and after a minute he gestured for the waiter to bring him a vodka and tonic.

"Do you know what's dumber than a stripper?" he asked the man when he brought the drink.

"What?"

"Nothing."

When Sonny left he went directly to the bank, and then he drove out to the casino. He wasn't comfortable walking into Big Billy Coon's back room. He hadn't been back since the day of the Breeders', and he knew that he'd escaped that day by a whisker. He was encouraged at once, though, to see that Billy wasn't there. One of the cousins, Leon, was behind the bar, and he was talking to a pretty native girl in a cowboy hat and tight black jeans. Sonny approached the bar.

"Billy around?"

"No."

The girl turned to Sonny, and he gave her a smile, which she returned. She had a small silver stud in her nose.

Sonny looked at Leon and asked, "You got the line for Woodbine?"

"On the board," Leon said. "I don't know if I can take a bet from you. I'd hafta call Billy and ask."

Sonny had a look at the board while Leon went to the phone. Fast Market was listed at a hundred to one. Sonny had never so willingly thrown away a thousand dollars in his life. He had no choice, though; he'd pay the piper and wait to hear from the cop that the complaint had been withdrawn.

Leon put the phone down and came back. "Billy says your credit's no good. Cash or nothing."

Sonny counted the money out on the bar. "The three horse in the seventh race. A thousand to win."

He saw Leon look to the board and saw his eyebrows arch.

"By the way, you can tell Billy that my gray's gonna win the race," Sonny said. "It's a lock. I'll pay him off out of the purse."

"Why you betting this horse if the gray's gonna win?" Leon asked.

"There's a woman involved."

"Oh."

Leon took the bet. Sonny looked at the woman in the cowboy hat. When he asked if he could buy her a drink, she said okay.

Pete made up a batch of his renowned chili, and after they watched the big bay stallion breed the multicolored mare, they went into the house to eat. Etta had left earlier, and there was just the four of them again.

They washed the hot chili down with cold beer, and then they played a few games of euchre. It was a down-home Saturday night, with nobody talking about what Sunday might bring.

Chrissie and Paulie partnered up, and they were the champions, winning four games out of seven. Chrissie played cards like she did everything else: she came out swinging with her trump and tried to hold on at the end. Paulie, in contrast, was patient and deliberate, Pete noticed. It seemed that the kid had a lot more going for him than he'd been led to believe.

Pete turned in shortly after eleven, and Paulie headed to

the couch a few minutes later. Ray smoked a cigarette and finished his beer and then got to his feet and said he would take a look at the horses.

"That stud's got a bad habit of getting stolen," he said by way of explanation.

Chrissie went along with him. The temperature had dropped sharply after the sun had set, and the night was clear and cold. The moon was up, and they could see the oak trees silhouetted against the sky, lined up along the lane like scarecrows in a corn patch.

There was a whole barn full of horses now, what with the new foal and the bay stallion. All were quiet, even the rambunctious filly. The air was cold enough that the horses' breath could be seen trailing from their nostrils.

The stallion whinnied when he saw them, and Chrissie walked over to his stall. "Feel like a cigarette, fella?"

Ray went into the stall with the gelding and walked him around a bit. The horse was limping still but didn't seem to be in any real discomfort. Ray hoped that the limp wouldn't disappear altogether overnight. He had brought a carrot from the house, and he broke it in half and fed half to the gelding, holding the horse by the halter while he did, leaning into him. "Don't tell fancy Dan over there," he said to the horse, indicating the bay. "He thinks he's something." Then he gave him the other half and left the stall.

Chrissie was still looking at the stallion, and she seemed to be deep in thought when Ray walked over.

"Well?" he said.

"Well what?"

"Getting cold feet?"

"Nope. You get me in the starting gate with this fucker underneath me, and I'll do the rest."

They stood there silently in the dim light for a time. There was a swallow swooping from beam to beam, its shadow casting a strobe across the single bulb above.

Ray had a sudden thought, and he put his hand in his pocket and pulled out a package of bubblegum and a small ball bearing. "I almost forgot," he said, and he handed them over.

Chrissie took the gum and put it in her pocket, and she had a good look at the ball bearing and then put it with the gum. She didn't say anything.

"Looks like Pete and I might be heading out to Texas when this is over," Ray said after a while.

"He told me."

"That okay with you?"

"Come on, Ray." She smiled. "My daddy's not gonna come after you with the shotgun."

He shrugged his shoulders, looking at her.

"You and I are all right," she said. "Did you think I was in love? It's not always about love, Ray. Sometimes it's just about finding a little comfort. And sometimes it's just plain fun."

He nodded and looked at the big bay horse.

"Sometimes it's a combination of all three," she continued. She looked away, then added, "I admire you, Ray. I think you're an honest man."

"Well, this honest man is about to fix a horse race."

"So's this honest jock."

"I appreciate what you're doing here."

"I have my own reasons for that. But forget about me—you better worry about what you're gonna do with whatshername—the horse painter."

"Her name's Etta."

"I know what it is."

They were interrupted by the sound of the gelding's snoring. Chrissie pushed away from the rail and walked over to the horse. Ray watched her, in her jeans and her boots and Pete Culpepper's wool coat. She reached into the stall and ran her hand softly over the sleeping horse's forehead.

"You know what I was thinking earlier today?" Chrissie

said. "This gelding's never been worth any more than what—ten grand—in his life. And he's the sweetest old boy I ever been around."

"Yeah?"

"Now this bonehead," she said, walking back and leaning on the stall door and indicating the stallion. "He's worth—I don't know—five or ten million. And he's nothing but a spoiled, arrogant prick."

The stallion chose that moment to try to nip her with his teeth. Chrissie rapped the horse sharply on the nose with her fist, and he threw his head in the air and turned away.

"What's your point?" Ray asked. "That horses are no better than people?"

"I guess. Kind of makes me sad, you know. I always figured they were."

Paulie was already awake when Ray came down in the morning. It was barely dawn. Paulie had the coffee perking, and they each poured a cup and then headed out. A considerable frost had accumulated overnight, and Ray had to scrape the windshield of the Caddy before they left.

Paulie had left a message for Dean to meet them at the Four by Four restaurant at the intersection of the highway and Crooked Creek Road. There was no sign of Dean when they got there, so they went in and ordered breakfast.

The waitress was bringing their food when Dean walked in, wearing a ratty green parka and work boots with no laces, a ball cap pulled down low. Incognito, Ray guessed. Dean saw them and then threw a cautious glance around the restaurant before he walked over and sat down. He appeared to be in possession of some attitude.

"Well, here I am," he announced.

"Did you talk to your mom?" Paulie asked.

"How else would I know to come here?" Dean asked. "Idiot."

Ray reached over the table and slapped Dean hard across

the side of the head. The smack resounded around the little restaurant, drawing stares. Dean put his hand to his head and looked angrily at Ray.

"What the fuck—?"

"Keep the name calling to yourself," Ray said.

"Jesus," Dean said.

"He won't help you either," Ray said. "We got a job for you. If you do what you're told, you might get off this horse-rustling charge without going to the hoosegow."

"I don't have the horse," Dean said sullenly. "Sonny stole him back."

"Well, as far as the cops are concerned, you're still the thief," Ray said. "You do what I say, and you might walk away from this."

"What do I gotta do?"

Ray reached into his shirt pocket and pulled out a pair of twenties and a ten and placed the bills on the table in front of Dean.

"Take this to Big Billy Coon's backroom totes," Ray said. "Bet fifty to win on the three horse in the seventh race at Woodbine. And listen—you tell Billy Coon that you got the tip from Sonny. Billy has to hear that, okay?"

"What the fuck's Sonny up to now?"

"Even Sonny doesn't know that, not this time," Ray said. "And you don't need to. All you gotta know is the three horse in the seventh race. Collect your money—'cause the horse is gonna win—and then make yourself scarce for a few weeks. I think I can square things with Jackson on the legal end. If he doesn't see your face for a couple months, he might forget about putting you in the hospital for whacking him with that shovel."

"What's this about?" Dean asked.

"It's about you getting out of a bad situation," Ray said. "Don't ask questions."

"I wanna know—"

"You heard him," Paulie said. "Don't ask questions."

Chrissie and Pete had breakfast, and then they loaded the gelding in the old trailer and hauled him over to Woodbine and housed him in the barn there. It was her luck that Juan Romano was strutting around the barns, all puffed up because he was riding the Stanton gray in the big race, and he saw them installing the gelding in the barn.

"Is true then," he said. "You are running this horse?"

"What's it look like?" Chrissie said.

"Estas loca," Juan said. "Look like to me."

He walked away with his little smirk on his little face. The look never went away, even when she'd decked him. But his ass had been in full retreat at the time. Chrissie would have followed him now, but Pete grabbed her by her jacket collar.

"Get in the truck," Pete told her. "We don't need trouble today."

They drove back to the farm. Ray and Paulie were already back, and they had the stud in the corral where Etta had just finished turning the bay into a chestnut. The horse's mane had been cropped short and darkened, and now she was coloring the lower legs to match. The horse did indeed look like a genuine chestnut, at least at a glance.

Pete Culpepper glanced at Ray, and Ray showed him a gambler's smile, a look that said the time for second-guessing was past.

The hardest part was always the deciding anyway.

Ray drove to Woodbine by himself that afternoon, arriving just as the fifth race was finishing. He parked in the main lot and took his leather jacket from the backseat, put it on, and smoothed the collar down. He watched the sixth race from the rail and then walked to a high vantage point on the west end of the grandstand. From there he had a view of the main track as well as the saddling barn and the paddock, where the entries were preparing for the Stanton Stakes.

The mounts were already saddled when Ray took his position. All but one, that is. Pete Culpepper brought Fast Market to the saddling barn late. Ray watched as the identifier checked the identifying tattoo under the gelding's lip and then motioned for Pete to get the animal saddled. Still, Pete took his time. The other horses were in the paddock parade by the time Fast Market reached the saddling stall. Jackson Jones, wearing a blazer and slacks, spoke briefly to his jockey aboard the big gray colt and then slipped through the rails and headed for the clubhouse to watch the race.

By the time Pete led the gelding into the paddock, the other horses were filing into the tunnel that led to the track. Chrissie, wearing silks altered to boast Pecos River Ranch, was waiting for Pete in the paddock. As Pete gave her a leg up, he looked into the grandstand, directly at Ray. Ray nodded, and then he turned his attention to the main track.

The track ponies and their riders had been mingling just outside the tunnel, sitting their western saddles aboard quarterhorses and older thoroughbreds, and they were just now hooking up with the entries and leading them to the starting gate.

Ray saw that one track pony rider was a little removed from the rest. His mount was considerably bigger than the others, and it was wearing a western saddle of tooled brown leather, the cantle and horn pronounced after the Mexican style. Although the horse was chestnut brown, it looked a lot like the thoroughbred Jumping Jack Flash. And the rider, though he'd gone from a porkpie to a Stetson to a riding helmet, was a dead ringer for Paulie. Ray stood watching until Paulie looked up and found him.

Ray turned back to his right then. Chrissie and the gelding

were still in the paddock, Chrissie sitting the horse while Pete Culpepper made a pretense of adjusting the girth strap. Finally, Pete straightened, and he looked up to where Ray stood. Ray glanced back to make sure Paulie was watching yet. Then he flipped the collar of his jacket up.

Pete stepped away, and Chrissie touched the gelding with her heel and headed him into the tunnel. Paulie, on the other side, moved the big chestnut to meet her.

Then it was clockwork. Ray watched as Chrissie rode a chestnut gelding into one end of the tunnel and a chestnut stallion out the other. Chrissie was still adjusting the just-switched saddle as she pointed the horse to the starting gate. She glanced up at Ray, and then he turned and made his way up the grandstand, where he intended to keep an eye on Jackson Jones.

Chrissie held the horse back, and when she reached the starting gate the other entries were already in. When the stallion balked going in, she told the starter to open the gate, and the horse fell for the ruse and walked right in.

A second later they were off.

The horses broke clean, and Chrissie settled her horse along the rail and saved ground. He was bound to run, and it took all her strength just to hold him in. She kept him tucked behind the one horse, giving him nowhere to go. The pace was lightning quick. Juan Romano had the big gray running third, and he too was holding the animal back. He had a lot of horse, Chrissie could see.

He just didn't have enough horse.

At the three-quarter post the field was still tight. Romano made his move in the clubhouse turn, moving the gray colt outside and running down the leaders with ease, taking a four-length lead heading into the stretch. When Chrissie came out of the turn she was maybe eight lengths behind

Juan Romano and the gray. She stood in the stirrups, and she leaned forward and tucked her face between the ears of Jumping Jack Flash.

"Okay, brat," she said to him.

She switched the horse to his right lead, and then she finally let the animal do what he'd been fighting to do for eight furlongs. She let him run.

She kept him hard to the rail, and she touched him just once with the whip. They flew by Juan Romano and the gray colt Rather Rambunctious on the flat, Chrissie hunched over the newly minted chestnut's neck, a smile on her face, the whip held lightly in her right hand. Chrissie had a fleeting glimpse of Romano's disbelieving face as she thundered past him, and she laughed out loud.

"*Vaya con dios,* shithead," she called.

She actually pulled the horse up, and they still won by ten lengths. A couple hundred yards past the finish line, Chrissie jumped to the ground and lifted the horse's left front hoof up, as if in alarm. She turned and gestured excitedly toward the tunnel and then quickly popped the bubblegum and the ball bearing from her mouth into her hand and wedged both tightly into the frog cleft of the hoof.

Then she grabbed the horse's reins and led him off the track, still gesturing to some anonymous presence in the tunnel. The crowd, which had been screaming as the longshot had crossed the finish line, fell silent as the horse, limping badly now, was led away.

Ray watched from the clubhouse, where he had positioned himself about thirty feet away from Jackson Jones. Instead of watching the race, Ray had kept his eyes on Jackson. The first look of suspicion had crossed Jackson's face when they had to trick the horse to get him in the gate. Ray saw Jackson, binoculars in hand, looking down in puzzlement.

About the time that Chrissie and the chestnut left the big

gray in their dust, Ray saw Jackson head for the escalator. He looked like a man who had come across some disagreeable and unidentifiable odor.

Jackson started down to the track, and Ray followed. They watched as Chrissie jumped off the chestnut and then led him limping away. When Jackson got to the rail, Juan Romano charged toward him on the gray.

"That no gelding, Mr. Jones. What the fuck goin' on?"

Jackson went over the fence and headed for the tunnel, his long legs covering ground. Ray followed, but he kept his distance.

Then Pete Culpepper walked out of the tunnel, leading his gelding Fast Market by the reins and watching in concern as the horse limped toward the winner's circle. Chrissie was walking alongside, carrying her saddle. In the tunnel Paulie had been sponging the gelding with a mixture of warm water and soap since the race began, and the horse appeared to be awash with sweat. As they arrived back at the finish line, Chrissie veered off and went to weigh in.

A moment later Paulie loped out of the tunnel aboard Jumping Jack Flash, the horse wearing the western saddle once more. He headed for the barns, where he loaded the still saddled horse onto Pete Culpepper's trailer and jumped behind the wheel of Pete's truck and was off.

Jackson had changed course by now, heading for the winner's circle, and never saw Paulie make his move. Chrissie weighed in and then returned to Pete and the horse in the winner's circle, where she made a show of examining the gelding's leg.

Jackson had looked on critically as the gelding had limped across the grass. The horse was pretty lathered up, but his breathing was easy. Now Jackson stepped through the rail and walked over, looked to see that the animal was in fact a gelding, and then ran his hand across the horse's withers.

"Get your fucking hands off the horse," Chrissie snapped.

Jackson looked at her. "Why isn't this horse breathing hard?" he demanded.

"I guess he didn't have much competition," Chrissie said.

Jackson touched his fingers to his nose, smelled the soap from the horse.

Pete walked around the gelding and stood in Jackson's path. "Something I can help you with?"

"This horse never ran that race," Jackson said.

Pete nodded at the electronic board in the infield. "Tote board says he did. Matter of fact, tote board says he won."

"This horse couldn't beat that gray in a hundred tries," Jackson said.

"It would seem that way on paper," Pete said, and he spit a stream of tobacco onto the manicured infield. "That's why you don't run horse races on paper."

Sonny had arrived at the track shortly past noon and headed straight for the clubhouse lounge. He watched the card on the closed circuit, sitting at the bar and betting at the automated teller there. He passed the afternoon alone. He'd arrived expecting to meet Misty, but she hadn't shown. He'd been into the vodka since waking up at eleven.

After the sixth race he gathered his change and stood up, intending to head down to the paddock to see his horse off, and to let himself be seen doing it. When he turned, though, he saw Etta Parr sitting at the end of the bar. She was wearing jeans and a man's leather jacket, and she looked good. She looked damned good.

"Hello, Sonny," she said when he saw her.

"Well . . ."

"Where you off to?"

"See to my horse," Sonny said. He was taken aback by her friendly tone.

Etta indicated the television. "You can see your horse from here. Let me buy you a drink."

"You want to buy me a drink?"

"It's time the two of us quit scrapping, Sonny. I think we can put it to rest today."

Etta bought the drinks, and they sat side by side at the bar and watched the race together. Sonny was smiling as he saw the big gray leading the field at the turn, and then he stared in complete disbelief when his horse was caught. Etta sipped her drink and watched him in amusement.

"How'd your horse do?" she asked when the race was run.

"He got beat," Sonny managed to say.

"Now that's a shame."

"Sonofabitch." Sonny watched as the winner limped back toward the infield. "Jesus Christ—that's the three horse."

"I believe it is," Etta said.

Sonny reached into his jacket pocket and pulled out the tote ticket from the casino. He grinned at Etta. "Well, I just happen to have a thousand dollars to win on that particular horse. At a hundred to one." Then he realized something else. "And . . . my gray finished second, so I get the place money on that. I'm a goddamn gambling marvel. Wait'll that snotty fucking Indian gets a load of me."

"You know, Sonny. If you weren't such a despicable human being, I would kiss you right now."

Sonny looked at her warily; then he smiled. "And why's that?"

"Because, I believe a man should get kissed when he gets fucked." Etta stood to go. "And you just got fucked."

When Jackson came out of the barn he still wore the confused look on his face. If any of the grooms or walkers had seen anything, they weren't talking. But they would eventually, Jackson knew. Whatever happened, he'd find out sooner or later.

A hot walker approached with the gray. Jackson looked the horse over, occasionally throwing dark glances over to the track where Chrissie and Pete were tending to the gelding, who was just now getting his picture taken for winning a race he never ran.

When Jackson finally walked away he came upon Ray Dokes, leaning against the corner of one of the barns, a rolled-up racing form in his hand and a strangely contented look on his face.

"Hey, Jackson."

"Ray," Jackson said, and he stopped, his eyes at once suspicious. "What're you doing here?"

"Trying to make a dollar at the wickets, like everybody else. I actually had a few bucks on that old chestnut over there. Talk about a Cinderella story."

Jackson turned back to the gelding, more puzzled than ever now.

"You train that big gray, don't you?" Ray asked him. "What's he called—Rather Rambunctious?"

Pete was walking the limping horse back to the barn now, taking it slow. Chrissie was striding off in the other direction, her saddle in her hands. She had a mount in the last race.

"That's right," Jackson said.

Ray watched as Pete Culpepper and his horse disappeared into the barn; then he turned back to Jackson and he smiled. "Finished second, didn't he?"

22

When Ray woke up it was full light. He lay in bed for a time, trying to gauge his hangover, and when he realized that it was not particularly debilitating he got up and went downstairs. Pete was still in bed, indicating that his condition was somewhat more critical than Ray's.

By the clock over the fridge it was nine-thirty. Ray put coffee on and then stuck his head in the living room. Chrissie was sleeping in her clothes on the couch, and the kid Paulie was on the carpet beside her, the Hudson Bay blanket across him. The Walker hound was alongside Paulie; he looked up at Ray and gave his tail a single thump and then lowered his head. Sleeping in seemed to be the order of the day.

The kitchen table was covered with bottles—beer, rum, whiskey, dead soldiers all. The ashtrays were full, and apparently someone had scrambled up a mess of eggs at one point. Ray cleaned up, and then he got the phone book from the drawer by the fridge and found the number for Stanton Stables. He wasn't sure how to get in touch with Jackson Jones. The phone rang three times, and then Jackson himself answered.

"Jackson, it's Ray Dokes."

"Oh," Jackson said, his voice unsure.

"I've got your horse."

The line was silent for a few seconds. Ray could imagine Jackson on the other end, digesting this piece of information.

"How would you happen to have my horse?"

"That's the wrong question, Jackson. You should be asking me how you go about getting him back."

"How do I go about getting him back?"

"I'll bring him over this morning. There's just one condition."

"What's the condition?"

"No questions asked. And no charges against anybody. Is that a problem?"

"Not if the horse is healthy. Is he healthy?"

"Hell, yeah. He ran a mile and a quarter yesterday in two minutes flat."

Ray hung up the phone and then grabbed his jean jacket and went outside. It was cold and gray, and there were snow clouds building to the west. The horse trailer was still hitched up to Pete's pickup. Ray got in and backed it around to the double doors of the barn.

Inside the barn it was warm from the heat of the animals. The stallion was standing in the corner of the stall, his eyes blinking at the daylight. As he looked for a lead rope, Ray's eyes fell on Pete Culpepper's old western saddle in the corner. Ray looked at the saddle for a moment and then looked at the big bay stallion, and the horse looked back haughtily, and then Ray nodded, and damned if it didn't appear that the horse nodded back.

Snow was beginning to fall when he came out of the barn. He led the horse to the house and tied the reins to the railing of the front porch. Then he went inside to get a heavier jacket and his ball cap. He pulled on a wool coat and searched the house in vain for his Tigers' cap before settling for Pete's Stetson.

It had been a few years since Ray had ridden a horse, but he hadn't forgotten much. There wasn't a hell of a lot to forget, the only important rule being don't fall off. The big saddle was custom-built and generous, and sitting it was like sitting in an easy chair. The stallion was his usual contentious self at first, chomping the bit and twisting his head around to try to bite Ray's leg. Reaching the side road, Ray galloped him out for a mile or so, and after that he settled down.

It was maybe fifteen or sixteen miles to the Stanton farm, Ray figured. Except for the last couple miles, he could keep to the side roads all the way. He kept the horse on the grassy shoulder, holding him alternately to a walk or an easy lope. The snow fell steadily, but Ray was comfortable in the heavy coat and the hat.

They passed, horse and rider, through farm country where family farms still existed, although many of the owners were specializing these days, cash croppers and dairy farmers, fallow hog operators and turkey ranchers. But it was farm country and always had been. Many of the families had been here for more than a hundred years, and although they'd had to change with the times, they were still on the land.

"Maybe do you some good to see a little bit of how real people live," he said to the horse. "Life ain't all rolled oats and horny mares, you know."

The animal offered no response, just kept the pace, his ears up and forward at every little thing, acutely aware of his surroundings. Whatever his personality defects, the horse was an intelligent animal.

"You and Sonny probably deserve each other," Ray continued. "You were both born to it. Neither one of you ever did a lick of work in your life and probably never will. I got half a mind to take you up to Kitchener and sell you to the Mennonites. They'd teach you something about honest work. A few days in a hay field, and you wouldn't be so quick to kick and bite at people."

They were passing a brick ranch house near the town line when a German shepherd came bounding down the drive, all bared teeth and loud bark. Ray touched the horse with his heel, and the animal jumped beneath his hand; he seemed to go from a walk to a gallop in a single stride. Ray had to grab the saddle horn to stay aboard. The dog was left in the jet stream.

Ray gave the animal his head then and let him run. He put his weight in the stirrups and leaned forward over the horse's neck, and he felt the sheer explosion of power beneath him, the horse's head reaching out, ears flattened, the huge leg muscles eating up the ground underneath. He let the horse run until he ran himself out and finally chose to stop on his own, pulling up finally into a trot, his head high, snorting loudly and proudly, sidestepping a little as if he was on parade.

"Well, all right," Ray said then. "All right."

Jackson sat in his office, watching periodically out the window where the snow continued to fall heavily. After two hours he began to think that Ray Dokes wasn't going to show. He'd been under the impression that the horse wasn't that far away. He'd received a call an hour earlier saying that the old man had regained consciousness in the Bahamas and that they were shipping him home later in the week. Jackson had no way of predicting the old man's mental capacity, but chances were he'd at least be ahead of Sonny.

Then he caught movement out of the corner of his eye, and he looked out to see a strange sight coming down the lane. A snow-covered man on a snow-covered horse.

Jackson grabbed a hackamore from the tack room and met them at the corner of the barn. Ray reined the horse to a stop there, and he looked down at the big man, pushing the Stetson's brim back with his thumb.

"Howdy," he said.

Jackson brushed the melting snow from the horse's neck to get a better look at the chestnut brown of the coat. Some of the color came off on his hand.

"Sonofabitch," he said.

"Yup," Ray said, sitting the big horse like he'd just come off the Chisholm Trail.

"Sonofabitch," Jackson said again, like there was nothing else he could think to say. And then, with something close to appreciation: "You beat him with his own horse."

"We still got a deal?"

"I gave you my word, Ray. You better hope the racing commission doesn't find out."

"I figure if Stanton Stables doesn't complain, then nobody else will. Nobody else has reason to."

"Sonny might, if he figures things out."

"I doubt it."

Ray got down off the horse. He unfastened the cinch and pulled the saddle off and set it on the top rail of the fence. Jackson pulled the bridle from the horse and slipped on the hackamore.

"He's a hell of a horse," Ray said.

"I know it."

"He's a bit of a peckerhead."

"I know that too."

Ray took the bridle from Jackson and looped it over the horn of the saddle. When he turned he noticed that Jackson had a cell phone clipped to his belt. Ray pointed with his chin to the house and asked, "Sonny here?"

"He'll be sleeping," Jackson said.

"Lend me your phone, will you?"

Jackson gave him a look and then handed the phone over.

"What's Sonny's number?"

Jackson told him, and Ray started for the house. Climbing up the front steps, he punched in the number and then sat down in one of the big wicker chairs while it rang. After five rings Sonny's voice message came on and Ray hung up and dialed again. He did this four times, and then he heard Sonny's aggravated voice: "What?"

"It's Ray Dokes."

There was a long silence. "What do you want?" Sonny demanded at last.

"There's a couple things we have to talk about," Ray said. "I understand you've been harassing Etta Parr."

"I hold a note on her farm. I wouldn't call it harassment."

"I would. Well, she's got the money to pay you off. And then you'll have no reason to go near her again."

"If I get my money. I doubt she's got it."

Ray stretched his boots out and looked over as Jackson, who had been watching Ray in wonder, now turned and led the big horse into the barn.

"Sonny, I want you to think back three years," Ray said then. "Remember that meeting we had at the golf course? After you raped my sister? Remember that, Sonny? Well, I have to believe that was maybe the worst day of your life. But I'll tell you what—if you go near Etta again—I mean, if you even so much as drive by her house—then I'm gonna find you and give you a brand-new worst day of your life. Understand?"

Sonny was silent on the other end.

"I'm gonna have to hear you say you understand, Sonny."

"So long as I get my money," Sonny said, trying to maintain an attitude.

"You'll get it. Now the second thing. Remember that big bay you had stolen? The one you were gonna electrocute up at Burnside's place? Remember that horse, Sonny?"

"What about him?" Sonny asked after another long pause.

"Well, I painted him brown and won the Stanton Stakes with him yesterday."

Ray could hear Sonny's breathing change on the line.

"Well, I guess you'll be going back to jail then," Sonny said.

"I don't think so. You see—nobody knows it was me who put in the fix. And I have it on pretty good authority that you collected a large sum of money from Billy Coon on the race. And I also heard that other people bet the horse with Billy, on a hot tip from you. Now what do you think Billy Coon's gonna do when he finds out it was your stallion that won the race under a phony name? I figure Billy and the cousins might take you out to the rez and make beef jerky out of you, Sonny."

"You think you're pretty fucking smart."

"Tell you the truth, I don't. But then everything is relative. Anyway, I want you to remember what we talked about here today, Sonny. I really think you should take it to heart."

Sonny realized that the conversation was about to end and he got brave. "I'll catch up with you one day, Dokes," he said. "You're having fun today, but you're fucking with the wrong man here. Eventually I'll find you, asshole."

"I'm sitting on your front porch, Sonny. Come on down."

Ray hung the phone up and reached out to place it on the railing. The snow was tapering off now, and he could see a sliver of blue sky on the horizon. He lit a cigarette and propped his boots up on the railing.

Sonny hung the phone up, and after a moment he got out of bed quietly and walked carefully to the window, the pain shooting through his knee as it did every morning. By moving to the right edge of the window and sliding the blind back with his fingertips, he could just see the end of the porch below. A pair of boots were propped on the railing there. The man wearing the boots, Sonny knew, was the architect of the pain in his knee. Sonny stood anxiously watching the boots, and after a moment he began to wonder whether he'd locked the front door when coming in last night. He considered for a moment going down to check it, but he knew that the action would put him within six feet of the man wearing the boots, and Sonny just didn't have the parts to make such a move.

So he watched and he waited, and after about twenty

minutes he saw Ray Dokes walk down off the porch and start across the yard. When Ray got to the fence he lifted the saddle from the top rail and then he cast one last glance at the house. Then he threw the saddle over his shoulder and started down the lane.

Sonny got dressed and went downstairs and ate a bowl of cereal. After a time his nervousness passed, and he began, as was his way, to focus on the positive aspects of the past twenty-four hours. For one thing, he'd gotten himself straight with Billy Coon, and it hadn't cost him a dime. He had that crazy fucking stripper to thank for that; Sonny still couldn't figure that one out, but he didn't really care one way or the other. So long as he made out on top.

And he had his horse back. Ideally, he would have liked the animal to turn up dead, but this could work too. The horse could win some big races as a five-year-old and then turn out to be a top stud after that.

The land deal in Holden County was on shaky ground, it appeared, if Homer Parr's place was in fact out of the running. But that could be a blessing as well. Sonny had lately begun to second-guess himself with regard to his grand plan for Holden County. Maybe he would just pull back a little, take the land he had, and concentrate on building the golf course. Hell, he could even design the thing himself. Any idiot could design a golf course.

He began to warm to the idea, and he stood in the kitchen looking out the back window to the rolling field behind the barn, and in a matter of moments he managed to convince himself that he would be a natural at course design. Soon he was mapping out the front nine in his head, and before long he was diverting creeks and elevating tees and creating pot bunkers.

Sonny made just one crucial mistake while mapping out the front nine for his new course. He should have done it while looking out the front window. Because then he would have seen the black Navigator coming up the drive. He would have seen the vehicle park in the yard, and he would have seen its occupants pile out.

As it was, Sonny didn't see Billy Coon and the cousins until they were standing in the kitchen beside him.

It was Wednesday before they sorted out all the financial arrangements. Ray showed up at Etta's shortly before noon. She was in the backyard, picking up branches from a windstorm the night before and piling them onto a small fire she'd built on the edge of the orchard. The snow from Monday was melted already, and the grass still showed green.

Ray parked behind Etta's car and got out. She looked at him and then dumped an armful of branches on the fire and came over. She was wearing jeans and a khaki jacket and Ray's old ball cap.

"That was quite a storm," she said.

"Fifty-mile-an-hour winds, the radio said."

"Well."

He sat down on the picnic table. "I brought your money."

She stood in front of him and looked into his eyes. "I've been thinking about that. I can't take that money."

"There you go, thinking too much. You made a decision, and you're gonna stick to it. Are you better off with it or without it?"

"With it," she admitted.

"Do you intend to spend it on frivolous purchases?"

"Hardly."

"Then here you are." He took an envelope out of his pocket. "Besides—you can't say no to Robin Hood."

She smiled. "When'd you see Elizabeth?"

"I just came from there."

"How is she?"

"She's the same as she's been, and I guess she's the same as she's always gonna be. Maybe it's time we learned to accept that certain things are just the way they are."

"Maybe," she said cautiously.

He reached forward and put the envelope in the pocket of her coat. "There's enough there for the mortgage and an extra ten grand. Buy Homer some new golf clubs for Christmas."

"Homer's golfing days are about finished."

"Then buy your boyfriend something. The salvage man."

"The salvage man is a priest, Ray."

"Oh . . . well, I didn't know that."

"There's a lot you don't know." She came forward and kissed him on the mouth, briefly and sweetly, then she stepped back.

"You and Mr. Culpepper headed for Texas then?"

"Tomorrow morning."

She sat down beside him on the table, and she slipped her arm through his. He could smell the wood smoke on her.

"And what will you do in Texas?" she asked.

"So far all I've heard is that we'll be drinking bourbon and eating rattlesnake chili."

"Well . . . it sounds like a shit kicker's theme park. What about your parole officer?"

"I told him I had a job in Timmins, working the mines. He said I could check in by phone. I expect they have phones in Pecos."

"I expect they do," she said in a drawl.

"Are you mocking me?"

"No. Well, maybe a little," she admitted. "You just keep finding new ways to get yourself in trouble."

He stood up then and smiled at her.

"What about your tractor?" she asked. "It's yours now, bought and paid for."

"I was thinking maybe you'd hold on to it for me."

"Does that mean you're coming back?"

"I guess maybe it does."

When Ray got back to the farm the first thing he noticed was that the real estate signs were gone from the front of the property. He drove down the lane and parked in the yard. Pete had his truck up on jacks, and he was checking the brakes in preparation for their drive south.

Ray walked over. Pete was replacing the rear brake drum, apparently satisfied that the linings would get them to southwest Texas. He slid the drum on and then fitted the wheel over the lugs and threaded on the nuts. Ray handed him the wheel wrench, and he tightened the nuts.

"What happened to the For Sale signs?" Ray asked.

Pete released the jack, and the truck came down with a thud. Then he straightened up and wiped his hands on his jeans. He gestured to the barn.

"Chrissie's gonna rent the place for a time," he said. "That way I can leave the horses and the old hound, and she can look after things. Don't forget, we got a mare in foal."

"We?"

"I got the taxes paid off. We might just decide to head this way again come spring."

"What about that woman's been waiting on you?"

Pete shrugged. "You never know—I might not be near as charming as I remember."

The door to the house slammed, and they turned to see Paulie, hurrying to the barn, a bucket of water in his hands, steam rising from the bucket. Paulie had the Stetson jammed down tight to his ears and his tongue clenched in his teeth.

"Paulie's gonna stay on here awhile," Pete said then.

Ray watched as Paulie disappeared into the barn, and then he looked at Pete and he smiled.

They ate in town that night, the four of them, at a steak place by the tracks that was done up like a warehouse. It used to be the mercantile. It was a pretty quiet evening, and Pete picked up the bill. When they got back to the house Pete and Ray packed up what they needed to pack, and then they sat in the kitchen and had a rum and Coke with Chrissie and Paulie. They sat there at the old arborite table, not saying much, and it felt like the end of something, but it felt like the beginning of something too.

Pete headed off to bed first, and Ray went maybe a half hour later. Chrissie and Paulie were still at the table, playing cribbage for a nickel a point. Pete and Ray were up early the next morning and they put a pot of coffee on, and while they waited for the coffee to brew they loaded their bags in the back of the truck.

They were on the road at first light.

ACKNOWLEDGMENTS

Thanks to my editor, Jennifer Barth, for her insight and patience. Thanks also to the indispensable Ruth Kaplan; my jockey advisor, Laurie Gulas; the good doctors Beth Blake (people) and Roberta Borland (horses); and my horse-painting expert, Mori McCrae. My eternal gratitude to my friend Jennifer Barclay.

Finally, special thanks to the pride of Maryland, Ann Rittenberg, whom I am pleased to have as an agent, and honored to have as a friend.

ABOUT THE AUTHOR

All Hat is Brad Smith's third novel. He lives near Canfield, Ontario.